GETTING
lucky

Other books by A.R. Casella and
Denise Grover Swank

Asheville Brewing Series
Any Luck at All
Better Luck Next Time
Getting Lucky
Bad Luck Club

GETTING lucky

A.R. CASELLA AND

NEW YORK TIMES BESTSELLING AUTHOR

DENISE GROVER SWANK

To my father (aka Fod), for giving me such a messed-up sense of humor I think it's funny to dedicate a book that starts with a one-night stand to him. Also for his love of Lurch, which inspired his role in this book.—ARC

CHAPTER

One

They'd had her at petting zoo.

Although Maisie O'Shea hadn't been to a Buchanan Brewery party in months, let alone one of their notorious staff parties, she'd finally relented. Because she was feeling lucky—adopting out four puppies and finding a foster home for a senior dog in one night would do that for a woman—and maybe a little reckless. Because it was a beautiful night in November, cool but far from cold, perfect for an outdoor party. And because she'd really, really wanted to see what kind of animals would be in a petting zoo put together by the Buchanan staff.

"I thought there were just going to be goats," Jack Durand commented, his eyes wide.

She patted his back. "Amateur. You'll get used to it."

Jack had moved to Asheville just two months ago to join the brewery as events director. Although his half-sister Adalia was good people and had become a close friend, Maisie could count on one hand the number of times she'd spoken to him. She took him for something of a straight man—the sort of stoic, humorless figure who watched in silent judgment as the world went mad around him. Then again, she was in the habit of making snap judgments about people, and she had to admit they weren't always correct.

Jack just stared into the pen for a moment. And it was a sight to see. There were four goats, a pygmy and three full-sized ones, but someone had also brought a donkey, and a goose wandered around at the other animals' feet, its neck occasionally darting forward for a vicious peck. They'd been corralled behind what looked like two zip-tied plastic baby playpens, which would almost certainly collapse sometime in the night. Especially since someone had inadvisably placed the food table directly next to it. One goat was already pressing against the plastic side of the gate, which had been insufficiently staked into the ground, attempting to reach for what looked like a breadstick. Whoever had set up the lighting in Dottie's back yard had done a poor job of it—half the yard looked like it was in full daylight, and the rest was cast in shadow. At least the animals were in the daylight part. If you were going to get attacked, it was best to see it coming.

"Aren't geese mean?" Jack asked.

"Positively vicious," she responded with a grin. "I'll bet Lurch was supposed to get a duck."

Lurch, the former head brewer at Buchanan Brewery, wasn't known for his intelligence. Then again, he hadn't been hired for it. Rumor had it the old owner, Beau Buchanan, had brought him on as a thank-you for helping him out of a lurch, and so the name had stuck.

She glanced at Lurch, who stood to the side of the zoo, talking with someone who looked like an animal wrangler, and thought, *Must've been one hell of a lurch.*

Dottie burst out of the house, accompanied by a woman with long white hair that had been piled into a bun on her head. The woman held a canvas and what looked like a collapsible easel. A large, sagging bag hung from her arm.

"Is she going to be painting out here?" Jack asked, although his voice wasn't pained like Maisie would have expected. Just interested.

She patted him on the back again. "I'll tell you what— it's going to be a long night for both of us if you keep asking questions like that."

The woman set up what was indeed a painting station in a patch of light right next to the makeshift animal pen, just in front of where they stood. Meanwhile, another former Buchanan staffer, Josie, had set up shop behind a couple of crates fronted with a handwritten sign that read, *Palm Reading. 13% Accuracy Guaranteed. Be prepared for the bitter truth.* She stood in near darkness, but a little lantern under the sign made it readable. An overturned goldfish bowl with a small tea light under it apparently served as some sort of crystal ball, but what a palm reader needed a crystal ball for was anyone's guess.

No, thanks. Josie had read her palm a year ago, and once was enough. Dottie had all but shoved her into the line at a party much like this one, and Maisie, rolling her eyes, had succumbed to the pressure. They all knew Josie's fortunes tended toward dark. The victim before Maisie had been told that he'd contracted syphilis from a Norwegian prostitute, only for his wife to pour a beer over his head—apparently he *had* been to Norway recently. So she'd prepared herself for something like that. Or to hear that she was going to die in a Zamboni accident or have her arm bitten off by a killer whale. But Josie had taken one look at her palm and said, "You're in love with someone, and he has no idea. But he's going to marry someone else, and you're going to die alone."

No words could have cut into her more efficiently. Because she had been in love with her best friend, River, for years—more or less—and she'd gone to some lengths to ensure no one knew. Not River, certainly, and most definitely not Josie.

And from the slightly bored, slightly high look in Josie's eyes, Maisie couldn't be certain if she knew or was only delivering another flip yet devastating fortune.

So no, no palm reading for her.

Rich, deep laughter drew her eyes to Jack.

"So you *do* laugh," she said.

"Is there any other appropriate response?" he asked, waving a hand back toward the petting zoo.

The goat had nudged the gate far enough that he'd managed to reach the breadstick, but the goose had jumped onto his back—its wings must have been clipped, which sucked, but there was no clipping those instincts—and was pecking at the breadstick with fervor. The goat looked rightfully terrified and was jostling around to get the bird off its back. Meanwhile, the artist was painting furiously. She'd only gotten in the outline of the goat so far, but she'd painted an obscene amount of blood on its back. Did she *hope* it would come to that?

This could only be the infamous Stella. Adalia had visited her studio a couple of months back while planning the Asheville Art Display—the event they would be celebrating at this after-party…if the back yard didn't explode into chaos before it officially started.

Dottie was looking over Stella's shoulder, nodding knowingly. "Marvelous, marvelous."

Although what was so marvelous about it, Maisie would never know. She might not be an artist like Adalia, but she knew what she liked to look at. Bleeding animals didn't make it on the list.

The goose was pecking the goat now, as if encouraging him to get another breadstick to avoid becoming a replacement meal. Maisie winced. It looked painful, and she didn't care if it made her a bleeding heart that she didn't want to watch.

The animal wrangler was still deep in conversation with Lurch, their voices raised. The sweat on his face indicated he was questioning his life decisions, as well he should.

"Hey," Maisie called out, clapping her hands. They all turned to look at her, puzzled. "Is anyone going to help that goat?"

"Help him?" the artist bleated. "He's my muse! Diego *knows* that. He's doing this for me."

"I take it Diego's the goat?"

"No, he's the goose," the artist said, giving her a look that suggested she was stupid. "I would *never* name a goat Diego."

The animal wrangler's lack of response indicated he was only there for the donkey.

Looked like Maisie was going to have to handle this up close and personal. Luckily, years of running a dog shelter made her the right woman for the job. In the early years of Dog is Love, before she had a volunteer network, she'd done nearly everything herself.

She marched up to the animal pen with purpose, and to her surprise, Jack was right beside her.

"I don't need your help," she said.

Which was when Diego pecked her shoulder, making a liar of her.

"Oh, this is good!" Stella exclaimed from behind her.

Jack made a grab for Diego, but the bird hustled out of reach, somehow managing to stay on the goat's back.

The goat rammed the gate, clearly panicked by his persistent rider, and his pygmy buddy joined in, hitting the gate at a lower height. Still, the goose clung on, giving its mount another good peck. This one created a welt, easily visible under the bright lighting.

"We've got to get him off," Maisie said. She made another grab, got another peck. She was about to say screw it and step into the danger zone beyond the baby gates, but Jack started to sing softly, crooning under his breath. An old Mamas and the Papas song about shining stars and dreams. Her mother used to sing that to her when she was a toddler, sleepless at night, and for a second she just gaped at him, mouth open. Just like that, her initial impression of him floated away, leaving something like wonder in its wake.

Then the goose came to him—it *came* to him.

He gently lifted it off the goat, who took a mouthful of his dress shirt for his efforts. At least he'd taken off the jacket. It seemed to think the shirt was tastier than the breadstick, or maybe it shared her sudden curiosity about what was under that shirt. Jack looked to her for help.

Bread wasn't great for goats, but they could eat it in small quantities, and desperate times and all that. She grabbed a handful of breadsticks from the table and lured the goat away from Jack—only for the rest of the animals to come charging over, butting the straining baby gate.

"Don't let Grumpy eat wheat!" Stella shrieked. "He's gluten-free!"

Maisie exchanged a glance with Jack, who was still holding the goose and miraculously didn't have a bloody face.

"Which one's Grumpy?" he asked.

"It's clearly that one," Maisie commented, nodding to the one in front. Part of Jack's shirt was hanging out of his mouth—he'd chomped the sleeve—and he had a look in his eyes that implied he would happily chomp Jack's arm to get more of it.

"Nah," he said, rearranging the goose. "That one's got to be Dopey."

Stella had finally left her painting for long enough to approach the gate, and the one she tugged away from the buffet was the little pygmy.

"I would have pegged that one for more of a Tiny Tim," Jack muttered in an undertone.

Huh. So he *did* have a sense of humor. And a lovely singing voice. And a talent with animals, obviously. Not that she hadn't already known that part. Jack lived with Adalia, in a house the Buchanan brothers and sisters had inherited from Beau, their grandfather, after he passed away. They'd also inherited his cat, the infamously evil Jezebel, who needed a double dose of sedatives to be brought to the vet. According to Adalia, the hell cat cuddled with Jack as if she were sweet as sugar.

And there was something else she knew about him. Adalia had told her that he had a little sister, one he'd helped raise, and she was about to move in with them. Which meant he was a pretty solid guy. One who was good with kids, no less.

Looking at Jack now, holding that goose as if it were a puppy, his face stretched in a rare smile, she felt a powerful punch of attraction. With his dark hair and soulful dark eyes, Jack Durand was a handsome man, something she hadn't noticed until this very moment. Of course, maybe she was just feeling the effects of her months-long man drought. Ever since River had accepted the brewmaster job at Buchanan Brewery and started seeing Adalia's sister, Georgie, she hadn't had the heart to go on a date or engage in one of her usual casual relationships.

She hadn't had much of a heart left to do anything.

But she'd come to terms with it, mostly. Josie was probably right—the man who'd played such an important role in her life had fallen in love with someone else.

So why not have some fun? No one needs to know.

Because from the way Jack was looking at her, with a crooked smile that spoke of attraction and amusement, he wouldn't be opposed to the kind of fun she had in mind.

Because he's Adalia and Georgie's brother, you idiot.

Then she heard the pop of a breaking zip tie, and the plastic baby gates came down, the animals rushing in a stampede over the fallen plastic. The next instant they were treating the buffet table like it was a trough. It had probably been inevitable, the way things were set up, but Maisie hadn't helped things by dangling a carrot—or some breadsticks, as it were—in front of them. Oops.

There was a backyard fence, so there was no real danger of them getting away. The only threat to their safety lay in whatever delicacies Dottie had included in the spread, but they were probably safe. Goats could eat practically anything.

"Oh, that happened earlier than expected," Dottie said without a hint of alarm. "I was hoping everyone would be here by the time they got out."

The animal wrangler finally shook out of his stupor. "You said nothing like this would ever happen again!" he shouted at Lurch.

"And you believed him?" Maisie asked in amusement, glancing at Jack again. The goose flapped its wings a little, and Jack shrugged and let him loose.

"Doesn't seem fair that they should enjoy the feast without him."

"I predicted all of this!" Josie said victoriously from behind her booth. "Feel free to approach my station for a painfully accurate reading."

"She shouldn't feel so vindicated," Jack said in an undertone. "I think anyone could have predicted this wouldn't go well."

Maisie laughed out loud at that, then laughed a little harder when Stella bustled up to the buffet, shrieking, "No! Blitzen is lactose intolerant." She released Grumpy to go after Blitzen, a rotund goat with a brown and black coat, only for Grumpy to immediately latch on to a breadstick and chow down.

The donkey wrangler had apparently had enough of this circus and departed without another word, literally riding off on his donkey to wherever he'd parked his trailer. Maisie and Jack exchanged a look, both of them laughing now, but they stepped forward to help wrangle the animals. By the time they got the goats back into the pen, Jack's dress shirt was torn in three different places, and the bottom of Maisie's dress was covered in some kind of bean dip. Lurch tried to do his part, too, and lunged for Diego, somehow managing to get a goose footprint on top of his bald head, made with some kind of red dip, it looked like. Apparently it burned—Dottie was sometimes big on making things look like they tasted—because Lurch shoved Diego at Jack before running to the ice bucket someone had put out for beer and sticking his whole head in.

As soon as the goats were contained again, Stella had run into the house in dramatic fashion. Maisie had thought she was going inside to change her clothes, but the back door opened again, and when Stella walked out, she looked much the same as when she'd gone in—dress eaten away in parts by Grumpy, a green stain on what remained of it. She was carrying a blank canvas, and she hurried over to her abandoned easel, threw the painting in progress on the ground, and started painting on the fresh one.

"She's inspired!" Dottie announced joyfully. "I can't wait to see what comes of this!"

She seemed genuinely excited, like she cared not one bit that the buffet table looked like a swarm of locusts had descended on it. People hadn't even started arriving for the party yet.

Josie sat silently in her booth, staring into the fishbowl as if studying all of the secrets of the universe.

"Dottie, do you have any clothes Jack and I can change into?" Maisie asked. "And maybe somewhere safe we can stow the goose?"

"Oh, Diego can go anywhere," Stella said, waving a hand dismissively. "He's sweet as can be."

"That poor goat would beg to differ," Maisie said, although perhaps she was just arguing for the sake of arguing. The "poor" goat in question had bitten her leg.

Stella glanced at them and then tipped her head. "Oh, don't be surly. Just look at the way he's cuddling with that fine man." She lowered her paintbrush, her gaze narrowing on Jack. "You know, I had my heart set on the other one—the one named after a fish—but his girlfriend is a harridan." The harridan being Adalia, and the "fish" being Finn, Adalia's boyfriend. "You'll do just fine. You're the Buchanan bastard, aren't you?"

Something flashed in Jack's eyes. Probably he'd been called that before.

But he just said calmly, "I prefer to be called that for the content of my character, not the circumstances of my birth."

Which was just about perfect as far as responses went.

"Stella," Dottie snapped in what was maybe the only time Maisie could remember hearing her lose her temper. "That's an awful thing to call my grandson. Now, I don't want you to leave, not when you're clearly in the throes of inspiration, but you should apologize."

Jack wasn't her grandson, not really. But Dottie had been Beau's partner for something like twenty years, and it was clear she saw his grandchildren as her responsibility.

Stella let the paintbrush fall—literally fall—into the grass, spraying red.

"I *am* sorry," she said, walking toward Jack with arms extended. He took a step backward, almost tripping on the baby gate, and Maisie moved in front of him.

"Don't come any closer," she said. "If you think Adalia's a harridan, you'll find my bite is much worse than my bark."

The goose in Jack's arms nudged Maisie with his beak, but she didn't yield any ground. Jack had apparently shifted the bird into the crook of one arm, because she felt his other hand wrap around her hip. Maybe he was just trying to keep her from walking into the goose's danger zone, but his firm touch was putting her into a whole different danger zone.

"Oh, so he's yours, then," Stella said with a pout. "I never get to have any fun." But she paused, then said, "Like I said, I'm sorry. I have an artist's temperament, I suppose."

Maisie didn't attempt to hold in a guffaw. "And I'm sure it allows you to get away with all manner of things."

Lurch looked up at them, head sopping wet from his dip in the bucket, water dripping all over his shirt. "I sensed that when I first saw you," he said to Stella. "The artist thing."

What gave her away? The paint all over her clothes and hair, or the fact that she had a literal easel out on the lawn?

"Oh, aren't you a big, strong man?" she said.

Maisie was half tempted to stick around to watch what was sure to be the strangest mating dance known to humankind—or animalkind for that matter—but the other guests would be here soon. Even if she was mostly resigned to the whole Georgie and River thing, she didn't want to have food on her dress in front of Georgie, who never seemed to have a single hair out of place.

"Dottie?" she pressed.

Dottie had been watching the whole Lurch–Stella exchange with fascination, but she shook it off and gestured for them to follow her into the house. "It's those pheromones Stella wears," she said in an undertone. "They bring men to their knees."

Jack shot her a dubious look, but his next comment was for Maisie. "Thanks for saving me back there."

"No problem," she said, her mouth tipping up at the corners. He still had the goose cradled against his chest, his grip gentle but firm. She wondered if he'd hold a woman like that too. "You let Adalia get away with fostering a dog while you were away for the weekend. Stella would have eaten you alive."

"Now, children," Dottie said, tutting her tongue. "That artist's temperament *does* get Stella into trouble sometimes, but she's a good-enough sort. I wanted to do a little something for her since Adalia was hesitant to allow any of the goats at the Art Display."

Maisie snort-laughed. She could imagine it now—the puppies barking at the goats, the goats chowing down on paintings. It would have been chaos.

"So the after-party was her consolation prize?" Jack asked. The goose in his arms looked cozy enough to take a nap. Who *was* this guy?

"And so are you, apparently," Maisie said with a wink. "Sounds like she had her heart set on Finn." Finn was handsome, but to Maisie he'd always been "just Finn," the way she hoped River could someday be "just River." She wasn't quite there yet, but she was trying.

Dottie pointed down the hall. "Help yourself to anything that appeals to you, dear. You know your way around. I'll get Jack and Diego here sorted."

Maisie met Jack's gaze, taking in the amused tilt of his mouth, the dark wells of his eyes. "Good luck," she said. "You might just need it."

Once in Dottie's room, she let herself into the closet and flipped through the clothes, feeling the bittersweet wash of memories. How much time had she spent here over the years? Dottie was River's great-aunt, but she'd raised him since he was a teenager, and Maisie and River had been so close growing up that this house had been like a second home to her, just like the O'Shea house had been a second home to River. Most of these outfits were ones she'd seen before. Birthday parties. Halloween parties. Just-because parties. Dottie Hendrickson was a woman who liked to celebrate.

She found a green summer dress, one that would be a little long on Dottie and maybe just a tad short on her, and took off her ruined dress and put it on. It fit, and when Maisie looked in the mirror, she wasn't ashamed by what she saw.

But you're not blond, and your hair will never be orderly, and most of all, you'll never be her.

Which she was okay with, really. She didn't want to be someone else. She liked herself just fine the way she was, and to hell with anyone who didn't. But she couldn't help feeling a little heartsick. Because for years she'd thought her life would be one way, and now she knew she'd been lying to herself, which was the worst kind of lying a person could do.

"Get it together, Red," she told herself, tapping the forehead of her reflection. It was a nickname her dad had given her for her hair, which had been fiery since birth. Out of three O'Shea sisters, she was the only one who was a true redhead, although her younger sister had strawberry blond hair.

She slipped out into the hall and nearly tripped over a warped floorboard when she saw Jack. He'd changed into a long-sleeved thermal T-shirt and a pair of jeans. If he'd looked good in a suit, he looked even better like this. The sleeves hugged his arm muscles, making her want to pull the shirt off to get a good look at them. And the way he was eyeing her said he thought she looked pretty good in Dottie's dress.

But then she realized that he was wearing River's clothes. Was that why she was suddenly so attracted to him? He had dark hair like River too, and although his eyes were several shades darker, they were still brown. Was she just looking for an imitation of River in someone else? Would she spend the rest of her life doing that?

Josie had been right: she was totally screwed.

CHAPTER

Two

Jack stopped in his tracks the moment he saw Maisie emerging into the hallway. He'd noticed her before—hell, how could he not? She was loud and confident and didn't take crap from anyone. Sure, he'd found her attractive the first time he'd seen her, but she was River's friend, and there was *no way* he was getting in the middle of that. He and River hadn't gotten off to a great start with the brewery—admittedly Jack's fault—and even though things were better, it didn't feel like they were on solid footing yet.

But…holy shit.

She was all legs in that green dress that brought out the green of her eyes, glittering like emeralds. Her red hair was slightly more contained than usual, but her curls still spilled everywhere. The silky material clung to her curves—and damn, did she have curves—but his gaze was drawn back down. Her shoes didn't exactly match the dress, but who cared when she had legs that went on for miles…

"So you're a leg man?" she asked in a wry tone, her hand propped on her hip, which only drew the hem higher.

Busted. He grinned, dragging his gaze from the newly exposed skin to her face, which now wore a smug expression.

"I appreciate every part of a woman's body," he said in a tone that bordered on cocky, which wasn't usually like him.

"Ah, you're a politician, then." Her voice had a hint of sharpness, and he knew she was testing him.

He took a step toward her. "Because I didn't directly answer your question?" he asked with a lifted brow. "You're asking me to choose a specific body part, which is impossible. But when you wear a dress like that..." His voice trailed off, letting her fill in the rest, because he was busy imagining that hem going higher... "After our near-death experience, I feel like I need to buy you a drink."

Because against his better judgment, he really wanted to continue this conversation.

She studied him for a moment. Then her mouth twisted into an amused grin. "Okay, goose whisperer. As long as it's not some of Lurch's punch. The name changes, but the hangover stays the same."

"Not to worry. I've been warned," he said, gesturing for her to head down the hall.

She turned and started for the living room, and his gaze landed on the swell of her butt, the silky fabric hitching up slightly as she walked.

He sucked in a deep breath and forced himself to stare at the back of her head, which was only slightly better. Her mass of curls made him wonder what they'd look like spread out on a pillow as he...

Shit. *No.* This was *Maisie.* River's friend. Hell, she was one of Adalia's best friends too. If they started something and it didn't work out, it would mess up *everything*, and Jack was tired of watching the world blow up around him.

Hell, he was digging himself out of a trench hole at that very moment.

No, no thinking about Iris tonight. He'd spent the past six months worrying about Iris—make that the past seventeen-odd years—and there was nothing he could do for her right then. He'd deal with his sister's issues tomorrow.

Still, he found himself following Maisie like she was the Pied Piper, because while his head told him that continuing this was a *very* bad idea, his hormones strongly disagreed.

She stopped in front of the fridge and opened it, scanning the contents while he stood on the other side of the open door.

"Dottie has some of River's new IPA out back," he said. "I brought it over and put it in a bucket of ice."

She made a face. "Didn't you see Lurch put his head in that bucket? Anyway, I'm not in the mood for beer."

He released a chuckle. "Is it *possible* to be a member of the Buchanan family, honorary or otherwise, and not be in the mood for beer?"

She turned to look at him, her eyes dancing. "So you're telling me you want beer 24/7?"

He grinned. "I like to brush my teeth with Hair of Hops, and I pour Cesspool of Sin in my Cheerios for breakfast."

Her smile spread as she rested her forearm on the fridge door. "So you're a Buchanan through and through?"

That sobered him. While his father was Prescott Buchanan, Jack's last name was Durand. A stipulation his father had made when his attorneys had worked out the child support arrangements. He wasn't a Buchanan, and although he'd thought that working with his siblings at their grandfather's brewery might change that, he felt like more of an outsider than ever. It wasn't his half-sisters' fault. It was his past that held him back, reminding him that sharing DNA with someone didn't ensure any kind of relationship.

"Hey," Maisie said, worry filling her eyes. "What that woman said was wrong."

It took him a second to realize she was talking about the goat lady—Stella?—calling him a bastard. Strangely, that part of being the product of an affair didn't bother him, but he saw no point in correcting her. He forced a smile. "I've heard plenty worse. So if we're not drinking beer, what are you searching for?"

She leaned back down, searching the fridge. "I was hoping Dottie might have a pitcher of margaritas or sangria or something."

"Sounds a lot like punch. Maybe you're not so averse to Lurch's drink after all," he said with a laugh.

"News flash," she said as she stood upright and closed the door. "He makes it from beer."

"Rumor has it there were other ingredients in it at the last party," Jack said. "Beet juice and dandelion wine, to name a few."

Her face scrunched in disgust, and she went from looking fierce to unguarded in the blink of an eye. "That's gross."

He shrugged, still grinning like a fool. "I'm only reporting what I heard. I wasn't there, and if I had been, I wouldn't have been first in line to try it. But I only recall seeing beer and Lurch's punch out back, so if you're in the mood for something else, I'll see what Dottie has in her liquor cabinet and make you something."

"You're gonna make me a drink?" she asked, raising her eyebrows. "I think I saw this play out in a Lifetime movie once. The guy made the girl a drink, and when she woke up, she'd been sold into some sex cult."

He laughed as he looked in the cabinet over Dottie's fridge, where most people kept their liquor. "That doesn't sound like a Lifetime movie to me," he said, pleased when he saw several bottles. Vodka. Gin. Rum. Triple sec. "And I used to be a bartender. I take it you like sweet and fruity drinks?"

Her brow shot up. "Are you judging me, Mr. I-Watch-So-Many-Lifetime-Movies-I-Can-Spot-a-Fake-Plot? Seems like *I* should be judging *you*."

Turning to face her, he shook his head. Damn she was prickly, and for some bizarre reason he liked it. "Judge me all you want, but I'm not judging you. I'm just trying to figure out what to make you."

Her face froze and her irritation faded. "Oh."

He laughed, then spotted some lemons on the counter. "How about a lemon drop martini? I'm limited on a few key ingredients, so it won't be my best, but I guarantee it will be better than Lurch's punch."

An appreciative look filled her eyes. "Okay, then. Wow me."

He laughed again, and damn it felt good. His life had been serious for far too long, but Maisie brought out a playful side of him that had been buried forever. Tonight he wanted to pretend that he didn't have a narcissistic mother and a seventeen-year-old sister who felt like the world was caving in on her. He was going to pretend he wasn't creeping up on thirty without much of an idea of what the hell he was doing. Tonight, he was just a man who was captivated by a beautiful woman.

After slicing the lemon, he pulled the bottles of vodka and triple sec out of the cabinet. He rooted around the kitchen and found a mason jar and lid, plus a bottle of agave nectar since he didn't have any simple syrup. He added the ingredients to the jar and shook it up with some ice, while Maisie watched him with an amused grin.

"Were you like those bartenders in *Coyote Ugly* who took their shirts off?"

"Sorry to disappoint. That would violate *many* health code standards."

"So you're a rule follower," she said, studying him more intently.

"Why do you feel the need to label me?" he asked, searching for an appropriate glass to pour the drink into and only finding a wine glass.

But Maisie must have realized his dilemma because she snatched the mason jar from his hand and took the lid off.

"You're supposed to pour it into another glass."

She looked up at him with a smug expression. "See? Rule follower."

Then she took a sip.

Was it wrong that he watched her lips as they cradled the rim of the jar? Or that his gaze drifted to her bare neck as she swallowed? Shit. That should *not* be turning him on, yet here he was, shifting uncomfortably and grateful his boxer briefs had shrunk in the dryer, binding him more tightly than usual.

"I don't follow all the rules," he found himself saying in a husky voice.

She lowered the jar and stared up at him. "Oh, yeah? Prove it."

Jesus. What was she doing to him? Was she insinuating what he hoped she was? He took a step toward her, closing the distance between them and wrapping an arm around her back. When she didn't protest or knee him in the balls, he slowly pulled her flush against him.

"Was this what you had in mind?" he dared to ask.

Her emerald eyes were staring up at him, hooded with lust. "Not exactly."

He started to let go of her, because while every signal she was sending him said yes, *not exactly* constituted a no in his book.

"Don't you dare let go of me," she said, grabbing a fistful of his shirt to hold him in place. "When I asked you to break some rules, I figured you'd just run with scissors or hang the toilet paper upside down."

Despite himself, he laughed, because even though that had to be the least sexy thing she could have possibly said, it was so her. "Do you think I'm so uptight that I'd get all twisted over how to hang toilet paper?" Then he added, "And it's over, not under."

Her eyes lit up with mischief, and she reached up on her tiptoes, pressing her lips to his.

It was a tentative kiss, a questioning kiss. Was this what he wanted?

Yes. This was *definitely* what he wanted.

His arm tightened around her, and he deepened the kiss with a hunger he wasn't sure he'd ever felt for a woman before. He'd blame it on alcohol, but he hadn't had a drink all night.

Voices filtered into his brain and he lifted his head, knowing he should step away from her in case anyone walked in on them, but he wasn't ready to let go of her yet.

"Wow," she said softly. "Did they teach you how to kiss like that in bartending school?"

A slow smile spread across his face as his stomach twisted. "I didn't go to bartending school. On-the-job training."

She cocked an eyebrow. "You don't say."

Then she took a step back, her drink still in her hand. His eyes tracked her lips as she took another sip.

He was either going to have to go to the bathroom and deal with his *down-south* situation or take her home, because just being next to her was sending his hormones into overdrive, and right or wrong, he wasn't ready to walk away.

"Well?" he asked. "Is it better than Lurch's punch?"

Her eyes lit up. "I thought you didn't care if I judged you."

"I don't, but you have to admit, it would have to be pretty bad to fall below Lurch's standards."

She laughed. "It's better than what I get at Prohibition." He'd been in town long enough to know that was a Roaring Twenties-style cocktail bar. A popular one. Then she added, "But don't let it go to your head."

He put the bottles back in the cabinet, then motioned to the back door. More people had filtered into the yard, and miracle of miracles, the goats were still contained. He'd left Diego in the bedroom, and he suspected Dottie was going to come back to a situation. Still, he'd done as he was told. "I feel like I need to make an appearance out there. Would you mind being my bodyguard?"

She gave him a puzzled look. Then understanding filled her eyes. "Because they're staffers and you're Buchanan management?"

He shrugged, not wanting to explain. There was a fine line between getting along with your employees and earning their respect, between being their friend and letting them take advantage of you. He wanted the Buchanan employees to respect him, but he also wanted them to feel comfortable coming to him if they had a problem. Which involved out-of-the-office interaction from time to time. He hadn't wanted to come tonight, especially since he was literally picking his sister up at the airport tomorrow, after which his life would be devoted to getting her settled in. To making up for all of the things their mother had failed to be. But now…

Thank God he'd come.

"As for a bodyguard," she said, "it seems like I need you more than you need me. *Goose whisperer.*"

He grinned. "I was thinking about the goat lady. I need you to be my harridan."

A saucy grin lit up her face. "Oh, I can do that with one hand tied behind my back."

An image of Maisie with his silk tie around her wrist sent his blood pooling south at a rapid rate, and he started to conjugate Spanish verbs in his head, a trick he'd learned in high school. It usually served him well, but for some reason it wasn't working.

Maisie walked out the back door, leaving him to follow.

And he did, like before, only the pull was stronger this time.

At least he had the sense not to reach out and hold her hand or wrap an arm around her back like he was sorely tempted to do. Instead, he kept a small distance between them.

"So what does this mingling entail?" she asked as they passed a few people and stopped a few feet from the food table, which was all but destroyed. Jack hadn't eaten much at lunch and had skipped dinner. He suddenly realized he was hungry.

"You know, the usual. Small talk." But that seemed nearly impossible with Maisie next to him, and he'd sooner cut off his foot than walk away from her now.

"So should we approach someone?" she asked. Then her guard went back up. "Unless you think you should talk to them alone."

"Don't you dare leave me," he said, and it took everything in him to keep from reaching out for her hand. "I need you to protect me."

"From Stella?" She nodded across the yard toward the older woman, who had gotten out yet another canvas and was painting a naked Lurch riding a goat. Thankfully, Lurch was posing with only his shirt off, several feet to her side.

"Obviously," he said with a grin. "What if she finishes the painting and decides she needs a new model?"

He was about to lead her over to a small group of employees when River and Georgie walked through the back gate, looking happier than ever, if that were possible. He'd seen the spark between them before anyone else, on the night of the will reading. Of course, Adalia and Finn were now running neck and neck for the happiest couple distinction, and while Jack was happy for his sisters, he realized there was a tiny spark of jealousy too. Some people took him for a loner, but that was more because he'd had to be alone most of his life than because he preferred it that way.

"Say," Maisie said, "you want to get out of here?"

He glanced down at her in surprise. "You want to get a bite to eat somewhere?"

"No," she said, her voice husky. "I was thinking my place. I have food…and other things."

Those words were like music to his ears, but this was dangerous ground.

"Don't think so hard, Jack," she whispered. "There's only one rule: this is just for tonight." She tilted her head up, her eyes glimmering with mischief and lust, her full lips slightly parted. "Deal?"

She was right. For once, he was going to stop thinking with his head and think with his… "Deal."

CHAPTER Three

They about-faced to cut back through the house, acting like bandits. And maybe they were—they were stealing away with Dottie's clothes, after all. But Dottie was the only person who saw them, and she just caught Maisie's eye and winked, which was basically like giving her blessing.

Not that Maisie had expected her to do otherwise. Dottie always seemed to be on a one-woman mission to get her laid. Or, as Dottie would put it, find her a man who was human. She suspected River's aunt knew more than she let on, which was unusual—Dottie usually liked to pretend she knew more than she did, not the other way around.

Once they were inside, Maisie set the lemon drop martini down on the kitchen counter.

"Don't take it the wrong way, but it turns out I'd rather take the bartender home than finish the drink," she said, grabbing Jack's bicep. It felt just as good as she'd thought it would. And as soon as she got him out of River's shirt, she could stop thinking about the fact that it *was* his shirt, questioning whether her attraction to Jack was about Jack or whether she was projecting. She didn't think she was. Not this time. Jack was sexy as hell, smart, and quick-witted enough to keep up with her. But she'd gone to see her older sister a couple of months ago, and Mary had told her, gently, that her last three boyfriends had looked like they'd come from an audition for the role of River Reeves. They'd even had the same kind of baggage. Broken homes, parents who'd adiosed.

Just like Jack.

Stop sabotaging yourself. A smoking hot man who can make you laugh also wants to make you moan. Forget River. Forget Adalia. And definitely forget Georgie. Tonight's for you. You, and this man with the ridiculous arms.

"I can't fault your decision-making," Jack said with a grin.

She heard voices near the back door. If anyone came in right now, it would destroy the spell between them, this bubble they were making, so she grabbed Jack's hand and tugged him toward the front of the house.

"You can follow me," she said as she led him out the door. "If you leave your car here all night, they'll assume you got eaten by Stella."

"All night, huh?" Jack said, his voice husky.

She could practically feel the prickles rising on her back. "Well, I wasn't planning on driving you back in the dead of night. Last I checked, I'm not a taxi service."

She came to a stop in front of her Jeep, and he stopped with her.

"Hey," he said, lifting a hand to her hip, his touch searing her. It had been much too long since she'd been touched like that, and she wanted those hands everywhere. They were strong hands, capable. "That's not what I meant," he said. "I'm just feeling pretty lucky. It's not every day a gorgeous woman invites me home."

"You mean it's only a once-a-week kind of a thing?" she asked.

He shook his head slightly. "After the goats and the goose and Stella…I'd say this is a once-in-a-lifetime kind of thing."

The way he was eyeing her up said he wasn't just talking about the circumstances.

She wanted to kiss that grin off his lips, make sure the kiss in the kitchen hadn't been a fluke—weren't you supposed to preview the goods before you went all in?—but they were in full view of anyone in the street, plus maybe some of the people out back, and she didn't want anyone to see them. She'd meant what she'd said: one night. The last thing she was equipped for right now was a healthy relationship. So she settled for touching those arms again, squeezing them.

"Which car is yours?" she asked.

He nodded to a Prius that had seen better days, and she reached around and patted her green Jeep, which had also seen better days.

"Nice car," he said, and she just nodded. It wasn't. But it had been her dad's car, and her parents had been gone almost a decade now. She'd drive it into the ground and then some.

"See you there?"

"I look forward to it," he said, in a deep, husky voice she felt down to her ovaries.

Down, girl.

He squeezed her hip and headed down to his car.

She drove carefully all the way home, checking her rearview mirror frequently to make sure he was still behind her. It had occurred to her belatedly that she should have given him the address, but Jack clearly knew his way around a car just like he knew how to stir a drink and calm a pissed-off goose. Every time she looked, she saw him there, right behind her. His expression looked intent, like he was planning all the things he wanted to do to her. Thinking about it gave her a full-body shiver. Her text alert went off a couple of times, and after she parked in her drive, she checked her phone.

They were both from River. *Where are you? Dottie says there was an 'incident' with the goats, and you left. Someone stowed a goose in my old room, and I'm thinking of declaring the space a loss.*

The second text was a picture of Diego sitting in the midst of a bunch of torn-up bedclothes and goose turds.

No mention of Jack. Somehow, she suspected it wasn't because Jack's absence hadn't been noticed too, but because River would never guess she might do something as impulsive as take him home.

She was tempted to text back: *Too bad. I stole the goose whisperer. Good luck getting the goose out now.*

But a quick glance in her rearview mirror showed Jack was pulling up beside her, and she turned off her phone instead.

They got out at the same time, almost clicking doors. It wasn't funny, not really, but she laughed anyway. Because she was feeling nearly giddy with the moment, something so unusual for her she felt a little beside herself.

Einstein must've heard the cars and her laughter—her corgi was old, not deaf—because he started barking at the door. Chaco, the little mutt she was fostering at home and leaning toward keeping, joined him.

"You know about the shelter, so surely this won't come as a surprise," she said to Jack, "but I have dogs."

"I would expect nothing less," he said. "How many do you have?" He grinned. "Five? Ten? Tell me you're not a hoarder."

"Just two at the moment," she said. "My dog, Einstein, is getting up there in years, and he's a grumpy old man. He doesn't like other dogs hanging around, but he tolerates Chaco because she's smaller than him."

She grabbed the belt loops of his borrowed jeans and pulled him closer.

Their faces inches apart, she said, "We're about to test your animal whispering skills on something other than geese."

She was referring to the dogs, sort of, but she also wanted to see what magic he could work on her.

He spanned the distance between them and kissed her, a hungry kiss that promised things she very much wanted. She was the one who pulled away.

"Let's go inside."

But she kept her fingers in his belt loops, because she wanted to, and he slid his arm around her, bringing his hand to rest at the small of her back. The heat that pulsed from it promised of things to come.

As they walked toward the door, Jack looked at the house, taking it in with the same intensity he seemed to approach everything.

"Big house for just the three of you," he commented. And even though he didn't know, had no way of knowing, it still felt like a blow.

"It's the house I grew up in," she said simply. Because *my parents are dead* wasn't exactly sexy talk.

Something told her that he might understand. That life had shoveled plenty of crap on him too. But that wasn't what this was about.

He looked at her but didn't say anything. It was like he was leaving her space to talk if she felt like it. That wasn't Maisie's way—if she wanted to know, she usually asked. But it was kind of nice, his discretion.

They reached the couple of steps leading up to the door, and Maisie put a hand on his chest—his incredibly firm chest.

"Fair warning. You may have some sort of talent with animals, but Einstein doesn't like men, especially men I bring home. I'm going to take him out to the clubhouse."

Part of her wanted to see if her dog liked Jack—given his ability with that goose, with Jezebel, it seemed possible—but she also didn't want Einstein to latch on to his ankle or stand at his feet barking up at him. It wouldn't exactly create a good impression, or contribute to the mood.

"You have a clubhouse for the dogs?" he asked, the corners of his mouth hitching up.

"It used to be for humans, but now it's just me. It would be kind of absurd to go out there by myself to, what, play solitaire?" She shrugged. "The dogs like it, and it gives me space for fosters if Einstein takes issue with them." But she remembered how it used to be, back when there were other people here, and it made her ache to think about it.

This was why she didn't bring men home much. Usually she went over to their places. That way she could leave whenever she wanted, and they couldn't see more of her life than she cared to show. But Jack lived with Adalia, and although Adalia was almost certainly going to be at Finn's house tonight, there was no way she wanted to answer the kind of questions she'd be asked if she tried to sneak out of the Buchanan house and found her friend in the kitchen drinking coffee.

"I'd want a clubhouse if I were a dog," Jack said, straight-faced.

It was an absurd statement, and it made her smile at him, pulling her away from her thoughts of the house and its history.

"Of course you would," she said. "Who wouldn't want a clubhouse?"

He nodded to the door. "I'm ready if you are."

The door was mostly glass, and she could see both of the dogs behind it. Einstein was barking louder now, his shrill bark—the kind he reserved for strangers—but Chaco had stopped barking and was wagging her tail maniacally.

"I leave Chaco to you," she said. "She's a bit of a sucker, and I think she's already in love."

She let go of him and opened the door, immediately swooping down and grabbing Ein. He stopped barking for long enough to lick her hand and then her face, but he immediately turned back toward Jack and let out a low growl. Apparently, Jack's magic didn't extend to slightly geriatric dogs. Or maybe the spell would simply take longer to set in. Ein was stubborn. He was a bit like her, which was one of the reasons she'd recognized he was her soul companion.

Jack had leaned down to Chaco, who instantly started licking his face, fuzzy tail wagging even faster.

He was speaking softly to her, his voice too low for Maisie to hear, and something about his gentleness moved her in a way she hadn't expected. In a way she wasn't supposed to feel about a prospective one-night stand.

He sang to geese and whispered sweet nothings to puppies. This man had hidden layers she'd only begun to tap, and part of her wanted to dig deep.

But Ein nudged her with his nose, and she shook the feeling off. "I'm going to take him out there," she said. "I'll be right back."

"Won't he get lonely?" Jack asked. "Should we bring Chaco out there too?"

Was he worried Chaco would sit in the corner watching them while they got down to business? It bothered some guys, having dogs around.

But no. There was a look in his eyes that said he was earnest, and she felt a kind of burgeoning fondness.

"Good idea. You can follow me. She's not going to run off."

Because she didn't quite trust Einstein not to harass Jack, she kept him wrapped up in her arms like she used to carry him around when he was younger—in that wounded time when they'd healed each other—and led the way to the clubhouse.

Jack whistled as they approached it. "Looks like a second house."

"I guess it was, back in the day. The people who lived here before us used it as a guest suite. There's even a bathroom. Not that I'd recommend using it."

"Noted."

She opened the door, letting out a musty odor with a strong hint of dog, and switched on the light.

"No perfume could cover that smell," she said. But she wasn't embarrassed. She'd told him what he was getting into.

"Doesn't bother me," he said. "It's an honest smell. I'd rather smell dog than some of the things I ran into at the bar."

She scrunched her nose. "I'll bet."

Chaco raced past her, heading straight for her favorite cushion and the koala bear chew toy she loved so much Maisie had bought her two, one for out here and one for inside. Yeah, she was a sucker when it came to them.

Ein whined a little in Maisie's arms. She gave him a little squeeze and an admonishing look and set him down. He threw a final grumpy stare Jack's way, seasoned by a low growl, then headed for his favorite bed. Chaco abandoned her perch to curl up at his feet.

Maisie shot Jack a look. But there was no hint of I-told-you-so in his expression. There was only heat. He held out a hand. "Shall we?"

Even though it was her house, and part of her was tempted to remind him of it, she shut the door to the clubhouse and took his hand.

They walked back to the house like that, hand in hand, almost like they were a couple instead of…well, whatever this was. It had no business feeling this nice. So Maisie turned to him with a wicked glint in her eyes.

"Want to play strip poker?"

He grinned back. "I thought you'd never ask."

CHAPTER Four

Jack had played strip poker once at a wild after-hours work party, back when he was busing tables at a chain restaurant his senior year of high school. No good had come out of it. He'd gotten drunk off his ass and lost everything but his underwear. But this was a different situation. Best-case scenario, he'd watch Maisie take her clothes off piece by piece, although, to be fair, there weren't many pieces. Worst-case scenario, he lost all of his. He couldn't think of a downside.

"You know how to play poker, right?" she asked with a sly grin as she climbed the porch steps. She started to reach for the door, but he stretched out his longer arm and opened it.

"I'm a man of many talents."

Turning around to face him, she took a backward step into the house. "And a gentleman too. Let's hope you're not so gentlemanly between the sheets."

When had he ever had this much fun with a woman? Okay, a woman who wasn't related to him, because Adalia could probably make a monk laugh in the middle of a week-long silent meditation retreat. "I can pretty much guarantee I'm not."

She sucked in a breath and he loved that he'd gotten the better of her, even if he was sure it wouldn't last longer than a second or two, three at most.

"Does that guarantee come with a return policy?"

He grinned. There it was. God, she was fun. "Satisfaction guaranteed."

"Promises, promises." She continued walking backward into the living room. The furnishings were older and well-worn, but the place was neat and orderly, with the exception of a few dog toys scattered around.

"You got a deck of cards?" he asked.

"Would I have suggested strip poker if I didn't?" she snorted, finally turning around and heading into the kitchen. "Want a drink?"

He watched her as he walked, the dress showing her upper thighs. "Got any bourbon?"

She gave him a surprised look over her shoulder. "No, but I have whiskey and gin."

"Whiskey will do."

"Goin' for the hard stuff," she said as she opened her fridge and pulled out a screw cap bottle of wine. She grabbed a wine glass out of the cabinet, gesturing to the fridge with her free hand. "The whiskey's up there. Just like Dottie's."

"Most people store their alcohol above their refrigerators," he said, reaching for the cabinet and sorting through the bottles. Some of them looked dusty and old, like maybe they were older than Maisie. Why had she kept them? "But the heat from the fridge can damage it. Especially opened bottles. It's better to store them somewhere cool and dry."

She gave him a sardonic look as he pulled out the Jameson. "Are you here to play strip poker or give me a lesson on storing alcohol?"

He turned back toward her and wrapped his free arm around her lower back, tugging her to his chest as he searched her face. "Definitely the former. The latter is pure bonus."

She studied him for a moment with an *Is he for real?* look. Then her eyes lit up. "You're just full of surprises."

"You have no idea." He leaned over and gave her a soft kiss, then sucked her bottom lip.

She reached her arms around his neck, eagerly kissing him back, but he took several steps backward, just out of reach. "Just giving you a sample of the goods."

She laughed, shaking her head. "Like I said. Full of surprises. You gonna pour that whiskey into a glass or drink straight from the bottle?"

He reached into the cabinet and got a juice glass, pouring a finger. He had no desire to get drunk. He wanted to experience every moment with her with his full faculties, yet there was no denying he liked the taste of bourbon. Or whiskey, in a pinch.

After she poured herself a glass of white wine—a moscato, he noticed—she opened a drawer and pulled out a deck of cards.

Holding his juice cup, he reached for her wrist, going for the hand holding the cards, and tugged her back to the living room while they stared into each other's eyes.

"Where do you want to do this?" he asked. "The living room or in your bed?"

Her tongue darted out and licked her lower lip. "My room."

"Tell me where we're going, Maisie."

"Or I could lead," she said in a challenge.

He'd suspected she had a strong independent streak, but this confirmed it. A slow smile spread across his face as he spun her around to be in front.

She headed up a staircase and led him into a simple room—a bed that looked too small for the space with a gray quilted bedspread, a nightstand with a modern-looking metal lamp, and a beaten-up dresser that had seen better days. Kicking off her shoes in front of what he presumed was her closet door, she set the wine glass on the nightstand and sat on the bed. She scooted backward, crossing her legs, and gave him the tiniest sliver of her black panties to view.

Patience.

Setting his glass down beside hers, he slid off his shoes next to the bed and sat in front of her, crossing his legs too. "You do know I have the advantage here," he said, taking the box and dumping out the cards. He started to shuffle them against his knee. "I have more clothes on than you do."

"Call it a handicap," she said, reaching for the cards and then launching into some fancy shuffling.

"Why do I feel like I've been suckered?" he asked with a laugh.

"One born every minute." She started passing out cards. "Five-card draw or Texas Hold'em?"

"Five-card draw."

She stopped shuffling. "Do you need a refresher of the rules?"

He laughed. "Deal already. I'm eager to get that dress off of you. I say the winner gets to pick the article of clothing that gets removed." He smirked at her. "And they get to take it off as well."

Her eyes lit up and she dealt them both five cards. "I can agree to those terms, and since we're not betting, we only get one chance to draw new cards."

"Sounds good to me." He picked up his cards, relieved when he saw he had a pair of fives, along with an ace of hearts, a ten of spades, and a three of clubs. He kept the fives and dumped the rest and drew three more. They were junk cards, but at least he had a pair. He glanced over at Maisie, who only exchanged one card.

"Okay," she said. "Show me what you got."

He lowered his hand. "A pair of fives."

Grinning, she laid out her cards—three eights, a ten of diamonds, and a king of hearts. "Like I said, show me what you've got."

He held his hands out to the sides. "I think the rules say you get to do the honors."

She shifted her legs, closing the gap between them, and leaned over. Placing a hand on his chest, she slowly lowered her hands down to his waist. She lifted the bottom of his shirt, tugging it up and over his head.

He resisted the urge to help, mesmerized by the sight of her. When he'd driven to Dottie's tonight, he'd never dreamed he'd end up sitting on Maisie O'Shea's bed, letting her undress him. Life had long stunned him with its ability to dole out unpleasant surprises, and it was a nice change of pace to realize it could go the other way too.

Pulling the shirt free from his arms, she tossed it to the floor, then placed her hands on his shoulders, running them slowly down his arms.

"Why, Jack Durand. It should be illegal to hide these arms under sleeves."

He laughed. "I'd hate to distract the employees at the brewery. Imagine what Lurch might do if he were blinded by my biceps. Peeing in the kettles was child's play."

Something he was only able to joke about now because they'd used that incident—vandalism? assault by piss?—to relaunch the brewery with all new beers. Everyone agreed it had been a genius relaunch, and only a few people knew the story behind it.

"Lurch doesn't work there anymore," she teased. "You really should keep up with the employee roster." She sat back down and scooped up the cards, then shuffled. "I think it's your turn to deal."

He took the cards from her, letting his fingers linger on hers. He really, *really* wanted to see what she was wearing under that dress. Did her bra match her panties?

He shifted to relieve his growing bulge, then shuffled and dealt. This time he had a jack and a queen of diamonds, plus a king of hearts and a two and a six. Maisie glanced up from her cards and looked at him, her gaze dipping to his chest and then lower. Her eyes lifted back to his and she smirked. "A girl can appreciate the view."

"She can touch too." He liked that she thought he was worth watching, worth noticing. He hadn't had a girlfriend in over a year, and he'd lost the last one because she'd gotten sick of competing for his attention. "Any woman in your life will always be second," she'd said, and since contradicting her would have been a lie, he'd let her leave. There'd been a few casual entanglements since, too short to be called relationships, but somehow they had only made him feel more alone. Being alone was something he understood, though, something he could accept. For now. Iris was almost out of high school. Out of his mother's clutches. Once she was free, he could relax, perhaps have a life…

He'd decided to jumpstart the process when his grandfather left the brewery to him and his half-siblings. It had seemed like his chance to make something of himself, but then his mother had gone off the deep end—again—and he'd been forced to sue her for guardianship. And now Iris was about to move to Asheville, something Adalia was on board with, thank God, which meant there'd be no time or room for a girlfriend. He'd spend the nine months before she went off to college trying to make up for leaving her with their mother and thinking it *wouldn't* come to this.

But watching Maisie now, realizing how absolutely perfect she was...filled him with a deep sense of loss. He may not have slept with her yet, but he already knew how hard it would be to leave in the morning...if she let him stay that long. God, he hoped she let him stay that long. He wanted every last minute he could get.

Suddenly, he didn't want to play this game anymore. He wanted her.

He reached over and took the cards out of her hand and tossed them down on the bed.

"Hey!" she protested. "I was about to take off your pants."

He cupped the side of her face, his fingers sinking into her red curls. "You don't need a deck of cards to get my clothes off, Maisie."

Her breath hitched and turned shallow.

"But we've got a major issue we need to deal with before they come off."

"What's that?" she asked, sounding like she was trying to be playful, but her voice was slightly strained.

"I only have one condom, and I plan to have you multiple times before I leave in the morning." He grinned. "Do you think you can order condoms on Instacart?"

She stared at him in disbelief for a moment. Then laughter spilled out of her, a rich, warm sound that stirred something deep down in his chest.

"Because if we can't," he said, "—and trust me, I'm willing to pay the extra fee for a small order—I'm going to have to go buy some."

"Don't worry," she said, grinning. "I've got you covered. Literally."

He laughed. God, she was perfect, but he'd spent his whole life waiting, and he didn't want another minute to tick by without seeing all of her. He pulled her to her knees, then rested his hands on her upper thighs and slowly slid them up and over her hips, dragging up the hem of her dress.

It was like unwrapping a gift. Her black panties were exposed first, then the creamy skin of her abdomen.

She was still, her expression serious as he pulled the dress over her head. He let it drop to the bed, mesmerized by the sight of her, the way her black bra clung to her breasts.

"Jesus, Maisie. You're gorgeous."

Her skin flushed, and she looked away, and he wondered how often men had actually told her that. Had they been blind or stupid? But the thought of her with another man soured his stomach. Maybe it was foolish given what they were doing here, what they'd agreed to, but he didn't want to think of her with anyone else.

He let his hands roam over her soft skin, then cupped her lace-covered breasts.

"You've got too many clothes on," she said, her voice rough.

"That's easily taken care of." He slid off the bed and quickly slipped out of his jeans before he sat down on the edge of the mattress, reaching for her.

His mouth covered hers, hungry and demanding. She hooked an arm around his neck, holding on to him as she let him know how hungry she was too.

He intended to spend all night showing her she was gorgeous.

His phone's alarm went off the next morning and he groaned, dragging himself out of a deep sleep. He hadn't slept much, and all he wanted to do was hold Maisie one last time before he left. He was already debating whether to skip going home to change before he drove to Charlotte to pick up Iris from the airport. But when he blindly reached for Maisie, he found her side of the bed empty and cold.

He sat up. Where was she?

Einstein and Chaco were on the floor, watching him curiously as he got out of bed and went to the bathroom. Jack and Maisie had brought the dogs back to the house sometime after midnight. Einstein had released a low growl at Jack, but he'd settled down quickly enough in response to Maisie's whispered words. Who knew if they were sweet nothings or threats—either would move a smart man, or dog, to listen to her. If her dogs were still here, maybe she was downstairs.

He headed down in his boxer briefs, the dogs trailing behind. She wasn't in the kitchen, and when he looked out front, his stomach sank. Her Jeep was gone.

Had she left already and not said goodbye?

"There's only one rule," she'd said. *"This is just for tonight."*

That had been the agreement, and he'd already reminded himself a half dozen times since their unfinished game of strip poker that he wasn't in a position to start a relationship, but it still felt like a punch to the gut. He really liked her, and he would have at least liked to say goodbye.

Maybe it was better this way. Somewhere around four in the morning, he'd wondered how he'd find the fortitude to leave her. Looked like she'd done it for both of them.

He went back upstairs and got dressed, then found a notepad and pen in her kitchen.

Maisie,

Confession: I really suck at this one-night stand thing. It seems crass to tell you last night was incredible, even if it was. I hate not being able to tell you goodbye, but I understand. I hope things aren't awkward between us, and maybe we can be friends.

"Really, Jack?" he said out loud. "You seriously just used the let's be friends line?"

Einstein released a low growl.

"I know, buddy. I'm a fricking idiot."

What he really wanted to say was, *Maisie, you're the most amazing woman I've ever met. I want more than just one night, and I think you do too.* Because sometime in the night she'd cuddled close to him, placing a hand on his chest like she wanted to feel his heartbeat. But it didn't matter, did it? He couldn't start anything. Not now. And the only rule she'd set was that their entanglement couldn't go on past a single night. He needed to suck it up and accept her terms.

Right?

But then something took hold of him, and before he could stop himself, he wrote:

But I don't want to just be friends. I want more. Much more. My life is a shitstorm right now, but you're the kind of woman who comes along once in a lifetime, and I don't want to lose the opportunity to see where this might go. If you can be patient with me, we'll find a way to make this work.

Still, this is about you too. You only wanted one night, and I agreed to that. It's not your problem that I suddenly want more. So if you want more too, let me know. But if you don't, we'll pretend like this never happened.

This is your choice, Maisie, even if I want you to say yes more than I've wanted anything in a long time.

Jack

He read the note, analyzing all the ways she could poke fun at it. Still, he wasn't sorry for laying his heart on the line.

Chaco jumped up on his legs and released a little whine. He squatted down and rubbed the little dog's head, but Einstein, who'd been right next to her, backed up, cowering, and eyed his hand like Jack might hit him instead of doling out pets. "I'd never hurt you, buddy," he said softly. "Hopefully, this isn't goodbye. If your mom lets me, I'll bring you treats next time, okay?"

Chaco looked up at him with adoring eyes, but Einstein still eyed him distrustfully. "I like you too, girl. And I'll find a way to win you over, Ein. If you and your mom just give me a chance."

Then he stood and walked out the door. He might be leaving a piece of himself at Maisie's, but he couldn't dwell on that at the moment. Now he had to find the fortitude to face his sister.

CHAPTER
Five

You weren't supposed to sneak out on a one-night stand if it was your own house. That was how you got burgled, or went home to find all the flour bags had been emptied onto the counter and the guy had finger-written expletives in it. Not that either of those things had happened to her, but her little sister, Molly, worked for a dating blog in Seattle, and she had stories.

Of course, Maisie knew Jack wouldn't do any of those things. It was far more likely she'd come home to find he'd cooked her breakfast.

The thought of coming home to find him in her kitchen, hopefully nothing on him but an apron, cooking pancakes or fake bacon, lit a little flame of hope inside her. That stupid flame was the reason she'd left like that, without leaving a note. Which was, objectively speaking, a shitty thing to do. She'd needed to leave—someone had found a two-month-old puppy locked in an empty apartment, and it had needed a foster home stat—but she could have woken him up. Or done *something*.

The reason she hadn't was because she was afraid—an emotion she reserved solely for her romantic life, it seemed.

Last night, she hadn't thought much beyond scratching an itch. Having some fun. Making the kind of memories that would get her hot and bothered the next time she needed a little self-pleasure. But it had backfired on her, and she couldn't stop thinking about Jack. And she wasn't just thinking about his head between her thighs, or the way those amazing arms of his had pinned her to the wall for their third round. No, she was hung up on his smile. On the way he'd cradled Chaco to his chest, humming softly, when they brought the dogs inside. How he'd announced, "Your sex banishment is over, kids!" and made her laugh so hard she actually snorted.

She wouldn't mind having him around some more. In her mind, she could practically see Molly rolling her eyes at her. "It's okay to admit you like someone, Maisie. The world won't end." Mary would pipe in, "If she hasn't told River after ten years, she's not gonna tell this guy after one night."

You said just one night. No takebacks.

Except it was a woman's prerogative to change her mind, wasn't it? And sure, Jack was Georgie and Adalia's brother, but maybe that didn't matter. She'd be seeing Georgie anyway if she intended to continue her friendship with River. And continuing their friendship would be so much easier if she was seeing someone else.

So maybe it wouldn't be so bad if Jack hadn't taken the hint and left.

He won't still be there, she told herself. *He's a sexy, confident man. The last thing he's going to do is stick around where he doesn't think he's wanted.*

When she neared the house, she saw there was a car in the drive, and for a second her heart lifted. It was the same color as Jack's car, but as she got nearer, she realized it was *River's* car.

He stood on the porch waiting for her, wearing a thermal just like the one Jack had worn last night, plus a pair of old jeans. Acting for all the world like it was normal for him to just show up. Which it had been. For years. Back in high school, they'd spent half their time out in what was now the dogs' clubhouse. Most of it had been spent studying, with Maisie tutoring River to help him catch up. His mother's free-range parenting had extended to education, and River's reading had been two grade levels behind, something that had filled him with shame. Although Maisie had quickly made it known she would eviscerate anyone who thought they could call him stupid and get away with it, she hadn't wanted *him* to believe it. But it hadn't just been studying. They weren't angels. They'd smoked the occasional joint in the trees beyond the clubhouse, hiding from Mary as much as they were from her parents. Snuck beers from Beau's stash.

But things had changed after high school. Her parents had died, and River had gone off the rails, hopping from job to job, mistake to mistake, and the only thing holding them together had been each other. Once, when they were twenty-one and a little tipsy off of Beau's beer, sitting in the clubhouse so their carousing wouldn't wake Molly, River had leaned in to kiss Maisie. She'd pulled back. Told him that she'd rather be his friend than one of his many ex-girlfriends.

He'd thanked her for that afterward, and then he'd seemed to forget all about it. But she hadn't forgotten. She'd had a crush on him at the beginning, when he'd shown up to Asheville Middle with his hair tucked behind his ears and those big brown puppy dog eyes with more than a hint of defiance in them…and their almost kiss had sparked something in her. Something that had waxed and waned over the years but never fully gone away.

Except when she saw him standing there now, so handsome in the morning light, she wished she were seeing a different man.

Sucking in a breath, she parked the car and headed toward the porch. Ein and Chaco were waiting behind the door, whimpering and padding the glass. River was the one man Ein loved, unabashedly, as if he took his cues from Maisie.

"This is a rather extreme reaction to an unanswered text," she said.

River reached for one of the disposable coffee cups he'd set on the little table between the Adirondack chairs. There was a paper bag there too.

At least someone had brought her breakfast. But she had that strange ache again, like she wished it had been Jack. Which was crazy. Jack didn't know that she liked the blueberry muffins from Beans and Buns. He didn't know anything about her—just like she didn't know anything about him.

Except that wasn't quite true.

"Better be the right one," she griped weakly, glancing at the bag.

"Yeah, yeah, got you the wrong muffin one time, and I'll never hear the end of it. What happened to you last night?"

She opened the door to let the dogs out. Ein raced over to River, tail wagging so wildly it looked like it would fall off. But Chaco didn't approach either of them—she just went to sit at the top of the steps, looking down at the drive.

Almost like she missed Jack.

Her first thought caught her off guard: *she's not the only one.*

Which was crazy, really. She didn't know him well enough to miss him, and Chaco had probably just seen a squirrel. Although she loved the little dog, not much of an argument could be made for her intelligence.

Except Chaco had been around for going on two months now, and Maisie had gotten to know her habits. If she wasn't looking for Jack, she was doing a good impression of it. And if that didn't tug the old heartstrings...

"Last night?" River prompted.

She settled into one of the chairs, motioning for him to do the same.

"I caught a whiff of Stella's pheromones, and it sent me running."

River chuckled as he picked Ein up. Her dog settled in his lap, sweet as pie now that he was with River. "You should have seen the nude painting she did of Lurch. Aunt Dottie kept going on about how accurate it was...which made me wonder how she knew."

"Maybe she and Beau were swingers," Maisie suggested. She took a sip of her coffee, savoring the flavor and the kick of caffeine. God knew she was going to need it. She and Jack had only gotten a few hours of sleep. "The lurch he helped them out of might have been a sex drought in their relationship."

He gave a dramatic shudder. "Now that's an image I didn't need. She says she wants Adalia to put Stella's painting in the next Art Display."

"I'd say we should warn her," Maisie said, "but I'd prefer to see the look on her face when she sees it for the first time."

"Probably pretty similar to her expression when Finn showed her his grandmother's ring."

Maisie laughed because it was funny, but honestly, Adalia hadn't been all that freaked out. She may have turned down Finn's hilariously quick proposal, but she was pretty much on the cusp of living with him. The only thing holding her back was Jack and his soon-to-arrive sister, whose name she hadn't thought to ask.

Was Jack back home with Adalia? If so, she would surely ask him about the party. What would he say?

She knew better than to think he'd tell his sister the truth. Which was good. Because she was about 99.5% sure that Adalia knew about the whole River thing. Finn had guessed, and even though he'd refrained from telling River, he wasn't exactly known for being a steel vault.

Something a little like panic stole over her. She really, really didn't want Jack to know, but she couldn't exactly ask Adalia not to say anything, if only because she and Adalia had never actually talked about it.

And what did it matter anyway? Jack was gone. Their deal was at an end. She'd have to see him again, obviously, and their secret would always give them a bit of a dirty thrill, but that was that. She shouldn't be thinking about him.

What if he left a note? a voice inside her whispered, kindling a little flame of hope. Chaco whimpered, still looking off in the distance.

"What are you thinking about?"

River was looking at her, really looking at her, as if trying to dig deep into her thoughts.

No, thanks. Finn and her sisters had advised her to talk things out with River, to be open with him. But she couldn't see any upside to that. He was clearly in love with Georgie. Maisie accepted that. Hell, she'd *encouraged* him, because at the end of the day she loved him, whatever that love meant, and she wanted him to be happy. Telling him about her feelings—her confusing, twisting, seething feelings, which even she didn't fully understand—would only make him feel like crap.

"You didn't take home that goose and cook him for dinner, did you?" she asked. "You know you're not supposed to do that with animals who have names."

He shook his head a little, acknowledging the joke with a small smile, but she could tell he was hurt. She'd iced him out for most of the summer, and although they'd since resumed their Tuesday Bro Club dinners with Finn—a tradition the three of them had carried on for years—there was a new distance between them. River was the one in a new relationship, but she was the one who'd inserted the space between them. For self-preservation. He didn't understand, of course, and thought it came down to a dislike of Georgie. Or some random gripe against him.

"There's something I need to tell you," he said in a rush, putting Ein down and getting to his feet. It was so like what *she* should say to *him* that her heart started pounding faster in her chest. Maybe he knew after all. What if he was going to tell her they shouldn't be friends anymore? Because that was one of her fears too—that he might decide it wasn't fair to Georgie for them to see each other.

Maisie hated feeling weak and vulnerable. *Hated* it. But there it was. She didn't want to lose him. She'd already lost so much.

"Oh?" she asked, standing too. Because she wasn't the type of person who took bad news sitting down. She'd rather be standing up, ready to launch into battle.

"I know you don't like Georgie..."

She opened her mouth to respond, although she wasn't quite sure what to say, but he saved her from saying anything. "I get it. I know it was weird in the beginning, her being my boss and all, and you were just trying to be a good friend. But I love her, Maisie, and I'm going to ask her to marry me."

With those words, it felt like he'd ripped all of her progress away, like tearing a Band-Aid off a raw wound.

What was it Josie had said?

The man she loved would marry someone else, and she'd die alone. Well, even a busted clock was right twice a day.

She'd expected this. Of course she had. She'd expected it from the day he'd come into the shelter beaming, talking about Beau's granddaughter like she was the Second Coming. But it still burned. Part of her had always thought they'd end up together in the end. That River would work out his abandonment issues. That he'd realize he was ready for a real relationship. That he'd try to kiss her again, only it would actually feel right this time.

But it hadn't happened like that. Because it had been a child's hope, one that didn't fit the woman she'd become. Still, the disappointment felt no less crushing.

She'd been a fool to think she could start something with Jack. Why would a man like him want a woman who was still hung up on his future brother-in-law? He wouldn't.

Einstein barked, as if picking up on her agitation, and jostled her to attention. She realized River was staring at her, waiting for a response.

She made it glib because she had to. "I feel like I'm the godfather and you're asking for my blessing."

"I am."

"You have it," she said. She meant it, too. It wasn't his fault she felt messed up. Nor was it Georgie's.

He cleared his throat, then said, "I want you and Finn to be my co-best men."

She laughed, both because of the way he'd put it, and because of the horror he was unconsciously putting her through. He wanted her to stand up with him while he married someone else. She knew what Mary would say—*You set boundaries with everyone else. It's past time you got started with him. He won't spontaneously combust if you tell him no.*

But River looked so hopeful, so intent, and if she said no, he'd want to know *why* she'd said no. She could pretend this really was about Georgie, but then it would drive a permanent wedge between them. And their friendship really was more important to her than these feelings she'd never asked to have.

So she looked him in the eye and said, "Does this mean I get to wear a tux?"

"If you want," he said, beaming at her. "I thought you were going to say no."

"Don't get ahead of yourself," she said. "I technically haven't said yes yet. And I'm pretty sure I can't until you're engaged." She lifted her brows. "For all you know, Georgie could say no."

But they both knew she wouldn't. River just shrugged and said, "Fair play."

"But I do intend to say yes once she does…on one condition."

"Why was I sensing there was a but?"

"I'll only do it if Hops is the ring bearer." Hops being the dog she'd basically forced River to adopt, not that he was complaining. Hell, Hops was now one of the mascots of the brewery, the other being the surly Jezebel, who represented their line of sours.

They started imagining out loud what Hops would look like as the ring bearer. Did they make canine tuxedos? (A quick internet search on their phones revealed the obvious: they did, and they came in all colors of the rainbow.) Would Hops carry the rings attached to the old sandal he'd imprinted on after River first took him home?

They ate breakfast, chatting, and some of the hurt and confusion Maisie felt drifted away, buried in the normality of the scene. She'd spent countless mornings just like this with River. Eating breakfast and drinking coffee. Bantering.

They said goodbye, and he hugged her, something she'd successfully avoided for months now. It felt crazy good—like stepping into your house after a long vacation—but it didn't make her want to ravage his mouth. Or lead him up to her bedroom.

Which only confused her more. She felt those things for Jack. Did that mean she was finally ready to move on?

But if that was so, why did it still hurt to think of River with Georgie? Of the two of them getting *married*?

"Good luck," she said softly.

"I make my own luck," he said with a grin. It was what she'd always said to him when they were younger.

After River left, she walked inside with the dogs, feeling every last minute of sleep she'd missed. The coffee wasn't helping, and the muffin had tasted like chalk.

Little bits of ripped-up paper littered the floor.

After glancing back at Chaco, the usual perpetrator of messes—Einstein was a senior citizen, after all—she followed the trail to see where it took her. Another ripped-up book?

But she found a torn and bitten note in Einstein's bed. The handwriting wasn't familiar, and her heart quickened in her chest. Jack. He had written a note after all.

She read it quickly, in a great gulp of words, but it ended on a cliff-hanger. He'd said something about being friends, then had written, *But I don't.*

But I don't what?

She wanted to find him, to ask. Or maybe piece together the tiny bits of shredded paper Einstein had so uncharacteristically left all over the house, but maybe it was best to just leave things as they were. To accept that he'd taken her at her word, and maybe feel grateful for it. Because if she was going to be the co-best man at Georgie Buchanan's wedding, odds were she would be seeing a lot of Jack Durand. And she wasn't at all sure how she felt about that.

CHAPTER
Six

Jack barely had time to shower before he ran right back out the door, grabbing two travel mugs of coffee from the pot he'd started as soon as he got home. He couldn't afford to get sleepy on the road.

He had a little over two hours to think about his night with Maisie, wondering if she'd read the note yet, hoping she'd text him some smartass reply.

You want more of this? It's gonna cost you. Or something equally sassy, to which he'd say, *I'm open to negotiations.*

But his phone stubbornly refused to beep, and he belatedly realized he hadn't put his number on the note.

What a moron. Maybe she'd find a way to reach out to him anyway. Come by his house. Get his number from Adalia.

But right now he needed to focus on Iris.

He hadn't been thrilled by his mother's announcement that she was giving him a sibling, but to be fair, he'd been an eleven-year-old boy, more interested in his new PS2 gaming console than in babies. Besides, his mother barely seemed to notice him. How would she handle a baby? And did the new addition mean he'd get even less attention from her? Even then, he'd known the cold, hard truth. She'd never wanted him for anything other than for the large child support check Prescott Buchanan sent her every month.

One afternoon, his grandmother had sat him down at her worn kitchen table with a batch of snickerdoodles—his favorite—giving him her *We're about to have a serious conversation* look.

"Jacques," she said slowly, pronouncing his name with her heavy French accent. "For the longest time, it's only been you and your mother."

"No, Mémère. It's been mostly you and me. Mom is too busy with her job and her love life to be bothered."

Which was a fair assessment. His mother couldn't seem to live without a man, and following her affair with Jack's biological father, she'd gotten a taste for men with money. And men with money didn't want a kid underfoot. As she got older, *she* didn't want a kid underfoot either, for fear it would reveal her real age. Rich men wanted hot younger women, and while Genevieve was still a beautiful woman, she was already fearful of losing her youth. So Jack lived with his grandmother most of the time, and he preferred it that way.

"Yes," she said slowly with a distant look in her eyes. "It has always been you and me, and you're the best gift your mother has ever given me. But soon, it won't just be the two of us. There will be three. And the new baby will be tossed into your mother's craziness. It will be up to you to make sure he or she feels loved."

He made a face. "I'm not taking care of a stupid baby."

She smiled knowingly. "You were once a stupid baby, and I took care of you."

He sighed. "Okay. I'll help take care of the baby."

Even if that was the last thing he wanted. He was biding his time until he turned eighteen and could escape. An infant brother or sister would only tie him down.

Reaching over the small kitchen table nestled into a bowed window, she patted his hand, her eyes brimming with tears. "You're a good boy, Jacques. Don't let anyone ever tell you any different."

He wished she'd remind his mother of that.

She took a breath, hesitating, then said, "I won't always be here to protect you and your new brother or sister, so I need you to make me a promise."

"What?" he exclaimed, dropping his half-eaten cookie onto the old china plate. She'd always used her china, saying beautiful things were meant to be used, not put on a shelf and admired. "Don't talk like that. You're going to be a *very* old woman."

She smiled softly, as though she was keeping a secret. "That is my wish as well, but promise me anyway."

His mother took promises lightly, but his grandmother had taught him that a man's ability to keep his word was one of the most important reflections of his character. For him, making a promise, especially to her, was akin to signing an oath in blood. Normally, he wouldn't agree to a blind promise—she'd taught him that as well—but this was Mémère. He'd literally give her anything she asked for. "Anything."

A soft smile lifted her lips. "When I am no longer around—hopefully, years from now—I need you to protect this baby. Just like I've protected you."

He stared at her in surprise, realizing what she had said was true. She had spent the entirety of his life protecting him, but he'd just seen it as loving him.

"I won't need to take care of the baby since you're going to live to be one hundred and two," he insisted, "but I'll help you. I promise."

Her gray eyes turned serious. "Not just help me, Jacques. If I am gone, I need your assurance that you'll protect him or her. Your mother's ten times worse now than when she had you. This child needs us."

He swallowed, realizing this was a grave matter. "I promise."

She sat back in her chair, relief flooding her face. "Thank you, Jacques. You *are* a good boy. I hope I can see you become a good man."

But she hadn't. She'd died the next year, when Iris was just three months old. Later, he found out Mémère had been diagnosed with inoperable cancer right around the time she'd sat him down for their chat. She had been living on borrowed time.

And that was how Jack had become responsible for his sister's well-being.

Iris's father was married, and he'd been about as eager to have a child with Genevieve as Jack's father had been, so he'd paid a small fortune to get her to sign a nondisclosure agreement. Which meant they'd lived fairly well when Iris was little. Not that Genevieve had changed overnight and become a good mother. Thank God she'd hired a nanny for Iris, someone who'd provided her with a bit of the stability that Jack's grandmother had afforded him. But the well had gone dry after Iris turned four, and the nanny had left. Jack had found himself essentially raising his sister by the time he was fifteen.

His mother had kicked him out the day after his high school graduation, telling him he needed to learn to make his own way in the world like her, which he'd found hilarious since she'd seemed to make her way mostly off the income he and his sister provided. He'd always wondered where the money had gone. His mother must have gotten thousands of dollars in child support a month, and she was a real estate agent who only worked with high-powered clients. Now he suspected she'd run through it all on alcohol and drugs and maybe gambling to self-medicate the bipolar diagnosis she refused to acknowledge.

It didn't take a genius to realize his eviction had coincided with his father's last child support check. He'd wanted to tell her off, to confront her with the cold, hard truth of who she was, but he knew she'd cut him out of her life, which meant she'd cut him out of Iris's life, which was unacceptable.

So he'd bitten his tongue and suffered her highs and lows, all so he could be there for his sister.

They'd continued to be close, very close. He kept her for occasional overnight visits, but most of the work he did was at night. Although he'd chosen his reading list from the syllabuses of his friends' classes, he hadn't gone to college. Instead, he'd worked his way up from busboy to waiter. Bartender to bar manager. It had paid off, and he was finally making decent money, a year out from Iris's high school graduation—which would free both of them—when he got the call from an attorney in Asheville telling him his paternal grandfather had mentioned him in his will.

And then his whole world had changed.

Part of him still wondered if he shouldn't have been so insistent about keeping the brewery, but it had felt like his chance to finally make something of himself. To live a life that was no longer dependent on his mother's whims. To be his own man. Iris was leaving anyway, and after she left for college, he didn't want to find himself in an empty existence that had suddenly lost its center. Then Iris had called during his and Georgie's disastrous walk-through of the brewery, less than an hour after they'd signed the papers to keep it. Genevieve had gone off the deep end and hit Iris and then smashed up the house. Jack had caught the first flight out of Asheville and rushed home to get his mother admitted to a psychiatric unit.

He'd spent the whole summer in Chicago, taking care of Iris, filing an emergency petition to get custody. His sister had been one hundred percent on board with the decision...until she found out Jack planned to take her to Asheville.

He'd considered backing out of the brewery, but he could hear his grandmother's voice in his head. *A man's word is the measure of his character.*

But which promise held priority? His promise to help run Buchanan Brewery or his promise to protect his sister? Surely the latter promise was more important—Georgie certainly didn't need him—and yet he couldn't find it in himself to step away. It wasn't just about the opportunity that had fallen into his lap—part of it had been his need to know them, the half-sisters and brother he'd never met.

His mother had been released from the hospital, now on medication to control her mood swings, and Iris had insisted that she wanted to finish out her senior year at home and look after her.

"We can't both abandon her," she'd said in a snide tone, a dig at his intended move to Asheville.

"You can come with me, Iris," he'd insisted. "The judge said you can decide who you want to live with."

"I know who I want to live with," she said sullenly. "And I know where I don't want to live."

So he'd reluctantly moved to Asheville, waiting until the very last possible moment, praying Iris would change her mind.

Then earlier this week, Iris had called crying, begging him to come home. Their mother had gone off her meds and was acting out worse than before, bringing men to their house and partying and drinking. One of the guys had made advances on Iris after she came home from a half-day at school.

Beyond furious, Jack had insisted on flying home to Chicago to press charges. Iris had already gotten out of the house, thank God, and was staying with a friend, but she'd refused to press charges, saying the guy had only tried to kiss her.

"I don't want to live with her anymore, Jack. You win. I'll move to Asheville. How soon can I come?"

He hadn't wanted to win. He'd only wanted to protect her, which was what he'd always wanted. His greatest hope was that she'd love Asheville as much as he already did.

He'd talked to her friend Janie's parents, whom he'd gotten to know well over the years, and they'd agreed to bring Iris to Genevieve's house to pack the rest of her things. Then he'd arranged for an eight a.m. flight out of Chicago to Charlotte.

He pulled into the airport parking lot, his stomach a ball of nerves when he saw that her plane had been scheduled to land five minutes ago. They'd probably arrive at the luggage carousel at the same time, but he'd planned on meeting her at the security exit.

He was late because he'd stayed with Maisie, which filled him with guilt, and then even more guilt because he wasn't sorry. Even if he never got another day or night with Maisie, he couldn't regret their night together. Which only proved it had been something special.

But when he walked through the door, he saw Iris was standing next to the carousel, surrounded by three large bags and a couple of small carry-ons. She looked lost and bewildered, and his heart wrenched.

He never should have left her with their mother.

"Iris," he called out, and her face swung toward him, her dark brown eyes brimming with unshed tears.

Her face crumpled when she saw him, and she burst into sobs.

He ran to her, gathering her in his arms and holding her close as she wet his shirt with her tears. She sobbed and sobbed as he stroked her long dark hair. "You're safe. I'm here. Nothing's ever going to happen to you again."

"Where were you?" she asked, her voice muffled. "I thought you weren't coming."

He tilted her head back and cupped her cheek. "I will always come, Iris. *Always.*"

She hugged him tighter, as though hanging on for dear life, and he wondered once again if he'd screwed up by coming to Asheville, because he knew beyond a shadow of a doubt that he'd screwed up by leaving her.

He wouldn't let her down again.

CHAPTER
Seven

Three weeks. It had been three weeks since Jack Durand had spent the night at Maisie's house. So why was she still dreaming about him? Why was she still smelling his scent, which had long since faded, on her pillows?

She hadn't seen him a single time in the interim. It was surprisingly easy to avoid someone when you really set your mind to it, something she'd already discovered in her months-long avoidance of River after he first hooked up with Georgie. But that had been a mistake, one that had hurt both of them, and her sister Molly was adamant that this was too.

"You don't know what the rest of that note said, Maisie," she insisted. "He probably said that he wants to keep f—"

"Little ears," Mary interrupted, covering her toddler son's ears.

Maisie felt a press of longing. It was Thanksgiving morning, and the O'Sheas were all supposed to be together—they were all supposed to be *here*, at their family house—but Molly had been given an assignment about holiday dating that required her to go on five Tinder dates on Thanksgiving Day (a huge opportunity, she insisted), and Mary and her husband had decided at the last minute to bring Aidan along to visit his paternal grandparents. So instead, she was sitting at her dining room table, looking at them through a computer screen.

"You might want to inform him he had another set of grandparents," Maisie had snapped upon learning the news. "Or that, I don't know, his aunt actually has a life outside of visiting him every few months. I promised to take him to the shelter. You said you were coming." That last sentence had gotten a little more pitchy than she would have liked. Dammit, she hated showing her cards—she much preferred knowing what was in everyone else's hands.

Mary had just shrugged as if it was out of her control, but Maisie knew better. Just like she knew Molly didn't *have* to do Datesgiving, as she was calling it.

They didn't want to come. And she knew they thought *she* was the one who needed therapy, that her wish to live at home, among their parents' things, was weird, bordering on creepy.

But her thoughts digressed.

"How did you know I was going to say something naughty?" Molly complained.

"Because I know you," Mary said with an eyeroll. "What are you going to do when you see him, Maisie?"

For a second, she almost asked *Him, who?*

Because she was going to see both of them today: Jack and River. Which had to be the worst idea she'd ever come up with.

But her sisters had bailed on her, and Adalia was hosting a big Thanksgiving extravaganza at Beau Buchanan's old house, and she hadn't really been *allowed* to say no. Adalia had told her in no uncertain terms that she wouldn't hear of it. Plus, she'd seen River and Finn on Tuesday night, and they'd agreed they would hunt her down like a couple of bounty hunters if she bailed.

To her surprise, River still hadn't told Finn about his engagement, which probably meant it hadn't happened yet. But it was going to happen soon, and she'd feel like she was sitting on the edge of her seat until it did. Which was, all in all, a very good reason to stay home today.

But you want to see Jack, a little voice insisted.

She did. But she wasn't sure what it meant, and they'd be surrounded by other people. By River and Georgie, Finn and Adalia, Dottie and whomever she'd been allowed to invite (although surely she'd gone rogue and invited some people on the Do Not Call list), as well as Jack's kid sister Iris. It had all the hallmarks of an awkward situation.

"Well?" Mary pressed. "What are you going to say to him?"

"I guess I'll start with hello."

Molly rolled her eyes. "Or you could pull him into the bathroom and lock the door."

"You seriously might have an s-e-x addiction," Mary said, scowling.

Aidan had run off, and it felt like Molly was meeting Maisie's eyes through the camera, the two of them sharing the same thought: why was their sister spelling it out if her son wasn't there to hear her? They both burst out laughing.

"It might not be a bad idea," Maisie said, pretending to think about it. "We *did* have some pretty great s-e-x against the bathroom wall."

"Oh, you two," Mary said, as if they shared an affliction and she pitied them. Truth be told, Maisie felt a little sorry for Mary, what with her husband Glenn's dad jokes and endless stories about his boring job in middle management. Which was judgmental of her for sure, but she'd never pretended to be a people pleaser.

"The truth is I don't know," Maisie said honestly. "I'm going there with no expectations other than to bring home some gross turkey for the dogs."

"And what are you going to eat?" Mary asked. "A dish full of potatoes?"

Maisie rolled her eyes. "I'll carve some delicate pieces of Tofurky, white meat only."

"It comes in different colors?"

Her elder sister had to be the most literal person on Earth, God love her. Maisie had been a vegetarian since she was ten—when she realized where the chicken on her plate had come from—and Mary still worried about her protein intake.

"On that note," Maisie said. "I have to go get ready. We're supposed to be over there at twelve, and I still have to make something."

"What are you making?" Mary asked.

"Mom's corn casserole, of course," Maisie said. Because it was what she made every year, for every potluck Thanksgiving.

A flash of something like sadness crossed her older sister's face. She opened her mouth to say something, but Molly interrupted.

"Wear something sexy!" she shouted, as if she needed to speak loudly to be heard through the internet connection. Given that she was the youngest of them, she really should know better.

"How about pants with an expandable waistline and a shirt from the shelter?" she asked, raising her brow. "Sexy enough for you?"

"Hubba hubba, ding-dong," Molly teased.

They exchanged their goodbyes and hung up. Aidan's "Happy Thankthgiving, Aunt Maithie" almost made her cry—he had a bit of a lisp, and even though her sister had him in speech therapy, she secretly thought it was adorable.

Einstein looked up at Maisie and whimpered. Chaco sat beside him, wagging her tail.

"Yeah, I know," she said in an undertone. "I miss them too. And I wish I could bring you guys with me." Einstein had taken an immediate dislike to Tyrion, Adalia's dog, when she'd briefly brought him home as a foster. Chaco would have been fine—she liked everyone—but it felt unconscionable to leave Ein alone, even if he didn't *know* it was Thanksgiving. Jack had been right. The dogs did better together.

"You'll get plenty of turkey." The other dogs at the shelter would get some later this evening. Dottie always made enough for them, and she'd promised to bring over a Tupperware. The shelter was closed for the day, but they were never truly closed. Even if no one was on full-time duty, they still had someone come by to check on the dogs every few hours. Thankfully, Maisie had a couple of very diligent full-time employees, plus a volunteer staff that generously donated their time.

Ein perked up at the mention of turkey, then followed her down to the kitchen while she cooked. She hummed to herself, startling when she realized what she was humming: "Dream a Little Dream of Me" by the Mamas and the Papas.

Although it pissed her off that she cared, Maisie had spent a little longer on her outfit than usual, ending up in a green blouse—Jack had said the color made her eyes pop—a pair of black slacks and a knitted cardigan. But she'd gotten a call from the on-duty volunteer on the way to Adalia's house, and she'd needed to stop by the shelter to give one of their anxious strays his meds. (The volunteer had been worried about getting bitten, which probably wouldn't have happened with that particular dog, but at the end of the day, they were volunteers.) So now her pants were covered in fluffy white hair (amateur mistake), and she was half an hour late.

The driveway was clogged with cars, so she parked a little ways down the block, did a half-hearted job of wiping the dog hair off with the roller she kept in her car, and grabbed her casserole dish.

She was somewhat tempted to change her mind now, walking up to the house, hearing the people bustling about and talking in the back yard. But she was Maisie "Red" O'Shea, and she wasn't about to wimp away from a little awkwardness.

Besides, she didn't need River and Finn searching all over town for her, singing the bounty hunter theme song they'd come up with while tipsy on margaritas.

It seemed like most of the action was in the back yard, but she headed for the front of the house, figuring she'd leave her dish in the kitchen or wherever the food was being prepared. And while she wasn't exactly a gourmet chef, she figured she should at least offer her assistance to whomever was in the kitchen.

She knocked, steeling herself for the possibility that Jack might answer. And okay, maybe she actually hoped it would be Jack…and that he'd be happy to see her.

But instead a young girl she'd never seen before opened the door, a look of skeptical boredom on her face. She was beautiful, with long dark hair and eyes as dark as her brother's—because this was surely Iris.

"They invited *more* people?" she scoffed. "Where are they going to find room for everyone?"

It was an obvious challenge, and Maisie knew better than to take it sitting down. She'd basically ushered her little sister Molly through her last year of high school, and Molly was nothing like Mary. Their big sister would have had a conniption fit—or several—if she'd known about some of what had gone down, but she'd been away at law school. (Maisie had refused to let her drop out.)

"Maybe we'll put out a kid's table," Maisie suggested, raising her brows. "Should solve the problem."

Amusement flickered in the girl's eyes, there and then gone, and she settled on an offended look.

"Who are you, anyway? One of Dottie's weird friends?"

"Dottie and some of the others," she said. "I'm Maisie, and I'll tell you right now, if weird people offend you, you're in for it today."

Iris stepped back with a beleaguered sigh, dropped a sullen "You said it, not me," and Maisie brushed past her.

She took a quick glance around the front room. River and Georgie sat on one of the couches, sides pressed together, but she barely had time to analyze whether that bothered her before Adalia's big husky barreled into her. The corn casserole went flying, and the dish—her mother's dish—cracked in two when it hit the hardwood floor.

It was foolish, really—it was just a dish—but it felt like her heart was being squeezed by a boa constrictor.

"Oh," she said softly, watching for a moment as Tyrion started to lap up the mess.

"I am *not* on cleanup duty until after dinner," she heard Iris say, maybe in response to someone asking her to help. "Jack said so."

Then River's hand was on Maisie's shoulder, his touch warm and comforting and safe, and she realized she was crouched on the floor next to the dish with tears in her eyes.

Tears that probably weren't just over a broken dish, to be honest.

If she hadn't known better than to believe in woo-woo nonsense, she would have thought this was bad luck. It sure felt like it.

"Hey," River said softly. "That was your mom's, wasn't it?"

Because he knew better than anyone that every last thing they'd owned mattered to her. They were just things, she knew that, but they were *their* things. They were all she had left.

"Sorry," she said, embarrassed that Georgie was seeing her like this. She shook it off and got to her feet. She shrugged at Tyrion, who was still lapping up the casserole. "At least someone got to enjoy it. That was probably my one major cooking effort for the year. Although I'm glad I don't have to pick up his poop later."

"Gross," River said, bumping her shoulder. Georgie came up to them with a dishcloth that was almost laughably inadequate for the task—or maybe not, given the speed with which Tyrion was eating.

"Thanks," Maisie said, reaching for it.

"It's okay," Georgie said. "I'll get the stuff spilled on the ground. Why don't you take the dish? Maybe it can be saved."

There was nothing on her face to indicate she was being disingenuous, so Maisie didn't question her motives, she just grabbed up the dish, trying to keep the goopy center contained, and shooed Tyrion away as she headed for the kitchen. Iris had gone off somewhere, probably upstairs.

River stayed behind, presumably to help Georgie, although she also thought she heard someone knocking at the door.

"Did my big lug do that?" Adalia asked, meeting her in the doorway to the kitchen.

Maisie pushed past her. "Sorry, this is still pretty hot. Kitchen emergency."

She barreled past Finn, who was doing something to a dish of squash—when had she ever seen him cook?—and headed straight for the trash bin. Georgie had updated the house some before leaving—after basically having her arm twisted by a fire Dottie had unintentionally started—but the trash can was still in the same place. Adalia handed her a spoon over her shoulder, and Maisie grabbed it and scooped the rest of the casserole into the trash. For a moment, her hands lingered over the trash can, her gaze locked on the broken dish.

She could glue it together again, but it wouldn't be useful for anything but decoration. And it wasn't exactly pretty, really—it was just old.

Maybe Mary and Molly had a point. Maybe it was time to let go of some things. She'd liked the way Jack looked at her, like she wasn't just one of those poor O'Shea girls who'd lost their parents so young. Like she was a woman who had baggage but didn't have to be defined by it.

"Do you want to save it?" Adalia asked softly. The door had opened in the great room, and she heard River and Georgie talking to someone, presumably another guest.

"Nah." But her hand refused to release the pieces.

Then she remembered that Adalia collected broken things, lost things, things no one wanted, and used them in her art. "Why don't you keep it? Maybe you can use it in one of your pieces."

Adalia took the remains of the dish from her and rinsed both sides off in the sink, looking them over with interest before glancing back at Maisie. "You sure? Because this is a seriously cool vintage dish, and I'm not going to ask you twice. I am totally, one hundred percent going to take advantage of you."

Finn moseyed over, having finished whatever he'd been doing with the squash.

"Oh man, was that the corn casserole?" he asked. He was a total glutton when it came to other people's home-cooked meals, and he'd eaten half of it himself the last time she'd spent Thanksgiving with her friends.

"The first casualty of Thanksgiving," Maisie confirmed. "Sorry, guys."

"Don't be sorry," Adalia said. A door opened and closed again. "It's my fault for not putting Tyrion outside. I just get a little twitchy when he's out there without Finn or me. God only knows where Jezebel is. She snuck out when River and Georgie got here, and I have a feeling she's going to come back with a live turkey at some point. Why don't you grab a beer and head out back? Take a breather?"

"I can help out in here if you want," Maisie said, glancing around. There were dishes piled everywhere, including some that were unmistakably Dottie's handiwork—a huge bowl of mac and cheese with a note reading "comfort" on the side, a vat of vegetables that read "health," and a huge bowl of mashed potatoes that read "happiness." And it wasn't a lie. Dottie made the best mashed potatoes on the planet, plus she always made a special vegetarian gravy just for Maisie, although Adalia, a pescatarian, would likely eat some too this year.

"We've got this under control," Finn said proudly, which was hilarious and kind of sweet. Before meeting Adalia, he'd struggled to make frozen pizza.

Adalia nodded in agreement. "Dottie's out there. Jack—"

At first she thought Adalia had started a sentence without finishing it, but then she realized her friend was looking over her shoulder. She turned around, and the sight of him almost made her stumble. Because he was staring at her with an intensity that told her he hadn't forgotten a single minute of the night they'd spent together. He had on a long-sleeved shirt that clung to those amazing biceps, covered by an apron.

So he'd been outside helping Dottie cook something—or maybe create something. She liked the thought of him out there with Dottie, playing along with one of her games or ideas. It endeared her to him.

As if you needed to like him more.

"Play any poker lately?" Jack asked, lifting his eyebrows.

She gulped back a laugh, all too aware that Finn and Adalia were looking at them strangely.

"Not for a few weeks," Maisie said. "But they say it's like riding a bike. You don't lose any *skills* if you take a little time off."

Something flashed in Jack's eyes, and he opened his mouth to say something, but she never found out what. Stella, of all people, barreled into the kitchen, followed by Lurch, who had a bright pink lipstick imprint on his bald head and a heavy-looking platter in his hands, covered by an aluminum tent. For a moment, the logistics of that kiss imprint boggled Maisie's mind—Lurch was about a foot and a half taller than Stella, which raised questions about other logistics too. Then her gaze landed on the painting in Stella's hand.

A naked Lurch stood next to a goose that looked like Diego, hand in wing as if they were shaking on something. Two goats stood behind them, one with a fork in its mouth, the other with a knife.

"It's called *Thanksgiving Dinner*," Stella said proudly, handing it to Adalia. "I know we got off on the wrong foot, what with the chemistry between me and your man"—she nodded to a flustered Finn—"so I brought you a housewarming gift. Well, two, I suppose."

Adalia's face lit up, which came as no surprise. Even if she didn't want a naked Lurch hanging up on her wall, it was exactly the kind of gift she'd find hilarious. "Let's hang it in the dining room so we can all admire it while we eat."

Jack's gaze shot from the painting to Maisie. Probably Adalia had thought he'd object, but he gave a wicked smile and said, "Sure. It brings up lots of good memories."

Finn and Adalia were looking at him like he'd lost his mind, but Jack didn't rush to explain himself.

"Oh, you were fond of Diego, weren't you?" Stella said, reaching out to touch his arm. And even though she was apparently Lurch's date for the evening, she hung on to that bicep for dear life.

Maisie couldn't blame her, but she cleared her throat loudly anyway, giving Stella a look intended to remind her of the warning she'd issued a few weeks back. She clicked her teeth together, miming biting. Sure enough, Stella pulled away, mouthing something that looked suspiciously like "harridan."

It was then that her earlier comment registered. "Wait, did something happen to Diego?"

Lurch lifted the platter and grinned. "You're looking at him."

CHAPTER
Eight

Iris was in a mood, and the house was pure chaos. Jack had almost packed his little sister into the car and run to IHOP, which had been their Thanksgiving tradition whenever their mother had other plans, but two things had made him stay. One, he really *did* want to have Thanksgiving with his newly discovered half-sisters despite all the craziness that seemed to entail, and two, Adalia had mentioned that Maisie was coming.

He hadn't heard from her, and although he'd thought about reaching out, she'd made her one rule pretty clear: just one night. She'd called him a rule follower, and he supposed that was true for the most part, but as far as he was concerned, she'd shown up on his home turf, which meant *his* rules.

Too bad he hadn't figured out what they were.

Now would be a *terrible* time to try to start something with Maisie.

Iris's move to Asheville hadn't gone as smoothly as he'd hoped. When she wasn't tearful and withdrawn, she was angry with Jack for moving to "this hippie town." He had to acknowledge that moving to a new city less than halfway through her senior year had to be awful, but he couldn't bring himself to go back to Chicago.

Did that make him a terrible person? He honestly wasn't sure.

Iris had begged him to let her move in with Janie and her family, something they'd agreed to, but Genevieve had been calling and harassing Jack frequently enough that he didn't dare risk it. Janie's family didn't deserve the hassle of dealing with his mother, and he wouldn't put it past Genevieve to try to coerce Iris back home. Turned out that Iris's father had caught wind that she wasn't living with her mother anymore and had cut off his child support checks. (Did he have someone watching her? Jack knew they weren't on speaking terms.) Jack noticed the asshole hadn't sent the money his way instead. Not that he would have taken it. At least Prescott Buchanan had met with Jack a few times when he was a kid, before Genevieve got pregnant with Iris (probably his mother's desperate attempts to rekindle something with his father). His sister had never once met her DNA contributor.

So Jack had told Iris that he was truly sorry, but their lives were in Asheville now, at least for the time being, and once she graduated from high school she could go to Northwestern University with Janie, just like they'd always planned.

If she got in, which was questionable since they had an eight percent acceptance rate, and she was blowing off a good portion of her homework.

Iris needed his full attention. He'd already dragged her away from her school and her friends. He couldn't add a girlfriend to the mix. It wouldn't be fair to Iris *or* Maisie.

All the more reason to blow off dinner and go to IHOP, and yet he hadn't left. He'd told himself he was sticking around because Adalia would hog-tie him to a chair if he suggested leaving—which was probably true—but he wasn't a total fool. He'd wanted to see Maisie again. To figure out if that spark was still there.

The answer had been obvious to him before he even walked into the kitchen. He'd glimpsed her through the back door, handing pieces of a broken dish to Adalia, and the surprisingly vulnerable look in her eyes had drawn him away from his post in the back yard.

He was supposed to be on Dottie duty. She was frying a turkey, and River and Georgie had decided she needed strict supervision. They'd all agreed to take turns babysitting her and the fryer; Georgie had even mocked up a schedule. But if he'd learned anything about Dottie Hendrickson, it was that she thought love trumped all other causes. If she'd known why he wanted to be in the kitchen, she would have pushed him inside with both hands.

He'd walked through the door, watching Maisie for several seconds before saying something. He hadn't planned to mention poker. The words had just flown out of his mouth.

Her sassy answer was more than what he could have hoped for—had she really insinuated she was willing to pick things up where they'd left off?

Then Stella had walked in with Lurch, touching his arm, and they'd blown everything apart by announcing that the goose Jack had charmed three weeks prior was going to be part of their Thanksgiving dinner.

Maisie gasped in genuine horror, and Adalia gave her a confused look. "Who's Diego?"

"The goose," Maisie said softly, gesturing to the painting in Adalia's hands.

"He'd outlived his usefulness," Stella said matter-of-factly. "I have a new muse." Then she gave Lurch an adoring gaze.

"Oh, my God!" Adalia shrieked and jumped backward as though trying to get as far away from the platter as possible, not that Jack blamed her. He might not be a vegetarian or even a pescatarian like Adalia, but he figured there were farm animals and pets, and it was best not to mix the two. Besides, he'd been fond of the little guy.

"She cooked a goose?" Finn asked in confusion, looking from Adalia to Maisie. It was clear he didn't understand the problem.

"Get that out of my house!" Adalia shouted, pointing her finger at the platter. She set the painting down, propping it against the cupboards, like she wasn't so sure she wanted to touch it anymore.

River burst into the kitchen with Georgie right behind him. "What happened?"

"She cooked a goose," Finn said, still not seeming to understand what all the fuss was about.

"Not just *any* goose," Adalia seethed. "The goose from her paintings!" She gasped. "Do you eat your goats too?"

Stella shrugged. "I believe in the circle of life," she said haughtily. "Diego would *want* us to have a delicious Thanksgiving dinner, looking at his portrait while we enjoy his bounty."

"But you *named* him," Maisie said, wrapping her arms across her chest. "You treated him like a pet. And now you want to *eat* him? Can you not see that this is massively screwed up?" She glanced up at Jack, her eyes glassy with unshed tears.

Was she thinking about Jack holding the goose in his arms? If not for Diego, he wasn't sure he and Maisie would have ever had their night together.

"The goose that destroyed my old room?" River asked, and Georgie gasped.

River looked like he wasn't sure how to react. Then again, Adalia had shown him the pictures. That goose had crapped on just about every surface in River's old room.

"Get it out!" Adalia repeated, pointing to the back door. "Now!"

"What's going on, dears?" Dottie asked as she walked through the back door into the now-crowded kitchen. "Oh, Stella. You made it."

"These young folk are carryin' on about me cooking Diego," Stella said with a scowl. "But I think their ingratitude really stems from this one"—she gestured to Adalia—"worrying that I'm gonna try to steal her man." She held up her hands in surrender. "I call a truce. Your man's off-limits today." She shot a dark look at Maisie. "I make no promises about yours."

"Maisie's?" River asked in surprise, then glanced at Maisie. "You have a boyfriend I don't know about?"

"No," Maisie barked, a little too quickly for Jack's taste, then turned her attention to Stella. "I thought you'd claimed Lurch."

"A woman can enjoy the company of more than one man," Stella said with an upturned chin.

"So they *are* swingers," he heard Maisie say in a whisper, nudging River.

Everyone remained silent for a moment.

"This town is so freaking weird," Iris said in disgust from the doorway. "This never would have happened in Chicago." Then she spun around and flounced off.

"I've heard Chicago is a very dry town," Dottie said absently.

Jack had no idea what that meant, and he wasn't sure he wanted to know.

A cat shrieked out back, and Jack realized if Dottie was inside, then no one was attending the fryer. With Jezebel outside, having snuck out the front door earlier…

Oh shit. They didn't need another dead pet at the party. Maisie would probably have a heart attack.

He raced out the back door just as Dottie said, "What's the fuss? Diego played his role in the great circle of life."

"That's exactly what I said," Stella agreed amidst a flurry of other comments.

But Jack had already left the kitchen, and he had much greater concerns than what was—or wasn't—on the menu for dinner. Jezebel was perched on the wrought iron bench out back, hissing at the fryer, which had overturned and caught a three-foot by three-foot section of the lawn on fire. The grease was slowly spreading down the hill, moving toward the kitchen.

"I smell something burning," he could hear Dottie say. "Is the stuffing still in the oven?"

"Addy!" Jack shouted. "I need a fire extinguisher! And possibly baking soda!"

He heard multiple gasps and cries inside, but his attention was focused on containing the fire before it reached the house or the fence. He'd seen an extinguisher when he'd helped clean out the shed to create a studio for Adalia a couple of months ago, and they'd put it in the detached garage. The door was locked, but it only took one good ramming with his shoulder to get it open. The extinguisher was on the shelf, thank God, so he grabbed it and ran back to the fire.

It had inched closer to the house, but his new concern was Lurch, who was holding the garden hose.

"Lurch!" Jack shouted. "Stop!"

Lurch waved as he turned on the faucet. "Not to worry! I've got this covered."

Then he sprayed a stream of water directly at the flames.

As Jack had expected, the reaction was instant. Flames shot up into the trees, sending Jezebel leaping off the bench in protest. He heard a few screams, and he pulled the clip out of the extinguisher and started spraying the flames closest to the older man as he made his way to the faucet and turned it off. Lurch's sleeve was smoldering, so Jack doused it with the extinguisher and then grabbed his free arm and dragged him to the porch, where everyone had gathered to watch the flames. "Get away from the house! Go out front, and someone call 911!"

But someone must have already called—likely one of the neighbors—because he heard distant sirens approaching them.

Stella and Dottie grabbed Lurch's arms and pulled him inside while River ran out the door with another, smaller, extinguisher. Finn was trying to herd everyone out front, and considering the resistance he was getting, Jack wondered if he had the hardest job.

Jack and River sprayed the flames closest to the house, but the water had spread the fire.

"River! Let the firefighters take care of it!" Georgie called out, her voice shaking with fear.

Then, as though obeying Georgie, River's extinguisher ran out. He took a few steps back toward the porch. "Jack, we can't contain it. Come on!"

But Jack wasn't ready to give up yet. His extinguisher was larger, and he was determined to save the house. It was his house, his and his sisters' and even the half-brother who still hadn't acknowledged him, and he wasn't going to give up on it. He'd hang in as long as he could, or at least until the fire trucks pulled up. The smoke burned his nose and he started to cough.

"Jack!" someone called out in a panic.

He glanced over his shoulder to see Maisie on the back porch with Iris. They were both watching with horror in their eyes, but Iris was sobbing loudly.

"Maisie!" he shouted. "Get my sister out of here! And make sure to tell the firemen it's a grease fire!"

"Stop, Jack!" Iris cried out. "Let it burn!"

Then his extinguisher ran out, and even though he was tempted to ask Maisie to get the industrial-sized bag of baking soda Adalia had gotten at Costco, he knew it wasn't enough to contain the fire, or even keep it from reaching the house.

Maisie ran down the steps and grabbed his arm with both hands, tugging. "Don't be a hero, Jack. Your sister needs you."

He glanced down at her in surprise, and then she was pulling him up the steps, and he was following. Just like he'd followed her through the party weeks before. Almost like he couldn't help himself. He wrapped his arm around Iris's back the moment he reached the top of the steps, and it caught him by surprise when a coughing fit racked his chest. Maisie and Iris led him through the house and out to the front yard.

Maisie tried to get him to sit on the front step, but he was determined to make sure the firemen knew what they were dealing with.

"Where are you going, Jack?" Iris called out as he pulled free and walked toward the fire trucks that were now parked at the curb.

"I told you we've been here before," one of the firefighters said to his buddy. "You owe me ten bucks."

"I only agreed to pay up if the crystal statue of the naked old guy is here."

"It's not," Jack said, pissed they weren't taking this seriously. "And it's a crystal dick, not a crystal statue. There's a grease fire in the back yard. An overturned turkey fryer. That guy over there"—he motioned toward Lurch, who was sitting under a tree—"needs to be checked out. He tried to douse it with water and may have been burned by the shooting flames." Then he started to cough.

"Sounds like you need to be checked out too," the first guy said.

"Just go save my damn house," he grunted.

"Jack, come on," Adalia said, grabbing his arm and tugging him away.

He was disappointed it wasn't Maisie, but she was sitting on the front curb with Dottie, who looked like she was about to burst into tears. Finn was trying to keep everyone gathered together in the front lawn, including Stella, who seemed far more interested in the firefighters than she was Lurch.

Maisie glanced up at him, her gaze letting him know that she wished she were tugging his arm too. She seemed to like tugging him around, not that he minded. He was tempted to go to her, to kiss her in front of everyone, but Iris was standing by herself, tears streaming down her face, and he knew what he had to do.

His ex-girlfriend was right. Until Iris left for college, anyone else would be in second place. And as much as it killed him to admit it, Maisie deserved more than he could give her.

He went to his baby sister and pulled her into his arms, comforting her. Then he felt something brush his legs, and he smiled when he realized it was Jezebel. Tyrion was trotting behind her, wagging his tail as if nothing had happened.

Adalia cried out, "Tyrion!" then dropped to her knees and buried her face in his fur. "I was so worried about you! They wouldn't let me go upstairs to look for you."

"That evil cat found the dog?" Iris asked in disbelief.

"Looks like it." Jack pulled away from Iris and sat down on the lawn to thoroughly examine the cat. When he declared her healthy, she nuzzled him under his chin.

"I swear you're a warlock," Adalia said in wonder. Finn was sitting down at the curb with Dottie and Maisie, but he kept glancing back at her.

"Animals have always liked him," Iris said in a snotty tone. "A real sister would know that."

Adalia's eyes widened slightly, but then she said in a sweet voice Jack knew it must have taken some effort to summon, "I'm Jack's real sister too. Same as you. And while we don't have as much history with Jack as you do, Georgie and I are trying to make up for lost time. But like I told you before," she said, "Jack's family is our family. We want to get to know you too."

Iris rolled her eyes. "Whatever."

Then she walked over to Jack's car and rested her butt against the side.

"I'm sorry, Addy," Jack said, horrified. It was like he'd left his sister in Chicago and some evil pod person had replaced her. What had happened to the sweet, funny kid he'd helped raise? But if he were honest with himself, she'd been changing over the last year as their mother had begun sinking into another depressive spiral. "I had no idea she'd be this surly when I asked if it would be okay for her to move in. We can move out if you want."

Adalia released a snort-laugh. "*Please.* You should have seen me when I was her age. I had a chip on my shoulder too. She'll come around. Give her time."

"I only have nine months before she leaves," he said, surprised to hear his voice hitch a little. Truth be told, part of him looked forward to his sister's graduation in the same way a prisoner looked forward to being released. Once she was an adult, on her own, he wouldn't have to worry about her so much. Of course, he knew it wouldn't matter in some ways—he'd feel responsible for her no matter where she lived. It had become part of who he was.

"Trust me, Jack," Adalia said. "Just love her and she'll come around. In the meantime, I feel like I'm looking at my teenage self in an alternate dimension, and I'm fascinated. Besides, I spend half my time at Finn's. Don't you think about going anywhere."

The firemen made quick work of putting out the fire, which had blackened the side of the house but not actually burned it. They gave Dottie a lecture about turkey fryers, but Stella kept interrupting to feel all of the firemen's arms. Lurch actually took photos of her posing with them, which Jack couldn't begin to understand. Then again, he'd never been the sharing type when it came to women. If he liked someone, he was all in.

The paramedics wanted to take Jack to the hospital to get checked out for smoke inhalation, but he refused since his oxygen saturation rate was fine. But they did end up taking Lurch, who had singed off his eyebrows and had burns on his arm. Thankfully, Stella went with him. One of the firefighters tried to get cozy with Georgie, asking her if she'd set the fire to summon him back, and River surprised Jack by getting between them, telling the firefighter she was very much taken. He had never seemed the jealous type.

The ambulance pulled away, followed by the fire trucks, leaving the Buchanans and their guests standing in the front yard, with a growing crowd of whispering neighbors watching them like they were a zoo exhibit.

"Show's over, folks!" Adalia shouted while giving them a salute. "Go enjoy your turkey and tofu dinners, just like we're about to go eat ours." Then she walked to the front porch and turned around to face her family and friends. "I spent all morning making this dinner, so don't you even *think* about leaving."

Then she disappeared into the house.

"You heard the woman," Finn said. "Trust me, you do *not* want her to go after you." But he grinned, like maybe he wanted her to go after *him*.

Iris rolled her eyes. "Old people are *so* gross."

CHAPTER
Nine

"It's time for us to announce what we're grateful for," Dottie said brightly. They sat around the dinner table, an unpleasant scorched smell in the air, and Maisie couldn't help but reflect that Dottie had recovered awfully quickly considering she'd been close to tears half an hour ago.

Dottie had leaned against Maisie's shoulder outside, feeling frail in a way that had scared Maisie—when had she gotten so old?—and said she felt guilty about nearly burning Beau's house down a second time. Which, to be fair, maybe she should. But then she'd gone on about it being a sign that Beau was displeased with her, that she hadn't done enough to help his grandchildren, and Maisie had told Dottie the truth: her theory was a bunch of BS. Because if Beau was pissed off enough to celestially cause fires, he'd do it in someone else's house. He'd been too fond of this place to watch it go up in flames, especially with his hell cat and the majority of the relatives he tolerated in the danger zone.

Dottie had found that line of argument strangely reassuring, and as soon as Adalia had announced they were having dinner, like it or not, Dottie had rebounded. She'd ushered everyone inside and helped warm the food.

Now they all sat beneath poor Diego's portrait on the wall—Adalia had insisted on hanging it up to honor him, although Georgie had put a Post-it note over Lurch's junk. They'd served themselves food and were eating a little half-heartedly, even though everything was good. Finn kept peddling the squash to people, grinning like he'd reinvented the wheel.

Probably Maisie should be mourning poor Diego, who hadn't had much of a life for a bird, other than those sweet seconds he'd spent in Jack's arms. Or yearning for her sisters, who could have saved her from all of this madness by actually coming home for a change. But instead she found herself staring at Jack's arm, propped up next to her on the table. She'd maneuvered to sit next to him, a decision of questionable wisdom, and she kept replaying the way he'd singlehandedly broken into the detached garage to get that fire extinguisher. She'd thought him sexy before, but now he was basically a hero, wasn't he? He'd slipped upstairs for a quick shower before dinner, and his hair was wet, something that somehow made him more appealing. Probably because of the whole sex-in-the-bathroom thing. He caught her looking, and a corner of his mouth ticked up before he got it under control. Careful not to reveal herself to Iris, who sat on his other side with a more pronounced scowl than she'd had earlier, Maisie trailed her fingers across his upper thigh.

She wasn't sure what the hell she thought she was doing—she'd said one night, and he'd written that "just friends" note—but she had been dreaming about him, and his note had trailed off in a strange way, and...

He jolted, and just as she was about to pull away—you didn't jolt when you were happy about something—he lowered his hand to cover hers, squeezing it and holding it for a second before he gently moved it. To be fair, if his sister thought it was gross for random adults to be nice to each other, she'd think it beyond disgusting to be confronted with proof that her older brother had a sex life.

"I'll start," Dottie said when no one offered to take the lead. "I'm grateful to be here with my nephew and four of my grandchildren, and all of our wonderful friends." The four grandchildren part was a puzzler, but Maisie figured she was including Iris in that number. Dottie *would* do something like that. "I know Beau would be proud to see us all sitting here together." She frowned a little. "Although I do wish Lurch and Stella hadn't had to leave early. Beau was always so fond of Lurch."

Maisie mouthed, "Swingers," to River, who stifled a laugh.

"River?" Dottie asked, turning to him.

He'd showered too, and the wet hair at the nape of his neck sent a little stab of memory through her. One time, when they were poor twenty-two-year-olds who couldn't afford real haircuts, they'd cut each other's hair. Maisie had done a pretty bang-up job, if she did say so herself—she'd just opened the shelter, and some of the dogs needed regular haircuts, so she'd had some experience cutting hair. River, on the other hand, had made her look like Bozo the Clown. But it hadn't mattered. She'd loved that stupid haircut because he'd given it to her. Because he'd spent an hour and a half trying to get the sides the same length—which was why it had ended up so short.

He cleared his throat, his gaze darting around the table, and she knew what he was going to say before he spoke. A grin broke out on his face. "I'm grateful that Georgie Buchanan has agreed to be my wife."

Adalia dropped her fork with a loud click and leaped—literally leaped—up from her chair. "Yes! I've been waiting for you to make an honest woman of her."

Dottie was grinning like the Cheshire Cat, and Maisie couldn't help but wonder if she'd planned his announcement—had she offered to give River an opening? Or had she just known he was looking for one?

Then everyone was getting up, Finn clapping River on the back and saying something about how he'd almost gone first—to which River huffed a laugh and said, "If you say so"—and Adalia squeezing Georgie and physically lifting her off the ground even though she was smaller, and Dottie flitting from person to person like a beneficent fairy, and Jack standing in the background a little awkwardly but with a sweet look on his face that said he wanted to take part and wasn't sure how. His reaction squeezed her heart in a way she wouldn't have expected given this was the moment she'd been dreading for weeks. No, for months. And it was then that Maisie realized she and Iris were the only people left at the table, one empty seat between them.

"I hate my life," Iris muttered.

"I did warn you," Maisie said, then added, "I think you could safely sneak away if you're done eating."

Iris tilted her head at the group of well-wishers. "Why aren't you over there acting like half of marriages don't end in divorce?"

Which was an opening of sorts. She shrugged. "Maybe I hate my life a little too."

Iris lifted her cup of sparkling cider—Jack had taken away the champagne Dottie had poured for her—and said, "To hating life."

"Nah," Maisie said. "I'm not drinking to that. I'd prefer to hope my luck will turn around." She glanced up. "Unlike poor Diego."

His anthropomorphized smile in the portrait gave her the shivers. She wouldn't want the painting in her house, staring down at her while she ate her breakfast.

Then Finn passed the table, pausing to look at her as he made an unnecessary summoning gesture to convey he wanted her to follow him into the kitchen. God, he was as subtle as a plane writing messages in the sky. Iris watched him with eyes that missed nothing before glancing back to Maisie to see what she'd do.

"We're going to go check on the dessert situation," she said, only to immediately get kind of pissed at herself for offering an explanation to a seventeen-year-old.

"Just so long as you're not cuckolding my 'sister,'" Iris said with air quotes.

"He's like a brother to me," Maisie said, waving a hand dismissively.

"I've learned people have really loose interpretations of family around here."

Maisie shook her head a little, a smile playing on her lips, and followed Finn into the kitchen. But the smile didn't last, because Finn could only want one thing. And God...he was not the person she wanted knowing her secret. But he did, and she needed to talk him off a ledge before he did something stupid like announce to everyone at the Thanksgiving table that Maisie had massively confusing feelings about the groom-to-be.

"What are you doing?" she hissed, pulling him to the back of the kitchen. It smelled worse in here, like singed hair. Lurch's eyebrows maybe.

"What are *you* doing?" he hissed back. "River says you're going to be co-best man. You still haven't told him."

It wasn't a question.

"Have you told Adalia?" she asked, dreading the answer.

"No," he said, surprising her. "But I want you to. This is driving me nuts. Do you know how hard it is for me to keep a secret like this?"

She did. And it wasn't really fair of her to ask it of him, so she just nodded. "I haven't had a girls' night with her and Blue for a while. Maybe I'll talk to both of them." She'd met Enid "Blue" Combs through the animal shelter, but they hadn't really become friends until Adalia brought them together. She saw Blue a little more frequently now, what with Adalia spending so much time with Finn, but she hadn't told her about the River situation. Maybe it would feel good to unburden herself.

"Good," he said with obvious relief. "Now let's go back out there, together, and you can congratulate them."

"Okay, bro, but only because you went full boss man on me," she said, giving him a little nudge. But she went with him willingly enough, smiling a little when she saw Iris had taken her advice and retreated to places unknown.

The rest of the party had returned to the table, although River, Georgie, Adalia, and Dottie were gathered around what looked to be Georgie's cell phone. Like before, Jack sat at a slight distance from the others. She was tempted to physically push his chair closer. Or maybe sit on his lap. He met her eyes and shifted slightly, as if inviting her to do just that. But instead she linked arms with Finn and hustled up to River.

"Co-best men at your service."

River cut his attention away from the phone, from which a handsome man with hazel eyes and dark blond hair was gazing at the Lurch portrait in horror. The Post-it had fallen off. That had to be their other brother, who sounded like he had a real stick up his behind, from everything she'd heard. But River was smiling at her, his expression hopeful, and he deserved her attention much more than some stuffed shirt in New York did.

"Congratulations, River," she said, all jokiness falling away. He hugged her, and she ignored the slight pricking of tears in her eyes and pulled back first. Georgie was holding the phone, which gave her the perfect excuse to just nod her congratulations to the bride-to-be.

Her nod was returned.

"And when do you plan on getting married?" came the brother's voice through the phone speakers. Even over the crappy phone speakers, he had a nice voice, Maisie would give him that. But she felt a prickle of defensiveness for River. This jerk clearly would have preferred to ask Georgie, in private, whether she had any second thoughts.

"As soon as possible," Georgie said, gaze locked on River's. "Just after Brewfest, we were thinking."

March. That was just a few months away.

"But I've already started planning the engagement party," Dottie said. "Early January would be a lovely time of year."

It would certainly be a *cold* time of year.

Georgie's eyes rounded with alarm, which was completely understandable given the smell of smoke still hung in the air from Dottie's last attempt to co-opt the planning for a family event. River took her hand and opened his mouth to let Dottie down gently.

But he didn't need to.

"I think we should plan it at the brewery," Jack said from behind everyone. His eyes glimmered with the idea. And he pushed his chair a little bit closer to the others. Turning to

Dottie, he added, "I'll take care of the logistics, but I'll need your help, Dottie."

River gave him a slight nod, a silent thank you, and Georgie actually mouthed the words.

Turning back to the screen, she said, "You'll come, won't you, Lee?"

He was silent for a few moments, as if trying to consider whether there was any way out, and then he nodded. "I will."

"And I'd like you to stand up with me in the wedding party," River said, glancing back at Jack. "Jack's already agreed to do the same."

He had? Maisie glanced at Jack, only to find him watching her, a gaze that seemed almost electric. A small nod. He knew she was co-best man, then, and that they'd be thrown together for this wedding. But it was hard to tell whether he thought that was a good thing—and even though her attraction to him had, if anything, grown stronger, she wasn't so sure either. She thought that maybe she needed to get through this, to see River married, before she could really move on.

A pained look crossed Georgie's face, but she said, "And I'd be honored if Victoria stood up with me. I know you two are getting serious."

A knock sounded over the phone's speakers, and a cold voice said, "Lee, are you on the phone in there? Your dad is about to make a speech, and it would look *very* odd if you weren't at the table."

A speech about what? Gratitude? That seemed rich.

Lee had the grace to look embarrassed, but he called, "I'll be right out," before he turned back to the phone. In a voice little above a whisper, he said, "We'll talk later."

Then he signed off.

They were all silent for a moment, the effects of Lee's disappearing act lingering like the stench of smoke in the air. Adalia was the first to speak.

"I hope that means Vic-*tor*-ia won't want to come."

"I want her to come for Lee," Georgie said. She paused, glancing at River, and from the look in his eyes, it was obvious this was something they'd discussed. "And Dad should be here too."

Adalia made a face. "I'd hoped to go the rest of my adult life without seeing him again."

She meant it too. She'd said as much to Maisie on more than one occasion.

"He's our father," Georgie said simply. Maisie glanced at Jack, whose expression had darkened, and she was tempted to say something in his defense. To say that the man had simply lent them his genetic material. That doing so didn't give him the right to torture them for decades. Then again, Maisie didn't know firsthand what it was like to have a terrible parent. She only knew the loss of two good ones.

"Well, should we have pie?" Dottie asked.

Then Finn started collecting the dishes, with River helping, and Jack got to his feet and started looking around the room for Iris, like maybe she'd hidden under a pillow.

Maisie came up to him and put a hand on one of his arms.

"She's upstairs," she said. "I suggested it might be a reasonable time to leave if she felt so inclined."

Jack swore under his breath, and it occurred to her that he was in a true predicament. He wanted to be with his family, but even though his sisters were all in the same house, Iris had isolated herself. It was either go upstairs and be with her or stay down here with Adalia and Georgie.

"I doubt she'd object if you brought her some pie," she suggested. "My sister went through the whole teenage angst stage, but it didn't do any harm to her sweet tooth. Bringing her brownies or whatever was always the best way to get her to talk."

"You have sisters too?"

"Yes, and my sisters are literally the most different people possible, so sometimes I have to be the go-between. Middle Child Duty, I call it."

His mouth twitched. "I wouldn't have pegged you for a peacemaker."

She smiled at him. "Now you're the one trying to put me in boxes. But you're not wrong. They didn't have much of a choice, though. Desperate times called for desperate measures."

"Desperate times, indeed," he said with a sigh. "This day didn't exactly go like I hoped it would." He met her gaze again, held it, and she felt tingles shoot through her body, like she had become effervescent. She had a feeling she knew what he'd hoped.

"It certainly didn't go as Diego had planned."

Jack barked a laugh, his gaze shooting to the *Thanksgiving Dinner* portrait. The Post-it had gone back up, but there was a little smiley face on it, which had almost certainly been Adalia's work.

"I'm surprised to hear you joke about it."

She shrugged. "Gallows humor. I think being Stella's muse is basically a death sentence. My hopes are not high for Lurch's future."

"No kidding," Jack said, leaning a little closer, his heat engulfing her. "I was looking forward to seeing you today."

"Were?" she asked. "Did that change somewhere between the fire and the most awkward video chat in history?"

"No," he said, "it didn't change at all. It's just…with Iris. It's not a good time for me to get involved with anyone." He looked at her again, regret in his eyes. "Today proved that. I told myself she'd get adjusted, that it wasn't selfish of me to bring her here, but I'm not so sure that's true."

The disappointment that washed through her was stronger than it should have been. After all, hadn't she decided they shouldn't pursue this attraction between them? Except she'd sought him out again, and here they were, standing much too close for two people who'd decided they didn't think it wise to start anything. Or continue anything.

"I get it," she said. "I don't know why you brought her here, but I expect you had your reasons. I was my younger sister's guardian for a little over a year after high school, and it's not easy. It consumes everything."

He gave her a look, like maybe he wanted to ask questions, but he didn't. He just reached for her hand and squeezed it.

"Wait," Dottie said, drawing their attention back to the dining room table. Maisie had a split second to notice Adalia was looking at her hand, which was clasped with Jack's, before she pulled away.

Then Dottie continued, "We didn't finish our discussion of what we're grateful for. Let's do it over dessert."

She sounded genuinely excited over the idea, but Maisie didn't feel like taking part. Suddenly, she itched to leave. To be with the dogs at the shelter. She'd already told a horrified Adalia that she would take the platter of Diego off her hands. She hated the thought of anyone eating him, but he'd already been cooked, and it would be more awful, to her mind, if he went uneaten. So the dogs would have goose this year instead of turkey.

"Iris is definitely not going to come down for that," Jack muttered, which gave Maisie an idea. He had to find a way to get Iris engaged in Asheville so she'd want to stay; Maisie constantly needed help at the shelter. Win-win.

Except she knew what Molly would say. She'd roll her eyes and say something like, *Having feelings isn't going to be your hamartia, you know. You want to see him too. This'll give you the chance...without everyone else around.* Her sister had learned that word in high school English—*hamartia, a fatal flaw leading to one's downfall*—and it had appealed to the drama queen in her. Of course, Molly wasn't one to talk. Her longest boyfriend had lasted all of two weeks.

She looked at Jack, saw the worried way he was eyeing the stairs.

"Does she like dogs?" she asked.

CHAPTER

Ten

"Why are you determined to ruin my life?" Iris asked in the petulant tone Jack had, unfortunately, grown used to hearing.

"I had no idea you'd taken drama classes the first quarter of the year," Jack said nonchalantly as he drove toward the dog shelter, refusing to let his sister see she was getting under his skin. "You really should consider getting a talent agent."

"Hardy-har-har," she groaned, but he caught the hint of a grin before she went back to scowling. "And you should take that stand-up act on the road." Then she quickly added, "But I refuse to watch any of your acts. I don't need more embarrassment. Thanksgiving may have been a week ago, but the memories will last a lifetime."

"That's okay," he said, making sure his voice still sounded breezy. "I'll stick to karaoke."

"*Karaoke?*" she asked, swinging her head around to face him.

He'd had a feeling that would pique her interest. "Addy took me and Georgie. You should have seen Georgie singing Bruno Mars's 'Uptown Funk.'"

Iris started to grin, but it didn't stick the landing. She remembered she was supposed to be mad and scowled again.

Seeing her struggle to keep the chip on her shoulder reassured him that she'd eventually come around.

"I can't see Georgie doing that unless she was drunk. She seems uptight."

While Iris was partially right, Jack still felt the need to defend his other sister. "Georgie's got a lot on her mind."

"Her wedding?" Iris scoffed.

"The brewery. It was a mess when we took over, remember? She put a lot of her own money into it, and it's just now starting to pay most of the bills, like the payroll. A lot of people need the brewery to work—you and me included—and it's pretty stressful." He still felt guilty about that. He'd put a lot of pressure on her not to sell, but they never would have made it this far if she hadn't invested the capital from the sale of her new age women's product company into the brewery. Sure, she'd met River because of it, but she'd gone through tons of stress those first few months while he'd flown off to Chicago to deal with a different kind of stress with Iris and his mother.

Iris was quiet for several seconds, then said, "So bringing me to this dog shelter is your lame attempt to make me feel like I belong in Asheville?"

"It's my lame attempt to help you make up for those mediocre grades."

"I already turned in most of my college applications," she said with a huff as she looked outside. "So there's no point."

"News flash—they still look at your grades for the rest of your senior year, Iris," he said, irritation bleeding into his tone for the first time since he'd picked her up after school.

She didn't respond.

"You like dogs, and this will be a great way to get some community service hours. And yes, I know," he added, "you've already turned in most of your college applications, but like I told you, they'll see your second quarter grades. Doing some good for the community might help offset the dip." And they needed her applications to shine. He'd saved up a little college fund for her, but it was nowhere near enough to pay for a degree at Northwestern. If she didn't want to take out loans she'd be paying until she was forty, she'd need a scholarship. It took grades and extracurriculars to get a scholarship. But she wouldn't thank him for saying any of that.

Jack saw the shelter up ahead, and as he pulled into the small parking area up front, he shot Iris a glance, asking her something that had been on his mind for weeks. "What's a harridan?"

"What?" she asked, scrunching her nose. "Why are you asking me that?"

"Because you scored a 32 on your reading ACT. So what's a harridan?"

She pushed out a breath in exasperation. "A mean, cranky woman. A shrew. Now why do you want to know?"

He'd gathered as much, but a slow smile lifted his lips. "I read it in a magazine."

Her eyes narrowed. "Since when do you read magazines?"

He reached for his door handle. "Since I moved to Asheville. Come on."

He got out, telling himself he only felt eager because, for all her objections, Iris actually looked a little excited as she got out of the car. The one-story building looked like it had seen better days, but he supposed most of the money they acquired went to the animals, not into beautification.

Iris joined him and they walked in together. A man with long white hair and a neatly trimmed beard sat at the front desk, his fingers flying over the keyboard of his laptop. He glanced up and smiled. "You must be our new volunteer."

Iris hesitated, then said, "Yeah. I'm Iris Durand."

Jack was relieved she sounded more like herself and not the changeling she'd become upon moving to Asheville. "I'm Jack," he said, "her brother."

"I'm Dustin," he said, walking around the counter. "Former volunteer turned employee." He said this last bit proudly, as if it were a new status. "So you know anything's possible." He winked at Iris, who responded with a flat expression.

Jack had been told he looked like that too, when confronted with something he didn't know how to react to. It had happened a lot in Asheville.

"Maisie asked me to let her know when you two showed up," Dustin continued. "Why don't you follow me?"

He led them to a door with a sign that said *Kennels*.

"I get to start out with the dogs?" Iris said in a hushed voice, and Jack was thrilled to hear her excitement.

He had warned her that her first day might be an orientation, that she probably would not be allowed to play with the dogs yet, but he knew how much she needed some simple enjoyment and the soul nourishment that came from doing something good. Somehow Maisie had known it too. She'd been the one to suggest it, after all.

He'd been skeptical at first, thinking that Iris would presume he was trying to pawn her off for free labor, and while she'd made a few smart-mouthed comments about child labor laws—he'd pointed out that she'd aged out of them when she turned seventeen—her objections hadn't been too adamant. Iris had always loved animals. She'd begged their mother for a dog for years to no avail, which Jack had secretly thought was for the best given their mother's instability. And while Iris claimed she hated everything about Asheville, he'd caught her snuggling with Tyrion on the sofa while she watched TV (always when Adalia wasn't around, of course).

Dustin opened the door, and the noise level shot up before they even walked in. It only got louder once they did. Multiple dogs were barking at once, in several different octaves. The kennels were along one side, and the long aisle ended in a wall with multiple windows. Maisie stood close to them, giving Jack a perfect view of her as they approached.

"I'll leave you to it," Dustin said, then headed back to the lobby.

Maisie wore a long-sleeved T-shirt, a pair of well-worn jeans, both of which clung to every delicious curve, and navy blue rain boots. Thoughts of her unclothed curves filled his head—his fingers digging into the flesh of her ass as he pinned her to her bathroom wall. Her legs wrapped around his waist...

Her hair was pulled up into a messy bun, exposing the delicate skin of her neck. Skin he remembered nipping and sucking.

Every ounce of blood in his body shot to his crotch, and he shifted uncomfortably. *Not now.*

But another voice insisted, *She's still interested.*

He'd mulled over their interactions on Thanksgiving so many times, it was like a video clip in his mind. He only had to press play to watch it again. The way she'd touched his upper thigh at dinner, sending desire pulsing through him in a way he didn't feel comfortable with, given how close they were to his sisters. How she'd stood so close to him after dinner, looking at him in a way that implied she'd prefer to go upstairs with him than stay for dessert. She still wanted him as much as he wanted her. Was it fair to hope she didn't meet someone else before Iris left for college?

She was holding a garden hose and shooting a spray of water into a kennel. She seemed intent on her work, and even though it was apparent this was one of the more unglamorous jobs of running an animal shelter, he liked that she hadn't pawned it off on someone else. Then he grinned, realizing she was probably about to.

She turned to face them, and he was once again blown away by her beauty. He'd met a lot of beautiful women, especially working as a bartender—women in slinky dresses with makeup expertly applied to accentuate their best features—but Maisie's natural beauty captivated him in a way he scarcely understood.

"Hey," she called out, her gaze lingering on Jack for a split second longer than necessary before she turned her full attention on Iris. "You ready to work with some dogs?"

Iris cast a glance at the empty kennel Maisie had been cleaning. "Yeah…"

Maisie laughed, and the familiarity of it did something funny to Jack's chest. The fact that he recognized it. That he'd heard it while he had her pinned to the wall with his arms and another part of him. That it was so natural and lighthearted it made him want to hear more.

"I'm going to show you how to do this, but not today. I'm going to have you walk the dogs while I clean their kennels." A soft smile lit up Maisie's face. "Keeping things clean is important, but the dogs need plenty of love and attention too."

Her gaze flicked so quickly to Jack, he almost missed it.

Maisie turned off the hose and walked to the next kennel. She grabbed a leash from a hook on the wall next to the door, then showed Iris the small whiteboard attached to the kennel gate. "These are very important. They'll tell you the dog's name and important information about them. This one is

Pete, and you can see that he jumps up on people. Some of the boards might tell you a dog's a biter. You steer clear of those ones, okay?"

Iris nodded. "Yeah. Okay."

Jack checked out the large black lab, who looked like he was over fifty pounds. He wasn't sure he liked the idea of Iris dealing with a huge dog jumping on her.

"When he or another dog tries to jump up," Maisie said, "turn your back to them as you say no. When he gets down, turn back around and reward him. We try to teach them how to obey commands like sit, stay, and heel, but we don't always have enough volunteers to work with them regularly. It's super helpful if the bigger dogs are somewhat trained so their owners can manage them. After you've been here for a while, we'll teach you how to train them too."

He liked that she didn't say "if"—she treated it as an eventuality rather than a possibility. Like she understood the gleam in Iris's eyes just as much as he did.

"How do I reward them?" Iris asked, her gaze on the lab, who was already jumping up against the cage, eager for attention.

"A pat on the head. Making sure you have a friendly pitch to your voice when you praise them. Sometimes treats, but it depends on the dog. We try to be careful with some of the overweight and elderly dogs, but we'll teach you as we go," Maisie said. "For now, I'll show you how to deal with Pete." She opened the kennel door and stepped inside.

Pete jumped up, his paws hitting Maisie in the chest and pushing her backward.

Maisie turned her back to the dog. He moved around her, trying to jump up again, but she repeated the maneuver, and Pete stayed down this time, nuzzling the side of her leg.

"Good boy!" Maisie said enthusiastically as she rubbed the top of the dog's head. Then she looked up at Iris with a smile. "Okay, your turn."

"Are you sure it's safe?" Jack asked, hating to question Maisie, but the last thing he wanted was for Iris to get hurt or to have an experience that kept her from coming back.

"Are you still here, Helicopter Brother?" Maisie teased. "You can come back at five to pick her up."

Jack's mouth dropped open. "What?"

"Your job is done. You delivered her safe and sound," Maisie said, then made a shooing motion. "Now it's my turn. And not to worry. I'll keep her safe and sound." She shot him a mischievous grin. "Probably."

Jack hesitated, and Maisie laughed. "She'll be fine. I promise. Actually, don't worry about coming back to get her. I've got to pick up Addy at your place for our girls' night with Blue, so I can drop her off."

Once again Jack hesitated, long enough for Iris to groan. "Jack."

But it wasn't the kind of groan she'd been making for the past month. She sounded more like the girl he'd known for seventeen years, not the pod person who'd shown up in her place.

"Okay," Maisie said. "Off with you."

"Okay…" He took a few steps backward, telling himself he was being ridiculous, but if he were honest with himself, he'd hoped to spend more time with Maisie. Sure, he couldn't pursue a relationship with her now, but he still hoped there was a chance for them in the future. Was it wrong to want an excuse to see her? Was it fair to either of them?

He gave Iris a soft smile, but she was already opening Pete's kennel to walk in. He caught Maisie's eye instead. He had trouble reading the look she was giving him, but at least she didn't seem pissed that he'd turned her down—or sort of turned her down—at Thanksgiving. He thought maybe she understood. And for now, maybe that was the best he could hope for.

CHAPTER
Eleven

Iris was different here. The dogs brought her to life in a way the madness of a Buchanan family gathering hadn't. And Maisie respected that. The dogs brought her to life too. She'd known that ever since Einstein had pawed at her leg, dirty and starving, beaten down by life. Helping him had given her purpose when she'd desperately needed it.

She'd let Iris show herself around mostly, recognizing that she wasn't the kind of girl who liked being corralled, something else she appreciated, but toward the end of their time together, she herded her over to the sink next to the windows at the far end of the kennels.

"Is this where the cleaning part comes in?" Iris asked, her tone making it clear she was less than excited by the thought.

"Only for our hands. I want to introduce you to someone."

She expected some sort of smart comment, but Iris just nodded, glancing back at Chewbacca, the part-chow, part-Chihuahua, all teddy bear dog they'd taken in a week ago.

"You're a fan of Chewie?" Maisie said, scrubbing her hands. She pulled back, leaving the sink for Iris, who shrugged.

"He's all right, I guess." But the sparkle in her eyes said she thought he was a whole lot more than that. And if she weren't already living with a dog and a hell cat, Maisie would have contemplated surprising Jack with another dog. He hadn't reacted so badly last time, had he? There was something sweet in the way he'd left the decision to Adalia—like maybe he knew how much she needed Tyrion, and vice versa, even though he'd been halfway across the country.

After Iris had washed her hands too, Maisie led her out of the kennel and down the hall, Dustin waving jauntily at them from the front desk. He'd volunteered so much Maisie had taken him on full-time as her volunteer coordinator-slash-jack-of-all-trades. A financial crunch when they were already hurting, but she'd needed the steady help, and retiree or not, he'd made it clear he wanted to be here. Privately, she thought he enjoyed talking to the visitors as much as he liked the dogs, but she was okay with that. *She* didn't feel that way, and someone had to make nice, especially with people who came in to surrender pets. Her other full-time employee, Beatrice, wasn't much for making nice either.

She waved back to Dustin, biting her lip to hold back a laugh when he winked at Iris. She didn't need to glance sideways to imagine the teen's look of horror. Dustin was technically Iris's boss, but Maisie felt no need to point that out. Because she'd decided to take Iris under her own wing.

She told herself it had nothing to do with Jack, and that was partly true—she saw herself in Iris, and she saw Molly in her too—but partly true wasn't the same thing as totally true. She'd sent him away earlier because Iris had needed him to leave. If it had been up to her, she would have kept him around. If it had been up to her, she would have led him into the playroom and locked the door behind them.

Then again, Jack had made it very clear that nothing more could happen between them, and he was right—not just because of Iris, but because of the whole screwed-up River and Georgie wedding situation.

She'd video-chatted with her sisters again after Thanksgiving, and while Mary had essentially gaped in horror the whole time, Molly had laughed so hard she'd peed a little in her yoga pants. She'd also recorded the whole thing, insisting she wanted to write about it for her blog (with all the identifying details changed).

"Don't you work for a dating blog?" she'd asked.

"Oh, some things are universally funny," her sister had said. "No one would mind. Plus, Datesgiving was a huge hit. Especially that guy who brought a wishbone and insisted I break it with him, then carried his half around in his pocket all night." A sly look had crossed her face. "Besides, you and Jack *are* sort of involved."

"Is that why he cringed when I grabbed his thigh?" Of course, that wasn't entirely true, but the outcome was the same. "You just need to accept it's not going to happen. And so do I. It's for the best anyway. I need to get through this wedding before I can move on."

Mary was the one who'd responded to that, shaking her head slowly. "Maisie, Mom would have told you that you can move on any damn time you choose."

Which was maybe the first time she'd heard her sister say "damn."

Shaking the thoughts away, Maisie led Iris to the back office and knocked twice.

"Dustin, for the love of God, I do not want one of your stinky cheese Danishes. I do not care that someone's filming a movie in Sylva, and I definitely don't care that you're wearing mismatching day-of-the-week socks. Now leave me in peace so I can crunch some numbers."

The corners of Iris's mouth twitched in a would-be smile, and Maisie smiled back and opened the door.

"It's me, Beatrice."

Beatrice shook her head in a manner that said she wasn't appeased. "Don't get me started on that boy. You puffed him up something good by hiring him."

She might like to call Dustin "boy," but Beatrice was younger than him. Not by much, but her hair was still black, interrupted by the occasional strand of silver, her dark skin barely wrinkled.

"Beatrice, this is Iris. She's our new volunteer. And Iris, this is Beatrice. Without her, nothing would get done around here. As a rescue, we're dependent on fundraising, and Beatrice is the one who keeps the lights on and the doors open. If you're interested in the business aspect of the shelter, she's the one you want to talk to."

She hadn't thought Iris would be interested in that, necessarily, but she only had two full-time employees, plus a part-time night manager, and she introduced all of the volunteers to them. There was another reason she'd brought Iris back to meet Beatrice, one she hadn't fully admitted to herself.

When she'd been down, Beatrice had pulled her up. She'd helped her establish all of this. This shelter. This life. And Iris was clearly struggling too.

"I'm glad to meet you, Iris," Beatrice said, her annoyance toward Dustin dissipating. "I work at home more often than not, but I'm always here on Thursday afternoons. And if you have any interest in the numbers, I'd welcome your help one afternoon."

To Maisie's surprise, Iris brightened. "Yes, I'd love that. I want to be a business major in school, and I *love* dogs."

"Good for you," Beatrice said. "Most kids don't know their a—butts from their elbows when they start college. If you know what you want going in, you're ahead of the rest. Are you coming in every Thursday afternoon?"

"And Tuesdays," Iris said, giving Maisie a rebellious look. They'd only talked about Thursdays, but she wasn't about to say no.

"Why don't you come by next Thursday when you get in, and you can be my new protégé." She smiled up at Maisie. "Maisie here was my first protégé, and she's not doing too poorly for herself."

Something like curiosity flashed in Iris's eyes, but she shut it down quickly.

"I'd like that," she said simply. And then, as if remembering some distant lessons of etiquette—lessons, Maisie gathered, Jack had probably taught her rather than her mother—she added, "Thank you."

"That's settled then," Beatrice said. "Now, I'll let you two go, but Maisie, you and I are going to have a serious discussion about putting locks on the office doors."

Maisie just waved her off, knowing she actually *liked* Dustin. They both did.

"See you later."

Iris didn't talk much as they headed out to the Jeep and piled in, but she scrunched her nose against the dog smell.

"I'm surprised you're not used to it after being in the kennels for so long," Maisie commented.

"I'm not sure it's the kind of thing you can get used to."

Which was something Maisie had said herself more than once, so she just nodded. "Fair enough."

"What did Beatrice mean," Iris said, "about you being her protégé? Do you work on the numbers too?"

Maisie pulled out of the lot, heading toward the Buchanan house. "No, but I had to learn some things to open the shelter." She shot a quick glance at Iris. "When my parents died, they left me that property." Iris's eyes rounded, but she kept going. "Well, they left it to my sisters too. They were going to flip the building and sell it. Beatrice was my mom's best friend, and she left her job to help me start the shelter. I think she did it because she wanted to take care of me. That's what she meant."

Iris was quiet for a moment. Then she said, "I'm sorry they're dead."

"Me too."

"I don't really have parents either," Iris said, picking at something on her shirt. Maybe an invisible thread, but given she'd been walking dogs for almost two hours, it could very well be a rogue tuft of fur. "I only know who my dad is because I went through my mom's phone and found his number. I...I tried to meet him, but he refused to see me. He said he only wanted to hear from me through his lawyer."

Maisie wanted to hug her then, and maybe toss some puppies at her, but she held back, both because she was driving and because doing any of those things would surely result in Iris pulling away.

"That sucks," she said, because it did. "But you have a brother who cares a lot about you."

"Yeah, sometimes too much," Iris said, looking up at her. Maisie only spared a quick glance at her, but there was something sharp in her eyes. A sort of scrutiny like she was studying Maisie for cues.

"Maybe he's trying to make up for both of your parents."

"I guess so," Iris said, "but it would be nice if he could just settle for being my brother."

"Give him time," Maisie said. Truth be told, the only thing Iris could do to get Jack to back off was to be happy. But she wasn't going to say that. Iris was too young to be burdened with that responsibility.

They were mostly quiet for the rest of the trip, although Iris surprised Maisie by asking some questions about a couple of the dogs. Chewie and the black lab she'd played with first, Pete.

"Do you think I could really help train them?" she asked as Maisie pulled into the drive.

"I do." Maisie shot a glance at her. "I didn't have a dog of my own until I was almost twenty, and I learned pretty quickly. You're a quick study. You'll learn too."

Iris glanced at the house. "Please don't tell Jack what I said to you. About my dad, I mean. He doesn't know."

Maisie mimed zipping her lips. "In the vault. And yes, I know I'm mixing metaphors. But that's how serious I am about keeping it quiet."

Iris nodded and then got out, heading for the door.

It came as no surprise at all when it popped open before she could get there, Jack peeking his head out like—

She stifled a laugh. Like a freaking jack-in-the-box. Probably he'd been waiting on the nearest couch the whole time Iris had been gone.

"See?" she called out, following Iris. "I told you I'd bring her back in one piece."

He glanced up at her, gratitude in his gaze, and something more—the same something more she saw whenever he looked at her—but then his attention shifted totally to Iris.

Helicopter Brother, reporting for duty, she thought to herself.

There was something so endearing about his concern, about this big, strong man who'd taken it upon himself to be both mother and father to his little sister. But if Jack was having problems connecting with Iris, he was taking the worst possible approach.

She didn't feel she could tell him that, though. Not yet, anyway.

"How was it?" he asked, hovering. "Did any of the dogs jump on you or bite you?"

Iris heaved a sigh and made her way through the door. Jack looked like he wanted to follow at her heels like a herding dog, but he held back and waved Maisie through. When she passed, she felt a whisper of his hand on the small of her back, there and then gone. It sent a pulse of heat through her, but she just stepped aside so he could pass her.

Iris turned to look at him. "I'm going to volunteer at the shelter on Tuesday afternoons too," she said. A defiant look crossed her face. "Maisie said I could."

"Sure," he said with a slightly baffled look. "That's great. Yeah."

"I have homework to do." She pushed past him, leaving him with a slightly lost look.

Adalia emerged at the top of the stairs, looking fresh and pretty in a bright turquoise shirt and a bohemian skirt. Maisie probably should have changed, but it wasn't like Adalia and Blue weren't used to her stinking of dog. Besides, she didn't regret bringing Iris home. She'd learned so much more about her, and about Jack.

Iris edged over to the far end of the stairs, like Adalia might have cooties.

"Do you want to make dinner with me tonight?" Jack asked her. "I thought we could cook together, like we used to."

"No, thanks," Iris said, in that careless way teens had about them, like she didn't know she was being cruel or maybe didn't care. "There's some leftover pizza in the fridge, and I'm going to video-chat with Janie."

"I'm glad you girls are still so close," Jack said hesitantly, "but aren't there some friends you'd like to hang out with in Asheville?"

Iris laughed, actually laughed, and then said, "Are *you* giving *me* social advice?"

And then she was gone in a thunder of steps.

The look on Jack's face...

Maisie wanted to say she'd cook dinner with him, gladly, especially if his cooking was anything like his bartending. But she already had plans, and she wasn't the kind of person who canceled on someone lightly. Besides, she'd promised Finn that she would tell Adalia and Blue about River, and she intended to go through with it. Maybe Adalia could help her figure out how many wedding-related activities a co-best man could feasibly shrug off.

But Adalia reached the bottom of the steps and slung an arm around Jack's shoulders as Tyrion, appearing from the kitchen, danced around them.

"Cheer up, Jacques," she said, a nickname she'd appropriated for him after finding out that his grandmother had been a French immigrant. "She'll come around. In the meantime, why don't you come out with us?" She glanced at Maisie, who was wrestling with how she felt about this development—on the one hand, she'd wanted to have that heart-to-heart with Adalia and Blue, but on the other...

She wanted to spend time with Jack, to get to know him better. To soak up his presence.

"Blue's not coming," Adalia told Maisie. "She texted you too, but I know you. Usually your phone is off at the kennel. It's something to do with a support group meeting, but she was a bit cagey about giving details. Obviously it's not AA."

Obvious, since they always went out for drinks, and Blue seemed to get tipsy off a single drink.

"Huh. We'll have to interrogate her the next time we see her," she said.

Jack smiled a little, as if amused, and she suspected it was because he was the type who'd allow someone to sit with their secrets. He would no more press someone for a confidence than he would let Iris go to a twenty-one-and-up concert.

"Well, what do you say, Durand?" she asked, letting her tone get a little playful. "Willing to let someone else make you a drink for a change?"

He glanced upstairs, looking a little twitchy at the thought of leaving Iris, but then something in his posture straightened and his gaze landed on Maisie. His eyes danced over her for a moment, like she was wearing a dress and heels instead of torn-up old jeans and a random shirt, then settled on her face. "Yeah," he said. "I guess I could be accommodating. Let me run up and tell Iris."

The second he was up the stairs and out of sight, Adalia turned to Maisie, raising her eyebrows.

"You're welcome," she said.

It took Maisie a second to realize what she meant— Adalia must have noticed something between them at Thanksgiving.

"So Blue didn't have a meeting?" she asked, shaking her head slightly. "That's some master-level manipulation."

"Oh, she does," Adalia said, "but it's ending early. She offered to meet us later."

"Adalia, I don't…" But she didn't have time to finish whatever it was she'd intended to say—and honestly, she wasn't sure—because Jack came down the stairs. And every bit of her seemed to lift in anticipation.

Great, Red, the first man you ever loved still has no idea, and now you're in danger of falling for a man who's told you it's a no-go.

But there was a naughty part of her that wondered if *everything* was a no-go, or just dating. Because they'd been plenty good at the other stuff.

CHAPTER Twelve

The ride to the restaurant was awkward. Adalia had insisted that Jack sit in the front seat next to Maisie because he had longer legs. Then she'd proceeded to pepper them both with questions, keeping them talking while she listened from the back like their would-be dating therapist. But the awkwardness hadn't kept him from noticing how close he was to Maisie. She was just inches away, and he clasped his hands in his lap to keep from reaching over and snagging her hand resting on the console. From the few glances she snuck in his direction, the impulse wasn't one-sided.

Once they got to the restaurant, Adalia immediately claimed the seat across from Maisie at the four-top table, leaving two empty chairs between them.

Jack didn't protest, although he was beginning to question the wisdom of joining them. Adalia was usually pretty chill, but her machinations were painfully obvious. She'd noticed him talking to Maisie on Thanksgiving. She must have decided to help prod things along. He suspected it had something to do with the fact that she'd started phasing *Emma* into her *Pride and Prejudice* watching schedule. Things he only knew about because Iris, who scoffed when Adalia put them on, loved those movies too. The real question was if Maisie was part of the attempted setup, but he quickly dismissed the idea. Maisie would have taken a more direct approach.

They ordered drinks and a couple of appetizers, chatting about Maisie's shelter and how much Adalia and Finn's art benefit had helped with funding. The contacts she'd made had apparently been just as useful as her share of the proceeds. However, she was maddeningly silent about Iris's afternoon, other than to say she'd enjoyed having her there and looked forward to seeing her next Tuesday. The drinks and fried cheese ravioli and spinach-artichoke dip arrived, and Adalia gave them a mischievous look and hopped out of her seat. "I'm going to the restroom."

"Do you think she's coming back?" Jack asked in a dry tone, watching her glance back at them.

"Hard to say," Maisie said, taking a sip of her peach Bellini. "It could go either way." It delighted him a little, the way a woman as tough and no-nonsense as her savored sweet drinks. They'd joked about putting each other into boxes, but he already knew no one category could contain Maisie O'Shea.

Setting her drink down, Maisie shifted to face him. "It's important you know that I had nothing to do with this. I know it looks a little sketchy since I offered to bring Iris home."

He shot her a grin. "I know this was all Adalia. Plus, she wasn't lying about needing a ride. Bessie really is in the shop."

"I'm glad to hear her orchestrations don't run so deep," she said with a smile. "In any case, I truly intended to drop Iris off and pick Addy up. It was supposed to be a simple exchange."

He laughed. "Is anything ever simple with Addy?"

She laughed too. "You have a point, but her heart was in the right place. She has no way of knowing that we both have good reasons not to get involved right now."

Both.

What did that mean?

But she took a big sip of her drink, indicating she'd said her piece, and he didn't feel comfortable pushing. He never had. When he was a little kid, he used to ask his mom all kinds of questions—why it rained and how yogurt was made and where she'd disappeared to for twelve hours without calling. Her answer to that latter question had put an end to his curiosity.

"I needed to get away from *you*," she'd said. He'd been six.

"Thanks for suggesting the shelter for Iris," he said. "She looked happier than I've seen her since she moved here."

"No problem," she said, then turned serious. "She's a good kid. She's lucky to have you for a brother. Addy is too."

He wasn't sure what to say to that. He felt like a huge failure in the brother department, and not just with Iris. "I don't know why she doesn't trash that hunk of junk she calls a car, and I honestly can't believe Finn hasn't gotten her a more decent one. The man obviously has money."

"You think he hasn't tried?" Maisie asked with a short laugh. "She refuses, of course. Not that I would expect anything less. Plus, she says her car is perfect for loading up literal junk. She'd be afraid to put her finds in a nicer car."

"I get that," he said with a frown, "but she should at least get a new engine. Maybe she'll have enough money after her art show in February. The current one is unreliable at best, and dangerous at worst."

"Dangerous?" Maisie said. "How do you figure?"

He frowned. "She works late at night in her studio, and her stupid antiquated cell phone doesn't hold a charge. She could break down in the middle of the night without a working cell phone to call for help."

"Because Asheville is so dangerous," she said with a smirk.

"Bad people are everywhere, Maisie," he said matter-of-factly. "It only takes one to cause irreparable harm."

She was silent for a moment. "Has someone close to you been hurt, Jack?"

"What?" he asked in surprise.

"Because you seem to see the boogeyman around every corner."

He was taken aback by that. "Is it wrong to care about my sisters?"

Regret filled her eyes. "No. Of course not. I was out of line. It's obvious you care deeply about your sisters' well-being and take your role in their lives very seriously."

"Why do I sense a but in there?" he asked with a scowl.

She glanced down at her drink, but then her eyes lifted and he found himself sucked into her deep green gaze despite his slight irritation. "I have two sisters, one older and one younger. Both of them love me, but they usually have very different ideas about what's best for me. They can't both be right. Sometimes neither of them is. Just keep that in mind with your own sisters, okay?"

What did she mean by that? His mouth parted to ask, but then she leaned closer and whispered, "I know for a fact that Finn's getting Addy a new phone for Christmas, so you can take that one off your worry list." Before he could react, she straightened up in her chair, giving someone a sugary smile over his shoulder. "Everything go okay in the restroom, Addy? You were in there for an *awfully* long time."

"They have really awesome soap, so I washed my hands for a full thirty seconds," she said with a grin as she sat in her chair. "How'd things go out here?"

"Peachy," Maisie said wryly, picking up her drink.

Jack didn't respond, his thoughts bouncing back to what Maisie had said. Did she disapprove of the way he was handling Iris? Was it wrong of him to worry about his sister? He'd failed to keep his promise to his grandmother—if he'd protected Iris the way he should have, one of his mother's many boyfriends wouldn't have made a pass at her—and that ate at him more than he cared to admit.

Still, he wasn't upset with Maisie for challenging him. In fact, that was one of the things he appreciated about her. She was up-front about her feelings, and he doubted she'd shy away from standing up for what she believed in. For *who* she believed in. After spending his entire life playing games with his mother and trying to decipher her every mood, he found Maisie's forthrightness refreshing. At least he'd always know where he stood with her.

He was withdrawn for the next ten minutes, and Adalia shot him several worried glances. Then Maisie's phone chimed with a text, and she glanced down at the screen and frowned. "I've got to make a call. I'll be right back."

"Everything okay?" Jack asked as she got up from the table.

She gave him a surprised glance, still clutching her phone. "Yeah, one of my foster dogs is sick. I just need to check in with the vet."

"Okay," he said, disappointment filling him at the realization she might have to leave.

"What happened while I was gone?" Adalia asked in a worried tone as soon as Maisie was out of earshot.

"What?" he asked absently, turning to face her.

"Come on. Before I left, there was so much chemistry between you two I was about to pull out my fire extinguisher, and now it's like it was doused by a tidal wave."

"It's a bit soon to be joking about fire extinguishers, don't you think?" he asked wryly. "We'll be lucky if Lurch's health insurance doesn't sue our homeowner's insurance."

Adalia cringed. "So letting Dottie fry a turkey didn't work out so well. It's hard to turn that woman down." She gave him a pointed look. "But don't change the subject. It's obvious there's something between you two, so why don't you ask her out?"

"Why are you putting this all on me?" he said, picking up his drink. "Maisie's a strong, independent woman. She's perfectly capable of asking me out."

Except for whatever reason she'd alluded to earlier.

"I know," she said with a frown, "which makes me think you've dissuaded her in some way."

Jack released a sigh. "Are you asking if I'm attracted to Maisie? How could I not be? She's an incredibly sexy woman."

Which made him wonder why she'd never dated River or Finn. The three of them spent a lot of time together, and while he was a firm believer that men and women could be friends, this was *Maisie*. As far as descriptions went, sexy didn't cut it. Smart. Funny. Sharp yet sweet, like candy covered in cayenne pepper.

Adalia clasped her hands together and beamed.

"But this isn't a good time for me to get wrapped up in a relationship, Addy."

She leaned closer. "Why? Because of Iris?"

"Yes, because of Iris. She already resents me for moving her here. Can you imagine the message I'd be sending if I spent half my time with a girlfriend?"

"That you're a well-rounded individual?" she asked sarcastically. "Look, no seventeen-year-old girl wants her older brother giving her all his attention."

He frowned. She probably had a point, but he couldn't help noticing that Maisie and Adalia were both finding fault with how he was handling his little sister, and it was starting to annoy him. Neither one of them had any idea what it had been like growing up with Genevieve Durand. Sure, he'd told Adalia some things, but she had nothing but a snapshot.

Iris needed to know *someone* put her needs first, and that someone had to be Jack. He'd already shaken the foundation of their relationship by choosing Asheville and the brewery over Chicago, but he saw it as a long-term solution, even if it hurt in the short term. Hopefully, Iris would eventually see it that way too.

"I'm not giving her my full attention," he said. "She spends a good portion of her time in her room. Without me. But she needs to know I'm there when she *does* need me. That she's my priority." Then, to drive the point home, he added, "If I'd known you after your mother died, I would have been there for you too, Addy. Just like I hope you know I'm there for you now." She'd told him that Georgie and Lee had gone off to college, leaving her to fend for herself with their father, another narcissistic asshole. If anyone would understand Jack's motivations, it was Adalia.

Surprise filled her eyes. She started to say something, but Maisie reappeared. "Another emergency resolved with a call. It's my superpower." She sat down, her brow furrowing as she glanced from Adalia to Jack. "Is everything okay?"

"Everything is perfect," Adalia said with tears in her eyes. Then she threw her arms around Jack's neck in an awkward hug. "Thank you," she said in a muffled whisper.

He hugged her back, saying nothing. Words were cheap. It was a man's actions that proved his merit. He only hoped he could prove himself to all his sisters. Only further proof that he shouldn't start anything with Maisie right now, but it would be a whole lot easier if she would stop looking at him like that...

CHAPTER Thirteen

Maisie had come back to find the mood between Adalia and Jack so serious they could have been at a wake. She preferred Irish wakes, full of dancing and drinking. Full of *life*. So she ordered another round for everyone.

Several sips in, they seemed to relax a little, and Jack started telling them about his bartending days. The stories were light and funny, but she found herself thinking about what his life had been like beyond the bar. He wouldn't have been able to see Iris as much as he did now. Was he trying to make up for that? Or had something happened to make him more protective?

She assumed something must have—both from what Iris had said in the car earlier and the fact that Iris now lived with him. It wasn't a normal arrangement for a sister to live with her brother when she had two perfectly alive parents.

"I'll level with you," Maisie said, leaning in a little. "I wish you'd made this." She nodded to her lemon drop martini.

"Oh yeah?" he asked, his eyes speculative. "Mine was better?"

"Much."

"It was so good you left it on the counter after taking one sip," he said, his eyes dancing. Because he remembered exactly why she'd left it, and so did she.

"It was a tragic mistake, and I think of it often. I should have taken the drink, tucked Diego under my arm, and run for the hills."

His gaze lingered on her lips, but Adalia coughed, shifting their attention to her.

"You okay?" Jack asked, patting her on the back.

"Yeah, my drink just went down the wrong way."

But something about the way she was coughing seemed fake. What had Jack said to her?

Before the bathroom break, she'd seemed so eager to set them up Maisie had half-expected the waitress to deliver a piece of chocolate cake in the shape of a heart with two forks, a hotel room key embedded in the middle. Now, Adalia was practically choking herself to end a flirty moment between them.

The cough stopped as soon as Jack's pats became harder. *Faker.*

"Maybe we should talk about the engagement party," Adalia said. "You know, since we're all in the wedding."

Huh. Maybe that was it. Maybe Jack had said he didn't want to get involved with Maisie because he couldn't commit to a relationship and they were going to have to keep seeing each other at wedding events. She couldn't fault such logic. Hell, she was in total agreement, but she still wished they could have a little fun.

"I don't know," Jack said. "I told Dottie I'd keep her in the loop." He eyed the door as if he feared she might come in and find them talking about it.

"You're afraid of Dottie," Maisie said with a grin.

"Of course I am," he said, "and I'm not ashamed of it." He took a sip of his drink, his expression contemplative. "She reminds me a little of my grandmother. I mean, my grandmother didn't push crystals on everyone she met or throw wild parties that always went horribly wrong, but she cared about people like Dottie does. She basically raised me." He was saying it for Maisie's sake, because Adalia was nodding in a way that spoke of foreknowledge.

"I'm sorry you lost her," Maisie said. Because she could tell he had—she heard it in his tone, soft and reminiscent. Jack was also not the sort of man who would've left his tottering, much-loved grandmother hundreds of miles behind with his mother, who apparently wasn't much of a nurturer.

He met her eyes, his gaze intent and serious, and simply said, "Thank you."

It was on the edge of her tongue to tell him that she understood the pain of loss, but she could tell he knew. So she simply said, "Dottie's like that for a lot of us. I'd never give her the satisfaction of hearing me say so, but it's like she has a sixth sense for who needs some extra love."

Adalia reached over and squeezed Jack's hand, and the quick motion startled Maisie. She'd forgotten her friend was there—for a moment, it had felt like she and Jack were alone at the table.

"Don't worry," Adalia said, "we'll only discuss it in general terms." It took a second for Maisie to realize she was still talking about the party. "Now, what can we do to ensure that Victoria and my dad almost certainly won't come?"

Adalia looked so serious, Maisie couldn't help but laugh. "I don't know if I want to help you," she said. "I look forward to meeting the infamous Victoria."

Adalia had told her and Blue dozens of stories about her, from the fact that she had a timeline for her relationship with

Lee to the fact that she'd monogrammed all of her bags with the initials VB, Victoria Buchanan, and pretended the store had made a mistake. She was so controlling Lee couldn't call either of his sisters without first ensuring she wasn't around.

Maisie couldn't understand why anyone would put up with that kind of behavior. Her sister Molly would quote the movie *10 Things I Hate About You* and suggest Victoria had beer-flavored nipples, although in the case of the debonair Lee, she suspected he'd prefer something snooty like port. But Maisie didn't think looks or prowess in the sheets were enough to compensate for someone being a blowhard. She'd sooner spend the rest of her life alone—*like Josie predicted*—than be with someone who tried to control her or keep her away from her family and friends.

"Trust me, you don't want to meet her," Adalia said. "Tell her, Jack."

"I didn't exchange a single word with her," he said.

"Maybe not, but you pay attention to everything."

He glanced at Maisie again, his gaze taking her in as if she were the bourbon in his glass. "You won't enjoy meeting her," he said at last. Then his lips twitched with a held-back smile. "But the rest of us would very much enjoy witnessing it."

"You think I'd eviscerate her," she said.

"I know it," he said, his eyes gleaming.

"And I'm counting on it," Adalia added, "unless, of course, we figure out a way to avoid her altogether, which would be preferable."

Maybe it was because Maisie had been thinking of an excuse to get out of it herself, but the answer came to her quickly. "That's easy," she said. "Forget having the party in January. Have it on Christmas. Or maybe just before. Yeah,

Christmas Eve. No way would she want to spend the holidays in Asheville."

Adalia's eyes lit up as if Maisie had just given her a gift.

"I don't know," Jack said, plucking at his napkin. "I don't want to sabotage the party. Georgie will be really disappointed if Lee doesn't show."

"Oh, he'll come," Adalia said. "But this'll give him an excuse to leave Victoria at home. He'd rather come without her anyway."

What kind of relationship was this, exactly?

"And Georgie might fool herself into thinking otherwise, but she'll be *much* happier if Dad stays home. We all will." This last was said in a small voice that indicated Adalia certainly felt that way.

Jack clearly saw it too, because he nodded encouragingly. "Let's float the idea. See if Lee's in, and if everyone else in the crew is going to be around. We can make it an open house type thing so family, friends, and people from the brewery can stop by."

He plucked at the napkin a little more, depositing the little shreds into a neat pile.

"Keep doing that and there won't be anything left," Maisie said.

He glanced up at her and smiled in the way of someone who felt seen. "I haven't told Iris yet, but Mom doesn't want her to come back to Chicago for Christmas. She's going on a cruise with a new…friend. Iris isn't going to like that."

"We'll cheer her up," she said, reaching out and putting her hand over his. She hadn't meant to, but there was something in his eyes. That sweet sadness for his sister, for himself.

"What about you?" Jack said. "Are you going to be here?"

"I am." The words came out before she remembered she was supposed to be getting out of this quagmire, not worming her way into it. But Molly was going to follow up the successful Datesgiving piece with the Twelve Dates of Christmas (Maisie had argued it was a blatant rip-off of the holiday movie, which Molly had openly admitted—"...but hey, free publicity!"), and Mary had invited Maisie to come stay with her family in Virginia. Maisie couldn't travel on the holidays, or at least not on a big one like Christmas. She usually gave everyone the day off and took care of the dogs herself. Although Mary would give her a sad look if she said so, it was fun. She liked the traditions she'd established with the dogs. Taking pictures with Santa Paws (okay, it was always just River or Finn in the suit with a tacked-on beard) and giving the dogs turkey and stockings full of chew toys and treats. So, yeah, she was staying.

"Then the important people are all available," he said. He meant the whole wedding party was available, because Georgie had picked Adalia, Dottie, Victoria, and Iris, and Maisie, Finn, Jack, and Lee were standing up with River.

Still, there'd almost been a sensual purr to his words, and if that didn't send tingles straight to her—

"Oh, good, you're still here," Blue said, bustling up to the table. With glossy, curly black hair and high cheekbones, Blue was a striking woman, and Maisie found herself glancing at Jack to see how he reacted.

But when she looked at him, he met her gaze. He hadn't looked away.

Something about the moment sent a stab of vulnerability through her, and Maisie turned from him, flagging down a server.

"Sangria," Blue said without glancing at the menu.

"So," Adalia said as soon as the server walked away. "Tell us everything about this support group-slash-cult you've joined. Although if it's a pyramid scheme, please don't ask us to host parties. I love you, but I refuse to sell crappy Tupperware for you."

"I'll keep that in mind," Blue said with a smile. But her gaze shot to Jack, and it was clear she didn't feel comfortable talking about her personal business in front of someone she didn't know. The realization that Jack and Blue were strangers to each other came as a bit of a shock. But just a few weeks ago she hadn't known Jack either, other than having seen him a couple of times in his role as Adalia's brother.

"I'm going to order an Uber," he said, slapping some cash down on the table. "I'd like to think some more about what we were discussing." He had to be talking about the party, and the possibility of holding it on or in the vicinity of Christmas, but for some reason he looked at Maisie as he said it. And she couldn't look away.

"I didn't mean to chase you off," Blue said, which was kind of funny, really, because Blue was the one they'd planned to meet in the first place. Leave it to Blue to apologize for attending her own girls' night. She was too damn nice, that was her problem.

"I'll see you ladies later," Jack said, and then they all said their goodbyes, and he left. His absence was so marked, it felt like his empty seat had turned into a black hole.

"What in the world is happening between the two of you?" Blue asked, fanning herself to mime the heat that had been passing between them.

"Nice try, Deflector," Maisie said. "You were telling us about your support group."

Blue looked to Adalia for help, but Addy shook her head. "We'll get to Maisie later. *After* we put your new group through the cult test."

"Sorry to disappoint," Blue said, "but it's not a cult." The server delivered her drink, and she took a long gulp. "You guys know I've gone on a lot of awful dates lately."

Maisie huffed a laugh. "That's an understatement."

Blue had reentered the dating world after some experience (heretofore unmentioned) had soured her from it, and every man she met seemed to be awful in a unique way. There'd been Leo, with his recycled tinfoil fashion creations, Rupert, who had a fake English accent but was from New Jersey, and David, who'd seemed normal and cute until half an hour into their drinks date when he'd revealed he was—shudder—a professional clown…and offered to dress up for her in the bedroom.

Blue nodded. "Well, I was on Craiglist…"

Adalia groaned out loud. "Don't tell me you went on a Craigslist date. That's how half the people in Lifetime movies get murdered."

Blue made a face. "No, I was looking for some affordable bolsters for my yoga classes, but I stumbled on this ad for the Bad Luck Club. It said it was for people who've had a bad run in life. With dating, or I guess work, or relationships or whatever."

"And you're telling us this now?" Adalia asked. "I would one hundred percent have wanted to come with you."

"I know," Blue said, looking down into her drink. "But you don't exactly have bad luck right now, do you?"

It was true. Adalia and Finn were gooey over each other in a way that would have been absolutely annoying if Maisie weren't so happy for them, plus Adalia had returned to her art and was preparing for a big show in February.

"What about me?" Maisie said. Although it was kind of funny to be hurt that your friend didn't think your luck was bad enough to warrant an invitation to a group of sad sacks.

Of course, she suspected that wasn't the reason Blue hadn't invited them. There was something from her past she didn't want them to know about.

"I figured you'd think it was stupid."

"Was it?"

"No, it was nice," Blue said warmly. "It feels good to talk to other people in the same situation."

"Did you meet a guy there?" Adalia asked.

"No, nothing like that. I mean, yes, there are guys in the group, but people don't go there looking for dates. We're discouraged from dating other members."

"So what did you do?" Maisie pressed. "Exchange stories?"

"I can't really talk about it," Blue said hesitantly. "That's another one of the rules."

It sounded like the founder had probably watched *Fight Club* too much, but there was something earnest about Blue's tone, and she didn't want to upset her by saying so. Or pressing her.

Adalia coughed into her fist. "Sounds like a cult."

"If it takes joining a cult to turn my luck around, I'll be the first to sign up," Blue said.

Which was puzzling really. Other than the bad dates, which, whatever, Blue had it pretty good from what she could tell. She was a beautiful, talented artist, in possession of a giant rabbit (thanks to Maisie) and good friends. What made her so unlucky?

Something had clearly gone down in her past, and while Maisie's usual habit would be to poke at it, she found herself thinking about how Jack would approach the situation.

He'd leave Blue alone, wait until she was ready to talk.

So Maisie cut off Adalia, who obviously intended to ask more questions, and said, "So I haven't told you guys this, but all of this wedding stuff is going to be a bit tough for me. I used to have feelings for…"

CHAPTER
fourteen

Jack left the restaurant and started walking, grateful for the cool night air. Although his situation hadn't changed, it was getting harder to stay away from Maisie. Which was unfortunate given he'd apparently be spending Christmas with her. No, doubly unfortunate given he was *excited* about it. After he'd walked a bit, stewing, he pulled out his phone and texted Georgie.

Addy and I were just talking, and we have an idea for your engagement party. Do you have time to talk about it tonight?

Truthfully, it had been Maisie's idea, but he sensed Georgie would more likely approve of it if he made it out to be a sibling collaboration.

She called him a few seconds later. "I thought Addy had a girls' night out?"

"Long story," he said with a short laugh, "but I got invited, and we got to talking about your engagement party."

"Must have been a sad girls' night out if you were talking about our engagement party *and* it's already over."

He laughed again. "They're still hanging out, but I decided to take off. Anyway, like I said, Addy and I had an idea. Would you and River be up for talking about it?"

"We're both here, so yeah, come on by."

"I need the address."

She paused. "Jack… Oh…I'm sorry."

"It's okay," he said, refusing to admit that it bothered him. River and Georgie had been to the Buchanan house plenty of times, but he'd never been to their loft. While he'd gotten to know Adalia fairly well, he and Georgie were still a small step above colleagues. Hence his blurted-out offer to plan the party. He'd done it to save her from the madness of a full-on Dottie party, but he'd also figured it would be a chance for them to spend time together. "Just text me the address and I'll head over."

"Okay."

He ordered an Uber to take him to Georgie and River's address and found himself at their front door less than fifteen minutes later.

Georgie opened the door seconds after he knocked, and it surprised him to see her in yoga pants and a long-sleeved T-shirt. She looked so much more approachable this way. At the brewery she was always so put together, even though she had obviously dressed down her business attire to try to fit the laid-back Asheville vibe. And she typically dressed up for family parties and gatherings too.

"Jack," she said with a bright smile. "Come in."

He walked through the door and the scent of something delicious filled his nostrils.

"I know you just left a girls' night out," River called out, "but did you have a chance to eat, or was it more of a cosmo diet?"

Jack laughed. "I confess I never made it to the dinner portion of the evening, but we had some appetizers. And for the record, no cosmos were involved."

"That's surprising," River said. "Maisie loves her cosmos."

Something about the way he said it irked Jack, but maybe that was just because he'd been thinking about Maisie's friendship with River and Finn earlier, wondering if she'd ever been involved with either of them. She and River had known each other longer, and…

And he was being an idiot. Even if they had meant something more to each other at some point, it was none of his business.

"Well, good, because I was hoping you'd join us for dinner," Georgie said as she held out a hand. "Here, let me take your coat."

He slipped out of his jacket and handed it to her. She opened the coat closet and hung it up as he walked toward the dining table, which was set for three.

River set a casserole dish on a trivet. "Good thing you said yes because we already set a place for you." He beamed. "You have impeccable timing. You'll get to try Georgie's famous pasta bake."

Jack closed the distance to the table, feeling guilty that he was about to eat a home-cooked meal while Iris was at home eating leftover pizza. But he knew she'd never want to come, and truth be told, he really did want to get to know Georgie better. Even if part of him still resented her a little.

"Have a seat," River said, gesturing to the chair closest to him.

He sat while River headed back into the open kitchen. "What can I get you to drink? A beer?"

"Water," Jack said. He'd already had enough bourbon at the restaurant.

River got him a glass of water, and Georgie brought out a basket of rolls before they both sat at the table.

"You didn't have to feed me," Jack said, his stomach growling at the smell.

"We've been wanting to spend more time with you," Georgie said, digging a serving spoon into the casserole dish and serving Jack some pasta. "Your offer to plan our engagement party was more than generous." She shot a look at River. "Especially since some of Dottie's more eccentric ideas might need a second eye."

He held up a hand. "Before you say that, you might want to hear what Addy and I were discussing."

"Shoot," River said, resting his forearms on the table as he gave Jack his full attention.

He made a face. "At the risk of sounding rude, Addy thought you might enjoy yourselves more if a couple of people don't attend the party."

"Oh?" Georgie asked in surprise as she scooped some of the pasta onto her own plate.

"Let me guess," River said, taking the serving spoon from Georgie. "Your father being one of them."

Jack shot a glance at his half-sister to gauge her reaction, but she showed none. "Yes, the other being Victoria." He paused. "But that's Addy's take on the situation. What do *you* want, Georgie? It's your engagement party. This is about you and River."

She hesitated for several seconds, keeping her gaze on her plate before lifting it to River. "I want the party to be a celebration," she said. "My father will detract from that."

"And Victoria…," River said, watching his fiancée for a moment before he turned to look at Jack. "Georgie's making a concession by asking her to be in the wedding. If she doesn't show up at the engagement party, I'm sure no one will be upset."

"But I want Lee there," Georgie said, turning to face Jack, "and they seem to be a package deal."

"Addy has a plan to keep Victoria and Prescott away but still get Lee to come."

"I'm all ears," River said wryly.

"We think you should have the party on Christmas Eve."

"Christmas Eve?" Georgie said, worrying her bottom lip with her teeth. "I'm sure everyone has plans."

"All the important people will be available," Jack said. "Addy and Finn. Maisie. And Addy's sure Lee will come, even though she doubts Victoria will."

"I guess she would know better than me," she said. "She and Lee talk much more often than he and I do."

Jack sensed she was unhappy about that, but he didn't hear anger in her voice. It was wistfulness, a feeling he understood all too well. He'd felt it for years after learning he had three other siblings. His visits with his father had ended by then, but a simple Google search during his sophomore year of high school had dredged up a photo of his siblings. He would have tried to contact them, but his mother had warned him she would have to pay back the hush money his father had forked over if he broke her NDA. And while Jack had long since stopped caring about pissing off Genevieve (he did a good job of that without actually trying), he hadn't wanted to risk what little security Iris had, so he'd kept quiet. But as far as he knew, nothing had prevented Georgie and Lee from reaching out to him once they'd learned about his existence a few years ago. They'd just chosen not to have anything to do with him. Hell, Lee had yet to look him straight in the eye.

But he shook that off, because Georgie had put a lot on the line to take over the brewery, and he knew it was partly for him. He appreciated that, even though it had obviously worked out pretty well for her.

"I know you're stressed about planning the wedding and getting ready for Brewfest, so this will be one less thing you need to worry about," Jack said. "I'll take care of it all, and if Dottie wants to help with the food, I'll make sure she sticks to a predetermined menu."

River chuckled. "Have you met Aunt Dottie?"

Jack's mouth lifted into a wry grin. "Addy and I will make sure the food is perfect."

Even if they had to cook it themselves.

Georgie gave River a long look. He reached over and placed his hand on hers and nodded. "I think we should take him up on it. Christmas Eve is perfect."

"Okay," she said, turning back to him. "Thank you, but I don't know how to repay you."

"We can plan *his* engagement party some day," River said.

"That won't be happening any time soon," Jack said, but he automatically thought of Maisie, which was beyond premature given he'd resolved to be single for the next eight months. Then again, eight months didn't seem too long in the scheme of things.

They chatted for the rest of the meal, discussing the wedding and River's plans for the spring brews. He still hadn't settled on a beer to enter into Brewfest, but he'd narrowed it down to three, and he was planning on using a Summer in January beer festival Finn had planned for Bev Corp as the dry run.

Georgie offered Jack a slice of chocolate cake for dessert, but he declined.

"I've got to get back to Iris. I hadn't planned on being gone this long."

"Dottie left the cake with us yesterday, so take some home with you, otherwise River and I will eat it all."

149

"Iris loves chocolate cake," he said. Then his mouth twisted to the side. "Or at least she used to before she moved here. Who knows what she likes anymore."

Georgie gave him a sympathetic look. "Hang in there. It's not easy being a teenage girl, especially moving midway through her senior year... Give her time."

"Yeah," he said. "Thanks." But he didn't feel like time was on his side.

Georgie wrapped up a large wedge of cake on a disposable plate, and he pulled out his phone and opened his Uber app.

"Did you park around the block?" River asked. "I didn't see your car."

"I took an Uber," he said. "I rode to the restaurant with Addy and Maisie and took off when their friend Blue showed up. I was just about to request a ride home."

"Oh, don't do that!" Georgie protested. "Let me take you."

"I don't want to put you to any trouble..."

"Don't be silly," she said. "I don't mind at all. Let me get my coat and my purse."

Before he could voice an objection, or decide if he wanted to, she disappeared into one of the bedrooms.

River gave Jack a slight nod as he started the dishwasher. "Thanks again for your offer to help with the engagement party, Jack. We truly appreciate it."

Jack got to his feet and leaned against the counter, feeling a familiar tingle of guilt. "Hey, man. I feel like I'm overdue with an apology."

River looked up in surprise. "What are you talking about?"

"When I found out you were supposed to inherit the brewery if we failed to place at Brewfest…" Jack grimaced. "I handled it poorly, and I apologize."

It had been one of the more eccentric tenets of their grandfather's will, along with his decision to include Jack, the unacknowledged Buchanan child.

River reached over and grabbed his upper arm. "I understand, Jack. No hard feelings."

"It's just…" He paused, then decided to plunge forward. "I don't trust easily, and I thought you knew about the will situation and possibly planned to sabotage us to get the brewery. The whole Lurch thing didn't help."

River grinned. "No, I imagine it wouldn't. You know, Aunt Dottie told me Stella's more inspired by him than ever now that he has scars. Of course, by scars she means one long mark on his right hand. Apparently, all of the animals in her paintings have scars now too."

"Huh," Jack said, wishing he could tell Maisie. She'd be amused. Probably. He doubted she'd gotten over the whole Diego thing. He and Adalia still had the Thanksgiving painting hanging up in the dining room. He'd wanted to superglue Georgie's Post-it over Lurch's junk, but his artist sister had disagreed on principle. (She didn't believe in ruining art.) Instead, she'd painted a single perfect fig leaf over it. He fully expected a conniption fit if Stella ever darkened their doorway again.

"Anyway, I digress," River said. "I'm just a lucky man. Turns out I got the woman of my dreams *and* my dream job."

"If I didn't know any better, I could accuse you of putting the moves on Georgie to hedge your bets."

River's shoulders tensed.

"Relax," Jack said. "I was kidding. I know you're in love with her, otherwise I never would have offered to plan your engagement party."

River offered his hand and Jack shook it.

"Is everything okay?" Georgie asked as she emerged from the hallway, slipping on her jacket.

"Yep," River said.

"Sure is," Jack responded.

She glanced between the two of them with a frown. "You ready, Jack?"

Jack grabbed the cake plate and lifted it. "Sure thing. Thanks again for dinner and dessert."

"Glad to have you," River said.

Jack headed for the door, and Georgie followed him out. They got into her car and drove in silence for a couple of blocks before his sister said, "You know, I was surprised when you offered to plan our party."

"Oh?" Jack asked, shifting in his seat. "Don't feel obligated to accept."

"Oh, no," she said. "It's just that you're closer to Addy."

He didn't know how to respond to that, because they both knew she was right.

"I admit that I've held back," she said quietly. "It's been busy with the brewery and River, but I could have made more of an effort to spend time with you. I haven't, though, and a large part of that is because I'm embarrassed and ashamed."

He nearly asked her what she was ashamed of, but she beat him to it.

"I knew you existed, Jack, and other than a small attempt to find you on social media, I never really tried to reach out to you."

"It's okay, Georgie," he said, even though he only half meant it.

"No, it's not. I should have found a way to get in touch with you. But I messed up, and then you left Asheville, and part of me worried you were running off on me. And when you *did* come back, I didn't know what to do about any of it. So I didn't do anything."

He stayed quiet.

"So for you to offer to plan our engagement party..."

"It's okay, Georgie," he said, feeling better after hearing her apology. She obviously meant it. "I knew about you three, but I was legally bound from approaching you. Or at least my mother was. I could have defied the order and tried anyway—
"

"No," she said emphatically. "My father would have legally pounced on your mother. You did the right thing. I have no such excuse."

"It's already done," he said. "We can't change the past. We can only move forward."

She nodded but didn't look entirely convinced. "You're a good brother to Iris. She's very lucky to have you."

His mouth parted, but he couldn't find any words. He was momentarily speechless.

"It can't be easy becoming a guardian to a seventeen-year-old girl. I know that's why you were gone this summer. You were being a father to her." She grimaced. "You could have told me, Jack. I would have understood."

"But I didn't know that at the time," he said. "And I'm pretty protective of her."

She released a short laugh. "Trust me, I get it." She paused. "River says she's going to start working with Maisie at the shelter."

"Today was her first day," Jack said, thinking about Maisie, his heart feeling both heavier and lighter at the same time. "But she wants to start working there twice a week."

"I saw you and Maisie at Thanksgiving," she said quietly. "Are you two seeing each other?"

"You mean dating?" he asked, caught off guard by her bluntness. "No."

She pushed out a sigh of relief. "Okay. That's probably for the best."

"What makes you say that?" he asked, toning his question down from *what the hell does that mean?*

A tight smile twisted her lips. "It's nothing." She pulled into Jack's driveway and shot him a glance. "I just don't think Maisie's in a place to start a relationship right now."

"*What?*"

"Look, I know I've missed out on a lot of years of being your big sister, but trust me on this one, okay?"

He was about to insist she elaborate, but Iris's face appeared in the upstairs bedroom window. She was bound to wonder why he'd left with Maisie and come home with Georgie. Besides, she seemed to resent all the time he spent with his "fake sisters," as she called them.

"Thanks for the cake," he said, holding up the plate. "And I guess for the warning, although I'd really like to know more."

"Oh, it's nothing."

But if it was nothing, she wouldn't have mentioned it, would she have?

It probably didn't have anything to do with River, because if he and Maisie had been involved at some point, that would be very much in the past. He and Georgie were getting married, and only a total jerk would ask a recent ex to be in the wedding party. But Georgie was making it sound like anything with Maisie would be complicated, and that was the last thing he needed right now. Maybe Georgie knew something from River. It tracked with what Maisie said earlier, about having her own reasons for staying away.

"Thanks anyway," he said, trying to keep his disappointment out of his voice. "You're filling in that big sister role pretty well."

She gave him an apologetic smile. "Just trying to keep you from getting hurt."

Now he was even more intrigued. Maybe Maisie had just gotten out of a relationship. If that was the case, he'd rather know. The last thing he wanted was to be her rebound. He was done being everyone's second choice. For once, he wanted to be first.

CHAPTER
fifteen

Maisie had always worried what would happen if anyone discovered her secret about River. Anyone other than Molly and Mary, anyway, because they'd known for years. But Finn had caught her at a low moment and guessed the truth. Now, Adalia and Blue knew too, and life wasn't any different. Adalia had kindly told her that she'd already guessed, and Blue had sighed deeply and said she understood the drive to keep a secret better than Maisie could ever know. Surprisingly, they had both supported her decision not to tell River.

Maisie had gone to Bro Club on Tuesday, after spending half of Iris's training session showing her the best way to clean poop out of the pens and the other half making up for it by teaching her how to train puppies to sit. Part of her had worried it would be weird to hang out with Finn and River, like maybe the fraying threads of Finn's filter would completely rip free now that Adalia openly knew what he had done, but he didn't say anything, and River was too pumped up about the plan to (hopefully) disinclude Prescott from the engagement party to talk about much else.

She hadn't told the others, but she'd had another reason for suggesting they hold the party on Christmas Eve. Christmas had always been a hard time of year for River. His mother had left him with Dottie two weeks beforehand…and he'd never seen her again. And while they were inviting Georgie's estranged father to all of the festivities, no one had breathed a word about Esmerelda. Nor would they, she was sure. Everyone involved knew better.

By the time Thursday afternoon rolled around, she was feeling pretty good, until Mary called her at ten until five.

"Hey," she answered, washing out some dirty bowls. Iris was with Beatrice today, and the other volunteer who was supposed to be helping out had called in sick, sounding so hung over she'd almost accused him of pregaming for SantaCon on Saturday. "What's up?"

It wasn't usual to hear from Mary at this time of day, on a workday, no less. Mary was a lawyer, and she always insisted on a firm separation between her work life and her personal life.

"I'm sorry," Mary said, sounding flustered, "but your gift got delivered early. The deliverymen were supposed to carry it inside for you, but apparently no one was home, and the dogs were barking, and they just left it there. That is so against the rules, and I'm going to write them a scathing Yelp review, but that doesn't change the fact that your gift is sitting out there."

"Um, I'm sure it's fine," Maisie said, not going into all the ways her sister's explanation was crazy. It was almost three weeks before Christmas, for one, and for another, the house was set back from the road enough that it was highly unlikely any teens would happen along and steal her packages.

"No, you don't get it." A pause hung on the other end of the line. "I got you a new bedroom set."

"What?" she squawked out, dropping a bowl to the bottom of the sink. One of their new rescues, a hound dog, started howling. "Can it, Ruby," she called out fondly.

"It's just...you still have the same furniture in there you've had since you were a teenager. You have a *double bed*, Maisie. Don't you want an adult set?"

She refrained from saying the obvious—if she'd wanted it, she would have bought it—because then Mary would make some stuffy sort of comment along the lines of *saving dogs never made anyone rich, Maisie, and you don't have to pretend otherwise.* And sure, no one would call her rich, but she wasn't some destitute pauper in a Charles Dickens novel, wearing rags and eating gruel. She sent her sisters rent checks for God's sake, to pay out their portions of the house, and she was never late. And okay, Mary had never once cashed one of the checks, but Molly needed the money and took it. As far as the shelter building went...they'd worked it out so it could be hers, fair and square. Molly and Mary had both gotten significantly larger portions of the life insurance money.

"How'd you even pick it out?" she asked. As a question, it was beside the point, but she was honestly curious. Mary's house looked like the love child of a hotel room and a museum, and she so did not share the same aesthetic.

"Molly did," Mary said, and if that wasn't a knife in the back... "Maisie, we're not telling you to get rid of the rest of the stuff, but there's nothing wrong with having a nice, updated room for yourself."

She wanted to argue. She'd opened her mouth to argue, but then she had a flash of that dish that had broken at Thanksgiving, and how good it had felt to hand it over to Adalia. Then another flash, of Jack's feet hanging off the end of her bed. Maybe they were right. Maybe it was time.

"Okay," she said.

"Okay?"

She could practically hear Mary's excitement, so she shut it down fast. "Only a bedroom set. And thank you. I guess."

"What are you going to do about getting it inside and getting the other furniture out?" Mary asked worriedly. "Do you think River and Finn would help?"

Yeah, she was pretty sure they would. But the last thing she wanted was for River to move a bed into her room. She might be feeling pretty good, pretty over things, but there was no point in pushing it.

"I'll figure it out," she said.

"Great!" Mary said. "Um. How are things going otherwise?"

Her voice sounded strained, though, and Maisie knew she was likely looking at the clock. Thinking about how she was really supposed to be working for another five minutes.

"It's okay, you can go," she said. "Love you."

Mary released a sigh of relief. "Thanks. Love you too."

As soon as Maisie signed off, she texted Finn: *Help a bro out? Some surprise furniture arrived at my house, and while Einstein is good at many things, he is no pack mule. There's a beer in it for you.*

He responded almost immediately: *Surprise furniture? I have so many questions. Unfortunately, no can do. In Charlotte for a meeting. River?*

"Ughhhh," she said out loud.

But it was almost five, and she wanted to see how Iris had fared with Beatrice today, so she gave Ruby some pets to stop her baying, then washed her hands and headed down to Beatrice's office.

She knocked on the door, surprised when Iris was the one who said "come in."

Both of them sat at their computers, Beatrice at her monitor, Iris pulled up to a laptop with an intent look on her face.

"Oh, is it time already?" Iris asked.

Which wasn't what Maisie would say if someone asked her to do accounting, but hey, she was happy for people who enjoyed that sort of thing. They made her work possible.

"Yup," Maisie said. "And knowing your brother, he's probably been out in the lot for five minutes already."

He'd gotten here early on Tuesday, at least. But he hadn't come in. He'd texted Iris to come out to him. Maybe he was offended by what she'd said to him at the restaurant. The stuff about Iris, at least. But if he were so easily offended, he surely wasn't a match for her, so she'd tried to shake off any hurt feelings.

"You got that right," Iris said with a sigh, shutting the computer and stuffing it into her bag.

"How'd it go in here?"

"I wish we could get rid of Dustin and keep her, that's how it went," Beatrice said with a smile.

Iris beamed back at her, and goodness, she hadn't known the girl had a look like that stuffed away.

"She came up with some great ideas for outreach," Beatrice said. "She's going to take over the Instagram account. About time we got a young person handling that."

"Hey," Maisie said, "I'm young."

Beatrice just gave her a look. Which, fair enough, the Instagram account had all of four pictures on it, and one of them was of Dustin eating one of his infamous blue cheese Danishes.

Maisie lifted her hands. "Okay, fair enough. I can't hashtag to save my life. Nor would I want to."

"Well, we're lucky we have Iris here," Beatrice said. "But I bet she'll be getting a letter from Northwestern any day now."

"Oh, did you do Early Decision?"

Iris nodded emphatically. "I've wanted to go there since I was ten."

Imagine that, having a university you'd wanted to attend since you were ten. Maisie hadn't finished college. She'd been at the end of her second year at UNC-Asheville when her parents had died. Although she'd stayed the course for a while, she'd failed some classes in the fall, and then the idea for the shelter had come, and she'd dropped out of school. Mary always made noise about her going back, but she didn't see the point. The shelter was her life. If she finished school, it would only be to make other people feel better about her life decisions, and that seemed like a pretty stupid reason for doing anything.

She had a sudden image of the several large pieces of furniture literally sitting on her stoop.

"Hey, Beatrice, you know everyone. You think you could rustle up a couple of people to help me move some furniture tonight? My sisters apparently took it upon themselves to get me some furniture for Christmas, but it arrived early, and it got left outside."

Beatrice twisted her mouth to the side, thinking, but Iris jumped in before she could say anything.

"Jack and I can help you. He used to move furniture as a side hustle."

She liked the image of Jack lifting her new furniture, those impossible arms of his looking even better while lifting…what came in a bedroom set, anyway? How much furniture were they talking? But then again, Jack had been weird on Tuesday, and if he was pissed at her or had resolved to stay away from her, she didn't exactly want to throw herself in his face.

"I doubt he'd like to do it in his free time," Maisie said, but Iris was already texting. God, she was fast. She found herself shifting on her feet a little while, waiting for the verdict, which pissed her off preemptively.

But Iris looked up from her phone and said, "He's in if there's pizza involved."

Maisie grinned. "What do you take me for? Of course there's pizza involved."

"That's settled, then," Beatrice said. She made a shooing motion. "Now y'all get out of here. I need to wrap things up for the night."

But she hugged both of them before they left the office, saying something softly to Iris that Maisie couldn't hear.

Maisie and Iris headed for the front together in silence, but Iris broke it by asking, "Jack said you have dogs, too?"

Interesting. What explanation had Iris given him for being at her house?

But she just said, "Yeah. They're going to love you."

Then they were leaving the building, and Jack was standing against his car, arms crossed in a way that made his biceps strain against his sweater, and she felt a suspicious flutter in her belly that she refused on principle to call butterflies.

"I hear you have furniture that needs moving?" he asked.

"I hear you're a man who knows how to move things."

"Ugh," Iris said with over-the-top disgust, "are you guys flirting? Let's get over there so I can meet the dogs."

Jack's face turned an adorable shade of pink, and he nodded to Maisie as he ducked into the driver's seat of his car. She found herself laughing as she got into her Jeep. To her surprise, she wasn't thinking about getting rid of the old furniture or adjusting to new stuff. She was just thinking about the fun she was going to have with Jack and Iris. And she was looking forward to it.

———————

"Um. Feel free to change your mind," Maisie said, gesturing to the enormous boxes and mattress and box spring set littering the front of her house. Why had they just left it here? She'd never heard of anything like that. Fear of Einstein and Chaco didn't properly explain it, what with the fact that the two of them, together, wouldn't be forty pounds soaking wet. There were so many things it looked like moving day. And sure, there was probably only a dresser, a bed, plus a couple of nightstands, but it was a lot for three people, and definitely a lot if two of them were volunteer helpers paid by pizza.

"Oh, he could probably do all of this by himself," Iris said dismissively, already heading toward the door, where Einstein and Chaco were pawing at the glass.

"You have a corgi!" Iris all but shrieked, her enthusiasm contagious.

So Maisie opened the door, and Ein and Chaco bustled up to Iris to give her licks and tail wags, Chaco only showering her with admiration for a moment before she defected to Jack.

He crouched down to pet her, saying sweet nothings in a soft, gentle voice that did things to Maisie. She couldn't help but think about the last time he'd been here, and when he looked up, she could tell from his smoldering gaze he was thinking about it too.

"What's his name?" Iris asked, jolting her attention away from Jack. Einstein was still loving up on Iris, a little lady's man like always.

"Einstein," she said.

Iris's eyes lit up. "Oh, did you name him after the corgi in *Cowboy Bebop*?"

"I did," Maisie said, surprised. Most people figured his namesake was the scientist, what with his old man ways. But the anime series, which could best be described as a space western, had been her favorite as a teenager, and to her mind, there was no other appropriate name for a corgi.

"It's one of Jack's favorite shows," Iris said.

"Oh?" Maisie said. She looked back at him. He'd stood up again, but Chaco was pressed up against his side, like she didn't want to break contact with him. "You didn't say."

He fidgeted uncomfortably. "I must have been...distracted."

They both knew by what, and Maisie had a flash of the multiple orgasms she'd had that night. Had she really thought it a good idea for him to carry in her bedroom furniture?

"Are we going to bring out the old furniture?" Jack asked. "Or do you just want us to put it in the living room or something until someone can show up and grab it? If I remember correctly, there's probably enough space."

Iris glanced at him with an assessing look, and it wasn't hard to imagine what she was thinking. Jack knew the dogs, and he'd seen the living room. But there were no cutting remarks, no teasing. It was like she'd made the observation and tucked it into her brain bank.

"Yeah, let's do that," Maisie said. "I'll donate the pieces to one of those places that does pickup."

"Pretty big Christmas present," Iris observed, glancing back at the boxes while she continued to give Ein pets.

Maisie sighed, shooting another look at Jack. "My sister Mary is what you might call the bossy type. She doesn't much approve of the way I live my life."

"So she got you new bedroom furniture?" Iris asked with understandable confusion.

"All of the stuff in here was my parents'. She thinks it's time for me to move on. Apparently, my little sister, Molly, agrees with her enough that she helped pick out the new stuff."

"How long have your parents been gone?" Jack asked softly. And it struck her that it meant something, him asking that question. He wasn't a man who pressed.

So she answered.

"They died in a car accident almost ten years ago." A corner of her mouth ticked up. "So really, maybe they have a point."

"Still," Iris said, giving Ein a final pat and getting to her feet. "They shouldn't press you before you're ready."

Meeting Jack's eyes, Maisie said, "Sometimes it takes me a while to come around to things, but I think I'm getting there."

"We're still talking about furniture, right?" Iris said, but there was no bite in her voice. She was just a teenager being a teenager.

"Yeah, that and a whole lot more baggage."

"We all have baggage," Jack said abruptly. The warmth in his eyes startled her, but he looked like a man at war with himself. "Let's move the stuff upstairs first. Then we'll take this in. Should I order the pizza?"

"Hey," Maisie said, giving his arm a fake punch, because, in all honesty, she really wanted to touch it. "That's my job. If I'm not the one who brings the pizza, what do I have to add to this moving party? You two are obviously the muscle." She gestured to Iris, who could probably, at most, move a nightstand.

"Fair enough," he said. "But only if you get half pineapple and pepperoni."

Iris made a face, and Maisie mimicked it. "I question your taste, but you do have those arms, so yes, I will make the call. Though I reserve the right to feel sad about it."

"Agreed," he said, reaching out a hand, and as she took it and shook, she had to wonder if maybe he wanted to touch her too.

CHAPTER
Sixteen

Moving Maisie's bedroom furniture was more complicated than Jack had thought it would be when he'd first offered. She hadn't known the furniture was coming, so she hadn't been prepared to move her old stuff out. The bed was made. Clothes were in the dresser. Condoms were in the nightstand.

He hadn't opened the drawer to see them. He was basing that assumption on memory. Unless Maisie had used the remaining packages since he'd last been there. The jealousy that raced through his blood at that thought caught him off guard. He wasn't usually the jealous type.

He paused in the doorway, bracing himself for the flood of memories. If Iris hadn't been behind him, he might have given himself a moment, but she had to be wondering how he knew Maisie's dogs and why he seemed so familiar with her house. He didn't want her to realize he'd spent some quality time in her bedroom.

And quality time it had been.

Maisie glanced around the room in dismay. "Sorry. I guess I hadn't considered this part. Maybe we should reschedule. It's not supposed to rain or anything, so the boxes should be fine outside."

Iris rolled her eyes. "Don't be dumb. We'll just strip your bed, stack your clothes on the closet floor, and grab a bag for the stuff in the nightstand drawers." She walked over to the nightstand closest to the hallway door. "Do you want me to get started on that one?"

"No!" Maisie and Jack cried out at once.

Iris's eyes narrowed as she glanced between them. "Okay..."

Shit.

He rubbed the back of his neck. "How about I go down and move the living room furniture around to make room for this stuff? Then I can unbox the new stuff out on the lawn."

"Yeah," Maisie said. "Good idea."

As he headed down the stairs, he heard Iris ask Maisie, "What's the big deal? Do you have sex toys in there? I've seen a vibrator, you know."

Jack did *not* want to think about how she could have seen sex toys. They'd likely belonged to Genevieve. Or maybe a friend. He wasn't sure which to hope for.

It didn't take him very long to move the living room furniture, and he used a pocketknife he kept in the glove compartment of his car to start unboxing the new stuff. Mary—or more likely, Molly—had good taste. The pieces were real wood, not the MDF stuff a lot of newer furniture was constructed from, and the finish fit with the farm-style look that was so popular.

He'd unboxed the headboard and dresser and started on one of the nightstands when Iris appeared in the doorway, the dogs at her feet.

"Maisie says she's ready to bring stuff down."

"Okay." He pocketed his knife and followed her upstairs, prepared for strange looks or a minor interrogation from his sister. Instead, she bounded up the stairs with more energy than she'd shown since moving to Asheville.

They started with the bed—the mattress and box spring, then the metal bed frame and headboard. After they got it down the stairs, Maisie headed to the front door to see what had been in the boxes, but Iris stopped her.

"No! It's like a makeover. We have to do a big reveal."

An amused grin lit up Maisie's face. "Are you in cahoots with my sisters?"

"No," Iris said. "I've just always thought that would be fun."

Jack tucked that thought away. Iris hadn't wanted to decorate her room in the Buchanan house, but maybe Adalia could help him and they could do a big reveal.

Or Maisie.

Iris was becoming attached to her, much more so than Adalia, so maybe that would be better. Or maybe he was just looking for an excuse to justify spending time with her.

"Okay, then," Maisie said. "I won't look, but I'm not sure you'll be able to help Jack get it all upstairs."

Iris propped her hands on her hips. "I'm stronger than I look."

Maisie laughed. "We'll see about that."

The dresser was harder to get down than the bed. It was a two-person job, and Maisie insisted on being the other person, saying Iris had her work cut out for her with the new furniture. They managed to get it down without crushing Jack (who held the bottom end) or putting a dent in the wall. They had gotten one of the nightstands down when the doorbell rang.

"I'll get it!" Iris shouted from the bedroom, which she'd been casing like an interior decorator. She raced down the stairs.

"I have to pay for it," Maisie insisted, but Jack had already gotten out his wallet, and he handed Iris cash as she brushed past him. They'd perfected that dance over many years of takeout.

"You can get it next time," Jack said, trying not to dwell on the possibility of a next time. "Let's get the other nightstand."

They headed up together, the early playfulness fading, the awareness of how close she was buzzing under his skin.

She walked over to the remaining nightstand and looked up at him with a mischievous grin. "Sorry that I almost corrupted your baby sister."

He laughed. "Did you, though? I guess she's seen a vibrator before."

"You heard that, huh?"

"Yeah, but thankfully not much else."

"I quickly steered the conversation to another topic. I was scared to death she was going to start asking me questions about you."

He grimaced. "Yeah. Me too. She really likes you, and I'd hate to ruin that if she thinks we've slept together."

"You think she'd be upset?" she asked in surprise.

"She already barely tolerates Addy and Georgie. I'm not sure how she'd handle a girlfriend. And right now, you're pretty much the only person she likes here in Asheville. I'd hate to take that from her."

Disappointment flickered on her face, but she gave him a wry look. "Just so you know, she really likes Beatrice, so there are two of us." Then she added, "But I understand."

Part of him wished neither one of them understood, that they'd say to hell with it and decide this thing between them was too powerful to deny. That love conquered all. But they weren't in love, just lust, and lust never conquered anything.

So why did he feel the loss deep in his soul instead of down south?

They carried the final nightstand down and found Iris in the kitchen, pulling plates out of the cabinet. "Do you want to eat now or after we haul the new stuff upstairs?"

"I'm starving," Maisie said, "but now I'm dying to see what my sister sent me. What if I hate it?" She said the last part with a grin, making it obvious she didn't expect to hate it, but he wasn't surprised she wanted to see it before going all in. He certainly would.

"Let me go unpack one of the nightstands. Then you can look at all of it." He glanced at Iris for her blessing.

"Good idea," she said, placing the plates on the table. "I'll help him make sure it's presentable."

Maisie laughed. "Presentable? I would hate to catch it with its pants off or without lipstick. Go work your magic."

Iris laughed. "Careful, or I'll make him box it all back up."

Jack headed outside and started working on the nightstand box as Iris surveyed the rest of the furniture. The headboard was lying on part of the box it had come in, and the dresser was perpendicular to the front door.

"I really wish we could get all of this upstairs before she sees it," Iris said wistfully. "But Maisie's right. I doubt I can help you get the dresser upstairs."

"I think she'll be fine seeing it outside, Iris," he said as he tore part of the box from the nightstand. "She's curious and doesn't want to wait. I can't say I blame her."

"But it's her Christmas present, and she didn't even get to unwrap it."

Crap. Why hadn't he thought about that? What if she'd wanted to unpack these things herself?

"You like her," she said softly, staring at him intently.

171

"What?"

"You look like someone stole your precious Prius. It bothers you that we might have ruined her present."

"I think that makes me a good person," he said.

"I already knew you were a good person," she said, then shifted her weight and asked, "Were you dating her before I moved here? It's obvious you've been here before."

And there it was. "Would it bother you if I *had* dated her?"

She hesitated. "I've never really known any of your girlfriends before." Her eyes widened. "Is that why she's so nice to me? Because of you? You two were flirting in the parking lot."

"No, Iris. We haven't dated and she genuinely likes you." Both things were true. He couldn't call their night together dating, and he wasn't about to admit they'd hooked up. "And we have mutual friends, remember? She's friends with River, Finn, and Addy."

"Not Georgie?"

He hesitated. "I'm sure they're friends too. But she and River and Finn have been hanging out for years. And the girls' nights with Addy started this fall before you moved here."

"Are you dating her now?"

"No. I'm not dating anyone." But his heart sunk, because it was obvious the thought of him dating Maisie bothered her. "How about I hold the headboard upright so she can get a better idea of what it looks like?"

"That should help," she said, slightly subdued. "I want it to be perfect for her."

"Sometimes we can't have perfect," Jack said. "Sometimes we have to settle for second best. Especially if the people involved are doing the best they can."

She gave him a long look. "Are you talking about you and me now?"

"Maybe," he said with a shrug. "But it's true just the same."

She pushed out a sigh. "Lift up the headboard, and then I'll go get her."

"Okay."

She went inside and he had the headboard upright by the time Iris walked out the door, tugging Maisie behind her. Maisie was covering her eyes with her fingertips and the dogs were jumping up on her, barking in excitement.

"If you let me trip, I'll give you poop duty at the shelter for two solid weeks," Maisie grumbled, but Jack heard the grin in her voice.

"I'm not going to let you trip," Iris said in an exasperated tone as she led her down the steps. "Okay. Stop right there and look."

Maisie dropped her hands and took in the furniture, showing no reaction.

Jack told himself he hadn't picked it out for her, so he had nothing invested in this, but he found that wasn't true. She'd said she was attached to the furniture in her house because of her parents, and this new set was vastly different from the stuff they'd hauled downstairs. What if she didn't like it? Would she feel obligated to keep it? He didn't want her to be unhappy.

But then a small smile lifted those kissable lips, and she glanced at him. Was she thinking about the new memories they could make in this bed? Was it wrong that *he* was?

"Well?" Iris asked, obviously wanting her to like it too.

"Relax, kid," Maisie said. "I like it."

"Whew," Iris said dramatically. "But obviously you can't use your old bedspread. You need a new one. And curtains too. It's a total redo."

"Slow your roll," Maisie said with a laugh. "One step at a time."

"How about you help Maisie figure out how to redo her room, and she can help you with yours?" Jack suggested, trying to sound nonchalant. But Maisie and Iris were coming to mean something to each other. And he sensed both of them needed this.

Iris gave Maisie a questioning look, and Maisie shrugged in response. "I'm game if you are."

Iris hesitated. "Okay, but we do your room first."

Maisie snorted. "That's a load of crap. We'll do it at the same time. Now let's eat this disgusting pizza combination that your brother picked out, then haul the furniture upstairs." She turned around to head inside, calling over her shoulder, "You're lucky I'm letting you eat before you finish the job."

"Hey!" Iris said as she followed her inside. "We paid for it!"

Jack laughed, loving that Iris liked her so much, not that he was surprised. Maybe the idea of the two of them dating would grow on her.

They grabbed slices of pizza as they sat around Maisie's table, the two women giving Jack grief about requesting pineapple, although Maisie conceded it wasn't that bad. But the best part was that Iris was acting happy. Genuinely happy. Maisie was obviously good for her.

When they finished eating, they hauled the new furniture in, which was a lot sturdier than the stuff they'd brought down to the living room. The nightstands, headboard, frame and even the mattress and box spring had gone up okay, but the dresser was tougher. They had to stop multiple times for

Maisie and Iris to shift their grip or take a break before they got it up the stairs and into the room.

They'd just gotten the dresser in place when Jack's phone rang. He fished it out of his back pocket, surprised when he saw Adalia's name on the screen. She usually texted.

"Hey, Addy," he said, wiping the back of his arm across his forehead. "Everything okay?"

"Everything is *far* from okay. It's a freaking disaster."

A million worst-case scenarios ran through his head. Jezebel had gotten into a fight with Tyrion. Or Dottie had decided to deep-fry Twinkies in the back yard. Or, God forbid, Lurch had peed in the kettles again. "What happened?"

"They're coming," Adalia said, her voice strained.

"What?" he asked in confusion. "Who's coming where?"

"Victoria and our father. They're coming to Asheville, Jack." She paused. "They're coming to the *engagement party*."

CHAPTER
Seventeen

"Our plan backfired," Adalia said, aghast. "Now we have to spend *Christmas* with them."

"Well, technically Christmas Eve," Maisie said. "Hopefully Santa Claus will take pity on us and whisk them away at midnight instead of leaving gifts."

"This is no laughing matter!" Adalia insisted, her voice so adamant, her curls bobbed.

Which only made Maisie want to laugh—not at her friend, but because it was sort of funny that a couple of *yes* RSVPs had led to this emergency summit in Beau Buchanan's old living room. How bad could two people be? Prescott Buchanan might think he was some kind of god, but he was just a man, like any other. And Victoria? Her boyfriend might let her boss him around, for yet-to-be-determined reasons, but she didn't scare Maisie.

Except Maisie didn't laugh, because her gaze found Jack. He'd gone silent and pale upon learning about his father's holiday plans. And why shouldn't he? Prescott might have been a bad father to the three children he acknowledged, but from what she could tell, he'd been a nonexistent father to Jack.

Great, you found another one with parent issues, she could practically hear Mary saying, but Mary could stuff a sock in it. It sucked, the way the Prescott news had punctured the little bubble she and Jack and Iris had been in all evening. They'd found their way to a comfortable place where Iris didn't feel the need to act out, and Jack and Maisie didn't feel the need to define whatever was growing between them, and then suddenly it had fallen apart. Iris's glower had come back the second she learned an "emergency" family issue had come up—"They're not *my* family," she'd said—and Einstein, who'd been tolerating Jack all evening, had randomly started barking at him until they left, all of them, for Beau's old house.

Finn still wasn't back from Charlotte, so Maisie was standing in for both best men. Except she was currently sitting, watching Adalia as she paced the living room, followed by Tyrion, who seemed to have picked up on her anxiety. Jack sat on the sofa next to Maisie, although he'd put a healthy distance between them, she'd noticed, and Dottie sat in a chair across from them, knitting an animal sweater. Given the size, she suspected it was for Tyrion, something that was completely unnecessary considering his thick coat. Jezebel watched them all imperiously from atop the kitchen cupboards.

They hadn't invited River and Georgie for the conversation. Adalia had insisted they develop a "strategy" before taking it to the happy couple.

In all honesty, Maisie could understand why Iris had run up to her room the second they'd arrived. Although Iris was technically in the wedding party, she'd only agreed on the condition that she didn't have to talk about the wedding up until the actual day. Which was a deal Maisie kind of wished she'd thought to ask for.

"I will *not* let them ruin this for Georgie," Adalia continued.

"Or River," Dottie said. She shot a look at Maisie, and it was obvious she was thinking about the holiday season many years ago when her niece had come to visit and then frittered off to places unknown, leaving her son behind. Maybe she assumed Maisie was thinking about that too, but actually her mind was on Jack. On what it would be like for him to drink beer and eat canapés with the father who'd so soundly rejected him.

"So we warn them off before the party," Maisie said. "I'd be more than happy to give this Victoria a talking-to."

There was that rueful half-smile on Jack again, and Maisie promised herself she'd get another full one before the night was through.

Dottie set aside her knitting and took a sip of her tea, which she'd doctored with a healthy pour of whiskey, Maisie had noted—she'd offered one to everyone, but Maisie had declined. She'd had one of Dottie's "medicinal teas" before, and it was not possible to operate a motor vehicle afterward. In fact, she'd probably have to end up driving Dottie home.

"This may be an opportunity, my dears," Dottie said. "No one's mentioned a bachelor or bachelorette party. We so rarely get to see our Lee." To Maisie's understanding, Dottie had met him all of once, but she spoke about him as if he were a dear friend. The lost Buchanan child. "And this may be our only chance to celebrate Georgie and River like they deserve, with the *full* wedding party." A crafty look stole over her eyes. "If we have the bachelor and bachelorette parties before the engagement party, it will give us a chance to talk to Victoria and Prescott individually. They need to understand, in no uncertain terms, that they are to behave or bear the consequences."

Adalia, who'd just taken a large gulp of the tea she was carrying on her walkabout, nearly choked.

"Wait a second," Jack said, and it struck Maisie that it was one of the first things he'd said since they'd arrived. "We're still ironing out the plans for the engagement party, and now we're planning more parties? This is all going down in less than three weeks."

"Oh, don't be silly," Dottie said, waving a hand. "Adalia's the maid of honor. She'll plan the bachelorette celebration, and Finn and Maisie will handle the bachelor party. I'll help all of you in an advisory capacity, of course"— meaning she'd try to take over—"but I plan on asking Prescott to have dinner with me that night so you young people can have your fun."

She said it in a way that charged up Maisie's curiosity. From what she'd heard, Prescott hadn't bothered to hide his disdain for Dottie at the will reading. Why was she so sure he'd accept her invitation? The implication was that Dottie had something on him...but what?

"Why don't we just have a joint party?" Jack asked.

"Because we need to separate Victoria and Lee if we're going to give her a talking-to," Adalia said, her eyes shining. "And because Dottie needs to work her magic on our father."

She said it with the faith of a convert.

"So you're on board with this?" he asked, his gaze starting on his sister and ending on Maisie.

She shrugged. "Sure. I won't have to spend time with either of them if Victoria's at the bachelorette party and your father's with Dottie."

"Oh no," Adalia said, setting her doctored tea down on the coffee table with an emphatic smack that implied she'd already imbibed plenty of it. "You're not turning your back on the bachelorette party."

"But I'm the co-best man!" Maisie objected. She waved a hand at Jack. "And River and Jack need a buffer." She'd meant they needed a buffer from Prescott, should he join them, but it hadn't come out right. A little rush of panic reminded her that this was *River's* bachelor party. She was supposed to be upset about that, wasn't she? Did she really want to be there with Jack? It sounded like a cluster of epic proportions.

"I need your help with Victoria," Adalia said. "If the message comes only from me, she'll go crying to Lee."

"And Lee doesn't know who I am," Maisie finished, inclining her head.

"Something tells me he'll know soon enough," Jack muttered, but he'd said it almost proudly, and Maisie felt a little swell in her chest. "But I *would* like it if you came to the bachelor party too." The swell got bigger, but his next words deflated it right back down. "And I'm sure River will be disappointed if you're not there."

"Okay," Adalia said, grabbing her drink and starting to pace again. Maisie couldn't help but smile when Tyrion, who'd sat down to rest, immediately leapt to his feet to join her. Oh, he was a loyal one. "So Dottie will take care of Dad, and Maisie and I will be on Victoria duty. We'll send Maisie over to your party after she helps with ours." She nodded resolutely. "We can do this. I'll call Georgie and tell her our plan."

Again, Maisie felt a compulsion to laugh, but she didn't. Because she *did* want the wedding to go well. She wanted it for River. And hell, she wanted the engagement party to go well for Jack's sake too. Something told her he was depending on it. He'd told her and Iris a little about the arrangements he made earlier, and it was charming, beyond charming, that he was going to so much effort.

Adalia walked off, apparently intending to call Georgie *now*, and Dottie finished off the last of her tea.

"Maisie, will you be a dear and drive me home?" she asked, just like Maisie had predicted.

"Of course," she said, but even as she went to grab her keys from her pocket, Dottie shook her head.

"No, not quite yet." She lifted the green sweater on her knitting needles. "Jezebel's run off somewhere, and I need to find her to make sure the armholes fit."

"Um, Dottie, that sweater's a little big for a cat. I figured you were making something for Tyrion."

Dottie clucked her tongue, getting to her feet. "Huskies don't need sweaters, dear. I would have thought you'd know that. This is a dress."

She disappeared into the house, leaving Jack and Maisie looking at each other. He had a flat expression, but she'd come to realize he looked like that when he hadn't yet decided how to react. So it didn't surprise her much when he smiled. This wasn't one of his big, unstudied smiles from earlier in the night, though—this one took work.

"A dress for a cat, huh? Maybe she's onto something."

"Probably not." She leaned into him a little before realizing what she was doing, pulled by the electric current between them. "I'm sorry he's coming."

"Who, River? He has to, given it's a celebration for his wedding and all." He'd meant it as a joke, obviously, but it still made her feel self-conscious and raw, which was probably the way she was making Jack feel by bringing up his father.

"It's okay," she said, "we don't have to talk about it. We can spend the rest of the time before Dottie comes back speculating about adding a cat clothing line to Dog is Love. It would totally be on brand, don't you think?"

181

He smiled again, and this one was more genuine, more him. "Yeah, I'm sorry he's coming too. Before the will reading, I hadn't seen him since I was eleven. He came to visit me a few times when I was a kid. At the time I thought he was trying to get to know me, but I eventually realized he was really testing me." He shrugged. "He made his call, and I'm grateful for it."

"What happened the last time he came to see you?" Maisie asked. Because she really was too curious for her own good. And also because she wanted to know how much of a hard time to give his father.

He scratched his jawline, drawing her attention to his heavy stubble. She wanted to feel it rubbing against her thighs again, but not as much as she wanted to hear his answer.

"He offered to send me to a prestigious boarding school, but only if I agreed to completely disavow my mother and sign an NDA of my own the moment I turned eighteen."

She bit her lip. "You said no because of Iris?"

"This was before Iris," he said, his eyes flashing. "I said no because screw him. He doesn't get to make the rules."

She leaned closer again, needing to be near him without understanding why she did, and he reached out and touched her thigh, his fingers searing her. He opened his mouth to say something, but the sound of approaching footsteps reached them, and he jolted away as if she were diseased. That stung a little, but she understood. It could have been Iris.

Instead, it was Dottie, her mouth pursed as she held what had been a cat dress and was now a snarled and ripped collection of yarn.

"I guess we have our answer on the cat dress," Jack said, giving her a look that she interpreted as a sort of apology. He hadn't liked being interrupted either, but she understood without him saying so that nothing else had changed. He was still hesitant to explore this thing between them.

"I guess we do," she said, getting to her feet. "Ready, Dottie?"

"I suppose so," Dottie said. "Really, I hate to say it, but sometimes Jezebel can be difficult, the dear."

Jack and Maisie exchanged another look and burst out laughing.

"Oh, you two," Dottie said, waving a hand. "Come on now. I need to get home so I can consult the books before I go to bed."

It seemed a pointless endeavor to ask which books. Undoubtedly they were wholly unscientific.

"Goodnight, Jack," Maisie said, wanting to touch him but feeling a little unsure of herself.

He studied her for a moment, then got to his feet and pulled her into a hug, those strong arms of his wrapping around her in a way that made her eyes prickle.

Oh God, did she have tears in her eyes? What was wrong with her?

"Goodnight, Red," he said softly. And if the tears hadn't been there before, that was enough to put them there. No one called her that anymore, and yet it felt strangely right coming from him. Almost like her father was telling her that he approved.

You've really lost it now. You're starting to think like Dottie talks.

But as she walked toward the car with Dottie, she couldn't help but look back. Jack waved to them from the door, and a sentimental part of her was happy to see it.

Once they were in the car, she expected Dottie to launch into some sort of lecture about the stars, but instead Dottie was silent for a few minutes. Finally, she said, "You know, there was a time when I thought *you* were going to marry my River."

And Maisie almost sideswiped a parked car.

Heart pounding, she said, "Crap. Dottie, don't say things like that while I'm driving."

Dottie chuckled softly. "The universe has a beautiful way of working things out, doesn't it? You were meant to join the Buchanan family all along."

"Are you talking about Lee?" Maisie said in disgust. "Trust me, I can tell he's not my type, and vice versa."

"No, I'm talking about Jack."

Which nearly led to another sideswipe. God, couldn't Dottie have waited for this heart-to-heart?

"Jack has made it very clear he isn't looking for a relationship right now."

"Oh, my dear, we're so rarely looking for the things we need."

There was a pulse of truth to that, so much so that she didn't question Dottie further, and they sat in contemplation of those words until Maisie pulled up to the little purple house where everything had changed for her. Twice.

CHAPTER
Eighteen

"Come on, Jack," Iris said. "It's for the dogs."

"Tell me again why the dogs care if I wear a fluffy piece of polyester on my face?" he asked, standing in a small walk-in closet at the shelter.

She rolled her eyes. "It's a Santa beard."

"Nooo...," he drawled, tugging at the itchy prop strapped to his face. "It's a torture device."

"To-may-to, To-mah-to."

But it wasn't Iris's voice.

He glanced over his shoulder at Maisie, who stood in the doorway watching in amusement. "Exactly how many people have worn this thing?"

She started ticking off her fingers. "River. Finn. Dustin—"

"Dustin? The guy who lives off blue cheese Danishes?" he asked in a panic.

"He never eats them while he's wearing the beard," Maisie said. A wicked smile teased her lips. "At least not that I know of. But the dogs were especially fond of him the last time he wore it. It could have been the cheese."

Jack made a face and tugged off the beard, tossing it back into the cracked plastic bin from which Iris had pulled it.

"It's for the dogs, Jack," Iris said again as she snatched it back out. "You know we got a crazy good response when I posted that photo of you with Ruby last week. This is bound to kick up the social media reach."

He gave her a skeptical look. "I thought you hated the attention that post got."

"Fine," she said with a groan. "I did and still do. Women were drooling over you, and it was totally gross, but I'm also a pragmatist. It got shared like five hundred times. If we can keep that up, imagine how many people will come in and adopt dogs or donate to the shelter."

"My little protégé," Maisie said, her voice full of pride.

Jack couldn't help thinking her plan had been influenced by Adalia. A week ago, Adalia had told Iris about her marketing campaign for the brewery. She took artsy photos of customers in the tasting room and paired them with simple comments about what they were drinking and why they'd come in. The campaign was simple yet effective—it made Buchanan Brewery seem approachable. Friendly. And one of the hashtags she'd created had gotten pretty big (#HomeSweetBrewery). They'd seen a gradual increase in visitors to the tasting room, a significant number of them out-of-towners, which suggested her efforts were working. While Iris hadn't completely thawed to Jack's Buchanan half-sisters, she at least respected Adalia enough to follow her advice. She'd applied what she'd learned to that photo of Jack holding Ruby.

Nevertheless, there was no disputing Iris had latched on to Maisie's attention in particular. She'd started off by working two afternoons a week at the shelter and then added shifts on the weekends. She'd even recruited several other high school kids and, thanks to a Nextdoor ad, a couple of retirees to help out with various projects.

All that volunteering had left her with little time to spend with Jack. But he'd found a solution: last weekend he'd started volunteering at the shelter too. He told himself it was because he wanted to be with Iris, and that was true, but he'd also hoped to see Maisie—and to his relief and consternation, he had.

His first day had been Sunday, and Maisie had arrived soon after they did. One of the volunteers had commented that she rarely came in on Sundays. Jack wasn't a fool. He knew she was there because of him.

Not that he'd complained.

He and Maisie had spent the afternoon cleaning out a storage shed. Alone. Innuendo had flown back and forth as they sorted through the boxes of junk that had sat in the shed since her parents had acquired the property. It was more fun than he'd ever thought he'd have in a dirty shed. They'd spent three hours talking about anything and everything, including his dysfunctional childhood and her idyllic one. But she'd avoided talking about her parents' death or what had come afterward, including the shelter's early days. Still, he'd picked up on some things. She'd taken time off college to finish raising her little sister, and she'd never gone back.

Jack was used to glossing over his past too, but for some reason he didn't want to do that with Maisie. Maybe it was because he was letting his seventeen-year-old sister hold his romantic life hostage, but he wanted Maisie to understand his need to put Iris first.

She'd listened, intently, with a gaze that made him think she was seeing into the depths of his soul. When he finished, she put down the rusted bicycle pump and took his hand, staring up into his eyes. The gold flecks in them had mesmerized him.

"You're a good brother," she'd whispered softly, her face cast in shadows in the dimly lit shed.

But he wanted to be so much more than that. Especially when Maisie's hand was cradled in his, and she was close enough for him to smell the green apple scent of her shampoo. He felt a closeness to her that he hadn't felt with anyone since his grandmother had died, and he didn't want to lose it. She was friends with River and Finn. Maybe she could be his friend too. At least for now.

It had taken everything in him to pull his hand free. "I want…"

"I know," she said with a weak smile. "I have the worst luck with timing."

Then she'd walked out, and he hadn't seen her until this afternoon, four days later, when she'd greeted them both, all smiles, and convinced him to play Santa for the dogs. And sure, he would have done it for Iris. But he was doing it for Maisie too.

"Okay!" Maisie exclaimed as she clapped her hands, shaking Jack out of his stupor. "When River does this, he usually squats next to them and we get a quick photo."

"No," Iris said, shaking her head emphatically. "That won't work."

"Why not?" Maisie asked with a laugh. "We've been doing it like that forever."

"My point exactly," Iris said. "Hardly anyone has seen them. Sure, you put some on social media, but taking photos and putting them up with hashtags isn't enough. People want pretty pictures now. *Artistic* pictures."

"You mean photos of hot men," Maisie said dryly, but her gaze shifted to Jack for a split second in a way that made his blood boil.

"Gross," Iris said with a shudder. "Stop saying that about my brother, but…" A pained look crossed her face. "It *is* true that the subject matter is almost as important as the quality of the photo. Addy gave me some pointers on how to get good photos with my phone, plus a couple of filters that will help with lighting."

That information caught Jack by surprise, but he was smart enough not to comment. Adalia's efforts were apparently paying off. She'd gone above and beyond to include his little sister, showing a level of patience that had surprised him. Iris saw much less of Georgie but seemed more tolerant of her than she'd been in the past, perhaps because Georgie had asked for her input with the bridesmaids' dresses. Both of those developments were surprising, but most shocking of all was Iris's acceptance of spending Christmas in Asheville instead of going back to Chicago as she'd originally pleaded.

Maisie crossed her arms over her chest as she gave Iris the side-eye. "It sounds like you have something in mind."

"That's because I do. Dustin was kind enough to get the backdrop set up."

Jack laughed as Maisie dropped her arms, obviously caught by surprise. "He *what*? You just got here, and he's not officially on duty today. When did you talk to him?"

Iris held up her phone. "There's this newfangled thing called texting. I showed him a few photos I'd found on Pinterest, and he said he'd hook me up."

"Why am I suddenly terrified?" Maisie asked.

"*You?*" Jack retorted with a laugh. "*You're* not the subject of the photos."

"I thought the dogs were the subjects of the photos," Maisie teased. "Are *you* available for adoption?"

Iris shook her head as if she found them tiresome and headed for the door with the beard in hand. "Come on. Let's get started. Dustin said he set up in the playroom."

She headed in that direction, well-versed on all the locations in the shelter now, and left them to follow.

"You forgot the Santa coat," Maisie called after her, picking up a flimsy red piece of fabric with tacky white fur attached to some edges.

"I'm supposed to wear that?" Jack asked in disgust. "How old is that thing?"

She propped a hand on her hip as she held up the coat. The way it was wadded into a ball didn't increase its appeal. "River wears it and never complains."

"Well, good for River, but I can't imagine Finn wearing it." He was too impeccably well dressed to agree to such a thing.

She made a face that told him he was right.

He motioned toward the jacket. "The only way I'm wearing that is if you delouse it first."

"Dramatic much?" she asked with a grin. "You're not going to catch lice." Her grin spread. "But I can't guarantee you won't get fleas."

"Maybe *you* should try it on first," he said, his voice turning husky. He hadn't meant for it to sound like an innuendo, more like a taunt. But now all he could think about was Maisie taking off her shirt, and what she might be wearing underneath. If anyone could make that Santa coat sexy, surely it was her.

From the way her mouth parted, a soft whoosh of air escaping her lips, he knew she was thinking about changing in front of him too.

"Are you guys coming?" Iris called out from down the hall.

"We're getting the Santa jacket," Maisie said, her gaze still locked on Jack's.

"Leave it," Iris said, her voice fading. "We don't need it."

A grin of victory spread across Jack's face, and before he could stop to think about what he was doing, he pushed Maisie backward a couple of steps until her back was to the closet wall. His hand grabbed her hip, pulling her to him to satisfy his desperate need to feel her close. His other hand cupped the side of her face, and she stared up at him in such shock he nearly laughed. It took a lot to catch her off guard, and he considered it a small victory.

He lowered his face, inches above hers, and slowly slid his hand up her side, stopping short of the curve of her breast.

"I've been aching to touch you since Sunday," he whispered. He knew he shouldn't be doing this. Hell, Iris was twenty feet away, but Maisie made him drop his usual reserve and forget reason.

Something flashed in her eyes and she grinned. "Just since Sunday, huh?"

He grinned back. God, he loved her quips. She always kept him on his toes.

His thumb brushed her lower lip, and she sucked in a breath. Images of that night at her house flashed through his mind. But he was greedy. He wanted new ones.

She nipped lightly at the pad of his thumb and the remaining blood flow to his brain shut off, and it all flooded down south.

He lowered his mouth over hers, and their lips came together in a crash of heat and lust.

She wrapped an arm around his neck, holding him close, as her free hand roamed his chest and arm.

"Jack!" Iris called out. "What's taking so long?"

Hearing his sister's voice was like being doused by a vat of icy water. He took a step back, horrified that he'd wanted Maisie so badly he'd been willing to do God knew what in the closet. What had gotten into him?

"Maisie. I'm sorry."

Anger flashed in her eyes. "Don't you *dare* say you're sorry," she hissed.

"We can't do this right now," he pleaded. "You said so yourself." At least she knew his reasoning. He still had no idea what was holding *her* back. Was it Iris? But he couldn't make that fit. Maisie seemed to genuinely like Iris.

"I know." She ran a hand over her head and then straightened her shirt. "Why don't I go out first? You can take a moment to get things under control." Her gaze shot to his crotch, and he had to close his eyes for a moment.

"Maisie," he said softly, pleading for her to understand, but he had no idea what he wanted her to comprehend. That he hadn't stopped voluntarily, maybe, which was an issue in and of itself.

"I know," she said again, sounding weary this time, and shot out of the room.

He took several deep breaths and headed to the bathroom, splashing his face with cold water and shifting things around. The last thing he needed was to draw his sister's attention to his crotch...or get it on camera.

He headed to the playroom, bracing himself for whatever his sister had planned. When he walked in, it looked innocent enough. A chair was covered in an off-white, fake fur throw. A scrawny four-foot Christmas tree was perched next to the chair, covered in dog bones and toys as ornaments. Several wrapped presents sat under it.

"What took you so long?" Iris asked, sounding annoyed. "Ruby is already getting antsy."

Sure enough, Maisie had Ruby on a leash, and the dog was trying to make a break for it.

"I had to go to the bathroom."

Iris shrugged. "Yeah. Good idea. Especially with all these dogs about to sit on your lap." She shot Maisie a challenging look. "No squatting. The setup is that the dogs are sitting on Santa's lap."

"So I'm supposed to sit in the chair?" he asked, gesturing toward it, hopeful Iris had meant it when she'd said he could go without the jacket.

"Yeah."

"He needs the Santa coat first," Maisie insisted, holding out the wadded ball of fabric. "His blue shirt's not going to cut it as Santa."

Iris made a face. "Actually...we're not going to need it."

"Ha!" Jack exclaimed in triumph and shot a smug look at Maisie.

"It's tradition," Maisie said, shaking the fabric. A three-inch piece of fur trim fell to the floor. "We can glue that back on."

"We're going to try something new," Iris said in an assertive tone.

"If it ain't broken, why fix it?" Maisie shot back, then added, "The jacket trim aside."

Jack was about to intervene, but Iris held her ground. "You're missing an opportunity, Maisie. You're barely bringing in enough money to run this place, and I have no idea what you're living on. Beatrice showed me that most months you don't take home your full salary. People *want* to like dog shelters, and they want to give their money to cute animals. You just need to rope them in differently. That

Instagram post last week got us attention. Did you know there was a ten percent increase in donations over the last week?"

"Everyone donates at Christmas," Maisie countered.

"No." Iris shook her head. "Beatrice showed me the books for the past five years. That money comes in the week between Christmas and New Year's. Charitable donations for tax write-offs. This was different."

Maisie turned to the side, and Jack could see she was struggling with the call to change. He longed to comfort her, but something told him she had to do this on her own.

"Okay," Maisie finally said. "We'll try it your way. *For now*. What's your plan? Because you obviously have one."

"We're going to call it the Dog Days of Christmas," Iris gushed. "In the week leading up to Christmas, we'll feature a new dog every day. We'll have a picture and a short blurb for each of them, encouraging people to *adopt not shop* and also to donate to the shelter. If this works, we'll look at bringing other guys in to model for future campaigns. Volunteers, of course."

"What do you mean *model*?" Jack asked, the hairs on the back of his neck standing on end.

"Here's where it gets slightly gross," Iris said with a gagging face. "I need you to take off your shirt."

"Say what?" Jack asked.

Iris held up her hands. "Before you freak out and think I'm a pervert, just know the shirtless part was Addy's idea."

Maisie burst out laughing.

"The Santa jacket is lookin' pretty good right now," Jack grumbled. On reflection, maybe Iris and Addy were getting *too* close.

"Not a chance," Maisie said, holding the coat behind her back. "You had your shot and you blew it."

"And no beard either," Iris said. "I texted Addy and she agreed that the beard was a bad idea. Especially *this* beard." She leaned over and pulled a Santa hat out of her bag. "Just the hat."

"I am not posing nude!" Jack shouted.

Maisie burst into laughter again.

"Ew!" Iris shrieked. "No one asked you to! Gross! You can leave your jeans on, just nothing above the waist except for the hat." She cringed. "Believe me, I'm not any happier about this than you are."

Actually, he was plenty happy that he could keep his jeans on, but he was even happier Maisie was agreeing to break with tradition. It was obvious she was mired in her past, and he wanted to help pull her free. Posing for some pictures was an easy price to pay.

He started to unbutton his shirt. "All right, ladies. Let's get down to business."

Iris made a gagging sound. "Now I feel like I'm shooting a porno."

The amusement in Maisie's eyes suggested she was enjoying every moment of his striptease, and the lust that washed over her face when he slipped off his shirt let him know she remembered seeing him bare-chested. Then her text alert went off and she pulled her phone out of her back pocket, her expression becoming pained as she stared at the screen.

"It's River. I have to call him." She hurried out of the room, and Jack wondered what that was about.

Something told him it was nothing good.

CHAPTER
Nineteen

SOS

Maisie and River had made a pact that they'd always drop everything and run out to call the other person if they ever texted that acronym. They both took the agreement seriously, and neither of them used it for non-emergent situations. The last use of SOS had been after Beau died. So it didn't matter that Jack was sitting there shirtless, about to cuddle one of her babies. (God, had Iris peeked into her fantasies?) It also didn't matter that he and Iris were looking at her like she was nuts. She had to make the call.

She ducked into Beatrice's empty office, not wanting to see Dustin right now. He'd expect to be patted on the back for his role in arranging things, plus he'd probably want to talk for fifteen minutes, and although she adored Dustin, she didn't have the time.

Hand shaking a little, she pulled up River's number and touched it. Beatrice's chair was comfortable—she'd rejected the somewhat crappy ones Maisie had bought for the shelter and brought in her own—but she couldn't see her way toward sitting.

"What happened?" she said as soon as he picked up.

He didn't tease her for starting their phone conversation that way or tell her it wasn't a big deal. Voice unsteady, he said, "Georgie's father called me. Me directly, not just Georgie."

"And?"

"He made it clear he doesn't intend to *let* her marry me. He told me in no uncertain terms I'm not good enough for her."

Anger uncoiled inside of her, sparking all the way down to her toes. "You're the man who saved his daughter's brewery. Of course you're good enough for her. And what the hell is this, the nineteenth century? She doesn't need his permission and neither do you."

She actually felt some righteous indignation on Georgie's behalf. Prescott Buchanan hadn't only been awful to Jack and Adalia, it would seem—he was an equal opportunity dick.

He barked out a humorless laugh. "Yeah, I don't intend to tell her that part. He doesn't want her working at the brewery either. He said he's ready to offer her a role in the family company." He was quiet for a moment, then said, "Georgie used to want to work with him. What if she takes it?"

And just like that, Maisie found herself stepping into the role she'd played several months ago: encouraging the man she'd loved to be with someone else. Only this time it didn't feel like she was speaking through the shards of a broken heart.

"She would *never* do that. In fact, you should tell her exactly what he said, because if you do, she's not going to want him at the engagement dinner *or* the wedding."

"I can't do that," he said. "He's already hurt her so much. He offered me a lot of money to stand down, and when I said

I'd rather die, he told me he could make my life miserable in other ways."

"River, you've got to tell her."

"It's too late, Maisie. They're going to be here in a little over a week. Plus, Aunt Dottie tells me she has a plan for neutralizing him. She insists she needs to have dinner with him, and it's the only way he's ever going to leave us alone."

Maybe it wasn't a half-bad idea to let Dottie do whatever she had in mind, but it was strange that she wouldn't come out and say whatever it was she knew. It wasn't like her to be so circumspect.

"You sure she's not just going to put a hex on him?"

He laughed softly, and it sounded real this time, like maybe he was relaxing a little. "That'd show him, all right."

"I still think you should tell Georgie."

He was silent for a second, then said, "I'll think about it. But I know she has this hope he'll come and be a real dad for once. And I really, really don't want to crush that."

"Oh, River, that hope is already dead." Because she knew a thing or two about hopes like that—the kind that were dead in the water. Harboring them only made a person bitter and lonely.

"Maybe you're right," he said. "Thanks, Maisie. How's the bachelor party planning going?"

"If you think I'm going to tell you anything now, just because you sound all forlorn, you have another think coming. But look, I need to run. Jack and Iris and I are doing a Christmas photo shoot for the shelter."

"Huh," he said, his tone thoughtful. "I have fond memories in that Santa coat."

"Yeah, you tell that to Jack," she muttered. "He refused to put it on. Speaking of which, I've got to go check on them."

A crash sounded from the other room, and she blurted out, "Gotta go. Bye!" and hung up.

Stuffing her phone in her pocket, she darted to the door and opened it. But she didn't need to check out the playroom to see what had happened—Ruby was darting through the hallway with the old Santa jacket gripped in her jaws like it was a chew toy, and Jack was racing after her, the fluffy white throw from the chair wrapped around his muscular shoulders in an attempt to hide his chest that only brought more attention to it.

Iris stood in the doorway of the playroom, a smile twitching on her lips as she watched him go.

"Did you get a good shot?" Maisie asked as she ran by.

"Perfect," Iris called after her, iPhone gripped in her hand.

Dustin had gotten in on the action up front, and he and Jack were trying to corral Ruby between them. The Santa jacket had lost several tufts of fake fur now, and it looked like what it was—a ratty old bit of red cloth.

When had it become so moth-eaten?

By the time she reached them, Jack had already pacified Ruby, and he was crouched on the ground hugging her, his perfect arms wrapped around her. Maisie motioned urgently to Iris, who still held her phone.

Then Beatrice's new protégé—really, had she needed to share *all* of the financial info?—crept up on him like a nature photographer approaching a lion in the wild and got several shots of Jack comforting Ruby. And Maisie knew that whatever photos Iris had gotten before, these were better. This was the Jack she'd been so enchanted by the night of Dottie's party.

A.R. Casella and Denise Grover Swank

He looked up, and he must have noticed the expression in her eyes, because she saw an answering gleam in his before he turned his attention back to his sister.

"Oh, come on. I don't need my own paparazzi." But she could tell he was pleased with Iris's mood—almost giddy— and the quickness with which she was moved to laughter.

Whatever funk Iris had been in was lifting. She'd made good on her offer to help Maisie find bedding for her newly redesigned bedroom, although she'd laughed off the design suggestions Maisie had made in return, calling them too old-fashioned, to which Maisie had replied that she'd spent her life in a house decorated by two boomers. Dustin, who'd stopped trying to help and was watching everything as avidly as if it were a Lifetime movie, snapped to it and said, "Here, let me get Ruby back to her kennel and get the next dog."

Jack got up, Ruby's collar in hand, and passed her over to Dustin.

Dustin's gaze shot to the Santa coat, which Ruby had dropped to the floor. "Was that *the* Santa coat?"

"Yup," Maisie said, trying not to feel a pang. It really was a mess. Now it was covered in dog slobber, plus the missing patches of white fluff made it look like it had mange.

"Huh. I think I forgot to clean it last year after my Danish fell apart on it. Maybe Ruby smelled the cheese. They say hound dogs have a good enough sense of smell to detect a scent from ten miles away."

Jack gave her a sharp-eyed look as if to say, *I told you so*, and suddenly she was laughing so hard she doubled over with it. Then Jack started laughing too, his eyes sparkling.

"You guys are nuts," Iris said, but she snapped a picture of them on her phone anyway.

Getting Lucky

Dustin started whistling "Santa Claus Is Coming to Town" and headed off to get Ruby squared away. But there was no missing his smile either.

"Do you want me to throw that away?" Iris asked, nodding toward the ruined coat.

It itched in Maisie's throat to say no, to *shout* it, but the response wasn't rational, and she remembered the freedom she'd felt after letting go of a few other things. The casserole dish. The old furniture she'd had in her room since she'd picked it out at sixteen with her mother. A box of old kitchen things she'd quietly donated to a women's shelter last week.

Part of her felt guilty for feeling good about those things, but she'd told Molly about it, and her sister had said, *They're just things, Maisie. Mom would have told you that. People don't live in things. They live in us.*

"Yeah," she said through a throat suddenly clogged with emotion. "Yeah, you can throw it away."

Iris grabbed it up like it was nothing—because it *was* nothing—and instead of throwing it behind the desk, she headed back to the playroom. "If you're going to hang out here until Dustin gets the next dog, I'm getting you a shirt, Jack. You can't just go around flashing your chest like that."

"Yeah, you might cause a riot," Maisie said to him in a soft whisper, because he had a look of righteous indignation on his face that almost sent her into another fit of laughter— he'd been bribed into stripping and then was chastised for it.

"Would you take part?" he asked.

"I'd be first in line. I'd trip everyone else."

"I bet you would." He paused, swallowed. "That was your father's, wasn't it? The Santa coat."

She felt seen in a way she wasn't sure she liked. What was it Dottie had said to her? *We're so rarely looking for the things we need.*

And because Dottie was so often right, Maisie didn't change the subject or refuse to answer. She just nodded. "It was. He used to wear it every year for the kids in our neighborhood."

She glanced back to the door to the playroom, but there was still no sign of Iris. Maybe Ruby had left a mess in there. Iris had proven surprisingly stoic about cleaning up messes. She'd commented on it once, and Iris had just given her a look. "After Jack moved out, I was the only one who cleaned up anything." She'd said it forthrightly, and that was that.

Maisie looked back at Jack, meeting his intent gaze. Taking in his chest and arms and all of him. And she knew with certainty that *he* was the reason this co-best man gig hadn't been as hard on her as she'd feared it would be. This was the man she needed. Not River. She loved River—she would always love River—but that love had changed.

"It's none of my business," Jack said, misinterpreting her pause.

"Maybe I'd like it to be," she said. "You're right. As you've obviously seen, I have trouble letting go. It feels like if I get rid of their things or change my life too much, they'll float away, and it'll be like they never existed. My sisters say I need to stop keeping vigil, but sometimes I'm not sure I can stop." She thought of River again and said, "But Iris is right"—she eyed the playroom again, taking in the door, still closed—"it's time."

He took her hand, pulling her to him just as commandingly as he had in the storeroom, but he didn't kiss her this time, and he didn't talk either. He just held her. He held her in a wordless silence that said it all, his strong arms wrapped around her, his chest warm against her shirt.

The sound of footsteps jolted her, and this time she was the one who pulled away from him, embarrassed to be seen so vulnerable by anyone—when had she last allowed that to happen?—and swiped at the tears that had escaped.

It was Iris, looking at them with eyes that saw everything. But she didn't tease, nor did she act repulsed. She just handed her brother his T-shirt. The shirt, sadly, went on.

Iris grinned at them. "If that last picture got five hundred likes, I'm sure this series will get a thousand."

Her words were optimistic, but that smile didn't quite meet her eyes. Maybe Jack had gotten it right and she was actually upset by the thought of them being together. Or maybe Iris had just been through so much change she wasn't sure she could take any more. Maisie understood that.

"What was that text about, anyway?" Iris asked.

It took Maisie a second to place what she was talking about.

Why was she interested in River's well-being? From what Maisie could tell, Iris was warming up to Georgie more slowly than Adalia, probably because Georgie was more of what Iris would call a "real" adult.

She rubbed her nose, thinking about the panic in River's voice. Although she was tempted to tell them, she knew he hadn't decided what to tell Georgie, and it would be a dick move on her part to spill the whole story. Not to mention it would be awkward talking about Prescott to Jack, knowing everything the man had done.

So she just shrugged. "Co-best man duties."

Jack gave her a look, like he maybe wanted to press her for information, but he only said, "Oh yeah? How's the bachelor party shaping up?"

It occurred to Maisie that Dustin hadn't come back yet, and she looked around for him, only to find him lingering in the door to the kennel, Chewie at his heels. If snooping were a criminal offense, he would have been in jail years ago. She waved him forward, wondering how much he'd seen. Hopefully he hadn't seen her tears.

"I can't tell you, can I?" she said to Jack, letting her voice drop into a flirty register. "I don't want to ruin the surprise."

"Now I'm intrigued," Jack said.

"Can I go to the bachelor party instead?" Iris asked for what was probably the hundredth time.

"Nope. Strictly twenty-one and up," Maisie insisted. But she gave her a wink to soften it. "Lucky for us, Dottie has had a *strong* influence on Adalia's plans. So you'll get plenty of mayhem. And you can help Addy and me torment Victoria."

"I can't officially sanction that," Jack said, but his slight smile gave him away.

"I'll take that as a yes," Iris said. "Do you guys want to see the pictures?" She beamed as she said it, proud of what she'd accomplished, and Maisie marveled at the change in her. So much of her sullenness had been stripped away. For a teenage Molly, the key had been writing. For Iris, it had apparently been dogs. Or whatever else was going on with her that they didn't know about. Because if she knew one thing about teenage girls, it was that they kept plenty of secrets.

"I'd love to see them," she said, her gaze shifting to Jack. His eyes were already on her.

"I'd like to see them because you took them," he said to Iris.

Dustin had never met a picture he didn't like, and Chewie was just happy to be included, so they all crowded around Iris to see the photos on her phone, and they truly were the perfect union of an ideal specimen and a talented photographer.

"These are going to make us money," Maisie said honestly. "You did good, kid."

"Maybe we can even make prints and sell them!" Iris said happily.

"Um, that's a hard no," Jack said.

"You won't do it for the dogs?" Iris said, and Maisie grinned at her.

"Keep working those heartstrings, kid. You've got a talent for it."

Then they scrolled to the last picture—the snap of Jack and Maisie laughing together, eyes and faces bright with it—and he reached around to touch the small of her back. It was a brief touch, but it told her all she needed to know: there might not be something between them yet, but there wasn't nothing either.

CHAPTER
Twenty

"Shopping in downtown Asheville is nothing like shopping on the Magnificent Mile," Iris said as she and Jack walked past a yarn store.

Iris and Jack didn't have many holiday traditions, but shopping on the Magnificent Mile in Chicago had become one of their favorites. It had started the year Iris was eleven. Their mother had made a last-minute date and dropped her off with Jack at work. It was a few days before Christmas, and Iris was upset that she hadn't bought any Christmas presents yet. Jack got someone to cover his shift, and the two of them went shopping and had dinner. Iris had loved it so much that she'd asked to do it again the next year. After that it had just become their thing.

Their mother had gotten jealous a couple of years ago and insisted on joining them, but Iris had convinced her to stay home by saying they still needed to find her a present. Wanting to dissuade future efforts to interfere, Jack had put extra effort into choosing Genevieve's gift that year. He really loved his time with his sister, and their mother had a way of ruining things, sometimes on purpose, sometimes because she couldn't help herself.

"I know," he said, "but the important part is that we're doing it together, right?"

"It's not like before," she said without any hint of anger or self-pity. "We're together all the time now."

He wasn't sure what to make of that. Did she want to go home? Or was she trying to tell him something deeper? It had been so much easier to read her when she was that mostly innocent eleven-year-old, excited by the window displays.

"I'm sorry we can't go back to Chicago for Christmas," he said. "I know you really wanted to see Janie, but maybe you can go over spring break."

"I wouldn't have seen Janie anyway. Her parents decided to take her and her brother to Disney World," Iris said, refusing to look at him. "One last family trip before college. So there'd be no point to going home."

Was she upset they weren't doing something like that? He'd never been able to bring her on a real vacation, not on his salary. And their mother had always preferred to go on solo vacations, leaving Iris with Jack or a nanny.

"Besides," she said, "Mom's not even going to be there. She's going somewhere with her new boyfriend."

"You found out about that?" He hadn't told her, and as far as he knew, she'd only talked to their mother a handful of times since she'd arrived in Asheville.

She gave him an exasperated look and rolled her eyes. "I'm not a baby. You could have told me."

"Sorry," he said. "I just feel like I've caused you enough grief. I didn't want to hand you any more."

She stopped and looked at a window display of an eclectic gift shop. "We both know that Genevieve didn't really want to see me. She doesn't want custody either. It's all a game to her. You're her opponent and I'm the prize, only if she won me, she wouldn't want me anymore."

"Iris..." His voice broke off.

"Relax, Jack," she said, making a brave attempt to sound nonchalant, but he'd known her for seventeen years. He recognized the pain in her voice all too well. He'd felt it himself more times than he could count. "I know you really love me, otherwise you wouldn't deal with all my crap."

He went to pull her into a hug, but she took off walking again, forcing a cheerful tone as she said, "I need to get Maisie a present. Have you gotten her one yet?"

He nearly stumbled on a crack in the sidewalk. "What? Why would I get her a present?"

"She's friends with Addy, right? They all seem like the kind of people who'd get each other gifts, and besides, we're seeing her on Christmas Eve. We *have* to get her a gift."

"Shared gift or separate?" he asked, trying not to panic, although he had no idea why the thought would make him react that way.

No, that was a lie. He knew why he was panicking. He'd already considered getting her a gift and wondered if it was appropriate.

Although he hadn't seen her since last Thursday, he'd given in to the temptation to text her on Sunday, when a work emergency had kept him from coming to the shelter with Iris. It was the first time he'd used her number, which he'd gotten from Adalia. They hadn't stopped texting since. It was Thursday now, one of Iris's usual afternoons at the shelter, but it had been the best time for their shopping tradition, and Maisie had apparently told Iris she'd more than earned a break.

"I already know what I'm getting her," Iris said. "Get your own gift. Come on."

She ducked into a store featuring handcrafted items from all over the world, and Jack smiled to himself. This was the perfect place to find Maisie a gift.

Iris knew exactly what she wanted. She'd seen a throw pillow she thought would go perfectly with Maisie's new bedding. And Maisie would love it even more knowing the purchase had empowered women in a developing country. Jack, on the other hand, was wandering the store aimlessly when something finally caught his eye.

"Is this for a special someone?" a friendly salesclerk asked. "That scarf was woven in India by women who escaped abusive relationships."

"I like the color," Jack said, feeling like a fool for saying it. It seemed insignificant compared to the story of who made it, but all he could think of was how close it was to the green of her eyes.

"Oh," Iris said, walking up behind him. "I like it."

"Yeah?" he asked, trying to sound nonchalant, but his heart was racing.

Why was his heart racing? It was just a scarf, yet he knew this was important. What he gave her mattered. It couldn't be so small it came across as insignificant, but he couldn't put too much money and effort into it, or he would come off as a stalker. The gift had to be just right.

"It's perfect," Iris said. "Let them gift wrap it for you."

"We have wrapping paper at home."

"Like I said," Iris said with a raised brow, "let *them* wrap it."

He laughed. "The was about as subtle as a sledgehammer. Thanks." He nodded to the saleswoman. "I guess I'll be getting it gift wrapped."

"Wise choice," the saleswoman said as she carried it behind the counter.

"Do you still need gifts for anyone else?" Iris asked, sounding happier than she had earlier. "We have more people to buy for than usual."

They usually just got gifts for the three of them, and their mother had told them years ago that she strongly preferred gift cards, but Iris was right. Their circle had expanded, and it now included his new siblings and their significant others as well as Dottie and Maisie. Jack worried Iris would be overwhelmed by the prospect, but now that she was finding her place in Asheville, she seemed to love the idea of a big celebration.

"I have something for everyone except for Victoria."

"And Prescott," she said, curling her upper lip in disgust.

"I won't be getting a gift for Prescott."

Iris put her hand on his upper arm. "He doesn't deserve one, Jack. He doesn't deserve *you*."

He gave her a tight smile. "Thanks."

A mischievous grin lit up her eyes. "I say we get Victoria a smelly candle. The smellier the better."

"I'm not so sure that's a good idea."

"Trust me," Iris said. "I've heard all about her from Addy. I know just which one to get."

It sounded like trouble, but you really couldn't get too upset over a terrible candle scent…or could you? While he didn't care much for Victoria's opinion, it wasn't Victoria who worried him.

Iris picked out a candle and declared it would be from the both of them. Jack took a big whiff before the sales staff started to wrap it and nearly fell over from the combined scents of dirty laundry and cinnamon.

"Are you sure, Iris?" he whispered as a second clerk rang up their purchases.

"Oh," she said with wide eyes. "I'm very, very sure."

"It's just…" He paused and took a breath. "I don't want to offend Lee."

Twisting her lips, she seemed to reconsider, then turned and looked him in the eye. "If he rejects you because you gave his girlfriend a candle that smells like a cinnamon roll that was left out for days in a pile of wet towels, then he doesn't deserve you either." She lifted one shoulder dramatically. "But he's not *my* brother, so feel free to blame it all on me. Guys have the women in their lives buy their gifts all the time."

"I'm not like those guys, Iris."

She turned and looked up at him, her eyes softening. "I know, Jack. Trust me. I know."

He wasn't sure what to say to that, but the salesclerk gave him his total, and he paid for the purchase. They grabbed their bags and headed out the door.

"I'm starving," Iris said. "Let's eat at that place with the great Southern food."

Jack laughed. "Which one? There are several here."

She named a restaurant a block away, so they headed over, enjoying the walk in the cool evening air.

"Remember our Magnificent Mile trip four years ago?" Iris asked with a laugh. "It was so cold we had to keep going into stores to get warm."

He laughed too. "I remember going into that Victoria's Secret store and buying a bra for the woman I was dating so I wouldn't look like a pervert shopping with a preteen girl."

"I was thirteen, so I was very much a *teenager*, not a preteen."

"I still looked like a pervert."

She laughed again. "Everyone knew you weren't comfortable being there. But Sally got a new bra out of it."

"Celia. And we'd only been dating a few weeks, so giving her a bra for Christmas wasn't the best move."

"You gave it to her for Christmas?" She shook her head, her eyes dancing. "Maybe you're not as smart as I thought you were."

"Let's just say I'm smarter now."

There was a ten-minute wait at the restaurant, so they stood on the sidewalk, watching the shoppers pass by. And while it wasn't the Magnificent Mile, there was a festive feel to it. Decorations and lights hung from poles along the streets, and the stores all had inviting displays. Iris seemed more relaxed than he'd seen her since she'd come to Asheville, but he knew better than to mention it.

Two women were walking toward them, carrying shopping bags, and the blonde leaned into her brunette friend, whispering something Jack couldn't hear. They stopped and giggled before one of them said, "Hey, you're the guy with the dogs on Instagram, aren't you?"

Iris practically bounced out of her skin. "Yes! He is!"

She'd been posting photos of Jack every day in her Dog Days of Christmas campaign, and the reach had been steadily growing, but this was the first time a stranger had recognized him on the street.

They eyed her curiously, and Jack realized they were trying to figure out Iris's relationship to him. She was too old to be his daughter and too young to be his girlfriend, and although they had similar coloring, few people put together that they were siblings.

"She's my little sister," he announced.

Iris shot him a dark look. She hated being called his *little* sister.

"Oh!" the women exclaimed, both of them relaxing.

"He's *very* single," Iris said.

Jack groaned inwardly as the attention on him intensified.

"I thought about adopting that black and white dog you were holding," the blonde said, tilting her head. "Shirtless."

"Most dogs are shirtless," Jack said.

"Oh, you're so funny!" the blonde said, then turned to her friend. "Isn't he funny?"

"Most of the photos were of Jack shirtless," Iris said. She shot him an *I told you it was a good idea* look. He was glad she thought so, because he was now having serious misgivings.

"Do you give tours of the shelter?" the brunette asked.

"Maybe you can introduce me to that cute little dog," the blonde said. "I'd love to meet her."

"Him," Jack said, really wanting to turn her down, but one of the purposes of the photos had been to give the dogs homes. Still, that didn't mean he had to give her a personal tour. "The shelter's open until six tomorrow. You should stop by. Lucky's a cutie."

"Will *you* be there?" the blonde asked, giving him flirty eyes.

"Unfortunately, no."

"But he volunteers on Sundays," Iris said.

"But not this Sunday," Jack quickly interjected. "Because of Christmas. So you should probably check out Lucky before then." He forced a smile. "Then you'll be able to have him home for Christmas."

She poured on the charm. "Will you come over so I can get more photos of you with her?"

"Him," Jack said. "And sorry. My schedule is booked solid for the next week."

"Wedding plans," Iris said, rolling her eyes in disgust.

She'd made it no secret that she thought having bachelor and bachelorette parties before the engagement party and *months* before the wedding was beyond ridiculous, and she never wasted an opportunity to let her feelings be known. He thought it was strange himself, but Dottie was involved, and he was used to the unusual when it came to her. He'd learned not to question it…unless a turkey fryer was involved.

"Well, maybe when you get back to your usual volunteering schedule," the woman said.

Jack tried to hide his disgust. She wasn't interested in adopting a dog. She was only using Lucky as an excuse. The buzzer in his hand began to vibrate, and he lifted it up in near triumph. "Our table's ready. Have a nice evening, ladies."

Then, before Iris had a chance to tell them he worked at Buchanan Brewery and suggest they go see him there, he grabbed her wrist and dragged her into the restaurant.

"Why didn't you get her number?" Iris asked once they were seated at their table.

"I wasn't interested," he said, opening his menu and hoping hunger would distract her.

"Since when are you not interested in getting attractive women's numbers?"

"I've got a lot on my plate right now, Iris."

She paused for several seconds, then picked up her menu. "You mean me."

"Not just you," he insisted. "The brewery too."

"Don't put your life on hold for me, Jack," she said, keeping her gaze on the open menu. "You should date."

He swallowed his rising excitement and said nonchalantly, "But you were so insistent that I couldn't date Maisie. I figured you'd prefer it if I didn't date at all. And I get it. You didn't move here just for me to be gone every night on dates."

"Every night," she scoffed. "One of your bachelor rules was to never go out two nights in a row so the woman wouldn't think you were an official couple."

He cringed. It was true. He'd given himself a lot of rules after his last girlfriend had broken up with him because of Iris, yet when he thought of seeing Maisie out in the open, every single one of them flew out the window. "But you lost it when you thought I might be flirting with Maisie."

"She's different," she said with a frown. "She's *my* friend. I can't risk you pulling your usual cut-and-run crap with her."

His heart sank. "What does that mean?"

She glanced up in exasperation. "It means you're notorious for breaking women's hearts, and I can't risk that with Maisie. Can you imagine how awkward it would be for me if you tossed her aside?"

"Why are you presuming I'd toss her aside? And I actually disagree with that assessment. Every woman I've dated knew my limitations going into it."

"And I'm sure all of them were totally on board."

"Hey," he said, lifting up his hands. "I can't help it if they didn't take me at my word." Then, because he couldn't stand her thinking he'd mistreat Maisie, he said, "I would never do that to Maisie. Never."

She studied him for a long moment. "I guess we'll never know." Her gaze dropped to the menu. "Bacon-fried Brussels sprouts? Who in their right mind would think that sounds good?"

"I do," he said a little too defensively. "I like Brussels sprouts fried in bacon grease."

Her eyes flew wide. "Geez. Calm down. Fine. You made your point. I was wrong. Some people like Brussels sprouts."

That wasn't the only thing she was wrong about, but he couldn't guarantee things would work out with him and Maisie, and he didn't want her to think her friendship with Maisie was in jeopardy. The ground he was on with Iris was still too shaky for him to take that risk.

Which meant he had to keep waiting, at least for long enough to soothe Iris's fears. He'd never waited for a woman in his life. Maybe it would be good for him. He only hoped he didn't lose her before he got his chance.

CHAPTER
Twenty-One

Christmas had always been a special event in the O'Shea household, as distinctive for the month of celebration leading up to it as for the holiday itself. But Maisie had stopped decorating the house after Molly moved out. The effort had felt like too much for one person and a dog (two this year), and the prospect of a large, decorated, *empty* house had put a pit in her stomach. So she did her decorating at the shelter, and at home she had nothing but a couple of stockings up for the dogs. Before the conceit of the holiday engagement party, Mary had been after her to celebrate up in Virginia, but even if she'd felt comfortable pawning off all of the Christmas shelter duties, she wouldn't have gone. Because even if she didn't decorate anymore, she always lifted a glass of her mother's eggnog on Christmas. And because she visited their headstones on Christmas day with a wreath from her mother's favorite florist. And because in her heart, she knew everything was changing. She was ready for change, but that didn't make it feel any less like the very ground beneath her was quaking.

The day before the "guests" arrived, she settled onto the downstairs couch with a glass of mulled wine and video-called

Molly. Chaco curled up at her feet, and Einstein would never settle for anything less than her lap or immediately next to it. Of course, she had to lift him up because his little legs would only take him so far.

Her sister answered immediately, and from the flash of colors and sound around her, it was obvious she was at a bar. A man who looked like a catalog model for a second-rate department store sat on the stool next to her. His expression was slightly flummoxed; her sister looked bored.

"Um, if you're busy, I can call Mary," Maisie said.

"Oh no, I can talk."

The man's expression went from flummoxed to aggrieved. "I thought this was going well."

"Blake, here's a pro tip from someone who's been on a *lot* of dates. No one wants to spend half an hour listening to details about your 'medically necessary' nose job. Or the fact that you never wear the same underpants. Generally, if you find that you're the only one talking, something is wrong."

Maisie held back her laughter...mostly, but a little sputtered out. Ein gave a little yip as if laughing with her.

"But...we just got refills." Blake waved to their full drinks.

"And this round was on me." Molly lifted the drink with the hand that wasn't holding the phone, toasting him. "Now I'm going over there." She waved the phone, the image going temporarily blurry on Maisie's side. From what little she could see, there were plenty of empty spaces at the bar. Then again, it was before five in Seattle. Leave it to Molly to go on a date before Happy Hour officially began. "You can stay here or go, but I recommend you finish the drink. The *He Sees You When You're Sleeping* is very good. Trust me, I've been drinking a lot of them lately."

Without further ado, she walked away and got settled at the far side of the bar.

"So, how's it going?" Molly asked eagerly. "Have you talked to Jack?"

"That is a *terrifying* name for a drink," Maisie said, "named after what has to be the most disturbing holiday song of all time. I had to ban Dustin from singing it at the shelter."

"The whole Santa conceit is creepy if you think about it too much. I don't want anyone to watch me while I'm sleeping." She raised a hand. "And before you say I used to wish I'd wake up to a sparkly vampire stalker, I was a *teenager*. Teenagers exercise super bad judgment. And I sense you're deflecting my question."

"Maybe," Maisie admitted. "How are the Twelve Dates of Christmas going?"

Molly laughed, a sound Maisie would never tire of hearing. Her sister's spirit was irrepressible, although in those long, tearful days after their parents had died, it had felt like there'd be no more laughter for any of them. And the first time they *had* laughed, their good humor had almost felt like a betrayal.

"Well, you just witnessed part of the latest disaster."

"Hey!" she heard from the other end of the bar. But it was said sulkily, and Maisie wasn't worried the man would try to retaliate in any way. Besides, her sister was equipped with Mace and self-defense moves. She could take care of herself.

"Do you intentionally choose people you're going to dislike?"

Molly's lips tipped into a little smile. "Sometimes." She inclined her head a little, as if to indicate Blake was one of those sometimes. "It makes for a better story. The guy I brought here yesterday was a life insurance salesman." She gave a dramatic shudder.

"Hey! Dustin was an insurance salesman in his pre-Asheville life." Maisie shrugged. "Although, to be fair, while I love the man, I can't think of anyone who'd willingly date him."

"Dustin's a sweetheart," Molly said. "This guy kept going on about his brilliant idea to send coffin-shaped postcards out with his sales pitch."

"Yikes." Then the other part of her statement penetrated. "Wait, you went to the same bar?"

Molly's smile stretched wider. "Yeah, it's part of the story. It's the same location, but with different dates."

"That sounds horrible. Are all of them at four in the afternoon?"

"Nah. I've experienced this bar at every possible day and time," Molly said, lifting her drink. "Now tell me what's going on with you. I see that look on your face. You're fretting about something."

"A lot of things actually," Maisie said, taking a sip of her drink too. "I haven't seen Jack since last Thursday, but he started texting me."

He'd had a brewery disaster to deal with on Sunday, some sort of commotion in the tasting room caused by none other than Stella and Lurch. Apparently, Lurch had created a distraction so Stella could remove some of the remaining paintings from Finn and Adalia's Art Display from the wall and hang up a few of her own in their place. But his idea of a distraction had been to release a rat—a pet rat, as it turned out, and thus easily rounded up, but even so. Dottie had apparently taken him aside and given him a long talking-to. Somehow the incident had ended with one of Stella's paintings being hung in the tasting room, alongside the much nicer work she'd tried to replace. Maisie had seen a snap of it.

The goats were all wearing Santa hats and holding forks and knives, surrounding a frightened-looking hen in lederhosen.

Apparently, it had sold to a tourist within two days for an obscene amount of money, and now Stella had another painting hanging on the wall. It just went to show that karma was a crock.

But she hadn't learned all of that until later. Her heart had sunk when Iris came in without him, but she'd done her best not to show she was disappointed. The last thing she wanted was for another person to communicate to Iris that she wasn't enough. Two deadbeat parents had been doing that for her whole life.

Instead, she'd swept Iris up in a wave of enthusiasm and introduced her to their new border collie mix, Alfred, who was going to need a *lot* of walking.

Iris's mood was so buoyant it had surprised Maisie.

"What's gotten into you?" she'd asked.

"I got some good news from back home," Iris said.

But the good news clearly hadn't come from her mother, since Maisie already knew from Jack that their mom had basically told them to get lost for the holidays.

"Is that the kind of teenager statement I'm supposed to pursue until you 'relent' and tell me what's going on, or do you genuinely want to keep this quiet?" she asked.

Iris had laughed at that, and buried her face into the dog's fur.

"I wouldn't do that until he's had a bath," Maisie said. "Dogs have been known to roll around in poop." When Iris pulled back in horror, she had to laugh. "He's clean. I'm just messing with you."

"I'll tell you," Iris said. "But not yet."

"It's a deal," Maisie said, and they shook on it. "Just promise me it's nothing dangerous or illegal."

"No, it's nothing like that," Iris said with a glow so bright it could light a city block. And because Iris was a good kid, once you got beyond her surface surliness, she believed her. So she hadn't mentioned anything to Jack when he'd texted to explain why he didn't show. Not that she'd been able to think of anything but him given he'd ended the Lurch story by saying, *I missed seeing you today.*

She'd replied: *Same. I had the door to the storage closet open in anticipation. I even unearthed an old Santa hat you can wear for a follow-up photo shoot.*

It had taken him a while to respond to that, but he'd eventually come back with: *I haven't been able to stop thinking about you.*

But your situation hasn't changed.

I'll be honest: I don't know what to do here. You make me want more than I can give you right now.

What she wanted was *him.*

She related all of this to Molly, ending with the fact that they'd been texting, off and on, ever since. Their exchanges were somewhat flirty, because they couldn't seem to not flirt with each other, but they were mostly conversational, deepening the connection between them. She'd learned he was a voracious reader, something she thought incredibly sexy, and that his sci-fi appetite went beyond *Cowboy Bebop.* And he was so invested in making the engagement party special for River and Georgie, he'd spent several evenings and weekends planning it, including Tuesday night, the last time Iris had been to the shelter.

"God, men are so *stupid*," Molly said with feeling.

"Hey, I'm right here!" someone said in the background.

"I'm not talking about you," her sister said, rolling her eyes as she projected her voice. "The world does not revolve around you and your thousands of underpants, Blake."

Turning back to the phone, she said, "Well, it's obvious he has all the feels for you, Maisie. He's just being dumb. He'll come around." She smiled. "Just make sure to 'accidentally' lead him under some mistletoe. Did you get him a present?"

"Yeah. I'm getting everyone presents, although Lee, Prescott, and Victoria are all getting the same thing." She grinned wickedly. "Donations in their names to Dog is Love." Her gaze fell to Ein and Chaco, snuggling close.

"Diabolical! I love it. And what are you doing for Jack?"

"I haven't fully decided yet." She rubbed a finger around the rim of her glass. "But I was thinking about maybe giving him one of Dad's watches." Molly's eyes widened, and Maisie immediately backtracked. "Is that weird? It's too much, isn't it? Or is it cheap of me to regift something?"

"No, Dad had some really nice watches, and you know Mary and I already took the things we wanted from the house. This just tells me that you're really serious about this dude. Not that I blame you. I saw those pictures. Hell, everyone in my office saw those pictures."

"Yeah, I know," Maisie said dryly. "I noticed that half of our Instagram traffic was from Seattle. Thanks for reposting them."

"You did us a favor. People love seeing hot guys holding dogs."

Maisie felt a little prick of jealousy. But while she didn't love the thought of other women checking him out, no one could deny the results. It was the best quarter they'd had in a long, long time, and she knew she had Jack and Iris to thank. Well, along with a little assist from Molly.

"It's not just the watch," she admitted. "I've been going through their things," she said through the burn in her throat. "I've put together a lot of boxes for charity. It seemed like a good thing to do for the holiday. And I'm going to give some of Mom's vintage stuff to Adalia for her sculptures." She swallowed. "Most of the furniture's going to go too. I already went to a couple of places to scope out some new pieces."

"Oh, Maisie," Molly said, "you don't know how happy I am to hear you say that. This is good. This is what Mom and Dad would have wanted."

"I know that." And she did. She always had. But for a long time it hadn't been what *she* had wanted. There'd been a solace in hanging on.

"Onward and upward," Molly said, repeating the phrase their dad had always used.

"Onward and upward," she repeated through her throat, thick with emotion.

"Anyway, I've got to go. I need to take an Uber to my next date. This one's a legit, for-real date." Maisie heard another aggrieved sound in the background, presumably from Blake. "Get this. The guy's a hot veterinarian. I know you'd approve."

"Have fun," Maisie said. "I love you."

"Love you the mostest," Molly said and made a dramatic smooch at the phone before ending the call.

In the wake of their conversation, she felt not just alone but lonely. And the house's lack of holiday cheer started to bother her. Perhaps it had been a mistake not to decorate. Maybe the only people here were her and Einstein and Chaco, because they certainly counted, but shouldn't they have some joy too?

If she was going to decorate, it would be much more fun to do it with someone else, but Adalia was busy with preparations for the unwanted guests—if you asked Maisie, Adalia was investing way too much thought into the bachelorette disaster; for the bachelor party, Maisie had booked a tour of the local breweries and called it a day—and

Blue had become enmeshed in this Bad Luck Club. Jack had run with his idea of setting the Christmas Eve engagement party as a pop-in, pop-out type event, so at least Blue was coming to that. But she was spending Christmas day with a couple of the other members of her club. Maisie hadn't asked why she wasn't spending it with her family instead. She understood without asking that it was the kind of thing Blue would share when she was ready. The holidays were a minefield of emotions for most people.

So instead she tapped her phone for a moment and then texted Jack: *Would you and Iris be up for some decorating fun? I need some help from Santa.*

CHAPTER

Twenty-Two

Jack studied the text on his phone, then glanced up at his sister, who was icing sugar cookies. It was nearly eight, which was later than he'd usually suggest an outing, but knowing her, she wouldn't go to bed until midnight or later, and who was he kidding? He really wanted to see Maisie. They'd been texting all week, but he hadn't seen her since the photo shoot…and the kiss.

And if Iris came with him, he wouldn't have to worry he'd be on anything but his best behavior.

Which was why he found himself saying, "Hey, Iris. Maisie just texted and invited us to come over to help her decorate for Christmas."

Her head jerked up, a tube of red icing in hand. "She hasn't decorated yet? It's, like, three days before Christmas!"

"Hey," he said with a shrug. "All I know is what she said."

She scrunched up her nose. "Why'd she text you and not me?"

He resisted the urge to cringe. "Maybe because it's so late. She probably wanted to text me to make sure it was okay."

"Yeah," she said, shifting her weight to one side. "Maybe."

"Do you want to go? You didn't show much interest when Addy and Finn put up the tree a few weeks ago."

She gave him a guilty look. Adalia and Finn had tried to make decorating the Christmas tree a family activity, complete with warm cider and cookies they'd baked together. Finn's excitement about the whole thing had almost been comical. According to Adalia, his parents had always used a personal shopper to buy his gifts, which they'd had professionally wrapped. A chef had made their Christmas dinner. None of that sounded especially bad to Jack, but the situation admittedly lacked warmth, something he'd always had from his grandmother. And then with Iris.

But the family-bonding Christmas activity had gone down before Iris's recent thaw toward Adalia, and his sister had silently put up a couple of ornaments before asking if she could be excused to do homework.

"Well…" she said sheepishly.

He hadn't meant to make her feel bad, so he jostled her arm and said, "It's okay, Iris. There was a lot going on and…" He pushed out a sigh. "I get it. That being said, this is up to you. If you'd rather stay here and decorate your cookies, I'm good with that too." He grinned. "I will gladly keep eating them."

"I'm cutting you off anyway," she said with a laugh. "Three's plenty. We can't risk you getting flabby for your puppy pictures."

He groaned. "You really need to ask Finn and River to do their share. They were Maisie's friends first."

"That's the lamest excuse ever, but I plan to ambush them at the engagement party. Wait until they have some spiked eggnog or whatever, then ask."

Jack gave her a look. "You know me better than to think I'd willingly serve eggnog. Are you bluffing?"

"I'll ask them. I promise! But for now, I say we go over and help Maisie. I kind of hate thinking about her decorating her house all alone." She glanced at the counter, covered with multiple tubes of frosting and stacks of undecorated cookies, as well as finished cookies on cooling racks. "I can pop the icing in the fridge and finish decorating in the morning, but I'll be leaving a mess." She made a face. "I don't want Addy to think I'm a slob."

He grinned, pleased by this further evidence that she cared what Addy thought of her. "She's staying with Finn tonight, so I doubt she'll ever see it, but you can shoot her a text to explain. She'll understand. In fact, she'll probably be excited to hear Maisie's decorating."

"Okay…you're right."

"I'll text Maisie to let her know we're coming over." He picked up his phone and saw the bubble indicating Maisie was typing another message, which appeared before he could type his own response.

Sorry. It's late. Forget I mentioned it.

Smiling to himself, he typed, *Too late to rescind now. We're coming over.* He noticed Iris piling cookies onto a paper plate. *Hope you haven't met your sugar quota of the day.*

In what sick world does such a thing exist? she responded.

He grinned again. *Do you have a fake tree?*

Of course I have one. How can we decorate without a tree?

Let me rephrase that, do you have one that's less than two decades old?

She didn't answer.

He looked up at Iris. "We need to make a stop before we head to Maisie's."

It was a miracle they arrived at Maisie's house only a half hour later, especially after their special errand, but it was a few days before Christmas and there hadn't been much of a selection left.

Maisie's front door opened and she appeared, wrapping an oversized cardigan around herself to ward off the chill. Her hair was piled on top of her head in a messy bun, but somehow she looked as sexy now as she had that night in the green dress. She was the kind of woman you wanted to come home to and kiss senseless…which was exactly what he wanted to do. But his little sister was his chaperone, and he couldn't.

He and Iris got out of the car as Maisie descended the steps, her two dogs following at her heels.

"What is on top of your car?" she asked, her tone a little accusatory.

Now he worried he'd overstepped.

"Surprise!" Iris said, holding out her plate of cookies. "We brought gifts."

Maisie took the plate and glanced down at the plastic-wrapped cookies. "This will go perfectly with the hot chocolate I have on the stove." Her gaze shot back to Jack. "But what's that on top of the car?"

As if she didn't know. It was every bit a challenge.

"It's a Christmas tree," he said. He'd been staring at her, so he shook himself out of his daze and started to untie the ropes. Chaco rushed forward in a burst of speed and started pawing at his pants, eager for a greeting. He stooped over and ruffled her ears. Einstein peed on the tire of his car, then came over and sniffed his hand.

Maisie's eyes were on the little dog, as if she expected he'd try to nip, but he surprised both of them by licking Jack's hand and wagging his tail. And when Chaco turned to shower her love on Iris, Einstein stayed put.

"I guess he's okay with me now that he's established where I fall on the food chain," Jack said, patting the dog's head.

He'd hoped to sneak a smile out of Maisie. Instead, she had a strange look on her face, bewildered almost, but she shook it off. "Don't try to change the subject. If you felt the need to get a tree, even though I have a perfectly good one, why'd you get *that* one? That tree's bigger than your car. It looks like the tree in *Christmas Vacation*."

"What's that?" Iris asked.

Maisie gasped. "Well, I know what *we're* watching over your school break."

Iris gave Jack a questioning look.

"It's a classic Christmas movie," he told her with a laugh. "You'll like it." Turning to Maisie, he said, "Iris and I always wanted a real tree, but our mother hated them. If we're going to help decorate on such *late* notice, we get to pick the tree."

She laughed. "Okay, but you have to come over and pick up all the dropped pine needles."

He stopped what he was doing and met her gaze. "Deal."

Although it wasn't much of a promise, it felt like it meant something. He *wanted* it to mean something.

"Do you need help?" Maisie asked. "I may not have arms like tree trunks, but it's not easy to pick up a hundred-pound dog."

"No one would ever accuse you of being weak," Jack said with a grin. "But I can do it. I'd *like* to do it." She looked at him for a moment, thinking, then nodded.

He got the ropes untied and pulled the tree off the roof, Maisie, Iris, and the dogs all watching him. After he wrestled it into the house, he carried it over to an empty spot in the corner by the front window.

The others trailed him inside, Chaco lying beside the tree and Einstein sniffing it suspiciously. He lifted one leg slightly, glanced at Maisie, and set it back down.

"I saw that," Maisie said. "Don't even think about it." Turning to Jack, eyes dancing, she said, "Um, slight problem. My fake tree stand, which is indeed from the 1990s, doesn't have a pan for water."

"Obviously, you don't know Jack very well," Iris said. "He's Mr. Prepared. The tree stand is in the car." Then she bounded out the door.

As soon as the door shut, Jack closed the distance between him and Maisie. Before he let himself think it through, he pulled her into his arms and kissed her.

She didn't respond at first, probably caught off guard, but it only took a second for her to wrap her arms around his neck and kiss him back. With her body pressed against him, his fingers woven in her hair, he felt more alive than he had in…well, since the last time they'd done this. She nipped his bottom lip, and he pulled her closer, needing more. Needing everything.

Except then he heard the car door slam shut outside, and he reluctantly pulled away. Both of them were panting a little. "I've been wanting to do that all week."

Maisie started to say something, her eyes full of lust, but Iris opened the front door.

"The guy at the lot promised this stand would work."

Maisie shifted her attention to Iris. "You went to a tree lot? Those places are rip-offs."

"And the trees in front of grocery stores are dry tinder waiting to shoot up in flames," Jack said. "The only way to get a fresh tree is to chop one down yourself, and since we didn't have time to go to a tree farm and our neighbor would hate us even more if we chopped her tree down, there were few options." He leaned his head to the side. "Although I suspect we might have gotten away with it if we'd told her Jezebel was in the branches and refused to come down."

Maisie laughed and the sound sank deep into his heart.

"Besides," Iris said, "the lot was raising money for a veterans' charity."

"Fine," Maisie said, rolling her eyes, but her grin let him know she was pleased. "Who am I to mock your gift? Especially when the profits go to a good cause."

Jack attached the stand and unwrapped the tree, but before he stood it up, he said, "Now just remember, it's only a few days before Christmas, so there wasn't much of a selection."

He lifted the tree, and the branches fell into place, revealing huge bare spots.

"You got me a Charlie Brown Christmas tree," Maisie said as she broke into laughter.

"We tried our best," Jack said, fighting his own laughter.

"Everything deserves to be loved," Iris said. "Even scrawny Christmas trees."

Jack heard the wistfulness in her voice, and his heart sank. Now he knew why she'd been so adamant it was *the one*.

Maisie pulled his sister into a sideways hug, keeping a hand on her shoulder. "Spoken like a fundraising chairperson."

"You hate it?" Iris asked.

"No, just the opposite," Maisie said with bright, shiny eyes. "I love it. It's perfect."

She'd already pulled multiple boxes of Christmas ornaments out of storage and stacked them on the sofa and coffee table. Iris pulled up some Christmas music on her phone, and the three of them began to string lights on the tree and fill it with ornaments. Some of them were handmade, and it was obvious a few had been made by the O'Shea girls when they were young. He felt another pang for Iris, who'd never done such a craft at home, but also for Maisie. For what she'd lost. Another ornament, which he hung, was a framed photo of the O'Shea family. Maisie stood in front with her sisters, their parents behind them. She looked a lot like her mother, but something about her father—the glimmer in his green eyes maybe, or the set of his jaw—reminded him of her too. He wished he could have known the people responsible, in part, for making Maisie the woman she was. He would have liked their approval.

When they finished, they stood back and studied their work.

"It's the most beautiful tree I've ever seen," Maisie said with tears in her eyes. Chaco yipped as if to say she agreed.

"I like it," Iris said with a soft smile and tears of her own.

Jack pulled Iris into a hug and kissed her forehead, then turned to Maisie, mouthing *thank you*.

She nodded, her chin quivering, and everything in him ached to hold her and reassure her that it was okay to move forward and leave the past behind. That she wasn't losing anything important, because the things that mattered couldn't be stored in boxes. He dropped his hold on Iris and was about to follow through on his instinct, but Maisie headed into the kitchen. "I think we've earned those cookies."

When he and Iris joined her in the kitchen, she was ladling hot chocolate into mugs and dumping mini marshmallows on top. She handed mugs to both of them, and they all sat at the table, choosing cookies from the plate.

Maisie bit into one and made a hum of pleasure in the back of her throat that had him squirming uncomfortably in his chair. "These are really good," she said. "I'm gonna need the recipe. The edges of mine always turn brown before the center is cooked."

"Your butter probably got too soft," Iris said. "You need to refrigerate the dough before you cut the shapes."

Maisie's eyes widened. "How is it you know more about baking than I do?"

Iris snorted. "I watch YouTube videos."

"Kids these days," Maisie said, but she grinned from ear to ear.

"What else do you usually do for decorations?" Iris asked. "I saw some stockings in the box."

Maisie's smile fell. "Let's not hang those. I think it's time to make some new traditions."

A mischievous look filled Iris's eyes. "You could put out reindeer food."

"Do I want to know what that is?" Maisie asked, sounding apprehensive.

"Don't fall for it," Jack said. "It's made of oats and glitter. Iris brought some home from preschool and dumped it all over my car. She was so upset because she thought Santa wouldn't bring her presents if she didn't have any. I had to look up the recipe."

"How old were you?" Maisie asked in wonder. "You must have been in high school."

"Yeah," he said, suddenly feeling embarrassed. "A senior."

"He's always been there for me," Iris said, blessing him with a look full of love. Then she turned to Maisie. "He was more of a parent than our mom."

Jack was shocked to hear his sister admit to his role in her life, not that he was surprised she felt that way. Iris was usually very tight-lipped about their mother with people she hadn't known for very long. The fact she was opening up to Maisie was a miracle, but it only drove home that Iris considered Maisie to be *her* friend and thus off-limits to Jack.

What was he going to do about that?

They took their mugs into the living room, and Iris helped Maisie sort through the remaining decorations, deciding what to keep and what to pack back up. Jack could see it was hard for Maisie, but she soldiered on as though she was a woman on a mission to face her future. They ended up hanging garland on the fireplace, and to his surprise, Maisie pulled the five stockings from the box and set them aside, announcing everything else in the box could be thrown out.

Iris, who was fluffing a tattered wreath, looked up, her eyes rounding when she saw the size of the box of discards. But she kept right on working, and when she finished, she hung some leftover ornaments on the wreath and then had Jack hang it on the front door.

"Your house is officially festive," Iris said.

Maisie released a contented sigh. "Maybe next year I'll plan far enough ahead so I can put Christmas lights outside."

Jack glanced up at her. "I'll be right back."

He hopped in the car while Iris and Maisie shouted after him. Ignoring them, he headed to the local twenty-four-hour Walmart. A half hour later he pulled into the driveway again, and both Maisie and Iris walked out to greet him. Chaco and Einstein trailed after them, and both dogs rushed him,

Einstein going so far as to lick his hand again. Apparently, he'd finally broken through with the dog.

"Where did you go?" Maisie demanded, her hands propped on her hips.

Grinning, he held up the two Walmart bags. "Again, the pickings were slim, so this will have to do."

Maisie herded the dogs back into the house, and he unpacked the boxes of netted lights and tossed them over the bushes in front of her house. He was relieved he'd remembered correctly that she had seven plants. Once the netted lights were in place, he linked them all together and connected them to the extension cord he'd bought. Iris and Maisie stood in the front yard while he crouched next to the outlet.

"This deserves a countdown," Maisie said. "Five, four."

Iris joined in.

"Three, two, one."

Jack plugged in the cord and...nothing.

Maisie laughed. "Are you sure the lights work?"

He shot her a dark look, then laughed. After he checked the plugs, he realized one of them hadn't been pushed in all the way. They had another countdown, shouting the last numbers, and when they got to one, Jack plugged in the last cord and the bushes burst into light.

He hurried toward Maisie and Iris, then turned to look at the bushes. While they were lit up in white lights, it looked like a half-assed effort compared to the bare two-story house.

"Well, it's not the house from *Christmas Vacation*," Maisie said in a teasing tone.

"I'll do better next year," he said, frowning as he studied the house. He knew she was stretching out of her comfort zone, and he really wanted to make it special.

"Jack," Maisie said, her voice tight.

He glanced down at her.

"It's better than I could have imagined."

He smiled even though his heart ached to pull her into his arms. He was about to say Iris be damned, but then he saw his sister watching him with narrowed eyes, as though she was trying to look deep into his soul.

So instead he grasped Maisie's hand and held on tight. It would have to do for now.

CHAPTER
Twenty-Three

Einstein apparently had a thing for Jack now. The only other man he did anything but tolerate was River. Maisie couldn't help but think it was a sign, even as her mind bemoaned the use of the word "sign" for anything other than a street directive. But she strived to, above all things, be honest with herself, and last night, standing outside with Iris and Jack in front of seven glowing bushes, her heart had felt full in a way she hadn't experienced in a long time.

"They would have liked him," she'd found herself saying to Mary and Molly this morning when she'd video-called them to show off the house.

"The important thing is *you* like him," Molly had said. "And that he has arms that could sail a thousand ships."

"I'm happy for you," Mary added. There were tears in her eyes, or at least it had looked like it. "The house is beautiful. I wish we were there."

And if that wasn't a Christmas miracle, Maisie didn't know what was.

"Remember," Molly had said to her before signing off. "Take down all the details you can this weekend. Record people if at all possible. This epic cluster of a gathering needs to be preserved for posterity. Future anthropologists will study it."

Maybe she was right. It certainly wasn't going well so far. She'd met the Buchanan crew over at Beau's old house so Adalia could drive them all to their destination—the Biltmore Estate—in Finn's Range Rover. The brewery tour didn't kick off until later in the afternoon, but the bachelorette party had begun early, so Finn had invited all of the guys, including Tyrion, over to his house to watch River's favorite movie. It was unclear whether Prescott was coming as well, although for the well-being of both Jack and River, she hoped the answer was a solid no. River had called her earlier in the morning, his voice a little panicked, to talk about Prescott again. She'd reminded him of what she'd said before— Georgie loved him, Prescott was a bully, and he had nothing to worry about. Besides, she would be there for most of it.

"Talk to Jack," she'd suggested to River. "You two have more in common than you'd think."

For a moment, she'd had a strange sliver of doubt. Hadn't it occurred to her in the beginning that Jack was a little too like River for comfort? But the feeling faded quickly, replaced by an ironclad certainty. Sure, they had some things in common, but they were hardly the same person. Jack's battles had been his own. Plus, he fit her in a way River never had—if River had seemed like the perfect match for her high school self, Jack was a better counterpart to the woman she'd become.

"Huh," River had said. "I hadn't realized you were such good friends."

"We've become close," she said, leaving it at that. Because it was the only way she knew how to describe what they were becoming to each other.

"Want to tell me about it?" he asked softly.

"Maybe later," she said. "Let's get through this first."

Because it certainly felt like something to "get through." The round of introductions had gone stiffly, with Victoria sniffing and saying something about being at a disadvantage since she had to remember so many names, when everyone else only had to remember one. Which was pretty amusing, really, given she'd met Dottie before—no one forgot Dottie—and she presumably knew what both of Lee's sisters were called.

"What kind of bachelorette party starts at three in the afternoon?" Iris bemoaned. "It's not like Georgie's eighty."

"No, that would be me," Dottie said with a sparkle in her eyes. "And parties that start early can very well become parties that end late."

"Let's hope not," Victoria said. Giving Dottie a speculative look, she added, "Maybe I'll join you and Prescott for dinner. I'm sure he'd welcome a friendly face."

"No, no. Adalia has planned a *long* evening of fun for you. I wouldn't think to ruin it with such serious talk."

Which only made Victoria look more desperate to know what the meeting was about. Not that the rest of them felt any differently.

At least the geriatric start time had ensured Dottie could be there for the bachelorette party. Her dinner with Prescott didn't kick off until seven. Apparently, they were going to an Ethiopian restaurant downtown, a fact that suggested Dottie really *did* have some dirt on him. Because from what Maisie had heard about the man, he likely didn't have an adventurous palate.

When Georgie declined to ride shotgun, Victoria turned up her nose and said, "Well, as the guest, I suppose *I* should."

It was obvious to everyone else that Georgie had declined so Dottie could be up front, so Maisie went ahead and said so. "Dottie's going to ride up front with Addy. You can sit back here with us bumpkins."

Which had earned her another sniff. If Victoria kept it up, Maisie was going to ask her if she had a secret drug habit.

Within half an hour, they were riding in a horse-drawn carriage on the Biltmore Estate. Apparently Georgie and Adalia shared an undying affection for Jane Austen, a predilection passed on to them by their mother, and the bachelorette party was, not surprisingly, *Pride and Prejudice* themed. It was something Maisie would have attempted to tease them for—or Addy at least—except she knew a thing or two about holding on to memories like they were gems. And she couldn't deny the whole thing had a festive feel, from all of the evergreen trees and holiday lights at the Biltmore to the carriage with the thick blankets and the plaid travel mugs of hot chocolate Addy had prepared. Apparently, there was a small amount of alcohol in Georgie's, to help her deal with the whole Victoria situation.

"You know, my family has a very close friendship with the Biltmores," Victoria said grandly as the driver paused the horse-drawn carriage in front of the estate.

"Um, I think you mean the Vanderbilts," Iris said, glancing up from her phone. Maisie sputtered a laugh.

"I said *exactly* what I meant," Victoria said, not backing down.

"Oh, how interesting," Dottie said. "I had no idea a Biltmore family existed. I'd heard the name of the estate was created by George Vanderbilt. If you have the *real* scoop, we'd love to hear it, dear."

Adalia let one peal of laughter escape before she turned it into a coughing fit. Georgie took another swig of her cinnamon schnapps-laced hot chocolate.

One of Victoria's now-infamous sniffs was followed by, "It's gauche to talk about it."

"Yes, let's not," Maisie said.

"Oh, I would *love* to hear more about the Biltmores," Adalia said through another round of laugh-coughing.

"They're a very private family," Victoria said, looking every bit like she knew she'd backed herself into a corner but wouldn't admit it upon pain of death.

"Yes, and I imagine they wouldn't like you name-dropping," Iris said, tucking her phone into her pocket as if the party had finally gotten interesting enough, or dysfunctional enough, to command her attention. "*If* they were real."

Victoria muttered something about young people and overactive imaginations, and that was that.

The horses continued along, bringing them past towering trees and sweeping fields. The scene was beautiful, and they settled into some innocuous conversation about Finn and Adalia's many visits to the Biltmore. They had annual passes and apparently used them often enough that the guards at the front knew them by name. Adalia's first idea for the bachelorette party had apparently involved everyone wearing nineteenth-century dresses, something Georgie had put the kibosh on. Maisie mouthed *thank you* to her, and Georgie smiled back at her…which had to be a first.

The highlight of the carriage ride, though, happened when the horse in back started to expel waste as it walked, the earthy smell of it drifting back toward them. Victoria released a scandalized gasp.

"What's happening?" she asked. "Is it…?"

"See, there are disadvantages to sitting in front," Maisie said cheerfully.

"We should complain to the manager," she said, her lips flattening into thin, colorless lines. "There's a time and a place for everything. This horse should have...evacuated its bowels before we arrived."

"There are some things that can't be planned, dear," Dottie said, giving her a surprisingly intense look. "You'd do well to remember that."

Something told Maisie she wasn't just talking about the bathroom habits of draft horses. Victoria had already mentioned, three times—she was counting for Molly—that she would plan her engagement festivities with Lee quite differently. And also that she couldn't possibly include either Adalia or Georgie in her wedding party since their blond hair clashed with her dark hair. Which was pretty amusing since Maisie had seen Lee on that Thanksgiving FaceTime call, and his hair was as light as his sisters'.

"This hot chocolate is *really* good," Georgie said with a hiccup.

The driver let them out in front of the Inn on Biltmore Estate, where Adalia had parked the Range Rover, but they weren't going anywhere yet. Their next stop was a *Pride and Prejudice*-inspired tea.

When Adalia had told her what she was planning, Maisie had asked, "Does that mean we get to take turns about the room and whisper behind each other's backs?"

"I knew you'd at least seen the movie!" had been Adalia's reply. Maisie hadn't let on until then—mostly because Adalia loved *Pride and Prejudice* enough for at least ten adults, and she'd gotten Finn into it too. An addiction like that needed no encouragement.

They disembarked from the carriage, Victoria giving another scowl to the offending horse, who nickered as if sensing evil, and headed into the inn. Once inside, they were ushered into a large drawing room, which really could have been pulled out of a nineteenth-century movie. A large tray sat on the round table in the midst of several uncomfortable-looking couches and chairs.

To Maisie, the sandwiches looked a little bland, the petit fours nowhere near as good as the ones she knew Dottie had carried over in the insanely large bag she had slung over her arm, but Georgie gasped with pleasure.

"This is perfect, Addy."

Adalia nearly glowed with the compliment. And it was such a nice moment that Maisie felt a little choked up, which was ridiculous, really. It had clearly been too long since she'd seen her sisters. And maybe, just maybe, she was getting into the spirit of things a little. Because seeing Georgie and River together didn't bother her anymore. She genuinely wanted them both to be happy, and she really, really wanted to be happy too. Maybe she was becoming a sap, because when she thought about being happy now, it was Jack she saw by her side. Stringing Christmas lights on her house with Iris shouting up instructions. Chaco and Einstein watching with wagging tails.

"Well, it's not tea at the Plaza, but it's about as good as can be expected, I suppose." Victoria shot an accusatory glance at the uniformed server, who looked like she wanted to fade into the wallpaper. Instead, she started pouring out cups of tea, handing them around as everyone got settled. Adalia and Georgie sat on one of the two-person loveseats, Iris and Dottie on another, leaving Maisie to take one for the team and sit with Victoria.

Victoria squirmed beside her, letting out an aggrieved sigh as she tried to get comfortable on the admittedly uncomfortable piece of furniture.

Maisie had half a mind to ask her if the stick up her butt was chafing, but instead she took the tea she was given and took a hearty sip.

"Do you need anything else?" the server asked, posing the question to Georgie.

"Coffee," Victoria said. "Three Splendas, no milk."

Of course she was asking for coffee at a Victorian tea. But the server was so eager to get out of there she eagerly took the excuse.

"I'm watching my figure," Victoria announced as Dottie pulled out one of her ever-present pieces of Tupperware and started adding delectable-looking treats to the serving tray.

"That's wise," Maisie said, serving herself a heaping plate of Dottie goodies, although she knew better than to take any of the red cakes. They were hot enough to get a five-chili-pepper rating at a Thai restaurant. "You'll want to fit into that wedding dress you've probably already ordered."

God help Lee Buchanan. This woman was a nightmare. Then again, Maisie maintained that it didn't speak well of him that he'd chosen her and stuck by her side. She was sorry for that—Adalia and Georgie clearly cared about their brother, and from a few comments Jack had made, she knew he was hoping to get to know him better. But she couldn't help feeling a little offended on Jack's behalf. His brother had made zero effort to get to know him.

Victoria gave Maisie's full plate a disapproving look as she selected a single cucumber sandwich and a piece of celery, something that looked like it had been intended as garnish. "Three of them, actually. I'm not ready to make up my mind."

Adalia laughed, not attempting to disguise her humor this time. "Are you waiting until he proposes to make up your mind?"

Georgie nudged her a little, a concerned look on her face. She was a peacemaker, and she clearly worried about offending Victoria for fear of alienating Lee. Which, fine. It hardly mattered if *Maisie* offended Lee.

"I get it," Georgie offered. "I still haven't chosen a dress, and I've dragged poor Adalia out to six different stores."

"I don't mind," Adalia said with a grin. "They give us free champagne."

"Only six?" Victoria said, aghast. "And you're trying to find a dress in this town? Oh no. You should get your father to send you to New York to take a *real* shopping trip."

She said it like Georgie was a little girl who needed a big, strong man to buy her something shiny. Good lord.

"She built and sold one company, and now she's running another," Maisie snapped. "I doubt she needs her father to buy her anything, let alone supervise her on a shopping trip."

Georgie's eyes flew wide. She clearly hadn't expected Maisie for stand up to her…and honestly, neither had Maisie. But she wasn't about to let Victoria ruin everything.

Iris started coughing suddenly, her face red, and Dottie patted her on the back. "There, there, dear, you got one of the red ones."

"Why…didn't…anyone…warn me?" she choked out.

"They're good for the constitution! They flush out all the bad energy. Everyone should have one." She glanced around the room, looking for another taker. Her gaze lingered on Victoria. "You could *especially* use one."

"What's that supposed to mean?" Victoria said, setting her plate down with a clink.

But the server arrived with her coffee just then. As she took it, she raised a brow and asked, "Three Splendas?"

"Yes, of course. Just the way you requested it."

Victoria frowned in a way that somehow failed to wrinkle her forehead. Wasn't she too young for Botox? Then again, Molly had interviewed a dermatologist who'd said women were coming in for treatments younger and younger. "Where's the milk?"

"Um, didn't you say you didn't care for milk?" the server asked hesitantly.

"Not *in* the coffee, but it should be served alongside it." She lifted a hand as if at wit's end. "Honestly."

"There's milk on the table," Iris said slowly.

"The milk for coffee and tea should be separate!"

It was such an insane statement that no one commented on it or asked her why. The server took off quickly, probably accustomed to dealing with the occasional irrational customer.

"Now, when each of you finish your tea, bring your cups to me," Dottie said expectantly.

"I realize we're in the middle of nowhere," Victoria said, "but surely the waitstaff collects the soiled dishes."

"She's going to read the tea leaves," Adalia said.

"Read them? What on earth does that mean?"

And Maisie, who'd never particularly taken with palm reading or psychics, especially given that the one reading she'd gotten had been so spectacularly bad, found herself in the position of defending Dottie's readings.

"Reading the future. Don't you want to know when you'll be getting engaged?"

"Oh," Victoria said, perking up. "And would you still know if I pour the tea into a different container, or do I need to actually drink it?"

"You need to drink it," Dottie said. "And really, you should anyway. It has chamomile in it. A very calming blend."

Adalia laughed a little at that, and Iris perked up from her phone, which she'd been bent over once again.

Who was she talking to, anyway? One of her friends? Or was she maybe texting with Jack? The thought was alluring, and she pulled out her own phone.

He'd clearly been thinking of her too, because there was a text from him.

Is it six yet?

At six, she would be defecting from the bachelorette party to join the guys for the brewery and bites tour she'd arranged with Finn.

She was about to type out a reply when Georgie announced, "I need to use the restroom."

"Really, Georgie, there's no need to tell everyone," Victoria said, shaking her head slightly. "There's a time and a place for such things."

"Just ask the horse," Adalia muttered, and Iris burst out laughing.

Cheeks slightly flushed, Georgie turned to Maisie. "Will you come with me?"

Maisie wouldn't have been more surprised if Victoria had started dancing on one of the tables. Why did Georgie want to talk to her? And alone, at that. But she was the bride, after all, and she could hardly say no.

"Um, sure," she said, pocketing her phone. "Just don't ask me to hold your dress while you pee. From what I've heard, that's only necessary for wedding dresses. Victoria knows what I'm talking about. She has three of them."

CHAPTER
Twenty-Four

Jack was starting to wish he'd faked the flu. It wasn't like he *needed* to be at River's bachelor party. While he and River were getting along better than they had before Jack moved to Asheville, they were by no means friends. Jack knew the only reason he'd been invited to participate in the wedding, let alone the bachelor party, was because he was Georgie's half-brother. While he could hardly get out of the wedding or the engagement party, considering he'd helped plan it, he'd seriously considered declining to participate in this afternoon's festivities. He'd gotten friendlier with Finn, but the thought of spending all afternoon and evening with River and Lee sounded exhausting, maybe even excruciating, but he didn't want to hurt his sisters' feelings.

Okay, that wasn't the only reason. He was also there to see the woman who'd helped plan it...the woman who wouldn't show up for several more hours. He'd considered begging off the movie portion and just showing up for the brewery tour, but it was the kind of rude, self-serving thing his mother would have done. And he never, ever wanted to be like her.

He told himself he was getting worked up over nothing, that the afternoon and evening would go just fine—he was fairly sure Prescott wouldn't be around—but his stomach still churned with anxiety. And it wasn't because of River.

Why did he care about what Lee thought of him? Jack had lived thirty years without an older brother and had done just fine. He didn't need Lee's approval *or* acceptance. But somehow it still mattered. Back in high school, he'd look at those pictures of the Buchanans and think about what it would be like to have a big brother, someone to help show him the way. Because his grandmother was already gone, and he was caring for his little sister, and dammit, at times he'd wanted the guidance of someone older. Now, of course, he realized how ludicrous that was—Lee was only slightly older than him, and he'd led a charmed life. He wouldn't have had any special insights into Jack's problems. Nor, in all likelihood, would he have cared.

Jack showed up at Finn's house a few minutes late with Tyrion in tow. He'd hoped Lee would already be there, but River was the first and only other guest.

Jack unfastened the leash, and Tyrion bolted for Finn, who bent over to rub his head, then took off for a water bowl by the back door, his eager lapping and splashing sounds filling the room. It was obvious the husky was used to spending time here.

"Jack, I'm glad you could make it," River said, but it sounded half-hearted and his gaze drifted over Jack's shoulder toward the street.

"Don't take it personally," Finn said in a low voice as he led Jack into the kitchen. "He's nervous about seeing Lee again. The two didn't make a good impression on each other at the will reading, and they haven't exactly hit it off over video chats since."

"Yeah," Jack said, "I know the feeling."

Finn grimaced as he stopped in front of a metal bucket on the counter. "I guess you do. I forgot you were there too." He gestured to the bucket, which was full of ice and bottles of beer. "Help yourself. There are some Big Catch bottles in there if you're interested in checking out the competition."

Jack pulled out a Big Catch IPA as he shot a look at River, who had shut the door and returned to the couch. "I thought some of River's other friends were coming."

"They're coming tonight," Finn said. "To the brewery tour. We'll meet them at the first stop."

An uncomfortable silence filled the air. River was staring at a blank TV screen, but his expression was fraught because of his nerves. Jack got it; he felt like River looked.

"So what movie are we watching?" he called out.

It seemed to take River a couple of seconds to register that the comment was directed toward him. "Uh...*The Big Lebowski.*"

"Ah," Jack said with a nod. "A classic."

Finn released a short laugh. "'Yeah, well, you know...that's just, like, your opinion, man.'"

Something about Finn's response seemed familiar, and then it hit him and he grinned. "A movie quote. Nice one."

Finn tipped his head to the side. "Something I picked up from your sister." Then he added, "Addy."

Jack laughed. "I figured. Doesn't seem like a Georgie thing."

He shot another look at River, who looked like a statue of some prey about to be devoured by a monster.

The doorbell rang, and Tyrion rushed over to Jack and began to howl.

Jack glanced down at the dog, surprised he'd come to him rather than Finn, but he leaned over and rubbed his head. "It's okay, boy."

River's back stiffened, insinuating he might not agree. He approached the door and opened it, saying in a deep voice that held a note of challenge, "Lee."

"River," Lee said in an equally authoritative voice from the front porch.

"Great," Finn mumbled. "It's going to be a pissing match." He glanced at Jack, raising his brow.

He shrugged and lifted his bottle to take a drink. "I peed before I left home." He gave a nod to the dog still standing next to him. "Tyrion too."

But he knew why Finn had given him that look. Everyone knew Lee refused to acknowledge him as a sibling. Hell, Lee might be one-fourth owner of the brewery, but he refused to acknowledge Jack as a business partner either.

River was still holding his ground in the doorway.

"Why don't you invite him in?" Finn said.

River backed up. "Come on in. Thanks for coming."

"Yeah," Lee said as he walked in, his gaze scanning the house. His gaze lingered on Finn and Jack for a brief moment before returning to River. "Wouldn't miss it." But he sounded like he *would* have missed it if he could have gotten away with it.

Tyrion released a low growl, but Finn grabbed his collar and bent down next to him, whispering something in his ear.

A wave of pain washed through Jack, catching him off guard. So the bastard still wasn't going to say anything to him. So be it.

Lee took a few more steps into the house, casting a wary glance at Tyrion. The dog had stopped growling, but his tail wasn't wagging. Which said plenty. He'd yet to meet a person he didn't like.

"I take it your father's not coming," River said as he shut the door.

Lee looked reluctant to move, as though he wanted to stick close to the front door in case he changed his mind and wanted to make a quick retreat. "No. He had some work to do this afternoon, and he's having dinner tonight with that eccentric woman from the will reading. Dottie Hendrickson."

"Dottie's my great-aunt," River said with a hint of warning.

Lee's eyes widened slightly. "Oh. Yeah. Sorry. Didn't mean anything by it. Half the people in Asheville are eccentric."

He shot a glance at Finn and Jack again, then back to River.

They all stood in silence for a few seconds before Finn gestured to the tub of drinks in the kitchen with his free hand. "We've got some beer here. Buchanan and Big Catch. Big Catch is the brewery River and I used to run." He gave Lee a questioning look. "Have you tried any of the Buchanan brews yet?"

Lee's shoulders tensed. "No."

"Hey," Finn said, looking over at River. "We should set up a flight for him. Like you did for Georgie the night of the will reading."

Lee's body stiffened even more as he swung his attention to River. "So that's how you got my sister to change her mind about selling the brewery? You got her drunk and seduced her?"

"Are you kidding me?" River said. He didn't raise his voice, but he didn't need to. He emanated silent rage. "I would *never* take advantage of Georgie that way!"

"So you're claiming you didn't get her drunk?"

Picking up on the tension in the room, Tyrion swiveled his gaze back and forth from River to Lee, then moved closer to Jack, pressing against his leg.

"I was there that night," Jack said, hating to get into the middle of this but feeling the need to set the record straight. "I wasn't there for the whole thing—I showed up after the flight—but Georgie wasn't drunk when I arrived. She was totally lucid when we discussed keeping the brewery."

"Like I should take your word for it," Lee sneered. "You got your way too."

"Now, everybody take a breath," Finn said in a tone a preschool teacher would take with two kids fighting over a toy. "I think there's been a misunderstanding."

Lee's eyes glittered with anger, and River looked like he was ready to deck him.

Jack was tempted to take his half-brother outside and beat him up himself.

"Maybe you all need to clear the air," Finn said, standing in the middle of the room. "Obviously, there are some perceived wrongs, and River *is* marrying your sister, Lee. I think it's safe to say we all care about Georgie and want her to be happy."

Lee didn't argue. Then again, he and Finn got along, apparently. Jack was pretty sure the six figures in Finn's bank account had something to do with it. And while he liked Finn too, he couldn't be anything but disgusted by Lee's snobbery.

"How about that drink first?" Finn said with a half grin.

"Got any whiskey?" Lee said with an air of challenge.

"Your choice is beer or water," Finn said. Then his eyes lit up with amusement. "Or the spiked lemonade Addy made last night."

With the amount of testosterone oozing out of Lee, Jack wasn't surprised he skipped the hard lemonade and went with beer. Nor was he surprised when he picked a Big Catch brew.

Finn had them all sit down in the living room while he dragged a kitchen chair in front of the fireplace like a mediator or an emcee. Lee sat in an armchair, and River and Jack sat on the sofa. Tyrion lay at Jack's feet, as though giving him moral support.

"Lee," Finn said in a firm tone. "It's obvious you think River has taken advantage of your sister, but I've gotten to know Georgie better, and she's not the type of woman who is easily duped. Am I right?"

Lee took a long pull from his bottle, then slowly lowered it and kept his gaze on his hand. "No. She's not."

"River," Finn said, turning to his friend. "I'm sure you can see how Lee might have gotten the wrong impression. He found out that you would get ownership of Buchanan if it doesn't place fifth or better in Brewfest, not to mention his sister put a ton of her own money into the brewery to bring it up to speed."

"She did *what*?" Lee barked, his face flushing.

Finn grimaced. "He didn't know?"

"He knew," River said in a short tone, then turned his attention to Lee. "Georgie told you. You just didn't listen."

"I knew she invested *some* money, but I didn't realize it was a *ton*," Lee said. "How much have you suckered her into investing?"

Jack wanted to stay out of this part too, but he was one-fourth owner of the brewery, which meant he had a say. "You have full access to the financials, Lee. Are you saying you don't look at them?"

"I've been busy," he said defensively. Then his eyes hardened. "But I'm sure *you* did your own fair share of pressuring."

"No, she did that on her own," Jack said. "I would have suggested loans."

"How much have *you* put into the business?" Lee asked.

"You know I don't have much money," Jack said, his voice cold. "I'm sure you had me investigated, if not before our grandfather's death, then definitely afterward."

Guilt flickered in Lee's eyes, but his expression quickly shifted back to anger. "Are you saying that surprises you?"

"No," Jack said, holding his gaze. "Not one bit. You learned at our father's feet, after all."

Lee started to say something, then stopped.

"Lee," Finn said, sounding less enthusiastic than before. "I've known River for six years. I *know* him. He has never loved a woman like he loves your sister. He would do anything to make her happy. Don't you want that for your sister?"

Lee gave River a hard stare. "I'm supposed to forget that you win the brewery if it fails to rank in the competition? Even after all the hard work my sisters have done?"

"I'm doing everything I can to ensure we place in the top five," River said. "And besides, if Georgie and I are married, she'll still be an owner. She won't lose in this, Lee, no matter what happens."

"But we might," Jack said, voicing a fear that had been simmering below the surface since he'd heard about Georgie and River's engagement. "Addy, me, and Lee...we're no longer part owners if we lose. We'll have done all this for nothing, especially since I've only just started to draw a fraction of my salary."

River started to say something, then stopped, swallowing.

Tyrion didn't budge from his spot at Jack's feet, but he glanced over his shoulder as if to check in with him.

"That's right," Lee said, perking up. "And who's to say you aren't marrying Georgie to hedge your bets? Win or lose, you still own part of it."

River ignored the comment and swung his gaze to Jack. "I'm not trying to screw you out of anything, Jack. I swear."

"Oh, yeah?" Lee said. "Then prove it."

River's body seemed to throb with anger. "I'm marrying your sister, Lee. I won't cancel the wedding to prove myself to you. *Or* Jack."

Jack sat up straighter and Tyrion did the same. "I never asked you to cancel anything. From what I've seen, you make Georgie happy. I would never take that from her."

He shot a glare at his half-brother.

Lee pushed out a breath, his brow furrowed, then held his hands out at his sides. "Finn's right. We all want Georgie to be happy. There's no disputing that." He narrowed his gaze at River. "But you seem to want my blessing."

"I don't give two shits about you or what you think," River said through clenched teeth, "but for some reason, Georgie does. Your approval matters to her." Then he added, "She's going to marry me regardless of what you say, but yes, she wants your blessing."

Suddenly, Jack realized why River had been so nervous. Not because he wanted to impress Lee, but because he knew his good opinion mattered to Georgie. It made Jack think more of River.

"Okay," Lee said with a hint of a smile. "I think we can work out an agreement."

"I'm listening."

"If you want to marry Georgie with my blessing, then all you have to do is relinquish your claim on the brewery.

Whether it places in the top five at Brewfest or not, it stays with the Buchanan siblings. Even after you two are married. You can have Buchanan Brewery *or* my sister, but you can't claim ownership of both."

Finn got to his feet. "Now wait a minute."

River's eyes narrowed. "No one owns Georgie."

"Fair point," Lee conceded, lifting a hand. "Poor choice of words."

River swallowed again. "Georgie means more to me than whether my name is on the ownership papers. I'll be happy as long as I can work there with her. But you have to *swear* that you're one hundred percent on board with this marriage, because like I said, your blessing is important to her, and I'll do whatever it takes to give that to her."

Lee shifted his weight with an air of confidence that reminded Jack of their father. "So, just to be clear, you're willing to give up any claim of ownership to Buchanan Brewery to marry my sister?"

River lifted his chin. "I'd give up everything and anything to marry her."

Lee stood, glaring at River.

River stood and held his gaze, issuing a challenge of his own.

"I'll have the papers drawn up and you can sign them before the engagement party tomorrow night," Lee said in a tight voice. "And *if* you sign them, I'll make a toast to the happy couple, giving you both my blessing."

"Even though you'll probably piss off your father?" River asked.

Lee shrugged. "Maybe it wouldn't hurt to keep him on his toes."

Finn looked surprised, and so was Jack. Both men had been privy to enough video conversations between Addy and

Lee to know he was an ass-kisser where their father was concerned. What had changed?

Lee extended his hand to River, and River clasped it. Both men put a lot of effort into their firm grips, enough so that Finn stepped in and broke them apart.

"Maybe now would be a good time to start the movie," he said. "I'll order some pizzas."

"Sounds good," Lee said, going back to his seat and focusing his attention on the blank TV screen. "I'll take anything as long as it's not hippie, new age, or vegetarian. And no pineapple."

"You know what I like," River grunted, returning to his vacated seat.

Finn grabbed his phone and started to place the call, then seemed to remember Jack. "What about you?"

"I ate before I came over." A lie, but he'd lost his appetite.

Jack's gaze swung from Lee to River. Both men were less tense after their discussion, but he wouldn't exactly call them friendly. Still, they'd reached an agreement, which was more than he and Lee had done.

Jack felt invisible. He knew he could make Lee acknowledge him, but what was the point? He'd suffered enough humiliation with Prescott—he wasn't going to invite any more from his half-brother. But wasn't his blatant dismissiveness a humiliation of its own?

Jack was close to making some excuse to get out of this torture session, but then he thought of Maisie and how excited she'd been to see him tonight. He'd stick through this for her and her alone.

CHAPTER
Twenty-Five

"Thank you," Georgie said, looking Maisie in the eye.

Which was about the last thing she'd expected Georgie to say when she'd dragged her to the bathroom. Of course, she wasn't sure what she *had* expected her to say. Except that it was probably about River, and she almost certainly didn't want to talk about it.

"For what? Being your bathroom buddy?"

"No," Georgie said, waving to the door. "For helping with Victoria. Lee hasn't told Adalia yet, but he's thinking of breaking up with her." She made a face. "I didn't mean to tell you that part. I think Addy put more schnapps in my hot chocolate than she let on."

"Why wouldn't he tell Addy that?" Maisie asked in genuine shock. "That would be, like, the best Christmas present ever for her."

Georgie shrugged. "You're no more surprised than I was. He doesn't usually confide in me. I think he probably wants to be the one to inform Victoria they're through. You know Addy wouldn't be able to help herself if she knew."

Maybe. Either way, it struck Maisie as another case of Buchanan dysfunction. Adalia had told her that the siblings had struggled to communicate with each other after their mother died, and although things had improved, clearly the struggle was ongoing. At least with Lee. Of course, her impression of Lee, whom she'd still never met, wasn't all that great.

Maisie had about a dozen other questions about the whole Lee/Victoria quagmire—why bring someone to a family event if you planned on breaking up with them? Why spend Christmas with someone you didn't love? And the real clincher: Why would anyone, for any reason, ever date Victoria?

But she settled for asking, "What do you think she's going to do with the wedding dresses? Shred them?"

Georgie laughed. "Or maybe she just repurposes them. They could be from her last would-be engagement."

"Imagine being the guy who goes home with her for the first time and finds a closet full of wedding dresses."

"And a fridge full of tiny jugs of milk."

Then they were both laughing, the kind of laughter that made you bend over with it, and it felt surprisingly good. Maisie had always hesitated to be alone with Georgie, and she was pleased to find she didn't mind it. That she *liked* her. Which shouldn't have been a surprise. Although Georgie had always struck her as a little too proper, she was Adalia's sister, after all, and River thought she'd hung the moon.

Georgie was the one who sobered first. "I'm grateful River has a friend like you. I wanted to tell you that too. You were there for him through a lot of hard times, and it helped make him the man he is. And I know you're the one who told him to talk to me after we had our fight this summer. I…I don't want you to ever feel uncomfortable around me. You'll always be welcome in our home. I hope we can be friends too."

She could just thank her, and that would be that. But even though she and Jack were a big question mark right now, she wanted to explore the curve of that question mark—just like she wanted to explore his body at much greater length. And that meant she needed to be straight with Georgie. Because Georgie obviously knew something, or *thought* she knew something. "I'd like that." She paused. "To be clear, I'm not in love with River. I'm interested in your brother Jack."

Georgie's eyes went comically huge, and Maisie would have laughed if the moment didn't feel so weighty. "You didn't expect me to be so direct, did you?"

"No," she said with a tentative smile, "but maybe I should have. You always have been before."

Except about this one thing, Maisie mentally filled in.

Georgie paused. "Thank you. I appreciate your honesty."

"In the interest of full disclosure, my feelings for River have been...confusing in the past, but I'm beyond that. I think I have been for a while, only I sometimes find it hard to move on from things."

The attachment she'd felt to River, to the idea of them possibly changing their friendship...it was no different than the old things haunting her house. And it was past time for her to let go of all of that. To accept the future in its frightening, maddening, and exhilarating uncertainty.

Georgie nodded like she understood, and maybe she did. From what River had said, she'd had no problem moving on from Moon Goddess, the company she'd founded and sold, but personal baggage always weighed more than the professional variety. "I get it." She paused, then added, "Jack's a good guy."

"He is," she agreed. "More so than he realizes. Now, do you really need to use the bathroom, or are you ready to go back out there?"

Georgie made a face. "Can't we just stay in here until it's time to leave?"

"Get ready for the long haul," Maisie said with a grin. "Addy planned a sleepover for y'all tonight."

Georgie blanched. "Surely Victoria won't stay for that."

"Although it disappoints me to say so, if only because I wanted to hear about her monogrammed pajamas and her sleep regimen, Addy wouldn't stand for it. She'll figure out a way to send her packing."

Still, they didn't hurry back. They both used the bathroom, then laughed about the three varieties of soap. Maisie suggested they use each of them to lengthen their trip, and so they did, both of them wrinkling their noses at the snowman scent.

"Why would a snowman have a scent anyway?" Georgie asked as they headed back to the tearoom.

"Only yellow snow has a scent," Maisie said. "And trust me, no one would want their hands to smell like that. Or if they did, they wouldn't bother washing them."

As they neared the room, shouting could be heard behind the door. They exchanged a glance, and Maisie opened it. Victoria was on her feet, waving a teacup in Dottie's face. Two additional teacups sat atop the table in front of Dottie, along with three saucers.

"Check it again," Victoria insisted. "You must be interpreting it wrong."

Dottie looked as calm as if she were meditating. "Dear, it's the third teacup you've given me, and the image is still the same. I suspect it would be if you drank the whole pot."

Victoria had downed three cups of tea in the time they'd been gone?

"But you said a fish can be a symbol of fertility. Maybe that's what you saw."

"Yes, but a fish *in water* symbolizes a goal that will be subverted. Of course, none of us know what that goal might be."

"How could it not be in water?" Victoria screeched. "It's at the bottom of a cup of tea."

Adalia huffed a laugh, and Iris grinned at her.

Maisie and Georgie exchanged a look and then headed into the room and took their seats.

"So, what did we miss?" Maisie said. "Besides Dottie dashing Victoria's hopes, of course."

"Mine had flying birds," Iris said, lifting her cup slightly. "It's a sign of good news."

Of course, she'd had good news already, from what she'd said the other day, although Maisie still didn't know what it entailed.

Dottie beamed at her. "Yes, I've rarely seen a happier cup."

How anyone could see anything in the small speckling of leaves that had escaped was beyond Maisie, but if it pissed Victoria off and made Iris happy, she wouldn't object.

The attendant knocked slightly on the door, then entered with a tray topped with three different small carafes of milk. The woman was clearly hedging her bets, which was not unwise. Of course, Maisie and Georgie had been gone awhile. For all she knew, Victoria had asked for a different carafe to accompany each of her cups of tea. The server was behind Victoria, so Victoria didn't see her when she flung the teacup at the floor. She'd probably intended to break it, but the floor was carpeted, and it merely bounced, flinging a few tea leaves up in the air.

"I'm tired of your game," she said in a huff, and headed back to her seat next to Maisie, sniffing in an aggrieved manner.

The attendant gasped, but she wisely didn't say anything as she lowered the tray of milk next to Victoria.

"Did you have to milk the cow?" Victoria snapped. Then she made a dismissive gesture. "I don't need it anymore. Take the coffee away and get me a vodka tonic." She pointed to the mess on the carpet. "And clean up that mess when you get back. It looks like someone dropped a teacup."

"Yes, ma'am," the woman said, backing away in the manner of someone trying not to enrage a psychopath.

"You threw it in front of all of us," Adalia said. "Are you suffering from memory issues?" Victoria's mouth dropped open, but before she could say anything, Adalia said, "Let's just move on to our private wine tasting. I think we could all use a drink."

"Yes," Dottie said, "quite. Doing this many readings at one time has made me very thirsty. Are you sure you wouldn't care for a red petit four, Victoria? Your energy could *really* use some cleansing. Even the tea leaves on the floor form quite a disturbing pattern."

"I only drink wine from organic grapes," Victoria said flatly. "Are the grapes one hundred percent organic?"

The server swallowed, the bottle she held hovering over Victoria's tasting glass.

"Yes," Maisie interjected. "And they play soft music to them to make the wine taste sweeter."

At a tight nod from Victoria, who gave Maisie a look to tell her she would personally hold her accountable if the wine was disagreeable, the server poured her a taste.

She checked her phone, but Jack still hadn't responded to her message—*I feel like I'm in the Twilight Zone. Victoria is something else. Can't wait to see you.*

Georgie had been sitting in the corner with her phone too, probably texting with River, and Maisie was half tempted to go over and ask her what was going on with the guys. Except Adalia looked like she was at her breaking point with Victoria, and if she stepped away for a second, she suspected Iris would help herself to the wine in her tasting glass.

She shot Iris a look. "It's not that good."

The server's immediate reaction was to smile—a slight tipping up of the lips before she turned her back on them to grab another bottle.

"Still, it's not fair," Iris said, rolling her eyes. "Teenagers can drink in Europe."

"Yes, well, in Europe, teenagers are seen but not heard," Victoria said with another of her sniffs.

"That's a very medieval attitude, dear," Dottie said, clucking her tongue. "Also, not very true from my observations. I do hope your parents didn't treat you that way."

Another sniff.

"Are you coming down with a cold?" Dottie asked. She rummaged in her bag and pulled out a small, unmarked bottle. "I have just the remedy for that."

Maisie missed whatever was said next, though, because her phone finally buzzed.

I'm going home, Maisie. I don't belong here.

Which meant Lee was acting like a douche-nozzle—big surprise there. The comment hinted at a deep hurt she'd sensed but not seen. His feelings toward the Buchanans were clearly a source of confusion to him.

Don't go anywhere, Maisie typed. *I'm leaving now.* It was five, so she'd get there early, but it took an unreasonably long time to leave the Biltmore anyway. The arrangement was that she'd drop Dottie off at the Buchanan house and then drive the Range Rover back to Finn's. The other women would be picked up by a car service when they were ready to go home, and the bachelor party would be driven around to the breweries in a van chauffeured by Lurch. An agreement Maisie had only consented to since Dottie had insisted he'd be on his best behavior.

She glanced up to see Iris studying her. Had she seen the messages? She knew Jack wasn't ready to tell Iris they meant something to each other, but the kid was smart.

"You're leaving?" Iris asked.

"Yeah, I think Jack might need a save."

"What about me?"

"Oh, you're strong enough to deal with anything this crew has to throw at you."

"I like that you see me that way," Iris said softly, her tone more serious than Maisie was accustomed to from her. "You see both of us better than most people do." She took something out of her bag, a folded note enclosed in an envelope. "Give this to Jack when you see him."

"A handwritten note? Did you body-swap with a boomer?"

"Ha. Ha. Very funny," Iris said, rolling her eyes. "No, but my brother might as well have. He insists on reading paper books instead of getting an e-reader, plus he's a letter writer. He always wrote to me three times a week when I was at sleepaway camp, even though we talked on the phone. And—"

Victoria spat out liquid, spraying Iris and Maisie.

"Was that poison?" she shouted, pointing a finger at Dottie. "Did you *poison* me?"

"Of course not," Dottie said calmly as Iris gave Victoria a disgusted look and grabbed some napkins off the countertop, silently handing one to Maisie.

"I should have warned you about Dottie's 'cures,'" Adalia said with a smirk that suggested she'd purposefully kept quiet. "They usually work, but sometimes they're worse than what they're supposed to fix."

Victoria got to her feet, giving Adalia a look of wounded dignity. "I'm leaving, but you can be sure Lee is going to hear about this. Your father too."

"I sure hope so," Adalia said.

"Don't you have anything to say for yourself, Georgie?" Victoria said, lifting an eyebrow. There were flecks of red wine all over her white cardigan, which slightly undercut the lofty air she was trying to put on.

"Have a good night, Victoria. I've heard the spa at the Grove Park Inn is really nice. Maybe you'll have more fun there."

Victoria made an unpleasant sound that reminded Maisie of a cat coughing up a hairball. "If I wanted to go to a spa, I would go in *Manhattan*." She glanced back and forth between Adalia and Georgie. "Honestly, it's as if the Buchanan blood skipped both of you."

Adalia lifted her glass to Georgie, who clinked it with hers. "You honestly couldn't have given us a better compliment," she said.

Another withering glare, and Victoria stormed off, heels clicking on the stone floor.

"Toodles!" Adalia called out after her. "See you tomorrow!"

"How long do you think it's going to take her to remember that we drove here together?" Maisie asked with a smirk.

"Now, girls," Dottie said, a touch of admonition in her tone. "Your father is a Buchanan, yes, but don't let that destroy your impression of the family. Your grandfather Beau was a good man."

"I know, Dottie," Georgie said.

Adalia just gave a "hm" and nodded. No doubt she was thinking of Beau's crazy will, complete with enough stipulations to have nearly given his attorney a heart attack when presenting it to the Buchanans. Or so she'd heard. Maisie had liked Beau, but he'd been far from perfect. He'd been warm, though. Something Prescott—and probably Lee—clearly lacked.

"I'm going to head over to the bachelor party a little early," Maisie said, pushing her nearly untouched tasting glass away. She tucked Iris's note into her bag, giving her a private nod. "That okay, Dottie?"

"Yes," she said. "I need to do some meditation to replenish my chi. That woman could drain all of the good energy out of a shaman."

"You said it, not me," Adalia said. She glanced from Georgie to Iris. "So it'll just be us sisters, huh?"

Georgie grinned.

Iris smiled too, like she was trying to fight it but couldn't quite muster the energy. "Does this mean I get to take part in the tasting?"

Adalia winked at her. "Maybe a little sip. But you'll have to earn it by painting your toenails with us tonight and watching terrible chick flicks."

"Done," Iris said, quickly enough that it was clear the thought of an evening with Jack's half-sisters didn't sound so terrible to her anymore.

"Ready, Dottie?" Maisie said, grabbing the keys from Adalia.

"Oh yes, I've been preparing for this."

"You're intentionally leading us on, aren't you? No one likes a tease, Dottie."

Dottie just gave her an enigmatic smile, and they said goodbye to the others, Dottie whispering something to Iris before they walked off.

"You still think Lee is 'a good sort'?" Maisie asked as they made their way to the Range Rover. "Because I'm thinking he must be a piece of work if he's spent months dating that woman."

"Lee is the most lost of any of them," she said with a sigh, patting her lilac hair. "Which only means he'll need the most help."

They got into the car, Maisie trying to process what Dottie was saying.

"How are you going to help him, Dottie? He lives in Manhattan, and he works right under his father's thumb."

"Oh, the universe has its ways." She made a swatting gesture, as if to hasten it along.

They started the drive back to the gates, the view pleasant even in the winter, if less stunning than in the other seasons.

"Well," Maisie said after a short silence. "Lee sounds like a dick. He's making Jack feel like he doesn't belong."

Dottie made a little humming sound under her breath. "So often we displace our own feelings onto others."

Maisie snorted. "You sound like Yoda, except without the weird speech pattern."

"I'll take that as a compliment." She paused. "Still, if everyone at the party is distracted, and you and Jack find yourselves able to slip away, you might want to stop by the restaurant. At seven-thirty, say. I don't plan on talking about anything of importance until *after* the meal. The food is quite good. Lurch gave me your schedule, and I believe you'll be at

Libations Brewing at that time. A short walk to Shebeen. I reserved a table for Prescott and me right behind the bar. There are some bushes that would separate us, but I don't imagine they'd block out any sound. It might be prudent to record the conversation, if you feel so inclined. I've heard it's easy to do that sort of thing these days."

"Dottie," Maisie said in disbelief, "did you just invite us to eavesdrop?"

"Well, my dear, if you need me to spell it out, you should hone your intuition. I have a friend who can help you with that."

Of course she did.

CHAPTER
Twenty-Six

Any other time, Jack would have loved watching *The Big Lebowski* for the umpteenth time, but he was distracted by a half dozen things, none of them good. No, that wasn't true. Tyrion hadn't left his side. He'd even followed him into the bathroom and watched him send Maisie a text.

Is it six yet?

She hadn't answered by the time he finished up and checked his phone.

"I hope that means she's having a better time than I am," he mumbled.

Tyrion released a small whine and rubbed his head against Jack's leg.

"Sorry, buddy," Jack said, squatting next to him and scratching both sides of his face. "It's not you. You know I love hanging out with you. In fact, I'm not sure I could have gotten through this afternoon without you."

Tyrion licked his face, and Jack laughed as he got to his feet. "Love you too, but we can't hide in here any longer. We better head back out there."

So he had. Finn had looked relieved to see him at least, like he'd thought Jack might have tried climbing out of the high, narrow window in the bathroom and pulling Tyrion through with him. They'd paused the movie for him, and the awkwardness was such a presence, it was like another guest. Poor River. It wasn't much of a party so far, and it probably wouldn't be as long as Little Lord Fauntleroy hung around. Finn was doing his best, talking about real estate in an animated manner that didn't match the subject matter, but not even Finn could add life to this party.

They finished the movie and Jack nearly groaned in agony when he realized they had over an hour to kill before Maisie and Lurch were supposed to show up for the brewery tour. It felt like he'd died and gotten stuck in the inner circle of Dante's inferno.

They sat in uncomfortable silence for several seconds before Lee pushed himself out of his chair. "I'm going to head to the bathroom."

As soon as he was out of the room, Finn and River exchanged a look. They were clearly dying to talk, but River cast Jack a sideways glance.

"I could use some fresh air," Jack said as he got to his feet. "I'll take Tyrion out to pee."

"You don't have to do that," Finn said, a guilty look washing over his face. "He's my responsibility."

"Nah," Jack said as he grabbed his coat off the rack and shoved his arms into the sleeves. "I take him out all the time. We're pals."

"Well, you don't need to walk him," Finn said as he and River started toward the kitchen. "Addy and I took him on a three-mile hike this morning. He's good."

"Okay," Jack said as he opened the front door. Once they were on the porch, he glanced down at Tyrion. "Don't worry. We'll be out here for a while, so you'll have plenty of time to sniff around." Could he get away with spending the next hour outside?

Tyrion was eager to check out the front yard, so Jack trailed behind, giving him plenty of slack on his retractable leash. He considered taking it off since Tyrion hadn't run off in over a month, but he didn't want to chance it.

Tyrion sniffed around for several minutes, peeing on a couple of trees next to the neighbor's yard, but then he went still and turned his attention to the street.

A black sedan was headed toward them, slowing down as it neared the house. Tyrion continued to watch, and a lump filled Jack's stomach when he realized who was driving.

The car parked in front of the house, and the driver's door opened. A distinguished older man in a tailored suit got out. He walked around the hood of his rented car and stood on the curb, his gaze scanning the house. His cold stare made Jack think he was inventorying the place, trying to figure out if it was worth his time to enter. He must have decided the pleasure he would take in making a bad party worse outweighed the possibility he'd catch some deadly disease from Finn's half-a-million-dollar house, because he started up the sidewalk. Then, halfway up the walk, he stopped and turned to face Jack.

Prescott Buchanan's lip curled as that cold, calculating gaze swept over his son.

Tyrion walked up beside Jack, pressing his solid body into Jack's leg.

"Don't worry. I have no interest in talking to you," Jack said in disgust.

His father lifted his chin and sniffed. "I guess you're not moving as far up in the world as you thought." An amused look filled his eyes as he nodded toward Tyrion. "You've been relegated to cleaning up dog waste."

Anger burned in Jack's chest, and his hand tightened on the leash. "I take it you've never had a pet, Prescott?"

The older man gave him a confused look, somehow still full of disdain. "*No.*"

"I'm not surprised," Jack said. "Pet owners are compassionate and empathetic. They treat other people with respect. You seem incapable of thinking of anyone other than yourself."

Prescott snorted. "Respect is earned, and letting my daughter fund your little brewery escapade reeks of opportunism, not that I'm surprised." Contempt filled his eyes. "You're a leech, just like your white trash mother, and while my father may have given you part ownership of a run-down brewery, you turned down the only offer you'll ever get from me."

Good thing Jack didn't want anything from him. A long time ago he'd wanted a father, but Prescott had made it crystal clear that wasn't on the table, and Jack had accepted it before he'd even turned ten. His mother had arranged those early visits from Prescott, but Jack had never asked for that. He'd never asked for anything, and he wasn't about to start now.

He opened his mouth to tell Prescott just that, but the front door opened, and Lee walked out onto the porch, his gaze firmly on his father.

"Dad. What are you doing here?" he asked in surprise.

Prescott turned his back on Jack and gave his attention to his son—the real one. "I finished my business and came by to check on things since you weren't answering your phone."

Lee crossed his arms over his chest. "I was busy."

An incredulous look washed over Prescott's face as he gestured to the house. "Busy in there…with *them*?"

"I told you we had plans."

Prescott's gaze narrowed. "Just because your sisters and the men they have lowered themselves to associate with feel they can take a day off, doesn't mean we can as well."

"It's a Saturday," Lee said, becoming irritated. "I'm spending time with the men my sisters are planning to marry."

Prescott's brow lowered and he gruffly said, "Adalia is *not* engaged."

Jack was still in the side yard, and while Prescott knew he was there, Jack was fairly certain Lee didn't. Should he make his presence known? Should he slink around the other side of the house so he didn't interrupt them? He decided he'd been there first, so he'd stay put.

Lee shook his head. "If you paid your daughters any attention at all, you'd see that Addy's crazy about Finn, and he's just as crazy about her. They're going to get married, Dad. It's just a matter of time."

Prescott's cheeks reddened. "Then you need to break them up. That boy encouraged her to drag our name into that article."

Jack nearly intervened—presumably by "that article," Prescott meant the *New York Times* piece about Alan Stansworth, the sleazebag who'd stolen Adalia's art—but then Lee surprised him.

"That's not happening," he said, shaking his head. "Finn makes Addy happy, and contrary to what you might think, she deserves happiness."

Prescott clenched his fists at his sides. "I gave you a simple job, Lee. Put a stop to Georgie's marriage before the engagement party tomorrow night. Have you made any progress?"

"No, Dad," Lee said, dropping his hands to his sides. "While you might have told me to break them up, I *never* agreed. I'll admit I had reservations about the guy, but after talking to him, I think he really loves her."

"*Love?*" Prescott asked in an ice-cold voice. "A good marriage is built on what each person has to bring to the table. Take Victoria."

Lee shook his head with a look of disgust.

"Victoria is an intelligent woman with important connections," Prescott continued. "She comes from a solid family. Marrying her will serve our business interests."

"I told you I don't care about that crap, Dad."

"Well, you *should*," Prescott snapped bitterly. "I thought I loved your mother, but all it got me was a house in the suburbs of Connecticut and three ungrateful children. Get your head screwed on straight, Junior, because Victoria's mother is planning *your* engagement party for New Year's Eve."

Lee's face lost all color, and he opened his mouth as if to protest, but Prescott turned on his heels, his shoes clicking on the sidewalk. He couldn't be bothered to give Jack a parting glance—confirming Jack's insignificance in his eyes. Good riddance.

Lee watched his father get in his car and drive off in silence, waiting several seconds before he sucked in a breath and squared his shoulders as though preparing to go into battle. But as he started to turn, he caught a glimpse of Jack and he froze.

"How long have you been standing there?" Lee demanded, his voice filled with rage.

"Long enough."

Lee's face reddened. "Do you make a habit of spying on other people's private conversations, asshole?"

"I wasn't spying. Your father knew I was here the entire time," Jack said, his back stiff.

Lee's jaw squared and his voice shook. "You may have fooled my sisters into believing you're part of this family, but make no mistake: you never have been. And you never will be."

Jack felt the pain of Lee's words as sharply as if he'd been stabbed with a dull knife.

Lee turned around and headed back inside, leaving Jack and Tyrion in the yard.

Jack drew a ragged breath, wondering again why he cared what either Buchanan man thought about him. For a split second, he wondered if he should relinquish his one-fourth share of the brewery, but he reminded himself that Beau had wanted him to be an owner. In this one respect, he was equal to his half-siblings.

Still, he had no interest in spending the evening with Lee. He wanted to go home—to whatever one-fourth section he owned—and forget Lee Buchanan existed.

He pulled out his phone and sent Maisie a quick text, softening his message.

I'm going home, Maisie. I don't belong here.

Her response was quicker than he'd expected. *Don't go anywhere. I'm leaving now.*

He cast a glance at the house, willing himself to go in, to be the bigger person and show Lee that he couldn't care less what he thought, but he couldn't muster the energy to do it. He didn't want to fight the Buchanan men. All he'd wanted was to finally have something of his own. To feel like he belonged somewhere. But they hadn't allowed him even that.

He tugged on Tyrion's leash. "Let's go home, buddy."

But for the first time since he'd arrived in Asheville, Jack felt the tiny prick of conviction that maybe Asheville wasn't his home after all.

CHAPTER
Twenty-Seven

River had called her twice within a matter of seconds, and even though she'd just dropped Dottie off and was on her way to Finn's place, she pulled over to take the call. Because she didn't have Bluetooth—another reason Mary had offered to give her a barely used minivan before her trade-in last June—and she'd promised herself years ago, after her parents' accident, she'd never take a call while driving.

"I'm on my way," she answered. "Everything okay?"

"No," he said bluntly. "I...I know something's going on with you and Jack. So I thought you'd want to know he just left the house. I'm not sure what happened, but I think he had words with Lee."

So much for Dottie's lost child theory. A surge of righteous anger took hold of Maisie. "I see. And where is Junior?"

A huff of laughter. "Finn took him outside to show him the back yard. I doubt it'll buy me much time. You know what Finn's back yard looks like."

"I thought Adalia was helping him plant things."

"Sure, but it's the end of December, and he still has a black thumb. It just took the plants longer to die this time."

Part of Maisie wanted to drive straight to Finn's house so she could let Lee know exactly what she thought of him—and also so she could save River from what had to be the worst bachelor party ever. Except Lurch would be there soon to take them on the Brews and Bites tour, and River had Finn. Jack had no one.

No, he had her.

"River, I'm sorry, but I'm going to be late to the bachelor party. We'll meet up with you later in the evening."

"He's special to you, isn't he?" River said.

"He is," she confirmed.

"I feel like I should tell you…" He trailed off, then cleared his throat. "I don't think I've always been good to you, Maisie. When we were younger, I let you be there for me in a way that wasn't fair. In a way that maybe held you back. That's never what I intended." Another pause. She fought the compulsion to fill it, her heart hammering. "I know you think I forgot about the time I almost kissed you, but I didn't. I just…you were right. You're family to me, and if anything had happened between us back then, it would have broken that. And *that* would have broken *me*."

"Did someone tell you?" she said softly, thinking of Georgie. She'd gotten the sense Georgie had been cool about the whole thing, but maybe she was wrong.

"No," he said. "I did some thinking after you avoided me this summer." He huffed a laugh. "And when I was feeling low about you blowing me off, Dottie suggested I 'dust' her old photo albums. I noticed something in those pictures. We looked at each other a little differently back then. Both of us. The things that happened that year…your parents dying, my screwups, it changed everything. I think we leaned on each other too much. But things changed after that day in the clubhouse… You opened the shelter, and I found Finn. And we both grew up. We changed. But you and Beau and Dottie…and Finn when he's not accidentally messing everything up…you're my family. You always will be."

"It's not what you think," she blurted. "I mean, yes, it messed with my head when you met Georgie. Neither of us had ever been serious about anyone else before. It was always you and me, together against the world. The people we dated were there, but they were in the background. They weren't important. And then there was Georgie, and suddenly you and I weren't us anymore, and I didn't know what to do about that. You're right, it wasn't healthy, but I didn't want it to change. Or I didn't think I did. You know how I am with change."

"I do," he said. "That's why I asked you to be part of the wedding. I thought it might help us work through this." He huffed out a breath. "Or, hell, maybe I was just being selfish again. I didn't want you to pull away. And I wanted you to get to know Georgie."

"I talked to her today," she said. "I *like* her, River. She's right for you." She didn't bother adding *in a way I never was*, because they both knew that. "And Jack…" She swallowed, then admitted out loud what she'd scarcely even admitted to herself: "I'm falling in love with him."

A pause, then he said, "I've seen the way you look at him. I'm happy for you, Maisie. I…I don't know him much, but he seems like a good guy. I'd like to get to know him better, for you and for Georgie. I should have done a better job of looking out for him today."

"It's your bachelor party," she said simply. "I want you to enjoy yourself. We're going to come. I don't know when, but we will. Fair warning, though. If Lee's still around when I get there, he might end up with a drink in or around his face."

"As long as I'm not the one to do it," he said, his tone not without amusement.

"Goodbye, River." Somehow it felt like more than a normal goodbye. Which was silly. She'd be seeing him later that night. But she was saying goodbye to the old way of things—to the days he'd described, when they'd leaned on each other so hard. Codependent, Mary had called it. It felt like a weight had lifted off her shoulders, but it crashed back down at the thought of the whole Jack and Lee episode. Why had Dottie managed to convince them it made sense to spend any more time than necessary with the other half of the Buchanan family?

"Bye, Maisie."

He hung up, and she tapped her finger on the side of the phone for a second before shooting off a quick text to Finn.

Whew, what a day. I'm handing you the best man baton. I'm going to be late. Jack and I will join you guys later. She paused, then added, *Get Lee drunk or get rid of him. I don't want him to ruin River's night.*

Finn's response was immediate. *Are you and Jack involved?* A pause. *Sorry, but Addy told me she thought there might be something between you two, and if there is, I think that's great.* Another pause. *I know, I know, we shouldn't have been talking about you, but it was in a good way, I swear. Duly noted about Lee. I've never seen him like this. Which, I guess I've never actually seen him before, but we've had video chats. I know you think he's just a dick, and honestly, maybe he sort of is. But something is up with him.*

Didn't need a novel, Finn, she texted back, smiling in spite of herself. She could imagine Finn texting up a storm while Lee feigned an interest in his shriveled evergreens or whatever—what even grew in December? Couldn't Finn have thought up a better excuse? *Just take care of it. Over and out.*

She thought of texting Jack, but she didn't want to give him the chance to tell her not to come over. Better to just go there in person. Talk it out.

So she drove straight to the Buchanan house and parked in the drive next to Jack's car. She'd had an image of hammering on his door, insisting he came out, but he was sitting on the porch with Tyrion at his feet and a purple ukulele in his lap. Strumming out a song. Which was so unexpected, she was a little thrown.

His eyes widened as she got out of the car, purse slung carelessly over her shoulder. He stood up and set the ukulele aside, which was when she caught sight of Jezebel's flashing eyes. She'd perched on the chair next to him, but she slunk to her feet too, falling in on the other side of him from Tyrion. It was almost like they'd appointed themselves his guardians, and if there was anything sexier than a man this loved by animals, she wasn't sure what it was.

He stared at her, eyes intense and dark and full of flickering emotion. And she knew she should probably explain why she was here, or maybe ask him what had happened with Lee, because River was right, obviously something had. Instead, she hurried up the steps and pulled him to her, right there on the porch, in front of whoever cared to look outside their windows or walk by, and kissed him, weaving her hand in his dark hair to pull him even closer. Pulling it a little too hard, maybe.

He released a little sigh—a sound of satisfaction or comfort—and kissed her back, his impossibly strong arms wrapping around her like she was his lifeline, pressing her to his body. His beautiful, hard body. Still, it wasn't close enough. Their kiss quickly became desperate and frantic, mouths clashing and moving like the kiss itself was an alive thing—something they could barely control. And then they were backing up into the house, Jezebel shrieking and darting inside when Maisie nearly stepped on her tail, Tyrion wagging his tail as if in approval as he ambled in after them. Jack went to pull away from her to close the door, but she refused, clinging to him, and instead he backed them up so their entwined bodies closed it, then reached out to flip the lock.

"I want you here," he panted.

"Good, because I'm not going anywhere," she said. He'd meant he wanted her against the door, she knew, and God, she wanted that too. But her words meant more than that, and the flashing in his eyes said he knew it. Those eyes saw everything, and right from the beginning, from that first day, they'd seen her.

She reached over to pull the curtains on the sidelight windows flanking the door and then grabbed the hem of his long-sleeved thermal shirt and pulled it over his head, biting her lip at the sight of his chest and his arms, as sculpted as any statue. She'd spent many, many hours dreaming about this— about the beauty of him unclothed—after not having appreciated it enough the one day she'd seen all of him.

"Quid pro quo," he said, reaching around to expertly unzip her dress. His hungry gaze took her in as if she were a feast for the eyes, and it struck her he'd always looked at her like that—even when he'd tried to stay away.

Another maneuver, and her bra joined the dress on the floor.

She reached for his belt, unfastening it as he stared at her with those beautiful dark eyes. Taking in the straining against his pants.

"Please tell me you have a condom."

He gave her a wicked grin that pumped heat through her. "You mean you're not willing to wait for Instacart?"

Afterward, they pulled on their clothes—Adalia's plans would keep Jack's sisters out of the house for another couple of hours, but it was possible someone might show up—and lay on the couch next to the Christmas tree, the twinkle lights casting a warm glow on them. Tyrion had curled up beside the tree, Jezebel perched on top of him like he was an ottoman.

"I'm glad you're here. Obviously. But I feel like I should ask why you're not at the bachelor party," Jack said, playing lazily with a lock of her hair.

"I guess I should be, technically speaking, but it was more important for me to be here with you," she said, turning so she could look at him. "River told me you left."

"Yeah." He sat up, pulling her with him. "Prescott stopped by to cause trouble, and I overheard him and Lee arguing. Turns out Prescott only came to Asheville because he wants to set up roadblocks for the wedding. He doesn't think much of Finn either."

"That's not exactly a shocker. Prescott called River a few days ago, and he basically told him as much."

Everyone knew Prescott was a dick—even she knew that, and she'd never had the displeasure of meeting the man. But she was pretty sure Prescott's dickishness hadn't been what sent Jack running. No, that had something to do with Lee.

"How does Lee fit into this?" she asked softly, reaching up to touch his stubble.

"Honestly, Lee surprised me. He actually stood up for Georgie and Adalia…" He stared off into the distance, his eyes glazing over.

"But?" Because with Lee, of course there had to be a but.

"But then Prescott left, and Lee told me what I already knew. He said I'll never be part of the family no matter how hard I try." He shrugged as if he didn't care, but it obviously stung.

"Well, he doesn't get to decide that," Maisie said tightly. "And he doesn't deserve you. I plan to tell him as much later tonight."

He smiled at her, then leaned in and kissed her neck, nipping a little.

She moaned because it felt good—beyond good—but she pulled back. "We need to talk about this. You said you didn't feel like you belong here, but I have news for you. You already belong. You and Iris. You're part of our crew."

She'd said it to encompass their group of friends. Finn and Adalia, River and Georgie. But she'd also meant her specifically, and the dogs. And she saw again that image of them stringing lights together next Christmas.

His eyes warmed, and he pulled her closer. "Thank you. I was feeling pretty low when I came inside with Tyrion, but as soon as I walked through the door, Jezebel knocked over the ukulele in the living room, and I found myself bringing it outside. Dottie left it on the porch for me a few months ago— one of her just-because gifts."

He traced a finger along Maisie's collarbone. "My grandmother always used to sing with me. I don't buy into Dottie's woo-woo stuff any more than you do, but it was almost like she knew. Anyway, I found myself thinking about Dottie and my sisters." He met her eyes. "About *you*. And I realized that I have the good opinion of everyone who matters. I shouldn't care about Lee any more than I do my father. It's just...I found out about Lee when I was still just a kid. I didn't have a father, and there weren't any other men in my life. So I had this image of a big brother who'd back me up and teach me things. Part of me still wanted it to happen."

"Oh, Jack," she said, and because she needed to, she leaned in and kissed him. "Trust me, I get it. I kept a moth-eaten Santa beard for ten years. And let's not get started on my closets. I'm going to recruit you and Iris to help me go through what's left. I'm pretty sure my Girl Scout badges are in there. It's hard knowing what to hang on to and what to let go."

She was tempted to tell him about her own struggle—about how hard it had been to see River find happiness with someone else. But she didn't want him to misunderstand. Besides, it didn't matter anymore, did it? It was in her past, and she'd moved on.

"I shouldn't have pushed you away because of Iris," he said. "I meant what I said in the note I left you after Dottie's party."

She lifted her brows. "It's a little late for you to tell me you just want to be friends."

"No, not that part of the note," he said, sounding a bit confused. "I'm talking about what I said at the end."

Ah, the mysterious end of the note, which had met its demise in Einstein's digestive system. She told him, and he laughed. "That's the equivalent of saying a dog ate your homework. I figured you weren't interested."

"Oh, I was, but I might not have been ready yet."

He gave her a look, like he maybe wanted to press her on that, but instead he played with another lock of her hair. "Iris will get used to the idea. I think she's mostly just worried that I'll mess things up, and it'll make things weird between the two of you."

"So don't mess things up," she said with a grin. "Speaking of Iris, she gave me a note for you." She got up and grabbed it out of her bag, then handed it over.

A.R. Casella and Denise Grover Swank

He read it, his eyes dark and full of emotion. When he was done, he silently handed it over to Maisie.

Jack–

I wasn't sure I wanted you to date Maisie at first, but that's only because I worried you weren't serious about her. You've never looked at any other woman the way you look at her though, and don't even get me started about the way you went off like a knight on a quest to get those Christmas lights. Maisie deserves the best. And you're the best. I just don't want to lose her. You've convinced me you're serious though, so you better make a move fast. Because people like her are rare.

I know you're worried about finally having a life of your own. Don't be. I'm almost eighteen, Jack, and I don't want you to be left with nothing when I go to college. I'm sorry I was a brat about it in the beginning, but I'm glad you came here to join the brewery. You did the right thing. And Georgie and Adalia aren't nearly as bad as I thought they were. Okay, fine, I'll admit it. They've grown on me.

This is where I should tell you that I got accepted to Northwestern, early acceptance. I know you're probably freaking out about the scholarships I probably wouldn't qualify for. But let's go back to the adult thing. I'm old enough to solve some of my own problems. I know you probably won't approve, but I got in touch with my father. He agreed to pay for my tuition, all of it, as long as I sign a nondisclosure agreement the moment I turn eighteen. Easy, since the last thing I want anyone to do is associate my name with his. I know you turned down Prescott's offer to send you away to school, so you probably won't be happy about this. You'll think I'm doing him a favor, but I wasn't going to claim him anyway. Let him think he won. That's not to say you should do the same thing. Your situation is different, and your deadbeat dad is making life miserable for your other siblings too. You want to fight him? Fight him. No one is as strong as you.

I love you, Jack. But I don't need you to be my father anymore. I'd like you to be my brother instead.

—*Iris*

So *that* was the good news Iris had received.

Maisie glanced up at Jack. His eyes looked glassy, like he was holding back tears. "Are you okay?"

"She's right. About everything. It's hard for me to see her as anything other than a kid. I've always thought things would be so much easier when she could take care of herself, but part of me feels a little lost when I think about her going away to school. Like I don't know who I am anymore without that role."

Which was the story of her life, really.

"But you came here anyway. You came to Asheville to stake a claim on your future. I know how hard that must have been, especially when you thought you'd have to leave her behind." She reached out and smoothed his hair. "After my parents died, I felt like the whole world turned against me. Mary was in her second year of law school, and she was going to leave Virginia so she could come home and take care of Molly and me. Maybe I should have let her, but she was engaged to Glenn already, and it would have totally disrupted her life. I was just partway through a liberal arts degree, and I lived on the other side of town. It had to be me. I *wanted* it to be me. Mary was always the responsible one, but I wanted to show her she didn't need to take it all on her shoulders. But getting Molly through high school, helping her with her college applications, it helped me get through the worst time in my life. I put my grief aside so I could get her through hers."

Suddenly self-conscious—was she talking too much?—she looked into his eyes, but his gaze was locked on her, his attention riveted. "I was only going to take a semester off, but then it became two and three, and then I got the idea for the shelter. By the time Molly left for school, I was fixed on getting the shelter up and running. So I had something else to focus on. I was worried that all the closeness we'd built would leak away, that we wouldn't need each other anymore. But Jack, that part doesn't change. Molly might live across the country, but we'll always have a special relationship because of that time when it was just the two of us against the world. That kind of bond doesn't go away. It's for life."

"You're right." He touched her cheek, his hand impossibly warm. "When did you stop putting it off?"

"Putting *what* off?"

"Your grieving."

The words pierced through her, a ray of light that both hurt and brightened. It made her see what had been happening these last months in a way she previously hadn't. The emotions she'd been experiencing were part of a process that had stalled out years ago.

"I guess part of it is happening now," she admitted.

Clearing out the house. Letting go. Choosing to be happy.

His fingers trailed down to her chin and cupped it. "I'm glad you can be as strong for yourself as you were for your sisters."

"So am I," she whispered. "And I'm proud of Iris for being strong too."

He looked down at the note, and his mouth ticked up into a small smile. "So am I. So damn proud. She's smart, and it was her decision to make."

"And what decision are *you* going to make?" she asked, tilting her head and studying him.

"About Prescott?"

"Yeah, because I'm pretty sure Dottie has some real dirt to dish. And I know exactly where they're meeting and when."

CHAPTER
Twenty-Eight

Jack had never been a fan of sneaking around and secrets, likely because they formed the scaffolding of Genevieve's life. "I'm not hiding behind some bush to eavesdrop on Prescott Buchanan. That would imply I give a shit about what he has to say, and I don't."

"Maybe so," Maisie argued, "but I could tell Dottie has a reason for wanting you there. She may be a little eccentric, but there's always some method to her madness." When he didn't answer, she added, "I think you have this picture in your head of us ducking beneath bushes like someone's nosy neighbor. There's actually a bar behind the greenery. Besides, I owe you a drink."

"We're supposed to be on the brewery tour you planned, which technically qualifies as you giving me a drink."

"Aren't you the least bit curious why Dottie wants us to come?"

She clearly was. It was hard to deny her when she looked at him like that, her emerald eyes sparkling, her mouth twisting with barely contained mischief. And, truth be told, he was a little curious too. Dottie had been with Beau Buchanan for decades. Who knew what kind of dirt she had on Prescott.

A small part of Jack, inherited perhaps from Genevieve and Prescott, longed for the power to put Prescott in his place. In the end, though, he didn't agree because Maisie looked especially sexy when she was up to no good, or because he wanted to ruin his father. He agreed because Prescott was determined to break up Georgie's engagement. If Jack found some dirt on him, he could hold it over his head to get him to leave Georgie and River alone—and Adalia and Finn for good measure.

They got dressed, and he let Tyrion out to pee before he put the pouting dog in his kennel.

"Hey," Jack said as he latched the door and then handed the dog a chew stick through the slats, "if I had my way, I'd be home with you all night. But you can't always get what you want."

Tyrion took the stick and seemed to forget his unhappiness, but Jack's disquiet didn't release its hold so easily. This thing with Maisie was new and exciting, but it still felt fragile. He wanted to let it evolve without bringing his messy family business into it. Then again, his messy family business was part of him. There was no escaping or hiding from it.

When he returned to the living room, she was standing beside the tree, smiling at an ornament Iris had ordered from one of those photo printing websites. It showed a shirtless Jack holding Ruby.

"Can I get one of those?" she asked, turning to him.

He pulled her into his arms. "Why settle for the picture when you can have the real thing?" He kissed her, slow and lazy, taking the time to do it thoroughly, while he pulled her body flush with his. "We don't have to leave," he said. "There are dozens of other locations in this house besides the back of the front door."

"While I'd like to explore all of them with you," she said breathlessly, brushing her fingertips along his cheek, "we can't stay here anyway. The ladies are having a slumber party. We're lucky they didn't walk in on us while we were sprawled out on the sofa."

"Then we can just go over to your place."

Her mouth twisted to one side, and for a moment he thought he had her, but she said, "Later. After we join the rest of the brewery tour."

"You still want to do that?" he asked, surprised.

"Kind of?" She shrugged, then pulled back and grabbed her jacket off the chair where she'd tossed it. "I *did* plan it with Finn, plus I don't want to completely bail on River. What if Lee goes off on him?"

Jack pushed out a sigh. She was right, and he felt like a heel for suggesting they skip it.

"Well, as long as you don't comfort him like you just comforted me, we'll be okay," he teased.

Her eyes widened slightly. She started to say something, but her phone rang. Grimacing, she pulled it out of her jeans pocket.

"It's Dottie." She answered the call and lifted the phone to her ear. "Yes, we're coming. We were just about to leave." She bent down and picked her purse up off the floor. "Okay. We'll hurry." She hung up and snagged Jack's wrist, pulling him toward the door.

They went in her car, leaving his Prius in the driveway. They were both quiet in the car, each of them lost in their own thoughts. Jack didn't want to sit in the same room as Prescott, let alone listen to him talk. He'd prefer to go back to a time when his father was nothing but a bad memory.

Maisie finally broke the silence. "Dottie said dinner was going faster than she'd planned. She escaped to the bathroom to make the call, but they've almost finished eating."

"So they had an entire dinner without discussing whatever she wanted to talk about?"

"She said she wanted to enjoy her meal first."

What could Dottie have to discuss with Prescott that would ruin her meal? She had to be the most patient, understanding, and forgiving person he knew.

Maisie got lucky and found street parking a half block from the restaurant and practically jumped out of the car.

"Come on, Jack!" she said, snagging his hand and sweeping him along toward the entrance. He matched her pace even though it went against his every instinct. He told himself he was doing it for her.

She rushed past the hostess and took him straight to the bar, claiming a high-top table next to a wall of fake greenery. He went for one of the chairs, but she steered him into the other.

A waitress came over to take their orders, and Maisie leaned in to give her drink order in a near whisper.

"Lemon drop martini for me, and…?" She raised an eyebrow to Jack.

"Bourbon. Two fingers. Neat."

The waitress nodded and turned away, while Maisie leaned her ear closer to the plant wall. It would have been adorable if he weren't acutely aware his father sat on the other side.

"How do you know we're at the right table?" Jack asked in a lowered voice.

"Because Dottie told me where to sit," she answered as she tapped her phone a few times, then set it facedown on the table.

Of course she'd planned it down to the table where she wanted them to sit. Maisie had probably texted Dottie that they were in position and ready.

Sure enough, Jack heard Dottie's voice clearly on the other side of the bush 'wall.' "Prescott, I'm sure you're wondering why I invited you to dinner this evening."

"Are you *senile?*" Prescott replied in an arrogant tone. "I've asked this exact question about ten times over the course of the last half hour."

His voice was louder than hers. And sure, he'd probably spoken louder, but from the crisp quality of the sound, Prescott was directly next to him, their seats separated by just the plant. Maisie had pushed him into this chair, which meant Dottie had even planned the *seating.*

"And as I told you, good things come to those who wait," Dottie said cheerfully.

"So something good will come from this?" he asked. "What could *you* possible give *me?*"

"Peace of mind," Dottie said in her soothing voice. "The knowledge that your eldest daughter will be marrying a good man. A man who loves her to the moon and back."

"A man who just happens to be your great-nephew," he sneered. "You're both after my money."

It sounded like Dottie blew a raspberry. "I don't want your money, and River certainly doesn't either. He wants to make a life with the woman he loves. Love makes a person rich, Prescott, not money, but you never have understood that."

"You're a fine one to talk. You stuck to my father for decades, hoping he'd cave and finally marry you. You were after *his* money. My father had many faults, but he was sharp as a tack. He saw you as a gold digger and strung you along, hoping to appease you without marriage."

Dottie let out a hearty laugh. "Oh, Prescott," she said while trying to catch her breath. "That was quite a story for such a droll, unimaginative man."

"You think this is *funny?*" he asked in a tone that probably made his subordinates quiver in their overpriced Italian shoes, but Dottie only laughed again.

"Some parts are humorous, and others are tragic. I still don't understand how the Buchanan good humor passed you by and went straight to your children. Your father was always such fun."

"My daughters might be flighty like their mother, but Lee is exactly like me."

"I wouldn't be so certain of that," she said, her amusement fading. "Lee just needs a chance to breathe." She paused, then said, "And Jack…he's a good man too. Your father tried to push you to have a relationship with your son, but I told Beau it would never work. Especially not with the strings he attached. You're not the kind of man who likes being forced to do anything, even visit your own child."

Beau was the one who'd made Prescott come visit him? That meant Beau had been aware of his existence for far longer than he'd realized.

"I told Beau you had to want it," Dottie continued. "That all you'd do was hurt the poor boy, but he was so insistent. It was one of the few things we disagreed over."

"There were only a few?" he asked in a snide tone.

"Believe it or not, Prescott, your father asked me to marry him many times. I was the one who always turned him down. I needed my independence."

"That, and his money was gone."

"Funny, he asked me while he still had it," she said. "He couldn't bear to ask me again after he gave you money the last time. That was most of what he had left."

Maisie's eyes widened and her gaze pinned Jack. He was just as stunned. Beau had given Prescott most of his money?

"You like to call yourself a self-made man," she said with a hint of judgment, which was more than Jack had ever heard her use, "but I know where you got the money to kick your commercial real estate venture off the ground. You broke your father's heart when you stole your mother's heirloom jewelry."

"She wanted me to have it," he countered.

"To hand it down to your children," she said in a stern tone. "Not to hawk at a pawn shop."

"I didn't take it to a pawn shop. I sold it to an antiquities house that deals with fine jewelry."

"Same difference. Whether they lay in a smudged glass case or on a bed of fine velvet, you sold the things your mother held dear. The pieces she hoped you'd give to your future daughters one day."

"I *did* give it to Georgie and Adalia in a way," he said in a pompous tone. "I invested it into a successful business."

"A business you purposely kept your daughters out of, although you actually did them a favor with that decision," Dottie said. "And if your business is so successful, why did you go to your father on several occasions, asking for money?"

He hesitated. "There were extenuating circumstances."

"Like fraud and misappropriation of funds?" she asked in a direct tone.

Maisie's mouth dropped open, and Jack's heart started hammering in his chest. His father had committed fraud?

Prescott was quiet for several seconds, then said in a tight voice, "Mistakes were made."

"Yes," she said. "That we can agree upon. Mistakes were made all the way around. I told Beau not to give you money the first time, when you and your partner were at risk of being indicted, but he couldn't bear the thought of your children living without you." Her voice broke. "Even then, he hoped you'd be a better father to your children than he had been to you when you were young, but you turned out to be much worse."

"You don't know anything about me," Prescott said in a controlled voice.

"I know more than you realize." She paused. "Did you know that Laura kept in contact with Beau?"

Prescott remained silent.

"They corresponded quite often," Dottie said in a loving tone. "She told him about the children and their activities. She knew that Beau desperately wanted to be part of their lives. It broke her heart that you forbade it."

"My father was *not* a good person."

"Your father had many faults, just like the rest of us. And yes, he was far too absent in your early years while he was setting up his business. When you left, he realized he'd taught you the wrong lessons. Not that hard work reaps great rewards, but that success matters more than family. He knew why you went into commercial real estate. You were looking at the dollar signs."

"There's nothing wrong with making a good living."

"There is if it's at the expense of your relationships with the people you love." Her voice turned sterner. "There is if you do it at the expense of other people."

"You're talking about the deal that went wrong," he said in disgust. "Those people knew there were risks."

"I was speaking of your *children*, Prescott. Especially Jack. That poor boy was saddled with a conniving mother and a bitter, resentful father. But yes, let's address the fraud charges you so narrowly escaped."

Maisie reached across the tabletop and snagged Jack's hand, squeezing it tightly.

"It was all that woman's fault," Prescott sneered.

"Yes, Genevieve was instrumental in that first escapade, but you were a grown man, Prescott. With two young children and an adoring wife."

Another squeeze from Maisie.

His mother had been in on the fraud? He knew it should surprise him, but it didn't. She was always looking for what she thought was the easy way out.

Prescott grunted. "I had two noisy toddlers and a wife who thought I was perfect. I had to provide for them, so I did what I could."

"Laura only wanted you to love her, Prescott," Dottie said quietly. "I read the letters she wrote to Beau. You broke her heart."

"I was never going to be good enough for her," he jeered.

"No," Dottie said, her voice dripping with disappointment. "You never were, only not in the way you think. She didn't want all the money you'd promised her when you married her. She only wanted the good man she saw beneath the bluster. That was the man she married."

Disgust filled Prescott's words. "I am no longer that fool."

"No," Dottie said, her voice breaking. "It's obvious that man is dead. Beau saw it too, and it broke his heart. That was why he didn't give you a thing. He'd already given you practically everything he had, and it was never enough. So whatever he had left went to his grandchildren. He hoped it would help lead them to the truth."

"The truth?" he scoffed. "What truth?"

"That love is the most important thing in the world. More important than money and material things. He discovered that at the brewery, and he hoped his grandchildren would find their place there too."

"The brewery is a waste of time and resources. It would have been far better to sell it."

"Better for you when you thought you were inheriting it," Dottie said, her voice cold. "I know you need the money."

"I don't *need* the money."

"I'm not a fool, Prescott. I know your business is in trouble. Again."

"Did your crystals and your tarot cards tell you that?"

"No," she said, "but a private investigator did." She took a breath. "You're up to your old tricks again, Prescott. Even down to using a young woman to help you commit fraud."

Jack's head was spinning, and every word Dottie said had it spinning faster. Dottie had hired a private investigator? Prescott was committing fraud?

Was Lee part of it too?

"You're bluffing," Prescott said, his tone equally icy, but Jack was sure he heard a tremor in his voice.

"Am I? I have photos." She paused. "Do these help prove my point?"

Maisie removed her hand from Jack's and leaned closer to the wall of greenery, peeking through an opening. She turned to Jack and mouthed, *She really has photos.*

Against his better judgment, Jack peered through a crack in the foliage and saw Prescott pick up several 8x10 photos from the table. He released a growl and ripped them in two, tossing them back down. "This only proves I'm sleeping with her. It doesn't prove anything else."

"Oh, Prescott," Dottie said, sounding close to tears. "Don't you see how far you've fallen if you think breaking your son's heart is a lighter offense than cheating people out of money?"

"According to the law it is."

Prescott was sleeping with Victoria?

Maisie's mouth dropped open, but she quickly recovered and made a retching face. Jack couldn't help but smile. He hadn't officially been introduced to the woman yet, but he knew enough about her to think Prescott deserved her more than Lee did. And that was saying something.

"You never learn," Dottie said, her sternness returning. "I let this go because I'd hoped your father's death would teach you the importance of family. Of love. But one of those photos you destroyed was from just last week. You've learned *nothing*, and it seems you're dead set on crushing the one child who has worshiped you since he could walk."

"What do you want?" Prescott asked. "Money?" He reached into his suit coat pocket and withdrew a checkbook. "I'm prepared to write you a check right now."

Dottie released a bitter laugh. "There you go again, thinking money can buy happiness. I don't want a penny of yours, even if I thought the check would actually clear. The only thing I want is for you to do the right thing. Give Lee his freedom."

"What the hell does *that* mean?"

"It means exactly what you think it does," she said softly.

They stared at each other for several long seconds. Then he scooted his chair back, loudly scraping the floor. "We're done here."

"You and I are done when you make this right," she said, staring up at him as he stood. "I'll give you until the new year to come clean to your children, and if you don't, I'll take what I know to the proper authorities."

He glared at her with so much hate, it was a wonder she didn't turn into a puddle of goo. But Dottie was made of sterner stuff than that. Instead of shooting daggers of hate, her eyes were full of pity. "For once in your life, do the right thing, Prescott. Don't bring Lee down with you."

Jack's heart beat faster again. Lee was in trouble, and against his better judgment, he wanted to help him.

CHAPTER
Twenty-Nine

"Do you think she has three wedding dresses because she's sleeping with three men? One for Lee, one for Prescott, and one for the third guy? Because there would be a strange kind of internal logic to that."

Jack just made a *hm* sound deep in his throat.

"At least he was going to break up with her anyway." She'd explained what Georgie had told her at the Biltmore, although she'd held back from sharing the rest of what they'd discussed. If Dottie hadn't called from the restaurant when she did, Maisie would have told him about River earlier. But now…well, he had enough baggage of his own to deal with at the moment. No need to throw more on the pile, especially since it was a nonissue.

"That's not the part that will upset him most," Jack said quietly.

No. A father's betrayal was much worse than that of a horrible girlfriend you'd already been looking for an excuse to break up with.

Dottie had called them over to the table after Prescott stormed out. From the look on her face, serene and kind of tickled to see them, it wouldn't have surprised Maisie if she'd asked whether they would like to see the dessert menu. Instead, she got up to hug them both, then told Jack in an undertone, "I want you to know that your grandfather very much wanted to know you. Your mother refused his many attempts to get in touch with you. I suspect she thought it would hurt her chances of a…congenial relationship with your father." It was clear she meant *getting money*, but Maisie was glad she hadn't outright said it. Jack had been through enough. After listening to Dottie and Prescott's conversation, he had the look of someone who'd walked away from a car accident in a reflective blanket. "But she told him you wanted nothing to do with him, and I'll admit he'd given up by the time you were an adult. He wasn't proud of that at the end."

"I…I didn't know," he stammered. "Any of it."

Dottie lifted a hand to his cheek. "That's why I'm so glad you made it in time. Now you have somewhere else you need to be." This she said with significance. "It's a short walk."

She'd slid them another set of 8x10s and sent them on their way.

Off they'd marched, following Dottie's tune, because hell, she clearly knew what she was doing. If you had to fall in line behind someone, you could do a lot worse than Dottie Hendrickson.

Maisie pulled Jack to a stop, and his eyes flashed to her mouth before lifting to meet her gaze again. Desire cascaded through her—inappropriate for the moment but undeniable all the same—before she got it under control. People parted to pass them, one person making a rude comment she threw back.

"But you're telling Lee, right?" she asked, guiding him over to the side of the building next to them. "There won't be a better time to talk to him than tonight."

He rubbed between his brows, as if in physical pain, then said, "As much as I don't want to be in the middle of this, I think I have to do something. Georgie and Addy love him."

She heard what he didn't say. Jack might not love him, not yet, but the little boy he'd been still wanted a brother, even after what had happened today. She'd intended to destroy Lee for the way he'd treated Jack earlier, and while she was going to give him a temporary pass—it wasn't every day you found out your girlfriend was cheating on you with your father, who, oh, by the way, was running some kind of scam that could get you arrested—his get-out-of-jail-free card would expire right quick if he crushed that tender part of Jack's soul again.

"Are you ready?" she asked.

And he actually laughed a little, deep in his throat. "Is there any being ready for this, Red?" He lifted a hand and stroked one of her curls, sending a jolt from her scalp down to her core.

"Stay focused. You're distracting me." But as she said so, she pulled him closer, hand on his firm butt, and kissed him.

He didn't pull away, and it felt good, impossibly good, to be out in public with him without worrying who would see.

"That's the kind of distraction I could use," he said when she stepped back. But she headed in the direction of the bachelor party instead of seeking out somewhere they could get horizontal, and he didn't object. He fell in beside her and took her hand, sending a thrill through her. Other than him, when had a man last held her hand? When had she wanted one to?

As they approached Libations, they exchanged a look, Jack getting that closed-down expression he seemed to roll out whenever he didn't know how to process something, that look she'd originally misread as aloof, and she laughed and opened the door. She hadn't let go of his hand. The bouncer,

Ed, was someone she'd known since elementary school, and he grinned as they came inside. With the way the building was designed, a bottleneck with the entrance as the neck, they couldn't see past him.

"We've been expecting you," Ed said. "I hear you're one of the ones who orchestrated this disaster. Fred says you better show up in the morning in a hazmat suit to clean up."

"That bad, huh?"

"I'm less worried about what's happened than what's about to happen. Which one of you knuckleheads thought it made sense to make Lurch the designated driver?"

She exchanged a glance with Jack.

"I guess Dottie can't get it right all the time," he said quietly, with a smirk.

Something crashed in the back, and Ed winced. "Better get that hazmat suit ready. One of those guys looks like he's ready to yack."

"Yeah, yeah," she said, and led Jack into the adjoining room. She *would* help if they needed it, but she was reasonably sure he was messing with her. Just before they reached the main part of the tasting room, she glanced at Jack. "What do you think we'll find back there?"

His lips lifted slightly. "Maybe Lurch made up with the donkey guy, and they decided to recreate the petting zoo."

"Or Stella came and she decided to do a live-drawing class. In the nude."

He cringed.

"Well, there's only one way to find out who's right," she said brightly.

They turned the corner, and Maisie burst out laughing. The place was somewhat crowded, but a bubble of space had been left around their group. Lurch's face had been marked up to look like a goat, and while the rest of their crew had tasting glasses, he had four different beers arrayed in front of him and was halfway through three of them. The group was gathered around the table next to the dart board, which had been plastered over with a taped-up picture of Stella hugging a goat. Darts were embedded in the wall on all sides of it, but none had made it onto the picture. Josie, who was for some reason in a fairy costume, stood next to Lurch, soothing him by the looks of it, and River sat a couple of seats down, surrounded by familiar faces from Buchanan Brewery and Big Catch. He looked like he was having a good time, at least.

"I should have bet money on it," she said. "Live art show. Although something clearly happened between Lurch and Stella." She shrugged. "It's surprising it lasted this long. Where's Finn?"

It was then she realized Jack wasn't looking at the sideshow at all. His gaze was on Finn and Lee. Lee was…was he *dancing*? A Beach Boys song was playing over the speakers, but no one else was swaying to the music, only a very, very drunk blond man who looked surprisingly different from the stick-up-his-butt stiff she'd seen on that Thanksgiving video call. Finn stood next to him, bobbing to the music a little, a slightly nervous look on his face.

She should check in with River first. It was his bachelor party, and she was supposed to be his best man. Co-best man. But he had a big grin on his face—a real grin, not one of his fake smiles—and the days of codependency were over. She and River both had new commitments. New people in their lives.

So she squeezed Jack's hand and led him through the crowd, releasing him when they reached the swaying pair.

When he saw her, Finn's eyes lit up like he was a kid who'd just found his mother in a crowded shopping mall. "You're here!"

She leaned in and hissed in his ear, "I said get him drunk or get him out. I didn't say get him so sloppy he's going to puke."

He shrugged helplessly. "He wouldn't stop. Like I said, something's going on with him."

Jack had come to a stop beside her. He was looking at Lee with a helpless expression that she understood all too well. They'd come here to talk to a sober person. What were they supposed to do now?

"It's you," Lee said, coming to a stop. He put a hand on Jack's shoulder. "My brother from a different mother." He paused. "Did you know the model for that awful painting at my sister's house is here? He's the designated driver, but he's been pounding beer for longer than I have." He started laughing, and the waft of alcohol from him made Maisie cringe. His mood turned more serious as he stared at Jack. He was looking at his face like he was searching for some resemblance between them. Their coloring was different, but it was there, undeniable as their identical noses. "Finn's right. I shouldn't have said that to you earlier. I don't know you, but you don't know me either. That conversation you overheard was personal."

If he had trouble with near strangers knowing his personal business, he wasn't going to enjoy talking about what they'd overheard at Shebeen.

A pause, into which Lee hiccuped. "I didn't expect to meet you like this."

Jack raised his brows. "Oh? I was under the impression you would have preferred not to meet me at all."

A shadow passed over Lee's face. "I almost went to your bar half a dozen times on my last business trip to Chicago."

Shock filled Jack's eyes. "But you didn't?"

"No, I was…" Lee trailed off, looking like he'd lost the point, or maybe like he didn't want to admit to his little brother that he'd been scared. And for the first time, Maisie felt something like sympathy toward him. Maybe he wasn't what he seemed, just like Jack wasn't the humorless, straightlaced man she'd taken him for.

"Why don't you take him to the bar?" she suggested, gesturing toward it.

"Do you really think more alcohol's the solution here?" Finn asked in an undertone.

She let out a little huff of laughter. "In lieu of one of Dottie's miracle hangover cures, I was going to suggest coffee."

"Who are you?" Lee asked, shifting his attention to Maisie. "You were at Thanksgiving, weren't you?"

Before she could confirm it, Jack put his free hand on her hip. "She's my girlfriend."

He said it hastily, then threw her a look, obviously worried about how she might react.

She just leaned into him and said, "I also have a name. I'm Maisie."

"Oh, you're the one who—"

Alarm knifed through her. Had Georgie told him something about her? Did he know she'd had feelings for River? She certainly didn't want Jack to find out from his drunk-as-a-skunk half-brother.

"—who's friends with Adalia," he finished.

The relief was real. And when Finn pulled her away, giving her a pointed look that was probably obvious to everyone, she let him.

"We need to go check on River!" he announced, speaking louder and more emphatically than was necessary.

Jack gave her a look like maybe he didn't want her to go, but he didn't attempt to pull her back or refuse. In fact, he hooked an arm around Lee's shoulders and helped him stagger over to the bar.

Maybe Jack would get enough coffee into Lee that he could relay the bad news. Or if their talk went really poorly, and he was feeling spiteful, he could just tuck the photos in his jacket into Lee's pocket to give him a surprise for later.

She chuckled to herself at the thought, which was the kind of thing Molly would have come up with as punishment for a vindictive ex. Oh God, Molly was going to be pissed, but Maisie couldn't let her write about this train wreck, even if the names were left out. It had become too personal for Jack.

"You think he's going to be okay?" Finn asked nervously as soon as Jack and Lee were out of hearing.

"Which one?"

"Both of them, I guess. I feel kind of bad about Lee. I gave him some high-gravity beers back at the house. He started drinking hard after Jack left. I think he felt guilty about how things went down...and he just kept going once we got here." He shot her a glance. "From what he said, I take it things aren't going great with Victoria."

She stifled a laugh.

Understanding flashed in his eyes, and he pulled her to a stop. "I can tell you know something, and I absolutely do *not* want you to tell me. I don't need any more secrets."

"Fair play," she said, raising a hand as her white flag. "Suffice it to say that their romance won't be long for this world. Dottie saw them breaking up in, like, five cups of tea."

"Good," he said decisively. "Because Addy hates her, and she sounds awful. Lee might be a stuffed shirt...well, most of the time"—he waved in the direction of Jack and Lee, who was singing loudly to Billy Joel's "Movin' Out"—"but he's not half bad."

"A rousing endorsement."

He shrugged. "You know what I mean."

"Has River been having fun?"

"Yeah." He glanced at the bar. "All of the guys from Buchanan and Big Catch showed up. It's a good crowd."

Something about the way he said it, and the look of little-boy longing he shot at the guys who used to idolize him, told her that some of the guys in the beer community still held a grudge against him for selling Big Catch Brewing to a corporate overlord.

"Still giving you a hard time?"

Another shrug. "You and River forgave me. That's what matters. Maybe they'll get over it too someday."

He started walking again, and she fell in beside him and gave him a little nudge. "Big talk for the guy who always wants everyone to like him. Being in love suits you."

He nudged her back, his eyes bright. "How about you?"

"Tsk, tsk. You said no secrets."

He looked like he was going to say more—of course he did, Finn always wanted to say more—but they'd reached Lurch's spot at the end of the table. He was talking to Josie while she swung a crystal pendant back and forth listlessly. Either she was bored or she was trying to read some sort of fortune for him. Maybe both.

"She drew the face on in permanent marker. Permanent!" he said, then paused to take a slug of the third beer on his makeshift tasting tray. "And she didn't tell me she was moving on until *after* she took pictures."

Maisie gave a shudder and glanced at Finn, who was steadfastly staring straight ahead.

"She's not the one for you, Lurch," Josie said. "The pendant never lies." She paused dramatically, then added, "She left you for a fireman, didn't she?"

"How did you know that?" he asked with wide eyes. The goat horns drawn onto his head winged upward.

"Lurch…" Finn interjected, "you've told all of us at least five times."

But Maisie's mind had skipped back to another time, another fortune. What was it Josie had said to her? *You're in love with someone, but he has no idea. He's going to marry someone else, and you're going to die alone.* She'd assumed it was about River, but what if it was Jack she was going to lose?

She gave herself a mental shake as she made her way to River. She'd really lost it if she was starting to look to Josie for spiritual guidance.

River turned as she approached him, and his face split into a familiar smile. She'd told Dottie once that one of her favorite things about River was that he had a different smile for every person, and this was hers—a little crooked, one side higher than the other, a flash of teeth. It was impossibly dear to her, just like he was, and she was relieved they'd aired out their dirty laundry without destroying their friendship.

They hugged each other, both of them holding on for longer than they normally would.

"The man of the hour!" she said, pulling back. "Are you having fun?"

He glanced around at the friends gathered around him. "Yeah, this is awesome, but I'm glad you're here. It felt like something was missing."

She knew he was saying it to reassure her that they were good, that their friendship was intact, and she appreciated it.

He glanced around the bar. "Speaking of. Where are Jack and Lee?"

"Talking it out," she said. "I hope. Either that, or they're in the alleyway having a fistfight that Jack is absolutely guaranteed to win."

He smirked a little. "Yeah, I can't imagine Lee getting his fists bloody." He nodded at Finn. "Did you tell her about what happened at the house earlier?"

"Which part?" Finn asked.

"About the agreement, I mean." He glanced at Maisie and made a face. "I didn't mention it earlier because—"

No need to let the world know about their conversation.

"Um. No," she interrupted. "What agreement?"

He glanced around again, then motioned for them to move to an empty spot at the end of the bar.

It didn't take him long to explain what Lee had asked for, and why. By the time he finished, Maisie was about ready to crack Lee like a nut, Victoria or no Victoria.

"And you let this happen?" she asked, turning on Finn.

He gave her a helpless puppy dog look that might have worked on Adalia but surely was not going to work on her.

Why hadn't Jack told her?

Because it's in his best interest for River to sign those papers.

If River didn't sign, then Jack could lose his stake in the brewery and possibly his job. He wouldn't, of course—River would never pull his job out from under him—but Jack didn't know him like she did. He'd pinned all his hopes on the brewery, and he didn't want to see them come tumbling down.

"I don't care," River said. "I really don't. If this is what it takes to get Lee's support, I'm all for it. God knows Georgie's father is still doing everything he can to tear us apart."

More than he even knew.

She just nodded distantly and turned from them to search the room for Jack and Lee. But her search was interrupted when she spotted someone else she knew—Blue, sitting with a brown-haired man in a brown shirt and khaki pants. Was she on a *date*? She didn't like beer, so it was the last place Maisie would have thought to look for her.

Blue hadn't been sharing her usual awful dating stories on the group chat she had with Maisie and Adalia. But if she was dating someone, why hadn't she told them?

She could practically see Mary giving her that disapproving look.

Because people worry you'll make fun of them, Maisie. You and Molly need to work on your people skills.

Really, fair enough, Phantom Mary. She and Adalia had made a few jokes about the Bad Luck Club—they'd sent increasingly wild theories about what it was—and Blue seemed pretty sensitive about it. Maybe this guy was someone she'd met there.

"Hey, guys," she said. "I'll be a minute. I'm going to go say hi to Blue and then find Jack and Lee."

River gave her a look. "Be gentle. Like I said, I'm okay with this. The guy's kind of a dick, but he didn't ask for anything I wasn't willing to give."

She squeezed his shoulder—"I know"—and thought, but didn't say, that it hadn't been Lee's right to ask.

"Should we head back over?" Finn asked, gesturing to the table they'd left. Maisie had to smile to herself because it was clear from the way he said it that he really would rather not.

"Not yet," River said. "Let's stay over here awhile and talk."

Maisie made her way over to Blue, whose eyes widened when she caught sight of her. There was a nearly untouched beer in front of her, but the man she was with had finished three quarters of his pour.

Blue didn't seem happy to see her. No, that wasn't quite true. Her first reaction had been the kind of happiness you weren't expecting, but it had given way to nerves.

"Hey, Blue," Maisie said as she got closer. "I guess I forgot to tell you the bachelor party would be stopping here tonight. Surprise!"

"Oh, are you with that group over there?" the guy asked, nodding toward the bar. He didn't say it with a tone, not really, but something in his face said he disapproved.

"Yeah, that's us," she said, holding out a hand and reminding herself to reserve judgment. "I'm Maisie."

He shook her hand. "Dan." He glanced at Blue. "And you're a friend of Blue's?"

Blue gave a pained smile. "Yeah, a good friend." An awkward pause hung between them for a moment. Then Blue said, "Hey, Dan? Would you mind getting me a glass of water from the bar?"

"No, not at all," he said, getting up. He was a tall man with dishwater brown hair and brown eyes fringed with long, sandy lashes. Good-looking, but in a somewhat generic way she wouldn't have expected from a man who'd gained Blue's interest. He turned to Maisie on his way past and said, "It was nice to meet you."

It kind of rubbed her the wrong way, like he expected her to be gone by the time he got back, but she just nodded and said "likewise" before turning to Blue with raised eyebrows.

"New boyfriend?"

Blue gestured for her to sit. Biting her lip, she said, "Sort of. We've been seeing each other for a few weeks."

A flash of hurt must have shown in her eyes, because Blue lifted a hand. "I'm sorry. It's just...I was nervous about introducing him to you and Addy. He's not my usual type, but the Bad Luck Club has helped me realize my old patterns weren't working for me." She waved toward Dan, who didn't stand out from the crowd of men he'd disappeared into. "Dan's a good guy. He hasn't asked to meet my friends or see my studio. He lets me be my own person, and that's what I need right now."

It was on the edge of Maisie's tongue to say it wasn't necessarily a great sign that he didn't want to take part in those aspects of her life. Although codependency was a trap she understood, it was possible to be part of someone's life without taking it over, and vice versa. But it wasn't really her business to say so, and she didn't want to give Blue any more reasons to pull away from her. From now on, any theorizing about the Bad Luck Club would have to be strictly limited to texts between her and Addy.

"Addy and I have been giving you a hard time, but we care about you. We want you to be happy," she said. "And if you like Dan, we absolutely want to hear about him. Even if he has a doll collection like the last guy you went out with."

Blue's mouth twitched. "No doll collection to speak of. He might be the most normal guy I've ever met."

Which didn't bode well for their relationship, in Maisie's opinion—Blue was one of the more unique souls she knew. But it didn't seem like the right time to say so. Maisie knew when to shut up—she just didn't often choose to.

"Well, I'd love to get to know him. Are you bringing him to the engagement party tomorrow?"

Blue played with her full glass of beer without taking a sip. "I wasn't planning on it. Do you think that would be okay?"

"More than okay. Jack got plenty of food for the party, and I've heard there's even some wine." She grinned at the full beer glass. "Plus, I'm sure Addy will want to meet him too."

Blue glanced behind her, her eyes widening. "Speaking of Jack...are you here with him?"

Before Maisie could answer, Jack came up beside her, Lee with him. If they'd had a fistfight, there were no marks she could see. Jack's expression was closed down, and it amused her to see Lee's look was identical. Still, she was somewhat pissed at both of them.

"Hi, Blue," Jack said. Then he turned to Lee, presumably to introduce him to Blue. But just then, Lee doubled over and vomited on Blue's shoes.

CHAPTER
Thirty

Jack jumped backward to escape the splatter, then felt like a jerk because poor Blue had gotten the brunt of the mess.

Blue let out a shriek, which caused Lee to cringe and back up himself, only he nearly fell on his ass in the process. Jack reluctantly reached out and grabbed his arm to steady him.

Maisie shot Jack a dark scowl as she got to her feet. "Get him out of here. I'll meet you at the car."

Jack didn't ask where she was going because it was obvious. She started dragging Blue toward the restrooms. Blue still hadn't said anything, but from the look on her face, it was unlikely she'd ever forget meeting Lee Buchanan.

"Shit," Lee mumbled, watching them hurry off. "Didn't mean to do that."

"God, I hope not," Jack said with a wry grin. "Let's get you outside."

Lee's unfocused gaze swung toward him, and his gray pallor made Jack tighten his hold on his bicep and drag him out the back door, rather than going the longer route through the front, in the event he yacked again.

It was a good call, because Lee bent over at the waist and vomited again in the alley four feet from the door. Jack wished he'd thought to grab the bottle of water he'd purchased for his brother only a few minutes ago. But Lee had promptly set it down and stumbled over to hug a man he'd mistaken for an old frat buddy. Only the man was in his seventies and sporting a T-shirt that read *Proud Liberal Snowflake.*

Jack had glanced away for a split second, looking for Maisie, and saw her and River hugging at the bar. It seemed to go on for too long, and there was emotion glimmering in her eyes, and for a split second he felt a stab of jealousy.

What the hell was wrong with him? River was marrying his sister, for God's sake, and he and Maisie were friends. Except a little voice in his head suggested his early suspicions had been right, and there were more layers to their relationship than either of them let on. That little voice still hadn't totally shut up, even after the situation with Lee had required him to rip his attention away. The older gentleman, who looked like he'd lived most of his life in the sun, told him his name was Tony, not Tripp, and he'd sooner burn Columbia down than go to school there. Lee had laughed and slapped the man on the shoulder a little too hard and said in all seriousness, "Thank God. I wondered why your face looked like a raisin." The bottle of water had been a casualty of the need to make a quick escape before Tony decked Lee.

Now, still hovering over the mess, Lee asked, "Why're you being so nice to me?"

"Because Addy would hate it if I left you like this."

"So you're doing this for my sister?" Lee asked with a hint of bitterness.

"*Our* sister. Partly." He paused, then added, "But I also have a soft spot for drunk losers, so there's that too."

Lee's gaze jerked up, fury in his eyes, but then he saw Jack's wry grin and his anger faded. "I guess there's some truth to that."

As much as Jack would love to rub in the fact that Lee wasn't looking so great right now, he took pity on him. It was obvious the guy was miserable—not just tonight, but in general—and for some reason, he found himself feeling brotherly. Maybe it was what Lee had said earlier about wanting to look for him in Chicago. Or the realization that he wasn't the only lost one and never had been. "Let's walk around to the front and meet Maisie so we can get you back to the hotel."

"Hotel?" Lee shouted, his voice unnaturally loud, as he stood upright and started to wobble. "It's too damn early to call it a night. I'm fine now. Let's go get another drink!"

"The only drink you need is more water. Come on." He grabbed his upper arm again and started leading him around the building.

"So you've got a girlfriend, bro?" Lee asked as he stumbled on a crack in the asphalt and nearly fell on his face. "My bad."

Jack released a snort. "Yeah, *bro.*"

And he had to question his sanity for not being in bed with her instead of here, rescuing the man who'd crushed him only hours earlier.

Lee came to a stop and grabbed the front of Jack's shirt, trying to maintain eye contact but failing badly since he could hardly keep his eyes open. "Let me give you some big brother advice."

His hand tightened, and he pulled Jack closer. The combined smell of beer and vomit nearly made Jack sick too.

"Don't trust her, bro," Lee said. "They convince you that you need them, then they cheat on you."

Little did Lee know, and while part of Jack longed to rip off the Band-Aid and tell him what he knew, now was not the time. Jack wasn't sure Lee would even remember once he sobered up.

"Yeah," Jack said with a bitter laugh. "You don't know the half of it. Come on, let's get you to the car."

Lee continued to mumble about women and cheating, then added, "Don't build your life on a lie, bro. Don't do it."

"Lie?" Jack asked, unable to stop himself as they rounded the corner to the street. "What lie?"

"That he…" Lee violently shook his head and nearly fell over again.

Jack grabbed his arm and righted him. Did Lee know about their father's misdeeds?

"Did you two take the scenic route?" Maisie called out, standing next to her car with the rear door open. She'd spread out some kind of tarp on the back seat that draped onto the floor. When Jack gave her a questioning look, she shrugged and flashed him a completely unselfconscious grin. "I'm used to hauling sick animals around."

"I am not a sicko." Lee pointed a finger at her face but misjudged his aim, poking her in the nose.

She easily batted it away with a short laugh. "Whatever, get in the car."

The two of them managed to get him belted into the back seat, but he was already slumped over and snoring by the time they closed the door.

"Do you even know where they're staying?" Maisie asked. "I could call Addy, but I'd hate to ruin her night."

Disappointment washed through him, but he knew what he needed to do. "Yeah, they're at the Grove Park Inn, but we can't drop him off like this."

"You want to take him back to your place?" she asked in disbelief. "*That* would definitely ruin Addy and Georgie's night."

"No, not my place..." he said slowly.

Understanding spread over her face. "Oh."

"It's a big ask, Red."

She studied him for a moment, and he was certain she was going to say no, but then she placed a soft kiss on his lips and stared up at him. Her eyes were always so expressive. Mischievous. Playful. Fierce. Angry. And now they looked adoring. He knew better than to think she was the kind of woman who gave out that kind of look often. When had he gotten so lucky?

"Do you have any idea how sexy a man who cares for wounded creatures is?"

"Lee's not a—" he started to say, then stopped. Lee was probably the walking definition of a wounded man. He ran a hand over his head in frustration. "Sorry about tonight. You can just drop us off at a motel. A cheap one's fine. It's not like Little Lord Fauntleroy will notice until morning."

She grinned at the nickname. "No, we'll go back to my place, but I might insist on putting him out in the playhouse where I keep the other sick animals."

He lifted his hand to her face, tucking an unruly red curl behind her ear. "No, you won't."

"Okay, I won't, but don't tell anyone. I'd hate to lose my rep as a hard-ass."

He laughed, sweeping her into a hug. A hug now, holding hands earlier. Jack's other relationships hadn't been like this. He'd never felt this pull to be physically close to a woman unless it was going to lead somewhere. But Maisie had always felt more like a partner than just a lover.

The thought caught him off guard, but as the idea settled in, he wasn't all that surprised. What was it Iris had said in her note? *You've never looked at any other woman the way you look at her.*

When he pulled back, he stared into her eyes in amazement, and a certainty he'd never felt before filled him—Maisie O'Shea was the one for him. It was much too early to tell her that, but he knew it to the marrow of his bones. Hope and peace settled in, making him feel like he'd finally found where he belonged.

Once Maisie started driving, he texted Iris to let her know he'd gotten her note and how much he appreciated her approval and support. He also let her know that he wouldn't be home until morning, but he was only a text or phone call away if she needed him.

I'm fine! she sent back. *I SERIOUSLY don't want to think about what you two are up to, but I don't want to hear from you until tomorrow, young man!*

Next he sent a group text to Georgie and Adalia, telling them that Lee was hanging out with him for the night and he'd explain everything tomorrow.

Lee slept the entire way to Maisie's house, but he woke up when Jack roused him, then stumbled upstairs to a spare bedroom Maisie directed him to over Einstein's barking.

"Is that a coyote?" he asked sleepily as Jack helped him into bed. Maisie came in a few minutes later, equipped with a glass of water and some aspirin—along with a small bucket—and they made sure he knew where to find the bathroom.

Then she linked her hand with Jack's and led him to her room, shutting the door behind them. They stood in silence in the middle of her room, the soft light of the bedside lamp spilling around them.

His mind skipped back to that lingering moment between River and Maisie earlier, like a broken record, but he knew he was being foolish. She was here with him now, staring at him with desire. She wouldn't want him like this if she had a thing for River.

"I like what you did with the place," Jack said, gesturing to the bed.

She grinned and reached for the button on her blouse. "Wait until you feel how comfortable the mattress is."

He turned serious. "Maisie, I'm sorry how tonight turned out."

"It's not over yet." She pulled her shirt over her head.

His gaze landed on her lace-covered breasts, and he instantly hardened. Earlier he'd been consumed by passion, but now he was consumed with something deeper he couldn't name.

They made love slowly, and he looked deep into her eyes as he entered her, wanting to take in every part of her. She seemed to sense the shift, gently cupping his face as though he were something to be treasured. Afterward, she lay in his arms, her head on his chest, and he thought, *I could get used to this*.

———————————

Lee was slow to wake up the next morning, and when he stumbled downstairs at around nine-thirty, his hair stuck up like a porcupine's quills, only at odd angles.

"Coffee?" he groaned.

Jack and Maisie sat on the sofa, sides pressed together, with their own steaming cups. Einstein was curled up against Jack's right side—much to Maisie's amazement—and Chaco was lying on his lap. Both dogs lifted their heads to study Lee,

Einstein releasing a growl in his throat that had Maisie putting her hand on his collar.

She flicked a direct gaze up to Jack, and he restrained a groan as he gathered Chaco in his arms and got to his feet, setting the little dog on the sofa next to Maisie before he followed his brother into the kitchen. He poured Lee a cup of coffee, using the biggest mug in the cabinet, and sat him down at the table.

Showtime.

"You need more aspirin?" Jack asked, refilling his own cup and putting off the inevitable for a few moments. He and Maisie had discussed how to handle this while lying in bed this morning. There was no perfect time to do it, and while Jack would have preferred to wait until Lee's head wasn't pounding, he didn't want Lee to go back to his cheating girlfriend—or their father—without the full knowledge of what was going on.

"No," Lee said, shaking his head, then wincing. "Mamie left a bottle on the nightstand."

"*Maisie*," Jack said, taking a seat opposite him. Einstein sauntered in and spun around in a circle next to Jack's chair before plopping on the floor at his feet. He gave Lee a glare, as if to warn him not to mess with Jack.

Lee winced again. "Sorry. Most of last night is fuzzy."

"What do you remember?"

"I remember going to a few breweries. I remember a guy marked up to look like a goat. There was someone who looked like my friend Tripp if he'd turned into a raisin. I remember dancing—oh God!—and then I threw up on some poor woman." He looked up at Jack in dismay. "Tell me most of that didn't happen."

"I wasn't there for much of it, so I don't know what happened before I showed up. Unfortunately, everything you just listed is true."

Lee covered his face with his hand and groaned. "I don't do this type of thing. Like *ever*."

"Maybe that's why you went so hardcore," Jack said, unable to stop himself from grinning. "It was about time you let down your hair." He gestured to Lee's bedhead and made a face. "So to speak."

Lee reached up to the top of his head and felt his hair, then rolled his eyes. Which brought on another groan.

"Lee," Jack said, his stomach tight with anxiety. This could go one of two ways—the first, Lee could refuse to believe him, evidence be damned, and leave in a fury, possibly punching him on his way out. Or he might accept the situation as it was without argument. Unfortunately, Jack didn't know him well enough to guess which scenario was more likely. He'd considered calling Addy and letting her know what he and Maisie had discovered, but Dottie had asked him and Maisie to be there last night, not Jack and his sisters, and that had to mean something.

Lee's face lifted, and the lost look in his eyes almost stopped Jack from continuing.

Almost.

"There are some things you should know," Jack said. He'd struggled with where to start, ease his way in or go straight for the jugular? There was a very good chance Lee might storm out, so he'd decided to lead with the part that could possibly keep him out of prison and reveal the rest in descending order.

He told Lee about Dottie instructing Jack and Maisie to sit behind the plant wall separating the dining area from the bar on the other side. "Your dad—*our* dad—has done some bad things, Lee. Both in the past and apparently in the present."

Lee shook his head. "Look, I know he's an asshole."

"No, this is more than just him being an asshole. I'm talking illegal stuff."

Lee's face paled. "What do you mean?"

Jack told him about Dottie and Prescott's discussion about Beau bailing him out decades ago because he'd committed fraud.

"With your mother?" Lee asked in disgust. "It was probably all her doing and he got caught up in it. Genevieve is a beautiful woman. I'm no fool. I know that's his weakness. I can see him falling for it."

Jack wasn't sure what to be more astounded by—that Lee knew what his mother looked like, or that he was trying to excuse their father's behavior.

"It wasn't the only incident, Lee," Jack said with a patience he didn't feel. To his surprise, he didn't feel vindictive or angry. Mostly he felt pity. "There were more occurrences. Sounds like Beau ended up giving him most of his money to keep him out of jail."

Lee shook his head. "No. Beau hated Dad. Refused to give him any help at all. Dad had to do it all on his own, but he said it made him a better man."

"Prescott Buchanan is a liar," Jack said. "He'd be nowhere without Beau. He practically admitted it himself."

"I'm supposed to just take your word for this?" Lee sneered. "How do I know this isn't your way of getting back at me for treating you like shit last night?"

"That's not my style, but I realize you don't know me well enough to know that," Jack said quietly. "You don't need to take my word for it, though. We recorded the conversation."

Lee went still. "Against my father's knowledge? That's illegal."

"No," Jack said, "North Carolina is a one-party consent state, which means only one person has to give consent, and Dottie asked Maisie to record it." Maisie had looked it up this morning to be sure it was safe to mention.

Lee studied him for a long second, then snapped, "So where's this recording?"

Jack pulled his phone out of his pocket and unlocked the screen. Maisie had shared it with him in the cloud, and he had the audio file queued up. "Before I play this, there are a couple of things you need to know. Your father's in trouble again. Legal trouble, and you're going to be caught up in it, and there's something else—"

"Just play the damn tape!" Lee shouted.

"Your funeral," Jack muttered, then hit play and set the phone on the table between them.

Parts of the file were hard to hear, but Prescott's booming voice had helped ensure the message was conveyed.

Lee listened with a flat expression while Dottie and Prescott discussed River and Dottie's relationship with Beau, but he perked up as the discussion turned to his family. He made a strange face when Prescott said that Lee was exactly like him. Flinched when Prescott admitted that mistakes had been made in connection with the fraud charges. Stiffened when Prescott and Dottie discussed Lee's mother. But when Dottie said that Prescott was up to his old tricks again with a new young woman, Lee's mouth dropped open in surprise.

"What woman?" he whispered, leaning closer to the phone.

There was silence and then Prescott's denial. Next were Dottie's fateful words, "Oh, Prescott. Don't you see how far you've fallen if you think breaking your son's heart is a lighter offense than cheating people out of money?"

Prescott answered, "According to the law it is."

Lee started to stand, then sat back down, his jaw tightening as he listened to the rest, until Dottie said, "Give Lee his freedom."

Their father threatened to leave, and Dottie issued her threat to go to the authorities if he didn't come clean by the end of the year. Then she implored Prescott not to bring Lee down with him. And the recording ended.

Lee was quiet for several long seconds. Then he swallowed. Still staring at the phone, he asked hesitantly, "What did he say to that?"

"After Dottie asked him to save you?" Jack asked, his heart breaking for his brother. Lee might be an asshole, but his entire life was being ripped apart. "Nothing. He got up and walked away."

Lee's gaze lifted to Jack's. "And the woman? Do you know who she is?"

Jack wasn't sure this was the right move, but Dottie had set this all in motion, and he'd known her for long enough to realize she knew what she was doing. She was right more often than she was wrong. So he pulled the photos out from under a stack of books on the table and slid them toward Lee.

Lee spread them out on the table, staring at them with a blank expression. The photos depicted a couple in the throes of passion, in varying states of undress, but it was obvious the woman was Victoria and the man was Prescott.

"I see." Clearing his throat, Lee got to his feet. He glanced off toward the living room, and Jack followed his gaze, not surprised that Maisie was nowhere in sight. They'd both agreed that Jack should be the one to handle this. Alone.

Lee started toward the front door.

"Where are you going, Lee?" Jack asked, concerned.

"I need to think."

"But you don't have a car. Let me drive you to the hotel."

Lee started to speak, then clenched his fists and released a bitter laugh. "That is the last place I need to go."

Jack understood that. "Then let me take you to the house."

"And tell our sisters about all of this?" Panic filled his eyes. "Do they know?"

"No," Jack said, catching on to how Lee had called them *our sisters*. "No. We recorded that last night. I tried to come straight to you to let you know, but you weren't in any condition to hear it."

Lee stared absently in the direction of the fireplace. "I'd noticed things that were off, but Dad always dismissed them. Dismissed *me*."

The word was bitter, and Jack wondered what kind of emotional abuse Lee had endured trying to gain their father's approval.

"I'm sorry, Lee."

Lee's gaze swung toward him. "Why'd you tell me this? Why not go to Addy and Georgie and have a good laugh over how stupid I am?"

"Addy and Georgie would never do that. They'll be worried sick. As for me, again, that's not my style. You may have been an asshole to me, but you definitely don't deserve this. I don't know what kind of legal trouble your father's in, but you can try to save yourself. Maybe go to the authorities and turn state's evidence or something."

"Turn on my dad?" Lee asked in disbelief.

"Lee, he's already turned on *you*."

He stared at Jack for another long second, then nodded. "Right."

And Lee opened the door and walked out.

CHAPTER
Thirty-One

Maisie's heart gave a satisfied thump as Einstein padded into the kitchen after Jack. When had Einstein ever left her for anyone? Jack had won him over thoroughly, it seemed.

You and me both, Ein.

Once the brothers were settled in the kitchen, she went upstairs, Chaco cradled in her arms, and headed to her bedroom. She left the door open a crack so she'd hear if the bad news sent Lee into some sort of ballistic rage. Not that Jack would need her help defending himself—those arms would protect him better than the baseball bat behind her bed—but even so. She'd whip that bat out if she needed to. Lee might be Jack's family, but she didn't trust him.

In the meantime, she figured she'd call Molly.

Her sister had already texted her this morning, even though it was only something like eight o'clock in Seattle. *You're killing me. Literally killing me. I need to know what's happening!!!!*

Which was a bit much considering Maisie had sent her several text updates the previous night, from *So, I see what you mean about having sex against a door* to *OMG, Jack's brother just puked on Blue's shoes.* But her little sister had always liked a good story, even before she'd become a blogger, and truth be told, she felt a powerful urge to see Molly's face. The previous day had changed her in ways she hadn't thought a single day could. It had felt...transformative, and she wanted to talk it out.

She set up her laptop on the desk near the window and dialed Molly, Chaco resting her paws on the edge of the desk as if she wanted to take part in the conversation. It came as no surprise when Molly answered right away.

"Thank God you called me, Chaco," she said with a wicked grin. "I was beginning to feel neglected. You love your aunt Molly, don't you?"

Chaco wagged her tail agreeably. She and Molly had actually never met—it had been much too long since Molly had come home, and Chaco was a recent addition—but they'd become steadfast video chat buddies.

"Should I leave the two of you alone?" Maisie asked, though she couldn't help but grin back.

"Just spill it. All of it," Molly said, making a sweeping motion with her hand. She was holding the phone with the gesticulating hand, and the picture went wild before settling back on her face. "Chaco's with me on this one. She wants to know what Mama's been up to."

"Only if you tell me about the real date you mentioned. The one that's not for the Twelve Dates of Christmas."

Molly pulled a face. "He seemed perfect until he tried to recruit me for his cult."

"You're exaggerating. Like with Blake and all his underwear."

"That was no joke," Molly said seriously. "Blake probably bears sole responsibility for one of our landfills." She shrugged. "Maybe you're right about the veterinarian, but I'm mighty suspicious about those self-betterment groups that peddle sunshine and probably sell uppers on the side. But I don't want to talk about me for once. I need this epic story you've been teasing me with for hours."

Molly's description made her think about Blue, who'd been quite rightfully horrified by the whole puking incident. Dan had been waiting with an aggrieved expression when they got back from the bathroom. He'd gotten Blue another beer on top of her untouched one, which seemed to represent a certain hardheadedness. He didn't want to know much about Blue's work or her friends, and he couldn't even be bothered to remember what she liked to drink? Upon learning Maisie's "friend" had vomited on Blue, he'd turned even colder. It had obviously solidified his bad impression of Maisie—just like his behavior had made her more certain she'd made the right call about him.

If the Bad Luck Club had led Blue to that gem, it might not be much of a winner.

But Molly cleared her throat, lifting her eyebrows in expectation, and forced her to table the thought. She'd promised Blue an explanation for Lee's behavior, but she could catch up with her later.

"To be clear," Maisie said, her gaze shooting to the pen and pad ready and waiting next to her sister, "this absolutely cannot go in a blog post, anonymous or otherwise. It's too personal to Jack."

Her warning only seemed to make Molly more eager, and because Maisie had never intended *not* to tell her, she started with Victoria's close, personal friendship with the Biltmores. Molly laughed plenty, made inappropriate comments even more, and cheered Maisie for talking so frankly with River and Georgie. And, of course, for the whole sex-against-the-door incident. When Maisie made it to the end, her voice almost hoarse from talking, Molly shook her head dramatically.

"That's one hell of a story," she said, "and it physically pains me that you don't want me to write about it."

"You'll survive. You can write about the cult."

Molly's only response was to make a speculative sound in her throat.

Something creaked in the hall, but when Maisie glanced over, she didn't see anything through the crack in the door. Old houses.

"That *would* be interesting," Molly continued. "But unfortunately *Beyond the Sheets* only does puff pieces. An undercover piece would be too in-depth for them." A pause. "I can't believe you and River finally had a real talk. That's about seven or eight years overdue." From the speed with which she'd changed the subject, it was obvious she didn't want to talk about work. Maisie wondered, as she had for some time, when Molly was going to get sick of working for *Beyond the Sheets*. It was fun, but fun only got you so far. Someday she'd want more of a challenge.

"Yeah, I guess it was time." Thinking about it, her throat got thick with emotion. "It went so much better than I could have hoped. I...God, as much as I hate to say it, Mary was right, we were codependent on each other after Mom and Dad died. If we'd gotten together, it wouldn't have been good for either of us. He thanked me for pushing him away that day. For not kissing him."

"You agonized over it for like a week. Okay, until a few months ago," Molly said, her eyes dancing. "Guess you made the right call after all, although you'll have to throw away all of those old notebooks with Maisie Reeves written on the margins. I'm sure you still have them."

"Nah, I went for River O'Shea. I've always been a modern woman," Maisie joked. "And I'll have you know I've started throwing things out." She waved at the room around her. "This is just the beginning. I'm done living in the past, Molly. I'm ready."

"And Jack? Is he going to be part of this splendiferous future? I know you were worried in the beginning because of Mary's whole thing about the guys you date being too similar to River, but she's full of it. Everyone has a type, Maisie, and there's nothing wrong with that. It helps keep us honest."

Chaco looked up at Maisie, wagging her tail, and she smiled at both of her girls. "I hope so, but we'll have to wait and see."

They talked for another minute or so, then signed off, Maisie promising to text her after the sure-to-be-disastrous engagement party. If it wasn't canceled, of course, and it really, really should be. She wasn't confident the Buchanan family could sit down to break bread together at this point without at least one person being poisoned or otherwise dispatched. She and Molly were supposed to talk to Mary in a three-way video chat tomorrow, although Maisie would be at the shelter on and off all day. She'd needed to take yesterday and today off, mostly, but she planned to make up for it by being the primary on-duty staffer for Christmas.

After they hung up, Maisie left the room and lingered at the top of the stairs for a moment, listening for sounds of conversation from the kitchen. There were none, so she headed down to the living room, Chaco climbing down after her.

Jack was pacing in front of the Charlie Brown tree, Einstein following at his heels, and from the look on his face—dark, tortured, *angry*—she knew it hadn't gone well.

Had Lee been fool enough to reject their indisputable evidence of Prescott Buchanan's wrongdoing? Had he managed to convince himself it was some other woman in those pictures, maybe someone else's voice on that tape?

Because people were good at convincing themselves to believe the things they wished to be true. She'd fallen victim to it before, and she never wanted to again.

Chaco gave a little whine, and Jack flinched—physically flinched—and looked over.

"So I take it everything went well?" she asked with a small smile, hoping to lighten his mood, but his gaze only darkened.

In the back of her mind she realized this foul mood he was in, this cloud he was under, wasn't because of Lee. Or at least it wasn't only because of Lee. It was because of *her*. And that meant...

"I overheard part of your conversation with your sister," he said in a ragged voice. "River's the reason you didn't want to start a relationship with me."

Part of her knew she should apologize for not telling him sooner. She hadn't wanted him to find out like this, and she wasn't even altogether certain of what she'd said to Molly. But she'd learned on her first-grade kickball team that defense was the best offense, and the lesson had stuck. "You know, when Dottie invited us to listen in on her conversation with Prescott, she wasn't suggesting we spy on each other."

His jaw flexed. "I came up to tell you Lee walked out. I *overheard* some of what you said, I didn't eavesdrop. And for the record, I didn't want to eavesdrop on Prescott either. *You're* the one who did."

He was right. But he'd said it with such acid, when just this morning they'd sat pressed together on the couch, drinking their coffee with the dogs. A unit. That moment of perfection felt so far away right now, and tears pricked at her eyes. Tears she couldn't bear for him to see when he was this angry with her.

"Why didn't you tell me? You've been so forthright about everything else. Why not this?"

If he'd said it more softly, with more understanding, she would have reacted differently. She would have let those tears fall, maybe. But it was almost an accusation.

So she steeled her back, trying to calm her hammering heart, and said, "Because it's not an issue. Yes, I had feelings for River in the past. I'll admit it was confusing for me when he first met Georgie...and even when they got engaged. Which I knew about weeks before you did. But we were *never* together. We've never even kissed. Have you told me about all of your old high school crushes?"

Defense, defense, defense. She knew what she was doing, and it made her sick inside. So she forced herself to stop. To take a breath.

Looking into his eyes, pleading with him to see her perspective, she reached for him. He let her take his hands, and something eased inside of her. "Jack, you're the one I want. I haven't lied to you about anything. The thing with River...it was hard to let go of it, just like it has been to sort through the things in this house. He was going through a tough time too after my parents died, and we leaned on each other harder than we should have. It was inevitable that I would feel that way about him. But we're not right for each other. It never would have worked between us."

She tried to communicate silently that she wanted a life with *him*. She could see that life so crisply. The holiday lights outside the house. Family dinners around the table, only they'd get a new table, one they picked out together. Iris would help her choose which things to keep and which to give away. Maybe Molly would too. And...

"I work with him," he said. "He's going to be my brother-in-law."

And it felt like something cracked inside of her. The vision that had been so clear moments ago felt like glass coated in grime. She dropped his hands. "Georgie doesn't hold it against me, so I don't know why you would."

He cocked his head. "Are you sure about that?"

"What's *that* supposed to mean?"

"Nothing," he muttered, but the look on his face said it wasn't nothing. Her fury must have shown because he sighed deeply. "She just told me that you might not be ready for a relationship."

It felt like a little knife of betrayal pierced her heart. "When was this? I talked to her yesterday, and I thought we were cool."

He squirmed. "Before that. She must have guessed your *secret*."

He said it like he'd found out she kept a secret collection of dead spiders in a Tupperware under her bed. Or that she was like Blake, only she kept the dirty underwear rather than throwing them out.

Jack had always struck her as someone who respected other people's silence. Someone who didn't press and push and bully. Someone who gave a person the time to share what they wanted to. Where was that man? Then she thought again about that agreement Lee had wanted River to sign, and how he hadn't seen fit to mention it to her.

"How about you, Jack? You have your secrets. You didn't say anything about that shitty agreement Lee wants River to sign. I'm guessing you didn't tell me because you *want* it to happen." Something flashed in his eyes, and Ein pawed at his pants a little. A bit of Maisie's anger leaked out. "And look, I get that, I do—it's your life, your work that's at stake— but how fair is it for you to keep secrets on your terms and not expect me to have some of my own?"

"That's completely different," he said. "I was going to tell you. I just didn't have the chance."

She just lifted her brows, letting her silence speak for her.

"Look," he said, "I feel like I'm not handling this well."

Again, she didn't say anything, because no, he wasn't. Neither was she.

"This isn't a good time for me to process this. I need some space to think, to—"

But she was already laughing, a bitter, humorless laugh.

"Oh, big surprise. *You* want space. You've been looking for every excuse you could find to stay away from me. Maybe you should thank me for hand-delivering one."

"I've been nothing but honest with you," he said, his face hard, closed down from emotion. "From the very beginning, I told you why I needed to wait."

The tears pressing at her eyes became more urgent, and she knew it wouldn't be long now before she lost the battle. She didn't want that to happen in front of him. Not now. Not when he was looking at her like this, like she was some bug pinned to a board.

Her eyes fell on the small pile of wrapped presents under the tree. She'd wrapped her dad's watch for him. It had felt like such a beautiful marriage of the past and present—giving something she'd cherished to the man she hoped would be her future, but now she wondered if she'd been naïve.

"I think you should leave," she said. "Since you're so desperate to get away from me."

Einstein whined, but he came to stand at her feet, gazing mournfully at Jack.

For a moment, Jack looked like he was maybe on the verge of tears too, but then something hardened in him again, and he nodded. "Yeah, I guess maybe I should."

And he just turned and left, leaving Maisie with her dogs and the heaviness of knowing he might not be coming back.

In a minute, she'd put herself together. Leave for the shelter so she could put in a few hours with the dogs, get their stockings together. Iris had helped her gather all the elements for them. But right now, she lowered herself where she stood, in front of the tree sparkling in lights he'd put there, and let the tears fall.

CHAPTER
Thirty-Two

Jack couldn't remember ever being this miserable. Not from anything Prescott or Genevieve had done. Not even from the realization that his problems in Chicago had very much followed him to Asheville. It struck him as odd that a woman he barely knew could make him hurt so badly. But that wasn't true. He knew her, and that was why he hurt so badly. She was the last person he'd expected to hurt him.

But as he stomped away from her house, realizing that she had driven him here and his car was parked several miles away at the Buchanan house, he told himself he had to put all of the emotions twisting inside of him away for now. His family disaster was still unfolding, after all, and as unbelievable as it was, he was supposed to be putting on Georgie and River's engagement party tonight.

Shit.

River.

Lee.

Jack had to make sure Adalia and Georgie knew about their father. Would Lee tell them? Where had he even gone? He didn't have a car either.

Maisie had accused Jack of running away, and maybe there was some truth to that, but this was how he'd learned to process anger. Any obvious shows of emotion had been like blood in the water with Genevieve, but she would occasionally cave if he went to her calmly and explained his side. So he had learned to internalize his anger and let it simmer until he could sort through the facts logically. If Maisie couldn't deal with that, then this was never going to work. If it was going to work at all.

Part of him wanted to say to hell with it all. How was he supposed to face River now? It felt stupid and petty, and yes, a little unfair, but he was jealous of the history they shared. Maisie had been in love with River for almost a decade, until she was forced to confront the fact that he loved someone else. Now Jack was supposed to believe she wanted *him*? He'd spent his entire life as his mother's consolation prize, and he wasn't playing that role *ever* again.

He'd walked about a half mile before realizing it was stupid to think he could walk the rest of the way. He had to get home, shower, then head to the brewery to set up for the engagement party. If the party was still happening. It was inconceivable to imagine it would, yet he didn't want to disappoint Georgie.

Damn, he really didn't want to break the Prescott news to his sisters. Maybe Lee had gone to tell them. Regardless, he needed to find out what was going on, sooner rather than later. He considered ordering an Uber, but he'd have to wait for it by the side of the road. Calling Iris was out. He'd get the third degree.

It wasn't like he had a lot of friends in Asheville, so he called the only person he knew who wouldn't make him feel worse.

"Hey," Finn said when he answered. "We missed you guys last night. We got kicked out of Libations after Lurch tried to start a conga line. And, get this, he and Stella got back together by the end of the night. Apparently, she told him she didn't want to break up with him after all. She wanted them to be part of a thruple with the fireman."

"Yeah, well…" Jack trailed off because he didn't really know what to do with that, then took a deep breath. "I need to ask a favor, man."

"Sure," Finn said, perking up. "Shoot."

"Can you pick me up? I'm kind of stranded, and I need to deal with a situation before I set up for the party tonight."

"Yeah, of course. Where are you?"

Jack scrubbed the back of his neck as he looked around. "About a half mile from Maisie's house. I'll send you a pin of my location."

"Did your car break down?"

"No."

"Did Maisie have to go to the shelter?"

He swallowed. "No. I don't want to get into it right now. Can you pick me up anyway?"

"Yeah," Finn said, sounding confused. But he didn't press him, and he didn't ask the dozens of questions that were probably lining up to leave his mouth. "Of course. I'm on my way."

When they hung up, Jack sent him his location but continued walking, planning to intercept Finn on the way.

About ten minutes later, Finn's Range Rover appeared around a curve, and he pulled to the side of the road when he saw Jack.

Jack climbed into the passenger seat. "Thanks, Finn, I really appreciate it." He grimaced. "Sorry if I came across as rude or abrupt on the phone."

"No problem," Finn said, making a U-turn and heading back toward their neighborhood.

They rode in silence for a few minutes, Finn squirming in his seat before he finally said, "I love Maisie to death, but she's not always an easy person to get along with."

"Was she in love with you too?" Jack scoffed, then instantly regretted it.

"Ah…" Finn said with a sigh. "She told you?"

"No, I overheard her conversation with her sister."

And wasn't that the worst of it? If it really wasn't a big deal, like she'd said, wouldn't she have told him herself? She'd apparently told everyone else.

A little voice inside him insisted that she hadn't had much of a chance. The last couple of days had been consumed with his family drama, and before that…well, neither of them had really been sure of what they wanted, had they? But those tangled-up emotions he'd tried to push away weren't so easily dismissed.

He turned to face Finn. "You knew we were seeing each other. Why didn't you tell me?"

"It wasn't my place to tell, Jack."

"So you let me fall in love with her, knowing I was her River surrogate."

Finn looked startled. "You're in love with her." But he shook it off, recovering, and said, "Never mind. And you're not River's surrogate."

"Apparently, one of her sisters gives her a hard time for always dating men who are similar to River. And I can see that. We have similar hair and eye coloring. We both come from messed-up families. Seems to me she just went for me because she can't have who she really wants."

Finn was quiet for a few moments. "I've known Maisie for six years. As you probably know, she and River have been friends since they were in middle school. They're close, but I've never seen her as happy with River as she is when she's with you."

"Yeah, that's because he didn't reciprocate her feelings. Of course she wasn't happy."

"I know it probably seems that way, but I've had some time to think about it, and while I know she loves him, I don't think she was ever really *in love* with him. Not like I think she's falling for you." He took a breath. "Maisie's one of the most amazing people I've ever known, but she has a hard time letting go of things. River was there when her parents died, and she clings to anything having to do with her parents."

"Is this supposed to make me feel better?"

"I'm getting to that part," Finn said. "The thing is, she's changing. We've all noticed it. She's clearing some of the old things out of her house and letting Iris take point at the shelter. Maybe it was River falling for Georgie that spurred her to change, but it didn't really start until you two started spending time together. I've seen her with other guys, Jack, and she never liked them the way she likes you."

Jack's heart warmed at the thought of that ratty old Santa beard at the shelter and the updates he'd noticed at her house. She'd even gotten a new set of plates in the kitchen to replace the cracked and chipped set she'd probably eaten on as a child. Then there was the fact that she'd invited him and Iris to help her decorate and put up the tree. Judging from the dust on the boxes of ornaments, no one had taken them out in years.

Maybe Finn had a point, but still, Jack had to wonder if she'd only moved on because she didn't have a choice. If they stayed together, was he going to freak out every time she went out for one of her Bro Club dinners with River and Finn? Every time he noticed her looking at River? It was something he needed to settle in himself before he talked to her.

Finn pulled up in front of the Buchanan house, and Jack frowned. "Is Addy here or at your house? I need to talk to her and Georgie."

Finn's face paled. "You're not going to tell Georgie that Maisie was in love with River, are you?"

"She already knows," he ground out, feeling another wave of annoyance that he'd apparently been the last to know, or close enough. "But no, it's not about Maisie. I need to talk to Georgie before the party. If she still wants to have a party."

"Then whatever it is, do *not* tell me," Finn said, holding up a hand. "I suck at keeping secrets."

"Have you or Addy heard from Lee today?"

"No, but Addy said Victoria is fit to be tied. She keeps calling her and Georgie every half hour or so, accusing them of hiding him from her."

"Lee doesn't need any help hiding from her." He glanced toward the house, preparing himself to go in and do Lee's dirty work.

"Addy isn't home," Finn said. "She and Georgie decided to go out for a spa day to recover from yesterday. They took Iris with them."

"What spa is open on Christmas Eve?" he asked in disbelief.

"The owner is a friend of Dottie's. She set it up."

Of course she did. She'd probably arranged it to give them some relaxation before the series of bombshells she knew was coming.

"I guess I'll call them then." He didn't want to tell them over the phone, but he could let them know he needed to talk to them ASAP.

Finn shook his head. "No cell phones. The spa takes them as soon as they walk in the door and keeps them until they leave."

"Which will be when?"

"Four-ish? It's an all-day thing." He paused. "Can't this wait until tomorrow?"

"No, it really can't, but I'm not going to bust into a spa either." He gave Finn a dark look. "I'll let Lee take care of it." He reached for the door handle. "Thanks for the ride. I guess I'll see you at the party unless you hear otherwise.

"Shit," Finn said. "Now I *really* don't want to know what's going on."

———

After Jack went inside, he tried calling Lee several times, but all of his calls went straight to voicemail. The first two times he didn't leave a message, but after he'd put off heading to the brewery for as long as he feasibly could, he finally said, "Lee, I realize this is all a huge shock, but your sister is about to have an engagement party with your father and your presumably ex-girlfriend in attendance. Georgie and Addy are having a spa day, so I can't reach them to tell them what's going on, but I feel like it should come from you anyway. Until I hear otherwise, I'm going to set up for this party, but call me as soon as you get everything sorted out."

Damn, he hoped Lee stepped up.

It occurred to him that he should call River and give him a heads-up that something was going on with Georgie's father and brother, but he couldn't bring himself to make the call. If that made him a bastard, so be it.

Thinking about River turned his mind, again, to Maisie. The two of them on the sofa this morning, with the dogs lounging around them. He'd had a fleeting moment of complete peace, of understanding what it felt like to have someone who truly cared about you. A partner, an equal. Someone to share his life with. He'd *liked* it. No, he'd reveled in it. But the sickening thought of being Maisie's second choice had poisoned the memory, and he wondered if it had been real at all.

The afternoon wore on, and he still hadn't heard anything from Lee or any of his sisters. He hoped Iris was having a good time, but he was worried about her reaction once she found out about this fight with Maisie. Would she blame him? Should he suck it up and call River?

Should he suck it up and call Maisie?

He didn't have much time to think about it because problems began cropping up. Someone had misplaced the centerpieces for the high top tables, and the boxes of wine he'd ordered from a local winery had never shown up. He'd decided to offer both wine and Buchanan brews at the party, and it had inspired him to strike up a conversation with the owner of Blush Winery. From his bartending experience, he'd learned people liked choices. Wine would be a welcome addition for certain events, like engagement parties, and they were in the process of working out a partnership.

He made a quick call to the winery, relieved when he got a hold of the owner, who quickly realized they'd never sent the cases. She didn't have time to run them over, but she offered to stick around until Jack showed up.

By the time he got back to the brewery, it was nearly five. He still hadn't heard from Iris, Addy, or Georgie, despite the fact that he'd sent all three a group text, telling them he needed to talk to them as soon as possible. The party started at six.

At ten past five, after Jack had called Lee again and left a more insistent voicemail, Dottie showed up. Her hair was freshly dyed a festive red, presumably for the holidays. She was wearing a flowing, gold lamé dress with a short train that flowed behind her and a green velvet hat with a large sprig of evergreen with red berries attached. She looked like a life-sized present.

"It's lovely, Jack," she gushed when she walked into the room.

Despite the stress of wondering if the party was happening, he was proud of how it turned out. The high top tables were covered in crisp white tablecloths, and the evergreen and candle centerpieces had finally been found and were arranged on the tables. The appetizers still needed to be placed on the serving tables, but the bartender had nearly finished setting up the bar in the corner. Georgie had given him the go-ahead to take care of everything, and he intended to do just that. He wanted her to be able to enjoy herself, to be happy, but he couldn't help thinking his responsibility for her happiness included making sure she knew about the situation with her father.

"Thanks," he said. "Have you talked to Lee today?"

She frowned. "No, but I presume you gave him the terrible news."

"Yeah, he didn't take it very well."

She nodded. "That's to be expected. That boy has been on a tight leash, and he's just discovered the man holding it is dragging him toward the gallows."

Jack grimaced. "Is it really that bad?"

"Oh, my precious boy," she said, her forehead creasing. "It's so much worse."

"Georgie and Addy don't know what's going on. I think Lee should tell them, but he's gone AWOL, and I haven't been able to get a hold of my sisters all day."

"That's because they're at the spa, dear."

"I know, but Finn thought they'd be done by four."

She shook her head. "No, the issue with the ostrich and the marbles put them behind schedule. The girls will be here shortly before six."

Ostrich and marbles? Jack knew there was a story there, but now didn't seem like the time to ask. "And Prescott?"

Her lips pressed together. "I would hope the man would have the decency to stay away, but no one ever accused him of possessing decency, so I suppose he'll show up around six-ten."

That sounded about right.

"If you need help, River should be here shortly. Since Georgie is running late, Adalia said she would bring her and Iris."

River was the second to the last person he wanted to see, Prescott being the first.

"Where's Maisie?" Dottie asked, glancing around.

"Good question," Jack said, walking over to the table that would hold the appetizers. He straightened the perfectly aligned chafing dishes.

"Isn't she coming?"

The thought of seeing her unleashed butterflies of anticipation in his stomach, but their wings were quickly crushed. "I'm sure she is, considering she's River's *best woman*."

"Oh dear," Dottie said, disappointment and then acceptance filling her eyes. "You know."

He turned around to face her. "That Maisie's been in love with River for half her life? Yeah, I got that bit of news this morning."

Dottie grabbed his arm and pulled him over to one of the few tables with chairs. "Sit."

"Dottie, I don't really have—"

"*Sit.*"

Since Dottie rarely gave orders, let alone in a stern voice, Jack knew better than to refuse.

She lowered into the chair next to him and held his gaze.

"Our Maisie likes to put on a tough front, but she's more vulnerable than most people realize."

"I know all about the situation with her parents, Dottie."

She gave him a look of reprimand, and he regretted interrupting.

"Maisie was there for River when his mother dropped him off in Asheville. She was his friend and defended him when some of the children made fun of him for being behind in school. She helped him catch up too. They were best friends all through school and then past graduation. River struggled to find his way, and she stood by him when others didn't. In turn, he was there for her after her parents died."

"I know most of this, Dottie."

"Maybe so, but I'm not sure you understand it all. Maisie lost her way after her parents died, and it was River who helped keep her afloat."

He closed his eyes. He really didn't want to hear how much River meant to her.

"Jack."

He gave her his attention.

"River and Maisie will always share a special bond. If you can't accept that, then you're not the man I thought you were. Georgie knew if she wanted her relationship with River to work, she'd have to accept it."

"She knew how Maisie felt from the beginning?"

"Of course she did. Women know these things. But she also realized it wasn't a threat to her relationship with River."

"I'm sure it was much easier considering River wasn't in love with Maisie. *She* was in love with *him*."

"Relationships are more complicated than that, my dear. At one time, there could have been more between them—on both sides—but that time has long since passed, and it's for the best that it did. For both of them. When Maisie's with River, she can live in her past. She can pretend her parents are on a trip instead of being buried at Riverside Cemetery. She can be the girl she was in high school. And River could do the same. While they both accepted each other for who they were, they didn't challenge each other to *grow*. Or more specifically, River never challenged *Maisie* to grow. She's been stuck in her tracks for nearly ten years." She reached over and covered his hand with her own. "Until you."

He thought about what Finn had said, how he'd claimed Maisie had only started changing things after she began spending time with him, but was that true, or did he just want to believe it?

"Because River moved on," he offered, mostly to see how she'd respond.

"Maybe," Dottie said, "or you could look at it another way: River set her free to realize he wasn't really what she needed. What she needs is a man who would make her want more than what she has. Who encourages her to leave her past behind."

He didn't say anything.

"She's falling for you, Jack, and she's very good for *you* too. All I ask is that you not hold her past against her, especially since she's trying so hard to break free from it."

He nodded. Talking about Maisie and River was eating out his insides, but he could see the truth in her words. Maisie had looked so raw and vulnerable when he'd confronted her, even as she snapped at him, and if he was being honest with himself, he realized part of that pain had stemmed from her fear of losing him. He didn't want to lose her either. He just needed to let all of these new revelations settle.

"You're a very wise woman, Dottie Hendrickson."

She graced him with a beaming smile. "Thank you for acknowledging my truth."

He laughed. "We still have to deal with Prescott and the party."

"Fate has a way of working these things out."

"Why do I think this will be an engagement party most people will never forget?"

She patted his cheek and winked. "Because *you* are a very wise man."

CHAPTER
Thirty-Three

Spending time with the dogs had always calmed her. They didn't ask for anything but love, and she'd always had plenty of that to give. Ruby licked her face, and Jackie Daytona, a small mix with a flattish face that spoke of her part-bulldog heritage, kept insisting on being picked up, not that Maisie minded. She hugged and petted all of them until her clothes were covered in fur, and then left the kennel and started stuffing the stockings in the playroom. Iris had gone above and beyond, like always, and for Ruby's stocking, she'd included a sweater with Jack's picture on it. Before, Maisie had laughed at the sight of it, but now it felt like a knife to her chest. Jack wasn't going to adopt Ruby. He already lived in a house with a big dog and dictatorial cat. It didn't matter how much Ruby loved Jack, how much she'd chosen him as her soul companion—she was going to be taken home by someone else eventually. Would she still pine for Jack?

Would Maisie?

The thought ripped a bitter laugh from her. Of course she would. And she knew a thing or two about pining. Except something told her this would be much, much worse than the pain she'd felt over River.

"Knock, knock," Dustin said, unnecessarily, as he pounded on the partially open door, swinging it toward her.

The look on his face was one he usually reserved for frightened or aggressive dogs, which told her a lot about the vibe she was giving off, but she couldn't bring herself to care.

"Would you like some help?" he asked for what had to be the third time. "Or maybe a Danish? I knew you were coming in to do the stockings at some point, but I figured you might bring Jack and Iris. I was actually expecting you all to come in much earlier."

She'd known he'd fish for information eventually. It was a testament to her resting bitch face that he'd held out this long. Still, she didn't want to bite Dustin's head off. He'd dedicated his whole Christmas Eve to the shelter so she could go to the engagement party.

The engagement party.

Would it still happen? It was past five, creeping toward six. It had taken her a long time to pull herself together.

Part of her thought she should warn River about the epic mess that awaited him. He'd texted her to check in— apparently Jack had seen Finn, and Finn had called River and told him something was up, although he'd refused to say more (apparently his ability to retain secrets was improving...she'd have to thank Adalia for that), but she couldn't bring herself to call him right now. Not after her fight with Jack. Not yet. Still, River was her oldest friend, and she'd already missed the majority of his bachelor party... Could she really skip the engagement party, knowing what she knew? Whether or not Lee showed, Prescott was sure to blow the whole thing to hell. She should go to offer her support.

Finn had texted her too, of course, telling her that he'd seen Jack and he knew her wink-wink-nudge-nudge secret was out, and if she wanted to talk, he was only a phone call away. Or he'd see her at the party.

Finn was right. Now that River and Georgie both knew, and Jack too, it really wasn't much of a secret anymore. There was freedom in that, but she feared it had come at a price she didn't want to pay.

"They're not coming today," she said, choking out the words. "The engagement party starts soon."

Dustin shuffled on his feet a little, one hand coming up to stroke his beard. "Now, I might be reading the room wrong, but it seems to me you're a little upset."

Another laugh ripped out of her. "Dustin, you excel at reading psychic energy."

He puffed up like bread dough left out in the sun. "I've always thought so. River's aunt gave me some suggestions the last time she came around."

"Sounds like Dottie."

"Well, if you need to talk, I'm two shakes of a dog's tail away," he said, laughing at his own attempted pun. "And if you need to leave, I'd be happy to take over."

"Thank you, Dustin," she said, meaning it.

He started to back out of the room but paused in the doorway. "For what it's worth, I hope you work it out, and not just because Iris knows how to make Beatrice laugh. There's something else I've read in your psychic energy—and Jack's. He's good for you. And he looks like a young Marlon Brando...you know, with dark hair."

Her heart was pounding in her ears, but she tilted her head and gave him a vacant look. "Who's that?"

"What?" he said, looking thunderstruck. "You don't know..." Her small smile finally penetrated. "Oh, you're messing with me. Well, you know where I am."

"I do."

He shut the door behind him, leaving her alone with the stockings. Only a few left. What would she do afterward? She could go home to Einstein and Chaco, but the prospect of spending the night sitting by the tree, alone, knowing her friends were at the party *with Jack* made her feel frozen inside. Maybe she should take the tree down so there wouldn't be such an ever-present reminder of him, but somehow she knew that would be worse.

Her phone buzzed again, and she drew it out with trembling fingers. She'd stopped thinking Jack would call. He had to be at the brewery now, making last-minute preparations.

He wouldn't want her there, probably. He'd said he wanted space. Time. Obviously, a few hours didn't qualify.

She'd thought about calling Molly back and telling her everything, but she hadn't. Because Molly was more sensitive than most people realized, and she'd think it was her fault. And Maisie wanted her to *like* Jack, because she still thought, she still hoped...

The text was from Blue.

Are we still on for the party? Ended up throwing away the shoes, but I didn't like them anyway.

Shoot. She'd forgotten she was supposed to call Blue today. Blue likely wouldn't want to go to the party if Maisie didn't. Adalia was Georgie's sister, and she'd probably be tied up the majority of the night. The last thing Maisie wanted to do was spend the night pretending to like drippy Dan, an uncharitable thought she forgave herself for given the circumstances, but she *would* like to talk to Blue. Blue was a good listener, and she was removed enough from the situation that she could be counted on to give impartial advice, unlike Dottie and Adalia, who had both made it very clear they wanted Maisie and Jack together.

Rather than text back, she called her, and Blue answered on the first ring.

"How'd it go with Jack last night?" she asked excitedly. "I was going to ask you more questions, but then...well, you know."

Of course, that was when the tears decided to make another showing.

"I'm in love with him," she said through sobs. "But I think I lost him. I think he's gone for good."

And then she told her everything.

———

"We can still change our minds and go to a bar," Maisie offered as Blue parked in a lot close to the brewery. Drippy Dan had been told to stay at home, not that he'd minded.

There you go, making assumptions again.

But at least she hadn't bad-mouthed him to Blue. She'd just thanked her, profusely, for listening to her fall apart. And for being enough of a friend to tell her it was more important for her to change her animal-hair-encrusted clothes than to be on time for the party. Blue had come to the shelter with a silky green dress, and Dustin had played Madonna's "Vogue" on his phone while Maisie changed. There was no getting past the fact that she had sensible wooden clogs on her feet, but Dustin had taken one look at her and insisted no one was going to look at her feet. He'd then sent them out the door with a couple of Danishes and hollered, "You go get your man!" like he thought he was in a romantic comedy.

"We *are* going to a bar," Blue said, returning her mind to the present. "I assume there'll be beer." She made a face. "Although maybe someone should cut Adalia's brother off this time."

"Fair point. But just in case, maybe you should stay out of spew range."

"If he shows up," Blue said quietly.

And Maisie nodded and repeated it. "If he shows up."

It wasn't her place to tell Blue his secrets, so she hadn't, but for all his flaws, Lee wasn't a drunk, she didn't think, nor did he have a fetish for ruining women's shoes. So she hadn't felt she was making excuses for him when she'd told Blue that he was going through a hard time. A really hard time.

Blue hadn't pressed. She'd just said she understood.

Looking at her friend now, across the front seat, she knew Blue understood her dilemma too. After Maisie had finished her sob story, sobs included, Blue had told her they were going to the party together, no Dan, because Maisie would regret it forever if she didn't fight for what she wanted. She'd said it like a person who knew from experience.

Maybe she was just stalling for time, but Maisie found herself asking, "Why'd you join the Bad Luck Club, Blue? What happened to you?"

Blue looked at her for a long moment, considering, then heaved a deep sigh. "We don't have time to get into it right now, but trust me when I say it wasn't just bad luck. I spent my whole life letting my father make decisions for me, and then I married a man who did the same thing." She winced. "Two men."

Maisie's mouth fell open. "You're a polygamist?"

Blue laughed at that, a tinkling, infectious laugh that almost had Maisie laughing with her. Except she sensed a hint of bitterness behind it.

"No," Blue said at last, "but some people would say I'm something worse. It's a rare woman who's divorced twice by the time she hits thirty." She looked down at her hands, as if searching for the ring she probably used to wear. Make that rings. "I should have told you and Addy, but I was embarrassed. I'm trying to get past that, though."

It took Maisie a second to find words. Not that she judged Blue. She didn't. This just wasn't something she'd anticipated. "I'm sorry you didn't feel you could tell us. I know I can sometimes come off as judgmental...that's something I'm working on too."

"It wasn't that," Blue said, looking up and meeting her eyes. "I wasn't worried about you two judging me. This was about me judging myself."

Maisie grinned at her. "Well, maybe you, me, and Addy can get drinks sometime soon, after this travesty of an engagement party, and we can be judgmental of your exes instead."

Blue gave her a soft smile. "You just want gossip."

"I'm dying for it."

"We'll see. In the meantime, stop stalling. We're already twenty minutes late."

Twenty minutes. A lot could happen in twenty minutes. Had Lee confronted Prescott already? What about Victoria? Would she show up in one of her wedding dresses and insist one of the Buchanan men make a solid commitment?

River had texted her again a little while back, after arriving at the party. He hadn't pressed her for details or asked why she wasn't there yet. He'd just asked if she was coming.

She'd replied in the affirmative, although she hadn't made the decision for him—she'd made it for herself.

And then her phone had died on her. There'd been no word from Adalia before it winked out. Presumably she was busy with Georgie and Iris, but it was still a little surprising. Were they at the party? There was no way of knowing without showing up herself.

Taking a deep, steadying breath, she opened the door. "Let's do this thing."

"There you are," Blue said, getting out too. "I've been waiting for your fiery redhead side to take over."

She'd been waiting too.

CHAPTER
Thirty-Four

When Jack still hadn't heard from his sisters at 5:55, he started to get worried, but Dottie waved off his concerns.

"They'll be here soon." She gave him one of her knowing looks. "I sense that all is as it should be with them."

"They're not answering any texts or calls," he said. "Shouldn't they have left the spa by now? Maybe I should go by and make sure everything's okay." It had bothered him a little that Iris had gone off for the day without checking in with him, but he'd told himself to calm down. She was almost eighteen, and next year she'd be in college. Besides, he was happy that she wanted to hang out with his other sisters, who were, after all, mature, responsible adults. Well, Addy was *most* of the time. But now the party was about to start, and he still hadn't heard from any of them.

He sent a quick text to Finn, asking if he'd talked to them. He didn't answer, but he walked through the door about a minute later with River in tow.

"Seemed easier to answer you in person," Finn said.

Both of the men were dressed in gray suits, although Jack noticed that River's looked more fitted than the one he'd worn to the will reading back in June. Georgie's influence, no doubt. He couldn't help smiling a little at that. In many ways, large and small, his relationship with Georgie had made him into a better man.

A lot like Maisie's influence was making Jack a better man. More grounded and happier. The urge to carve out a place for himself had driven him to Asheville, but when he was with Maisie, he didn't feel like he needed to carve or gouge or fight. He felt like he fit. He felt like he could finally just be.

Now that his anger and resentment had eased, all that was left was a sharp ache in his chest, along with the fear that he'd just ruined the best thing that had ever happened to him. A lump filled his throat. River gave him an apologetic look and was opening his mouth to speak when Georgie, Adalia, and Iris rushed into the room. All three had on dresses and heels, but it was their elaborate updos that caught his attention.

"Oh, my dears," Dottie gasped with tears in her eyes as she clasped her hands together. "You look beautiful."

Iris caught Jack's eye and winked, a signal they had developed from enduring life with their mother—*Have I got a story to tell you.*

She looked beautiful in her dark blue dress. And so grown up. And her hair—along with his other sisters'—looked better suited for a wedding than an engagement party. The way Adalia kept lifting her hand to her hair and wincing suggested that she was less than thrilled with it. Then again, she had short hair, and it would take many, many pins to hold it up like that, so maybe she was wincing from pain.

"Sorry we're late!" Georgie said as River walked over to intercept her.

"Everything okay?" he asked, wrapping his arm around her back in such a protective way, Jack felt like a Peeping Tom to their tenderness.

"It was crazy," Georgie said with a nervous laugh. "I almost felt like we were being held hostage." She shot an accusatory glance at Dottie. "Especially since Dottie suggested we bring our clothes *just in case* the appointment ran long."

Dottie beamed. "You of all people know the importance of being prepared." She gave a slight nod. "You're welcome."

Finn was staring at Adalia in amazement and reached out a tentative hand to touch her hair.

She slapped his hand away. "Don't you dare. There's so much hair spray holding all of this up, I'll fall over if it gets unbalanced."

"I wanted to call so you wouldn't worry, Jack," Iris said, looking guilty. "But they took our phones and then they couldn't find them when it was time to go. We still don't have them."

He pulled her into a hug. She'd looked so happy and confident when she walked in, and now she seemed nervous. He hated for anything to steal her joy, especially him. "I'm just glad you're here and that you had a fun day." He pulled back to study her face. "You had a good day, right?"

Her eyes lit up. "The best. You'll never believe what happened." She glanced at a Buchanan employee walking toward them. "But I'll tell you later. It's going to take a while to explain the ostrich."

He would have loved the distraction from worrying about Maisie, but a staffer pulled him away to deal with an issue in the kitchen. By the time he returned, some of the guests had arrived and were getting drinks at the bar. So far, there was no sign of the New York Buchanans, and he wasn't sure whether to be annoyed or relieved.

Iris's forehead furrowed. "Are you okay? You look upset."

He gave her a weak smile. "Long day."

She glanced around the room. "Where's Maisie?"

"Not here yet. I had to set up, so I've been here for a few hours. She's coming on her own." Which had been the original plan, but now he wondered if she'd skip the party to avoid seeing him. They'd left things badly, after all, and she knew as well as he did there would be plenty of drama to go around tonight.

A little voice in his head, the one that gave voice to all his doubts, whispered that maybe she'd been looking for an excuse to skip it. Even if Dottie was right and Maisie was mostly beyond the whole River thing, it might still bother her to see him officially move on. Except she'd shown no hesitation when they'd talked about the party earlier. No hint of regret either. Which meant if she missed the party, it was likely because of him. He pulled out his phone to text her, to tell her that she didn't need to stay away on his account. That he *wanted* her there. That he was desperate to talk to her and set things right.

But he'd only made it halfway through typing out a lengthy text that would have made Finn proud when Prescott and Victoria entered the room. Victoria's nose scrunched up as she surveyed the space, making it clear she found it lacking. Prescott marched right up to Georgie, ignoring the fact that she and River were in the middle of a conversation with another couple, and demanded, "Where is your brother?"

Georgie's mouth dropped open and she glanced to the side, her gaze landing on Jack.

"Not him," Prescott said in an icy tone. "Your real brother."

Jack flinched. He didn't give a shit what Prescott thought, but he was still sensitive to the opinions of his newly acquainted siblings.

"I have *two* real brothers," Georgie retorted. "One of whom has gone above and beyond to make this evening special for River and me. If you wish to have a discussion about our family, then it can wait until later." Then she turned back to the couple they'd been talking to, who looked understandably uncomfortable, and said, "I'm sorry, where were we?"

Prescott looked stunned that one of his children could dismiss him so efficiently, but Victoria wrapped her hand around his upper arm and tugged him toward the bar. "Come, Pressy. Let's get a drink."

Pressy? The way she clung to him, the way she looked at him so adoringly…how had no one seen the signs that they were sleeping together? Maybe Lee had seen them and dismissed them. It had to be hard to believe your own father would betray you that way, although Jack was only guessing. He wouldn't put it past Prescott to try to sleep with Maisie, if for no other reason than to hurt and humiliate him.

The thought of Prescott with Maisie was both nauseating and hilarious. Maisie had the best bullshit meter of anyone he'd ever met. One attempt to touch her, let alone kiss her, and she'd knee Prescott in the balls. He almost wished the fool would try it.

His lips twitched with a smile. God, he loved her fieriness.

But then he quickly sobered. If he loved that side of her, why had he held it against her in their argument this morning?

Prescott and Victoria got their drinks—a glass of wine for both, not that Jack was surprised—and moved to a high top table in the corner, surveying the room like they were a king and queen sitting on a dais. It astounded Jack that Prescott could act so high and mighty knowing that he was in deep trouble with the law, but then again, Beau had always been there to bail him out in the past. Who did he expect to bail him out this time?

A cold chill washed through him when he realized Prescott was now watching his oldest daughter like a stalker.

Was Prescott going to ask Georgie for help? If that was Prescott's plan, he was going to crash and burn, which gave Jack far more satisfaction than it should. Georgie may have sought his approval in the past, but Addy had told him their sister had grown since coming to Asheville.

About twenty minutes into the party, Jack was talking to Finn and Addy and a couple who worked at Big Catch (and had apparently forgiven Finn) when Maisie and her friend Blue walked into the events room.

Maisie stopped in the entrance and scanned the space, her gaze locking on Jack.

His mouth went dry, and his vision tunneled as he took her in. She looked sexy as hell in a slinky green dress that clung to every delicious curve. Her hair was loose, the curls brushing her shoulders and making him think of how he'd kissed that exact spot the night before. Then his gaze dipped to her legs, and he smiled a little when he saw she was wearing clogs. Maisie O'Shea was the only woman he knew who could wear them and still look so hot.

His gaze lifted to her expressionless face, and he took a step toward her. But River beat him to it and engulfed her in a hug. "There you are! I thought you were going to ditch me again."

It stung to see River touch her, hold her, even though he released her and immediately wrapped an arm around Georgie's waist. Did it still hurt Maisie to see them together? To witness their happiness from the outside? He couldn't tell from her expression. Then again, even though she was talking to them, her gaze was on *him*.

"You're the one she wants," Addy whispered next to him, and he realized he'd been flat out staring. When he glanced down at her, she added, "Finn told me about your fight." She shrugged with an apologetic grin. "He held out for a few hours, which has to be some kind of record for him, but he's an incurable blabbermouth."

"That's okay. I've never been a fan of secrets." Which was why he felt so uneasy about the ones he'd shared with his brother. "Have you talked to Lee today?"

She frowned. "No, and I'm actually starting to get a little worried."

Jack was too. "He and I discussed something important this morning, and I'd hoped he'd talk to you and Georgie about it before the party. But obviously it would have been impossible for him to get a hold of you."

She cast a glance at Victoria and frowned. "Ol' Vicky was losing her mind this morning. I can't decide if she was actually worried, or just pissed she wasn't controlling Lee's every move."

"Probably a combination of both," Jack said dryly, watching Maisie and Blue as they left River and Georgie and joined the line at the bar. "Only not how you think."

"What's that mean?"

He pushed out a sigh. "I'll tell you and Georgie everything, but not until later. I don't want to ruin her night."

"You mean Georgie and River's night."

He made a face.

"She wants *you*, Jack. I've seen it for months." She paused, then lowered her voice. "I think she loves you."

He loved her too, but he still felt unsettled, as if he'd been given the gift of his dreams on Christmas morning, only to find someone else's name crossed out on the tag. But he knew that was his own insecurities talking. He would get over them, but he wouldn't get over losing her. He couldn't let that happen.

Adalia put a hand on his arm. "You should talk to her."

"But the party—"

"We'll hold down the fort," she said. "Trust me, Georgie would rather see you happy than have the perfect party." She smiled up at him, and for a second he flashed back to the will reading. To the way Adalia had spoken about him and not to him. They'd come such a long way, and he couldn't believe how he'd lucked out in the sister department.

"Okay." He squared his shoulders and started toward Maisie, still unsure of what to say. He only knew he didn't want to be at odds with her a second longer.

But as he started across the room, Lee walked in wearing the same clothes he'd worn the night before. His hair looked like he'd repeatedly run his hands through it.

Oh shit. This did not bode well.

Prescott's back stiffened when he saw him, and he shot a dark, accusatory glare at Jack.

The asshole could go stuff himself. Jack was more concerned about Georgie.

Lee headed over to Georgie and grabbed her shoulders. "I love you, Georgie. You marry the man you love, you hear me?"

Her eyes narrowed in confusion. "Thank you…?"

Then she waved her hand in front of her face.

Lee turned to face River. "But I still want you to sign those damn papers, because it's not just about Georgie here. It's about protecting Addy and Jack too."

River turned serious. "I would never hurt Addy or Jack. I have no problem signing."

Jack was stunned, both because River had been so quick to accept the request, and because Lee had expressed concern for him for the first time.

"Have you been *drinking*?" Georgie asked, then threw a panicked look toward her sister. "Why don't you go sit down with Addy and we'll talk later, okay?"

As much as Jack wanted to talk to Maisie, he needed to deal with this situation first. He hurried over and grabbed Lee's right arm, nearly keeling over from the alcohol stench, and tried to steer him toward a high top table in the back of the room.

A server walked by, and Jack snagged her as she passed. "Chelsea, bring us a cup of coffee as soon as you can get to it." He shot a glance at the wobbling Lee. "Actually, make it a carafe."

Chelsea took one look at Lee, then rushed out of the room.

"Oh, my God," Addy said, taking Lee's arm on the other side. "Are you *drunk*? I've never seen you like this."

"You're just the person I need to talk to," Lee said, craning his neck to face her and nearly falling from the abrupt motion. "Georgie too, but she's busy."

"Now isn't a good time," Jack said, tightening his grip. "Let's wait until later."

"But you said I needed to be the one to tell them," Lee said, slurring his words. "The FBI agent thought so too."

Addy gasped. "Lee, are you in *trouble*?"

"He's going to be in trouble if he ruins Georgie and River's party," Maisie said, sweeping in. She gently pushed Addy out of the way and took Lee's arm in a tight grip. "I'm having a severe case of déjà vu. Jack, what do you say we take your brother outside to get some fresh air before he wrecks another pair of innocent shoes?"

His heart rate had picked up, and even though his focus should have been on Lee and the unfolding chaos, he couldn't help but be excited that Maisie had come over to help.

"Addy," Maisie said, "can you get your brother a cup of black coffee?"

"Already on it," Jack said.

Maisie gave him a dark grin, then turned to Adalia. "Jack and I have Lee covered. You make sure your dad and Vic-tor-ia don't ruin the party over this." When Adalia hesitated, Maisie said, "We know what's going on. He's okay. Trust us?"

"Okay," Adalia said reluctantly.

The fear in her eyes ripped a hole in Jack's heart. He wanted to reassure her, but he couldn't. The situation *was* as bad as she was imagining. For now, the less he said, the better.

Jack and Maisie escorted Lee out the back door and into the alley.

"It stinks out here," Lee said, his nose wrinkling.

"Yeah," Maisie said. "Kind of like you. I take it from the fact you're wearing the clothes you had on last night that you haven't had a shower today?"

"No time," he mumbled, then pulled away from them, pacing in anxious circles near the dumpster.

"You're going to fall, Lee," Jack said. "Why don't you sit down for a minute or just lean up against the wall?"

Lee shook his head. "No. I have to talk to Georgie and Addy. I have to warn them about the FBI."

"You talked to the FBI?" Maisie asked, her eyes wide.

"I called them." Lee held up his hand, using his thumb and index finger to mimic a phone. "They were super eager to talk to me. Flew right down even."

Jack's stomach dropped. "Oh shit."

This must be really bad.

"I made a deal," Lee said with a laugh. "If you'd told me yesterday whether I'd be making a deal with the FBI to turn on my father, I would have called you a lying asshole."

"You actually did call me an asshole," Jack said dryly.

Lee stopped and gave him a blank look. "Oh, yeah. Huh."

"We need to get him home," Maisie said under her breath. She was shivering from the cold. "Or at least to the Buchanan house."

"Good idea," Jack said. "You're freezing, so you go inside and I'll take him."

"They need you inside," she said. "You're the man who planned all of this." She waved back at the brewery. "I'm expendable."

"You're not expendable, Maisie," he said, his voice breaking. There was so much he wanted to tell her, but he didn't want to get into it with Drunk Lee about to barf again. "I'll deal with this mess."

"Alone?" she asked in an accusatory tone.

"You look way too gorgeous in that sexier-than-hell dress to be dealing with a drunk, but I *do* want to talk about what happened. Look, Maisie, I've been—"

He was about to say miserable, but Chelsea opened the back door carrying a tray with a carafe and several coffee cups.

"Adalia told me you were back here. I have your coffee," she said as she glanced around as though trying to decide what the hell was happening and if she should set it on the ground or on the dumpster.

But Lee took advantage of the open door and rushed through the opening faster than Jack would have expected from the intoxicated man.

Jack and Maisie raced after him, but by the time they reached him, he was already in the event room, confronting his father and Victoria.

"Lee," Victoria whisper-shouted, even though everyone could hear her. "You're drunk. You need to go back to the hotel and wait for me. You can apologize for everything later."

"And sit on the bed where you screwed my father?" he bellowed. "No, thanks."

There were several audible gasps, including from Georgie, who stood near the appetizer table.

Victoria's face paled. "What in God's name are you talking about?"

Lee reached into his jacket pocket and pulled out a folded wad of photographs. He tossed them onto the table in front of his father. "This should explain it."

Victoria shot Prescott a panicked look that suggested Prescott had kept quiet about his dinner with Dottie. She clearly didn't know news of their affair had gotten out. Her eyes flew wide as she opened one of the photos.

"That proves nothing," Prescott said in a bored tone. "I have a sex life. I'm allowed to sleep with women."

"You can sleep with other women, yes, but it's generally frowned upon to sleep with your son's girlfriend," Lee said.

"That's not me," Victoria said, taking a step backward as though the photos would bite her.

"I recognized that little mole, *Victoria*," Lee slurred. "The one on your back with the hair that grows out of it."

"My mole does *not* have a hair in it!" she shouted.

Lee released a harsh laugh. "Of course you'd deny the hair before denying you slept with my father. I knew you were screwing someone, but I figured you'd keep it out of my family."

Her eyes were wide, and Jack could practically see her flipping through her mental Rolodex of options.

"It was only one time," she said, tears pooling in her eyes. "It was a mistake, Lee-lee. I've regretted it ever since."

"That's bullshit and we both know it." Lee pointed at the photos. "Take a look. They're from different days."

"Okay, twice."

"Try again."

She winced. "Three times, but I was drunk and he took advantage of me the last time."

"You were more than willing *every* time," Prescott said.

"You thought you were just screwing him," Lee said, laughing, then shook his head. "But the truth is you're both screwed."

Prescott's face turned a dark red. "What have you done, Junior?"

"You were going to let me take the fall, but I turned it all around on you," Lee said. "Right now, the FBI is going through our offices."

"They can't do that," Prescott said, but uncertainty filled his eyes.

"They can if you give them permission, which I did only a few hours ago."

Prescott's face paled, and Victoria looked like she was about to pass out. But then Prescott's anger returned with a vengeance.

"What the hell have you done?"

"For once in my life, I made my own decision. Have a nice life in prison. Both of you." Then he turned around and headed for the exit, plowing into Blue.

She nearly fell over, but he grabbed her arms and kept her upright.

"Hey," he said, his eyes lighting up. "I know you."

A wry look twisted her mouth. "Don't throw up on me this time."

He made a face. "Then maybe I should leave."

Before anyone could stop him, he ran for the door.

CHAPTER
Thirty-Five

So much for saving Jack's party. Then again, maybe it had been beyond saving the moment Prescott and Victoria had RSVP'd yes. Everyone stood in the room in shocked silence, and Maisie fought the crazy urge to laugh or ask about the canapés. Blue was looking out the door after Lee, like maybe she was worried about him. Leave it to Blue to worry about a man who'd been falling down drunk both times she'd met him.

"Is it true?" Addy asked her father, her voice hard.

"This is ridiculous," Prescott said. "This is neither the time nor the place for this discussion. You're ruining Georgie's party."

"Answer her question," Georgie said, raising her voice with each word.

Prescott started to say something, then stopped and started again. "Your brother is exaggerating. I might be in a *small* bit of trouble, but I have it under control."

Dottie laughed. "A small bit?"

Prescott became enraged. "*You.* You did this."

He lunged for her, but River and Jack quickly bodychecked him, holding him back. Not that Jack needed the help. He could have held Prescott back with one arm. Still, she liked that they'd acted together, that they weren't awkward with each other.

"That woman is a conniving witch!" Prescott shouted.

Victoria, who'd turned the photos over as if to hide her indiscretion—or maybe the questionable mole—looked up with flashing eyes. "She *is*. She can read teacups."

That earned her a disgusted look from Prescott, who shook off River and Jack. They stood by, ready to grab him if he tried to go for Dottie again.

"I refuse to take any more disrespect from my ungrateful children. I'm leaving." He grabbed Victoria by the arm and headed for the front door, walking at a pace that indicated he would be driving straight to the airport in an attempt to waylay whatever was happening at his office. If the Feds hadn't been combing through his papers, catching every single altered figure, he surely would've stayed until the bitter end to make every last person miserable.

"Prescott, my shoes," Victoria squawked as she shuffled along in her three-inch heels.

"Good luck!" Addy called out after them. "I know for a fact there isn't another flight to New York until morning. Plenty of time for the Feds to find everything. Being arrested isn't a big deal, Dad! Happens to the best of us."

Maisie finally let herself laugh then, because Adalia would know. Of course, she'd been arrested for destroying her own art, which had been stolen from her. Not for stealing someone else's money.

Her father didn't turn back to look at her, but his scowl deepened.

Before he could leave in a huff, the door to the street swung open so hard it would have broken his nose if he'd been any closer. Too bad.

Lurch and Stella stood in the opening, Lurch's face still drawn up like a goat, along with a tall, silver-haired man with a chicken's face superimposed on his features with paint. Lurch had gotten the short end of that stick—at least the other guy's face could be washed. They had Lee with them, and the silver-haired fireman was holding him up.

Addy and Georgie hustled up to the front of the room, Finn and River with them. Maisie looked for Jack, assuming he'd head up there to deal with the situation, only to feel a sudden warmth at her side. When she glanced up, he was there beside her, his eyes on hers, a question in his gaze. He reached for her hand, and she gave it to him, his touch sending a rush of relief through her so great she nearly crumpled from it.

Blue grinned at her and stepped off to stand next to Iris. With her updo and dress, Iris looked like the adult she was becoming, but the wave she gave Maisie was all teenager.

"The party has arrived!" Stella said grandly. "I'll be painting faces for half an hour for my new project, but only if you're willing to pose nude." Glancing at Lee, she announced, "I've already found my first volunteer."

Lee pulled away from the fireman a little, wobbling alarmingly, and took a step toward his father. "And another thing. I quit."

"You're a disgrace," Prescott said, his cheeks flushed. "You'll be back, though. You wouldn't know how to stand on your own two feet if someone drew a diagram for you."

He gave Lee a withering look of contempt, which Lee responded to by wobbling a little more, looking just this side of nauseous. Really, if ever there had been a time to vomit, surely it was now.

"He doesn't need you," Georgie said, seething.

"He has us," Addy said, and they fell in on either side of him, each of them taking one of his arms.

"He's not going to stay here," Victoria said as if scandalized.

"And why ever not?" Addy said. "Looks like you're going to have to burn those wedding dresses and all of your monogrammed baby bibs. Either that, or you can take out a personal ad for someone whose last name starts with 'B.'"

She gaped, wordless, and Prescott gave her another tug toward the door. After ushering her through the opening, he turned back in the doorway, no doubt to make some final pronouncement regarding his ungrateful children, but Lurch slammed the door shut in his face.

"I'm buying you a drink!" Addy said.

Stella grimaced. "Now, don't you go trying to steal one of *my* men, girly, just because I like the look of yours."

She gave Finn another of her long, lingering looks, making him edge a little closer to Addy.

Then Jack was turning Maisie around, looking down at her with those deep, dark eyes. Reminding her of the night of Diego and the petting zoo and *them*. She hoped that had only been their beginning, and that this wasn't their end.

But it struck her that his sisters were over there with his brother, and he probably needed to help them work out whatever craziness was still unfolding.

"We have to talk," he said, squeezing her hand.

"Don't you need to deal with the fallout?" She gestured to the gathering at the front of the room. Stella was waving around a paintbrush she'd retrieved from her bag, going off about promises being promises while Addy lectured her about consent and Lee teetered some more. "If you're worried about Stella, I can go with you. But I don't promise I'll protect you from getting your face painted."

381

"I'm only worried about getting things settled between us. Everything else can wait. I shouldn't have let the party get in the way in the first place."

"You know the world is falling apart around us, don't you?" she asked, gesturing to the rest of the party. People were gawking openly, some taking pictures of Stella and her guys. If this wasn't on all the local news reports in the morning, it was only Christmas that had saved them.

"The world fell apart this morning, and I'm not doing anything else until we make it right."

As far as words went, they were perfect. It felt like someone had taken a big dishrag to the cloudy window concealing her future.

"There's somewhere I need to take you," she said.

The park was quiet and cold, its beauty lost to the dark and the winter. But she took Jack by the hand and led him to a wood bench. Christmas lights twinkled from houses in the distance, adding a little holiday sparkle to the view. They sat next to each other, sides pressed together, and he looked at her, waiting.

He probably wanted to know why she'd brought him somewhere outside rather than back to the warmth of her house. Which, fair enough. She was cold, despite having put on her dog-hair-covered coat. (He'd already seen the dress, she figured—might as well avoid freezing). But he hadn't asked questions in the car. They'd just sat in companionable silence, soaking in each other's presence.

No one had questioned Jack for leaving the party he'd put on. If anything, everyone had seemed pleased to see them go. She might have made a joke about that, but she wasn't quite ready to laugh yet. Not until they talked.

"This is where I found Ein," she said. "I was sitting on this bench, feeling more lost than I ever had. Molly had been getting into a little trouble at school, and I felt like I didn't have it together enough to take care of myself, let alone her." She looked down and smiled. "Then I felt something nudging my leg. I almost screamed, thinking it was maybe a bear, but I looked down and saw a filthy, starving, little dog. His skin was raw in patches, and he just looked...he looked like I felt."

"You found Einstein out here?" Jack asked in surprise. "I thought people bought corgis from breeders."

"They do," she said, "but there are plenty of people who buy dogs from fancy breeders and end up with buyer's remorse. They abandon them like they're nothing. Ein had a microchip, so I was able to contact his owners. They weren't even looking for him. I think they were relieved he ran off."

"That's why you started the shelter," he said. "It happened after you found Ein out here."

He was a good listener. It was one of the things that had endeared him to her from the beginning—the way he really listened to a person, both what they were saying and what they weren't. "Yes. I saved him, and he saved me. He gave me another purpose. Of course, I had a massive assist from Beatrice, plus my inheritance from my parents. But I knew from the beginning Einstein and I were soul companions, and he was going to change my life. It was what you could call a pivotal moment."

Something glimmered in his eyes, almost as if a string of twinkle lights had lit up inside him.

"I didn't think beyond one night when I took you home from Dottie's party. But it was another pivotal moment, Jack. Just like when Einstein found me." She smiled up at him, feeling tears in her eyes. "Dottie always told me I needed to find a human soul companion, and I did. I found you." A tear trickled down her cheek, and he traced it and wiped it away. "But I can tell you that I love you every day, and you might still wonder if I have feelings for River...because he's my friend and Georgie's your sister, and they'll be in our lives. I get that. I just don't know what to do about it. That's why I didn't say anything before I did. I was worried you'd push me away."

He was silent for a long time after that, and her heart thumped painfully in her chest. She could offer to give up her Bro Club dinners with River and Finn, or to avoid hanging out with River alone, but that was the kind of thing she'd end up resenting Jack for. She didn't want that for them.

"Did you just say you love me?" he asked, staring into her eyes. He took her hands, and the warmth of his fingers, the familiarity of them, grounded her. His eyes weren't expressionless, the way they got sometimes when he was overwhelmed. They were wells of raw emotion.

"I guess I did," she said with some amount of sass, and then she said it again, her tone completely serious this time. "I love you. And Jack, I know what you thought earlier, but you were wrong. River is my friend, and he'll always be special to me, but I've never wanted him the way I want you. He's not my soul companion. *You* are."

One moment he was looking into her eyes, and then he was pulling her onto his lap, claiming her mouth. His kiss was fierce and insistent, and it touched something deep at her core. When he pulled away, she was panting, no longer chilled by the cool air.

"I love you," he said. "I shouldn't have run away from you—I should have *listened*—but I let my past get between us." His brow furrowed with anger she knew wasn't for her. "That's how I always dealt with Genevieve, by taking off, but I don't want to do it anymore. That's not who I want to be."

She smiled at him, running a hand through his thick hair. "Well, you're in luck, because I can give you plenty of lessons about snapping at people until they quail in submission. Except I've been told that doesn't work out too well either."

"I'll hold you to it, Red." He reached up to caress her face and wiped away another tear that had escaped her eye. They were silent for a moment, just taking each other in, like they had in the car. Then he said softly, "I didn't know what I was looking for when I came here, not really, but I never imagined I'd find this. I always felt like I had to do everything alone, but you made me realize that I don't want that anymore. I want *you*. And if you really feel the same way, then the River thing isn't an issue."

She kissed him, a slow, sweet kiss meant to tell him that he was the one in her heart and he didn't have to be alone anymore. He had her, and they had each other, and that was enough to get them through this crazy life.

Then she pulled back and grinned at him, letting her sassiness roll out again. "Is this a good time to tell you that I think you should adopt Ruby?"

CHAPTER
Thirty-Six

Jack woke to the warmth of Maisie's soft body next to him. The sun hadn't risen yet, and she was still asleep. He told himself not to wake her. They were up late the night before, professing their love with both words and their bodies.

She rolled over and released a contented sigh as one eyelid cracked open. "You're not watching me sleep like a crazy stalker, are you?"

He grinned, his heart warming. "And if I said I was?"

Laughing, she pushed him onto his back and crawled on top of him.

"Merry Christmas," he said, staring into her eyes. The happiness he saw there made his chest puff with pride that he'd put it there.

Her smile softened into contentment. She lifted a hand to his face, and gently cupped his cheek. "Merry Christmas."

He kissed her then, because his lips hadn't covered hers for nearly six hours, and that was five hours and fifty-nine minutes too long.

She lifted her head a few inches and smiled. "What about morning breath?"

He wrapped his arms around her back. "Worth it."

He glanced over to the bedroom door and saw Einstein and Chaco watching them.

"Question," Jack said, brushing a strand of hair from her cheek. "Can dogs be taken from their owners for being exposed to live porn?"

Maisie laughed and lifted up on her elbow to check them out. "They probably have to pee."

When she started to get up, he pulled her back down. "I'll take them out. You go shower, and I'll join you when I'm done."

"Okay," she said hesitantly. "But maybe put them on leashes. In case they decide to bolt."

They didn't run off for her, but he knew her dogs were her babies, and he'd follow whatever rules made her feel comfortable. He put on his dress pants and shirt while she ogled him. Grinning, he slipped his feet into his dress shoes.

"You look like you're doing a walk of shame," she teased.

"There's absolutely not one ounce of shame from sleeping with you," he said, leaning over to give her another kiss. "I'll proudly wear this all day long."

"We should have given this whole morning situation more thought," she said, her eyes dancing with mischief. "Especially since you volunteered to go to the shelter with me."

He'd barely had the presence of mind to text Iris to tell her he'd be home late. She'd replied that if she saw him before brunch at the Buchanan house, which Finn and Adalia were optimistically calling the First Annual Christmas Brunch Extravaganza, she'd kick him in the rear end. "The only thing I was capable of thinking about was getting you home so I could strip that sexy dress off your gorgeous body. Promise me you'll wear it again."

"It's not mine. It's Blue's."

"Then I'll buy it from her." He kissed her again. "Just tell her what we did in the car while you were still wearing it." He cocked a brow. "She might not want it back."

She laughed. "You're terrible."

"You love every moment of it."

"Obviously," she said. "Now take those dogs out before I drag you back to bed and they pee on the floor."

Poor Ein looked miserable, so he hurried downstairs and clipped on their leashes to take them out, not that he was worried about them running off. They were so excited he was there, he could barely get them to focus on the task at hand.

"Come on, Ein. I really want to see your mommy naked again. Let's take that poop already."

It was another five minutes before they finally finished their business, and while he would have loved nothing more than to race up the stairs, stripping off his clothes as he took the stairs two at a time, he knew how much Maisie loved her morning coffee. He started a pot, then headed up to the bathroom, telling the pouting dogs, "I'll feed you later. I'll give you extra if you promise to stop trying to make me feel guilty."

The water was still running when he opened the door, the dogs sitting in the hall behind him, and he quickly dropped his pants and parted the shower curtain.

Maisie was standing under the shower in all her naked glory. "I was about to send a search party."

"Turned out Ein wanted time with me too."

She pulled the curtain to the side and laughed at the sight of Ein wagging his tail in the doorway. "It looks like he still doesn't feel he's had enough."

"Too bad," he said, picking up a bottle of body wash and squeezing some into his hand. He slid a hand over her shoulder.

"I already washed. Somebody took too long."

"You can never be too clean," he said as he glided his hand down to cup her breast.

She sharply inhaled. "I guess they *do* say cleanliness is next to godliness."

"I think that makes you a goddess."

She laughed. "It's about time."

They got dressed, then headed down to the kitchen, and Maisie kissed him senseless again once she realized he'd made coffee. She poured to-go mugs for both of them while he fed the dogs, and then they took off for the shelter. They took all the dogs out to pee and let them have some playtime before bringing them back in for breakfast. He was surprised when he saw so many empty kennels, and she told him they'd had a surge of adoptions after his Instagram photos.

Ruby was overjoyed to see him and covered him with kisses.

Maisie gave him a pointed look, which made him sigh. "I would...you know I would, but it's not a good idea right now with Lee staying at the house and everything up in the air. Plus, Jezebel doesn't like most dogs."

She huffed a laugh. "No kidding. I know, I just feel bad for her. A family was interested a couple of weeks ago, but they changed their mind."

"What can we do to find her a home?"

"Honestly, the Instagram posts have made a huge difference." She gave him an ornery look. "Quite a few women have specifically asked for you. I may need you to make celebrity appearances from time to time."

"You don't mind?" he asked.

She grinned. "First rule of running a shelter: tug the heartstrings. Second rule: do anything you can to seal an adoption." She gave his arm a tap. "Well, within reason. As long as you come home with me, they can look all they want."

Maisie was torn about when to give the dogs their stockings, but they worried they'd be late for brunch since they'd gotten a late start.

"Let's just come back later," Jack said. "You know Iris is going to want to be part of it. She can take pictures for Instagram." His lips tipped up. "Maximize the heartstring pulling."

"Okay," she said. "But let's make sure we do it this afternoon. I don't want to keep them waiting."

"Deal."

Maisie drove them to the Buchanan house, and Jack couldn't stop looking at her, her hair like a fire in the sun. He reached over and took her hand, shocked all over again that this gorgeous, feisty redhead was his.

"If you look at me like that at brunch," she said with a mischievous glint in her eyes, "Lee might take us out back and hose us down."

"I think he'll be feeling his hangover too much to notice me lusting after you." But the thought of Lee was sobering. The guy was in serious trouble, and he was going to need his siblings to help him through it. Would he want Jack's help too?

Everyone had already arrived by the time they walked in the door. Christmas music was playing, and the delicious smells made his stomach growl. Finn was sitting on the sofa with Addy on his lap. Tyrion lay on the floor at his feet, but he was staring up at Addy as though she'd hung the moon. Iris was in the overstuffed chair next to them, reading something on her phone, but her face lit up when she saw Jack holding Maisie's hand.

"This is the best Christmas present ever!" she exclaimed, launching herself out of the chair and into his arms.

He gave her a tight hug. Then she moved on to Maisie, whispering loud enough for Jack to hear, "I'm happy he's in good hands. Now I won't have to worry about him so much when I go to college."

Maisie laughed. "I'll make sure he's fed and watered."

Iris pointed a finger at her. "I'm holding you to it."

"Dottie says we can eat now that Jack and Maisie are here," Georgie said as she emerged from the kitchen wearing an apron, River on her heels. She shot Jack a look. "And don't let the apron fool you. Dottie cooked it all. We only got to arrange it on the counter."

"At least you were allowed to go into the kitchen," Addy complained. "She shooed me out."

"Too many cooks in the kitchen makes the soufflé fall," Dottie said, appearing behind River. "Besides, I had to pass all of my Christmas brunch traditions down to River's future bride."

Georgie's face flushed with happiness, and Jack was relieved the mess with her father hadn't stolen her joy.

They all headed into the kitchen, where Georgie and River had set up Dottie's food on the counter—under her watchful supervision—buffet style, next to a stack of plates. Jack wasn't surprised to see tented papers with labels next to every dish. A bowl of Jell-O salad said "Comfort," and a casserole dish with an egg casserole said "A hearty new year." A plate of banana muffins read "Prosperity," and a pitcher of mimosas was labeled "Peace," along with several other dishes and notes.

Jack wanted a jumbo-sized mimosa for all of them.

He was starving, but he made sure Iris and Maisie got plates first. He was about to make his own when he realized he hadn't seen his brother.

"Where's Lee?"

"Out back," Addy said, wincing. "He said the smell of food was making him sick."

He shot Maisie a pointed look, then said, "You all start without me. I'm going out to check on Lee."

"That's a good idea," Dottie said. "First let me make him one of my special cures."

Adalia pulled a face. "I can still taste it in my nightmares," she said, backing out of the kitchen. "I recommend that you all clear out of here for a minute. The smell alone might make you lose your appetite."

She was right. It looked disgusting and smelled even worse, but Jack had seen firsthand that it was a miracle drug. Once it was done, Dottie called him in, and he took it out back, holding the cup as far away from him as possible.

Lee was sitting in what was referred to as "Beau's chair." It was the one their grandfather had always sat in, and Jack found it amusing that the Buchanan siblings tended to automatically gravitate toward it. He was sure Dottie would have had something to say about that.

"Hey," Jack said softly as he sat in the chair next to him, still holding the cup a good distance from his body.

Lee lifted his bloodshot eyes but didn't respond.

"Do you feel as bad as you look?" Lee flipped him off, and Jack laughed. "I guess that answers that."

They were silent for a moment before Lee cleared his throat. "I owe you a massive apology."

Jack waved his hand. "Trust me, I've been flipped off plenty of times before."

Lee laughed, then reached a hand up to his head with a grimace. "Not for that. For how I treated you yesterday and the day before and all the days before that."

"You had some things to work through," Jack said. "I get it."

"It's no excuse. You're just as much a victim as the rest of us."

"Maybe so," Jack said, choosing his words carefully. "But going to the FBI had to give you some of your power back."

"It did."

"How much trouble are *you* in?"

Lee sighed and leaned over, resting his forearms on his thighs. "I think I'm fairly safe. I didn't know what was going on, and I gave them my full cooperation. My father and Victoria...let's just say I think their luck has run out."

"I heard you quit, but I guess that doesn't mean much given your father won't be the boss anymore. What does this mean for Buchanan Luxury?"

Lee released a bitter laugh. "After this, it no longer exists. There's no way any of our clients would ever trust us again."

"Well, I'm sure Addy has already told you, but I feel like I should too. You're welcome to stay here as long as you like," Jack said. "I mean, *of course* you can stay. It's your house too. I'm just saying, if you decide to hang out here while you figure things out, you'll be welcomed."

Lee gave him a long, hard stare. "Why are you being so nice to me after I've been nothing but a dick?"

"Because I respect Georgie and Addy's opinion. If they see good in you, it must be there." He grinned. "It's just buried under a pile of shit."

Lee's laugh turned into a groan again.

"Here," Jack said, shoving the glass toward him. "Drink this."

He took it, making a face as he lifted it to his lips. "So you came out here to poison me?"

"It's one of Dottie's miracle hangover cures. It smells disgusting and tastes even worse, but you'll be hangover-free within the hour."

"How is that possible?"

"Didn't you hear? She's a witch," Adalia said as she came out the back door. "Why didn't you give it to him when you first came out, Jack?"

He shrugged. "I had to butter him up first."

"Drink it," Addy said, placing a hand on Jack's shoulder. "Trust me. I'm living proof it works."

He gave her a dubious look, then chugged it down, looking like he was about to barf.

"When the feeling passes, come inside," Addy said. "We're dying to open presents after we eat." She glanced down at Jack. "And you need to get back to Maisie. She's about to give your food to Tyrion."

Jack hadn't even made a plate yet, so he knew it wasn't true, but he appreciated Adalia coming out to check on him. He went inside and scooped food onto his plate, then poured himself a generous mimosa. Iris and Maisie had saved him a spot between them, and for a moment he just stood there, holding his plate and cup, and watched them talking and laughing, savoring the knowledge that they were both in his life. That they were *friends*. Then he walked over and joined them, setting his things down on the table. He planted a kiss on top of his sister's head, then sat down and gave Maisie a quick kiss on the lips.

Adalia wolf-whistled as she stepped into the dining room, and Georgie beamed. Finn reached out for a fist bump from Maisie, and she rolled her eyes as she reciprocated. River just gave them a single nod of approval.

"All right, all right," Maisie said. "You have five seconds to get it out of your system, and then it all stops. Forever."

The whole table erupted in applause, Iris joining in. Maisie turned to her with a mock glare. "I expected better from you."

"What can I say?" Iris said. "I'm a hopeless romantic."

"You two are perfect for each other," Dottie said quietly. "Beau would be so happy."

The table grew quiet, and Jack lifted his glass. Although he'd never met Beau, the man had changed his life. Without his meddling, Jack would never have met Maisie or found a place among his half-siblings. "To Beau."

Everyone lifted their own glasses, repeating Jack's toast with a quiet reverence. "To Beau."

Dottie's eyes glittered with unshed tears. "I wish he could be here to see how happy you all are."

"Not *all* of us," Lee said bitterly from the kitchen doorway.

"Give it time," Dottie said.

Disgust filled Lee's eyes, followed by a rush of something like panic, and he raced up the stairs.

"He doesn't mean to be rude," Georgie said.

"Of course he doesn't," Dottie assured her. "Our Lee needs love and support. He needs time."

Georgie reached over and squeezed the elderly woman's hand. "And we'll give him plenty of it."

Adalia lifted her fork. "Speaking from my personal experience with Dottie's cure and the way he ran up the stairs, his most immediate need is a bathroom."

The other couples had all exchanged gifts at home, so Jack slid Maisie's gift under the sofa on the sly, catching her eye as he did so. She winked and pointed toward the dining room, where he could see her purse hanging from her chair. Later, after all of the other gifts had been opened, Lee wandered off, either to his room or the bathroom, and Addy turned on the TV and found *A Christmas Story* mid-film. Jack whispered into Maisie's ear, "Let's go open our gifts to each other on the front porch."

She grinned. "I saw your moves with the sofa. How about we meet outside with our presents?"

"Deal."

His was easy. He was sitting on the floor next to the sofa, so he grabbed the gift and went outside, suddenly worried it wasn't enough. He was resting his butt against the porch railing when she walked out, carrying the small, wrapped box he'd seen at her house.

"I want to open mine first," she said, setting her gift in one of the chairs and snatching his wrapped gift from him.

"Okay…"

She didn't waste any time before ripping off the paper. When she opened the lid, she carefully lifted out the scarf.

"It was made by impoverished women in Vietnam," he said in a rush. "So we're contributing to the livelihoods of women in need." He pushed away from the railing. "But that's not the reason I bought it," he said in a husky tone.

"Oh?" she asked as he took the scarf from her.

He looped it behind her neck and tugged her closer with the ends until she was flush against him. He held one hand up and brushed the soft fabric against her cheek. "I was right."

"About what?"

"It's nearly the exact color of your eyes."

She smiled and wrapped a hand behind his neck, pulling his face down to hers. "Your turn." She looked nervous. "I'm worried you won't like it."

"I'll love whatever you give me, simply because it's from you."

"You have to say that," she said as she pushed him down into one of the chairs and grabbed the gift up from the other. She hesitated, then handed it to him. "If you don't like it, I can get you something else."

"Maisie, I'm going to love it." He snagged her wrist and tugged her to him, settling her on his lap before he tore into the paper. He was surprised when he discovered an oversized jewelry box, and the gift inside left him nearly speechless. Having worked at a bar with wealthy clientele, he knew an expensive watch when he saw it.

Now he felt like an utter asshole for getting her a scarf.

"Maisie…"

"In the interest of transparency, you need to know I didn't buy it."

He grinned at her. "You stole it? There's a whole bad-girl side to you I didn't fully know about."

"I didn't steal it, and can I say you got far too excited over the possibility that I did?"

He kissed her, then pulled back, grinning like a fool. Maisie did this to him, but he didn't mind one bit.

"It was my dad's," she said quietly. "He would have liked you. A lot." She swallowed. "It sat in a box for years, like everything else. But what good is it to keep things in boxes? And…it felt right for my past and my present to merge into my future."

A lump filled Jack's throat. He was the luckiest guy in the world.

"You hate it," she said, horror filling her eyes as she misinterpreted his silence. "I didn't buy it, so I know that makes me cheap, but I—"

Jack kissed her hard. "*Maisie*. This is the best gift I've ever received. Thank you."

"Are you positive?" she asked, looking uncharacteristically unsure of herself. "I really can get you something else."

"Don't you dare," he said, removing the watch from the box. He slipped it onto his wrist and fastened the clasp. He tried to slide it up and down his wrist, but it barely moved. "It fits perfectly."

"It's like you were meant to have it."

He stared into her worried eyes. "I know it's hard for you to let go of the past, but you don't have to let go of everything, and I'll be there to help you. At your pace. There's no rush."

"Thank you, but I finally feel ready. I want to focus on the present…and on starting my future with you."

He smiled at her. "I already have plans for our future, starting tonight. Dirty plans."

She grinned back. "I should hope so."

The front door opened and Iris's face appeared. "The neighbors are texting River, telling him there's an indecent couple on Beau's front porch."

Maisie laughed.

"If they think we've been indecent, then let's give them something to talk about." He shot his sister a look. "Go inside, Iris."

She squealed, then slammed the door.

"Should I be concerned that your sister is excited we're about to do something indecent?"

"Probably, but it's too late to change her now. Just be thankful for her blessing." Then he kissed her with a hunger he'd suppressed for the last hour. She met his passion with her own, until they were both breathless.

"Do you think that was indecent enough?" Maisie asked playfully.

"I don't know, but I fully intend to keep on working on it."

EPILOGUE

"Oh my God, I forgot to ask. Does Molly like pizza?" Iris asked anxiously. She'd started reading Molly's column, and much to Maisie's amusement, she now acted like Molly was a celebrity.

"Iris," she said as she slung an arm around her shoulders. "If my sister didn't like pizza, I would disown her myself."

"She means it too," said Jack, touching her hip. They stood like that for a moment, the three of them linked together next to the dining room table, the dogs at their feet, sniffing hopefully at the scent of fresh pizza in the air, and Maisie felt a swell of emotion. Her house was becoming a home again. And now her sisters were coming to visit, finally, to spend New Year's with them. Although Maisie would have preferred to see her nephew too, Mary had decided—after a long bout of hemming and hawing—to come alone.

All these months without a visit, and apparently all Maisie had needed to do was find a boyfriend...a *real* boyfriend, as Mary referred to him...to convince them to come. Of course, she suspected Molly also intended to needle them all for details of the epic Christmas Eve engagement party that had ended up getting Prescott Buchanan and Vic-

tor-ia arrested…along with half a dozen other employees from Buchanan Luxury. Although Prescott and Victoria had both been granted bail, the evidence that had been collected against them, thanks to Lee, was fairly damning.

Didn't matter why they were here. If she was permissive of pandering and the occasional white lie to secure a dog's adoption to a good home, she was even more so of her sisters' behavior.

A knock landed on the door—the pattern one she and Molly had perfected in childhood and taught to River—and Iris flinched as if she expected Taylor Swift might walk through the door.

The dogs dashed toward the door, Chaco still wearing the jingle bell collar Dottie had gotten her for Christmas, much to Jack's annoyance. He'd told Maisie they should "lose" it on a walk, but she'd insisted they wait for at least a full week to ensure believability.

"Go," Jack urged her, smiling and giving her a little push toward the door. "You've been waiting all day."

She had. She would have gone to the airport to pick them up if Mary hadn't insisted on renting a car. Inside, Maisie was dancing in place like Ein, but rather than dash for the door, she tugged Jack with her and snagged a wide-eyed Iris too, bringing them both with her. Because they'd spent a lifetime being left out of things, and she never, ever wanted them to feel that way with her. Because they couldn't meet her mother and father, but Mary had their mother's practical outlook, bluntness, and complete inability to read sarcasm, and Molly had their father's slightly wild streak, and they all had the O'Shea laugh.

She released Jack and Iris to open the door, and Molly flew into her arms in a tackle hug that almost sent them both flying to the floor. Both of them burst out laughing, and Mary gave them a long-suffering smile. "You shouldn't encourage her."

Then Molly pulled her into the hug too, and Mary hugged them back in a way that said her bluster was just that. Ein and Chaco pawed at them as if they wished to be let in on the fun, and Molly squealed and picked up Chaco. "Finally, we meet in person!"

Which reminded Maisie.

She pulled away and reached for Jack and Iris, who stood to one side of the door, looking a little shell-shocked. Understandable. The O'Shea girls could be like a tornado when they were all together. She and Molly were the only ones who could pull Mary out of her ordered universe.

"Molly and Mary, meet Jack and his sister Iris." She could see them taking her sisters in, Molly with her long, wavy strawberry blond hair and hazel eyes, Mary with her short brown hair, which only showed hints of red in the sun.

"The famous Iris!" Molly cried, pulling her into a hug while Mary greeted Jack in a more sedate manner. Iris looked a bit startled but very pleased.

"Did you miss the New Year's Eve Countdown to be here?" she asked. From what Maisie had gathered, the gist of it was that Molly was supposed to go on several blind dates on New Year's Eve, with men chosen by her fellow blogger. Her goal was to guess which of them had been selected to be her date at midnight. Apparently they'd intended to vlog it.

Molly waved it off. "Yeah, but I get to meet you and your hunky brother instead." She winked at Jack. "I call it even."

"Shameless," Maisie said, giving her a little shove. She shut the door and turned to face them, her heart full.

"Maisie, the house…" Mary said, her head swiveling around to take in the living room.

"I told you I'd made a few changes," she said. "It's a work in progress."

She felt a prickle of defensiveness—did Mary disapprove?—but then she saw the tears in her sister's eyes.

Molly grinned at her. "This has to be a record. It only took you two minutes to make Mary cry."

That earned her a swat from their big sister.

"It's just…I'm so proud of you," Mary said.

"I'm proud of me too," she said.

Jack put an arm around her, and she leaned into him, suddenly feeling all of the emotions of having everyone here on the last day of the year, of feeling the new year unfurl before them. Of sensing possibilities rather than fearing the changes the future might bring.

Molly clapped. "I smell pizza, but before we eat or even bring in our bags, I think it's time for us to show Iris our surprise."

"What?" Iris said, flinching. She'd been leaning against the banister, and she almost fell. Flushing a little, she stood up straighter. "Why would you do something nice for me? You don't even know me."

Molly raised her hands up, palms out. "You underestimate how much our sister tells us. Plus, I only helped in an advisory capacity."

Iris swiveled to look at Maisie, who couldn't hold back a grin. She glanced up at Jack, and he gave her a little squeeze with one of those famous arms of his. "What'd you do now, Red?"

She could almost feel Molly and Mary exchanging a look. They'd never heard anyone but their dad call her that. Yeah, they knew she had it bad.

"Guess you'll all have to come upstairs and see."

She led the way, Jack behind her—she suspected he'd followed her so he could stare at her butt the whole way up—and then Iris and Molly and Mary. Chaco and Ein, who refused to be left out of the fun, came next.

When she reached the doorway of the spare bedroom, she felt a little prickle of nerves. What if Jack and Iris took her gesture the wrong way? Molly had egged her on, of course, but Mary had suggested it would be wise to consult Jack before moving forward. But there'd been too few good surprises in Maisie's life, and she'd wanted to pull one off for Iris.

Jack shot her a questioning look, and she moved closer to him, wanting to feel him at her side.

"Go on in, Iris."

"Why do I feel like I'm being set up?" Iris asked with no small amount of suspicion, glancing from face to face.

"Maybe because Molly is literally taking a video," Maisie said, giving her sister a look.

Molly kept at it. "She'll thank me later."

"Go ahead, Iris," Jack said. Something about his tone, soft yet strong, fatherly yet brotherly, was heartrending. Because Iris might think she only needed a brother in Jack, but that wasn't totally true.

Iris cracked the door open and walked in, leaving it gaping behind her.

She returned a moment later, her face unreadable in the way she and Jack always looked when they were overloaded with emotion.

Maisie found herself holding her breath. Was this good emotion or bad emotion?

Then Iris threw her arms around Maisie and hugged her, holding on tight.

When she pulled away, Maisie said, "I know Jack's been spending a lot of time here, and I wanted you to have your own space in the house. Because you belong here just like he does. You can decorate it however you want, but I figured you might prefer updated furniture."

"I love it. Jack, you've got to see this," Iris said. She glanced around at them all again, then cracked the door wider. "All of you, come in."

Maisie had spent yesterday afternoon moving the new furniture in, with help from River and Finn. She'd chosen the pieces based on Molly's advice, although Mary had been adamant about what was needed. Jack and Iris had been held up by Dottie, who was almost frighteningly good at keeping people busy.

"You did this?" Jack asked in wonder. "When?"

"Yesterday afternoon."

He shook his head slightly. "I should have been suspicious when Dottie said we were the only people who could help her organize her crystal collection."

"You *were* suspicious," Iris corrected him. "But it was Dottie, so we had to."

"And don't you forget it," Molly said. "Only a fool would cross that woman."

"Oh, I know," Iris said. "She basically got Beau's son arrested."

A gleam entered Molly's eyes, and Maisie gave her a warning look.

"Hey," Jack said, drawing her attention back to him. "Why don't we go out and bring your sisters' bags in from the car?"

Mary looked slightly pained by the suggestion, but she handed over the keys. "Thank you. That would be great."

She obviously knew Jack wanted a moment alone with Maisie and was taking one for the team. Maisie's heart started beating painfully. Would he be upset about the room for Iris?

Giving Molly a final warning glance, Maisie told Mary, "You keep an eye on her," and followed him out of the room and down the stairs.

He waited until they were outside and then turned to face her, his expression as stoic as his sister's had been moments before. Then he tugged her to him and kissed her, his hand burrowing into her hair to bring her closer.

When he pulled away, he just looked at her for a moment, his eyes warm now. Deep wells of warmth like a cup of dark coffee on a cold winter's day.

"I can't believe you did this for her. It's not even New Year's yet, and you already made her year."

"It's only fair," she said, reaching up to cup his cheek, loving the feel of his stubble. "Both of you have already made mine. You even found a home for three dogs last week."

One of them had been Ruby. She'd been sad to let her go, especially since she had such a powerful bond with Jack, but one of the members of Blue's Bad Luck Club had adopted her. Blue had confided that Ruby was now treated like the spoiled only child she was, and Jack had been invited to visit any time he liked.

Sometimes things didn't work out the way you planned. And sometimes it was much, much better that way.

"You know, this worked out pretty well for a one-night stand," she said, grinning at him.

"Who said anything about it being a one-night stand?" he asked with mock innocence. Then the humor slipped out of his expression. "I never wanted it to be one."

"Kiss her again already!" Molly shouted out of the open doorway. "The pizza's getting cold."

So he did, and they got the suitcases and walked back into the warmth of the full house, hand in hand, and Maisie felt full to bursting with happiness and love and hope. The future wasn't frightening anymore…it was glorious.

ABOUT the Authors

A.R. CASELLA is a freelance developmental editor by day, writer by night. She lives in Asheville, NC with her husband, daughter, two dogs, and a variable number of fish. Her pastimes include chasing around her toddler, baking delicious treats, and occasional bouts of crocheting. *Any Luck at All,* co-written with *New York Times* bestselling author Denise Grover Swank, is her first book.

You can find out more at www.arcasella.com

DENISE GROVER SWANK was born in Kansas City, Missouri and lived in the area until she was nineteen. Then she became a nomad, living in five cities, four states and ten houses over the course of ten years before she moved back to her roots. She speaks English and smattering of Spanish and Chinese which she learned through an intensive Nick Jr. immersion period. Her hobbies include witty Facebook comments (in own her mind) and dancing in her kitchen with her children. (Quite badly if you believe her offspring.) Hidden talents include the gift of justification and the ability to drink massive amounts of caffeine and still fall asleep within two minutes. Her lack of the sense of smell allows her to perform many unspeakable tasks. She has six children and hasn't lost her sanity. Or so she leads you to believe.

Find out more about Denise at denisegroverswank.com

Made in the USA
Coppell, TX
05 March 2021

51335748R00238